SMOKE
THE ARDELEAN BLOODLINE
BOOK ONE

SARAH JAEGER

BEARLY CONTAINED ROMANCE

© Bearly Contained Romance

E-Book ISBN: 979-8-9877001-0-5

Male Model Paperback ISBN: 979-8-9877001-1-2

Wolf Paperback ISBN: 979-8-9877001-2-9

Editing - Indie Edits with Jeanine

Proofreading - Marcelle of Books Checked

Book Cover - Sandra of Mando Designs

Traffic Director - Kelsey Schneider

 Created with Vellum

Smoke

To anyone who has ever felt like they weren't good enough.

You were then and you are now.

"Someone asked me how I manage my nerves. And I don't. I don't, I just do things scared."

— ELYSE MYERS

"Fate leads the willing and drags along the reluctant."

— SENECA

A QUICK NOTE ON CONTENT

This book is a traditional shifter romance book. As such, it contains events such as physical on-page violence and murder. These events may be handled or discussed in ways that may not be acceptable by all readers.

Smoke is a book based in a world very much like our own and deals with a wide variety of heavy topics. These topics may cause individuals to have negative feelings or reactions.

The list of topics includes, but is not limited to, mental health, suicidal ideation, drug and alcohol use, addiction, sexual intercourse, gambling, misogyny, use and deadly use of a firearm, body dysmorphia, talks of weight and weightloss, and suicide.

These topics are not always handled in the most politically correct way. As often seen in real life, my characters can sometimes be insensitive to those around them and their struggles.

None of these words written were chosen without thought. All choices were debated at length. Ultimately, it is my intent to highlight the struggles of humanity as we work toward acceptance of all the differences among us. Even if that means allowing my characters to be imperfect as part of their growth, as part of our growth.

And while it is never my intention to cause any reader any distress: reader discretion is advised.

If based on this warning, related to the potential triggers listed above, you have any additional concerns or questions that you'd like addressed, you may reach out to me via email: sarah@authorsarahjaeger.com or on Instagram: @author.sarahjaeger

CADE'S HOME IN WISCONSIN

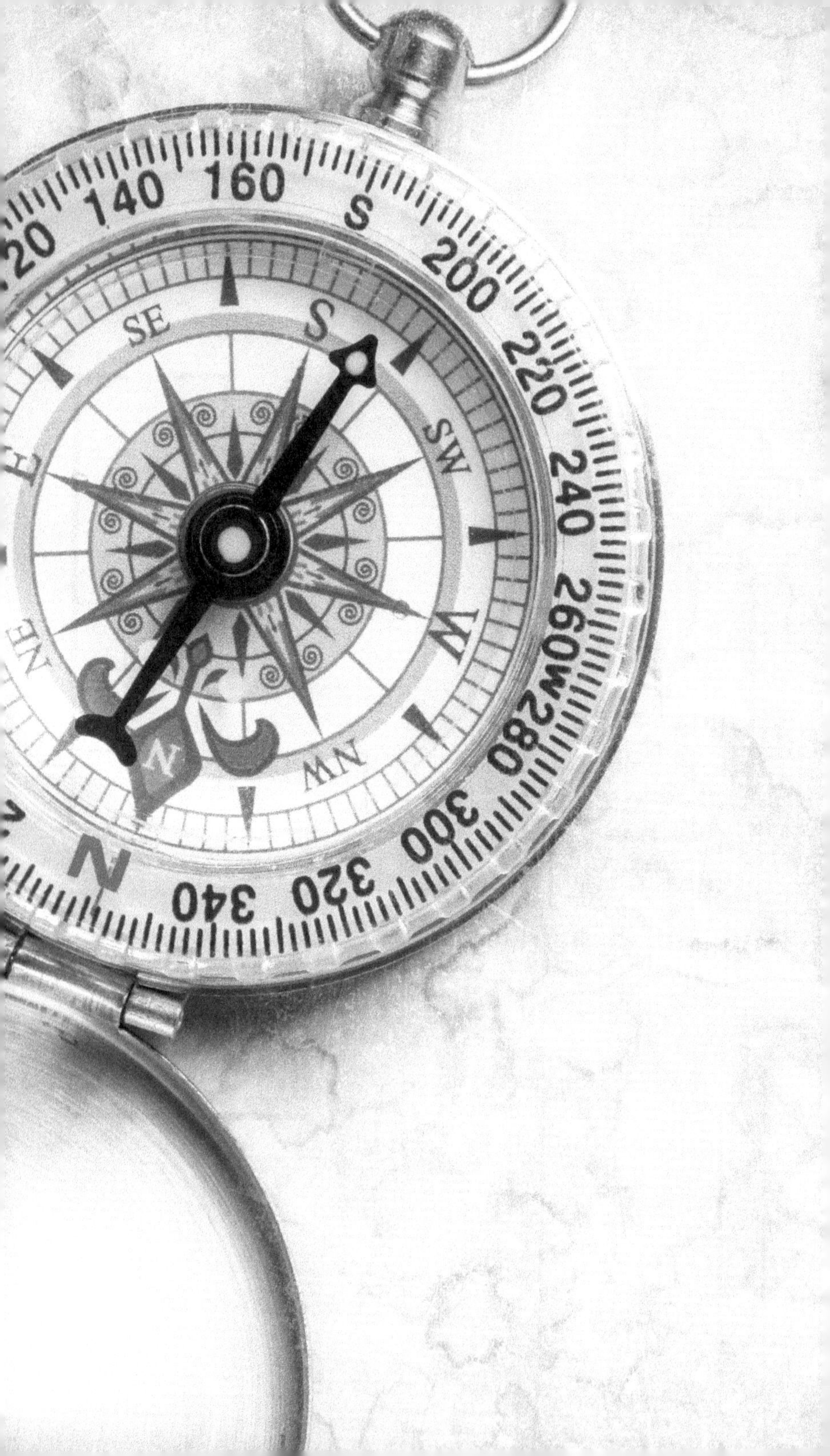

140
160
S
200
220
240
260
W
280
300
320
340
N
SE
S
SW
W
NW
N
NE
E

PROLOGUE
CADE

Eleven Years Earlier

Oddly, it's not remorse you feel when you commit patricide. As I stand here with the rich copper taste of blood in my mouth, it's relief. The world around me fades to a dull buzz. Focused on my father's lifeless body, I wait longer than I need to before I go; I need to be sure he won't get up. When my wolf and I agree that he's gone, I turn my back on his corpse. My wolf fades back, leaving me in my human form. Cold wind shakes leaves loose from the trees and dries the blood against my skin. Next to die, the wind tapers off in exhale; when it does, the sounds previously tuned out flood back.

My mother crumples with her arms wrapped around herself. She wails over the loss of her mate. On the other end of the patio, my younger brother Deacon stands with our younger sister, Kathleen, held tightly against his chest. Members of the pack and the council stand at the front between the curved staircases. I meet their darkened gazes with my own, yet most

1

of them fail to meet or hold my eyes. The heavy footfalls of running echo through the crisp air between our mother's sobs.

"Take another step, Robert, and you'll meet the same fate." I roll my head to look at him, daring him to make the next move.

My older brother, the coward, freezes a mere three steps from the bottom of the left curved marble staircase separating the upper patio from the lawn where I stand. My wolf, not sated from bloodshed, silently begs for him to take another step.

More moments of tense silence tick by. I stand there, unsure of what to do next. No one prepares you for this. I suppose no one expects a coup. No one tells you what to do after you win an Alpha challenge, mostly because no one expects you to survive.

It's a few moments longer before one of the council members proclaims, "The Alpha Ebenezer Vance Alden is no more. May his lineage, but not his acts, live on. Hail the ascended, Cade Alexander Alden, Sovereign Alpha of the Ardelean bloodline."

A chorus of acknowledgments stems from around the patio before me. Then, from behind me, through the trees, a chorus of agreements rise in an eerie howl from wolves who left the Equinox banquet earlier. They must have returned hearing of the chaos.

Robert's eyes burn against my skin as I walk to the staircase opposite him. I feel the intensity of his anger. The fact that I wouldn't sacrifice my little sister's life for his benefit should give him an understanding of where we stand as siblings. His days of being in charge because he's the eldest are over.

Fighting back a chill and the growing need to look over my shoulder at the blood-soaked earth, I make my way to the right-hand staircase and stiffly climb. Slashes and bite wounds, scabbing over, reopen as I force stiff muscles up each step. With curt, acknowledging nods, I walk past the council members and head into the house. Tracking mud and blood across the cool marble floor, I ascend to the second floor and into my bedroom suite to clean up. No one follows in my wake. I'm allowed to grieve for my future — the life that I just killed to have.

When the water runs cold and rinses clear from my body, I step out of the shower. As much as I'd love to sit in silence and process my new existence in life, it's not an option. Dress pants, a dress shirt, and a tie lay on my bed. The scent of Kathleen hangs in the air strongest where she stood pulling the items from the closet and then again where she stood laying them on the bed.

Screaming from down the hallway, toward the public spaces of our home, echoes into the room. Despite the scream being an indication that there may be danger, I can't be bothered to dress any quicker. In a house full of wolves, surely it can be worked out without me.

"He murdered my mate. You saw him. All of you! A wolf red as blood. He's a monster. That was no challenge. It was murder." Mother's hysterical voice echoes through the house from the grand entryway. "I'm no longer needed here. It's been my home for all these years. We've been so good to you all, and now I'm to be cast out by my own son. He killed my mate. Murdered him in cold blood."

Advancing to the noise, I find my place at the top of the stairs, and from my perch above, I observe her, with a haphazardly thrown together suitcase at her side, yelling nonsense. Tears stream down her face, disheveled hair and clothes hang about her, adding to the look of her insanity.

Accusations continue, "He'll kill you all next. That monster is unhinged. Tonight was just a tiny display of what he is. He's not like all of us. The Leviathan lives within him. We let you all believe Vance had The Leviathan, but it's been Cade. And now, there is no hope."

I stare at my feet, drawing a deep breath. My wolf, The Leviathan, huffs. He's unamused by her manipulative tactics.

I don't know what I'm doing, I warn The Leviathan as he pushes against my skin, urging me forward. *Okay. I'm moving.*

Squaring my shoulders, I descend to the foyer. My presence goes unfelt in the room while they focus on trying to make her calm down and see what little reason there is.

"Enough." The Alpha command comes out of me.

All eyes turn to me as mouths close into silence. My wolf basks in the attention, growing from it.

Deacon crosses the room and stands to my left, in the Second's position, with Kathleen on my right, in the Alpha Female's position. I bow my head slightly to both of them, accepting their show of support. My father's Second wears a scowl, clearly noting the snub of not inviting him to Deacon's place. My mother had held rank as both our pack Luna and Alpha Female. Even if I had offered the position to her, she wouldn't have accepted. The glare she's giving me is unsurprising.

"We've all had a long evening. Mother, if you wish to leave, I will not stop you. You're welcome to remain here, in the family home. If you choose to leave, Robert is free to go with you. Deacon, Kathleen, and I are to remain as the heads of the pack." I watch her carefully.

Her outburst may appear uncharacteristic to the pack and council. But I know the truth as I've seen this type of reaction hundreds of times before. Her dramatic manipulations won't lead to any more fights in this house. She's hidden this side of herself from the pack all our lives. This behavior won't go unchecked anymore.

She folds her arms across herself, trying to hide. "I will speak with the high council this evening."

"After I set my meetings for this week, you're more than welcome to." I drag my eyes away from her, looking around the room.

It's pin-drop quiet, even as I turn and head past the foyer to the library, where I'll set up my command center for the time being. Eventually, I'll have to take residence in my father's office, but for now, I want a neutral playing field.

In a split-second decision, I killed my father and any hope of a future outside this life. At eighteen, this life, this responsibility, and this chaos have become my entire world. The Leviathan doesn't see it as a mess, he sees it as our birthright.

PROLOGUE
THALIA

FOUR MONTHS Earlier

Dear Miss Thalia Clark,
Congratulations on your acceptance to our internship program. Please review the information below . . .

SHAKING MY HEAD, I can't believe it. I draw big breaths. *I did it.*

Grabbing my mail on my lunch break was the best idea ever. Letters for internships weren't supposed to go out until next week, but something deep inside told me to look today.

Slowly I fold the letter and tuck it back into my purse.

I want to tell someone, anyone. It's so hard making friends when you're a diplomat's kid. We moved too much. I had more tutors and private schooling than general classes. Any kids I was in school with were also kids of diplomats. It was a political minefield trying to make genuine connections and not fuel the political games.

Pulling out my phone, I check the time. It's just after 2:00 p.m. here in Washington, DC. The few acquaintances I have that I tell these sorts of things to are all ahead of me in the time zones. Most of my relationships that aren't tied up with academia are all online friends I've kept in touch with via social media. I shoot a few messages off to those in a reasonable time zone. But there's no one awake or free right now to really truly talk to.

I'll call Mom and Dad later; they wanted to discuss plans for next summer over the weekend. How is it already Thanksgiving? *Where did the year go?*

ALONE IN THE LAB, I'm looking through the microscope lens at a document repair I'm practicing on.

"Thalia."

I jump on the stool I'm sitting on and yelp. The stool nearly tips over, so I grab the countertop, trying not to fall off.

Well, I *was* alone.

"I didn't mean to scare you." Doctor Dorset tilts his head as he watches me.

His eyes on me don't feel right.

Panting from the shock, I opt to get down rather than right myself on the stool. With my feet on the floor, he's so tall I have to tilt my head to look up at him.

I smile and try to divert the tension. "You would think all this time in the lab, I'd get used to you not making any noise."

"Someday." He smiles, but it seems forced. "It seems that you've something to celebrate?"

I bite my lips together, thinking of the envelope tucked

neatly in my purse hanging on the hooks at the lab's entrance. *How does he know?*

"The chair of the board of directors called and asked me for my opinion on you. When I stated I enjoyed working with you and that you'd become a valuable asset to the team, well, apparently, it came down to you and another candidate." Doctor Dorset shrugs. "I was made aware that my number of summer fellows went up, so I could only assume the best."

Reading Doctor Dorset has always been difficult. As a freshman, he was intimidating but made me feel comfortable. Sophomore year we got closer, and he asked for some things, but he was respectful when I told him no. Until just after spring break, when he snapped and was completely against talking to or being seen with me. Now, this fall term, he's slowly warming up to me again.

This is so incredibly awkward. But I have to say something. "Thank you for saying kind things. This means so much to me."

"Of course, sweetheart."

Doctor Dorset calls me that, but it's weird coming off his tongue. It's been a long time since he's used the sentiment, and the last time was shortly before I told him no.

He steps into me, his hand gently reaching out toward my bicep.

Slowly, I step back, bumping into the stool. It falls with a clamor to the ground.

He steps around me to pick it up. After setting it upright next to me, he pats the stool for me to sit.

"Oh, no." I falter. "Uhm, I need to stretch. I've been working on this tear for a while."

"Excellent." Doctor Dorset's eyes seem to come alive. "Let's go to dinner. My treat, to celebrate your newest adventure."

Crap. I need an out. Biting my tongue for a moment, I bluff. "I just haven't had a chance to tell my parents, and I was going to share the news with them tonight at dinner. Dad's taking me to one of his favorite restaurants."

"Is he?" Doctor Dorset cocks his head and raises an eyebrow.

"Yes," I confirm, nodding.

"I see." Doctor Dorset sighs. *Does he believe me?*

"Well, thank you for the well wishes."

Moving as quickly as possible, I put away my work. All the while, Doctor Dorset watches me. It's uncomfortable, but I don't know what else to do.

Lab coat off and fall coat on, I grab my purse and escape the lab. Trying to put distance between us, I move as quickly as I can down hallways past other labs and classrooms until I get outside. Pulling my phone from my pocket, I look at it.

I flip through my contacts: Dad.

"Hey, pumpkin." My dad answers on the third ring. "Are you okay?"

"I'm fine, Daddy. Did I catch you at a bad time?" My voice shakes with excitement. I can't believe I did it.

"I have about ten minutes before my next meeting," he says. "Is this important? Can you meet me for . . . is that really the time? Can you meet me for dinner?"

Is it important? Should I just wait until this weekend? No. Now is good.

"Yeah, dinner would be good. I'll meet you at our place?"

"Mmhmm. I have to go. I'll meet you there," Dad answers before he hangs up on me.

There's a fifty percent chance Dad won't meet me there. He's super good at being a dad if he can ever remember to show up. But his meeting will run long, and then he'll get called into something else. There's no harm in going alone.

Walking down the street to the bus station, I stop and let the excitement finally hit me.

Mom and Dad haven't supported my choice to major in something other than political science or global studies. To be fair, I hid it from them. But, just as suspected, when they found out, I was 'a disappointment' and 'uninteresting to men of my level.' Why am I only worth the man I can marry?

I have an internship at probably the most prestigious institution for documents, history, and artwork in the entire country. They wanted me. I haven't even graduated. *They wanted me.* It feels so good to have achieved this. The culmination of my hard work and everything I'm passionate about.

I pull the letter out of my purse and look at it again. A dream come true is in my hands, waiting for me.

PRESENT DAY

CHAPTER 1
THALIA

YESTERDAY, life was *amazing*.

I had my first day of orientation as a museum educator intern at the Smithsonian, which has been my dream job since I was little. Well, right after I realized that being an archaeologist wouldn't be so fun, seeing as how it's spending every day outside looking at pieces of pottery and not discovering ancient civilizations and mummies, contrary to what my favorite movies led me to believe.

To celebrate my first day, I treated myself to a first-day dinner. I ordered the tortellini with parm-crusted chicken and even got a slice of peanut butter silk pie from my favorite restaurant, and then picked up the newest book in the series I'm currently reading. Despite wanting to stay up all night and finish the book, I went to bed at a reasonable hour to keep up with my newest self-care goals. It's been three months, and while I don't really notice a ton of changes from going to bed at a reasonable hour, it feels more responsible, so I take it as a win.

Today, however, life really sucks. I'm rousted from my bed

at 5:00 a.m. by banging at my door and a man shouting, "Washington DC Police!"

I begrudgingly shuffle to the door and barely have it open when police officers and private security team members flood my one-bedroom apartment. The only distinction between them is the lack of Kevlar and the word SECURITY on the back of some of the uniforms.

"Hey! No. What? Where are you —?" Stamping my feet, I try yelling at them to get out.

They rush in, ignoring me, despite my loudest objections.

"Clear!" one yells from my bedroom.

"Clear!" My shower curtain is slid back by someone in the bathroom. There must be at least twelve people rushing around my tiny apartment. It is absolutely against fire code.

They've confirmed I'm here alone. But now they're searching my entire apartment — for what, I don't know — while I follow them around, yelling at them to leave or give me more information.

"What are you doing?" I ask one in the living room as he's dismantling my library of books.

He doesn't answer, so I dart off to find someone else.

I've cornered an agent in the bathroom. I'm ready to barricade him in when another agent or cop yells over the top of my head, an order that we need to leave. *Yes. They do need to leave. Who are these jerks?* If it weren't for the fact half of them are police, I'd be calling 911. I'm sure my neighbors think I'm being murdered, or worse.

The agent from the bathroom shoos me back with his palms, and I rotate out of the door frame. *Shoot, there goes my chance!*

"Ms. Thalia Clark?" One of the uniformed police officers finally speaks to me, coming around the couch into my sitting area where I'd gone to try my luck with the man looking at my entertainment center.

"Yes. That's me." I try to focus on him, but people are still milling through my house. "What's going on? Why are you here?"

"Miss." A member of the fleet of men approaches the officer and me, splitting my attention yet again. He's wearing a polo emblazoned with SECURITY and starts talking. "I'm Michael with Corinth Security. We need you to come with us now. Your life is in danger."

"What?! Are my parents okay? What kind of danger?" I ask, but he's already moving on, shouting orders to his team. *Rude. What if they're not okay and no one is telling me? They have to tell you, right?*

The police officer tries ushering me toward the door and away from Michael. "Wait. No, I need to put on clothes."

"Make it quick, Miss Clark," the police officer says flatly. "We've got to go."

I'm barely allowed five minutes alone to change out of my puppy-print pajamas and brush my teeth. I try to find an outfit my mother might approve of, but the stress of starting my day with strange men in my apartment makes it impossible. Luckily, I'm able to toss my hair up into a messy bun and try to be presentable.

I'm flustered. My face is red and puffy, and I'm pushing back tears of panic. Children of politicians must be in control of their behavior. You're only allowed emotions in private, and even then, it's frowned upon. With two parents in politics, it's even more disgraceful that in the chaos of it all, I've failed rule number one this morning. I've fallen apart, gotten upset, and don't have the effortless grace that Mom expects of me.

As I'm rushed out the door, I manage to grab my phone.

Before I can unlock it, one of the private security specialists snatches it, turns it off, and puts it in a little black box. *Rude.*

"If you're going to take my phone, you need to tell me about my parents." I try to demand, but the six-foot man made of muscles isn't into answering questions.

My protests continue to go unanswered. My mounting frustration has me wanting to fight back, but I'm five foot two against a small army of well-armed individuals.

If my parents were dead, they'd tell me, right? I don't have any other family in the area they could tell first. Mom and Dad are probably the reason for all of this. But what caused this mess? Sans phone, I'm at the mercy of the officers and security team.

After what feels like twenty minutes from them barging through my front door, I'm whisked into the back seat of a black town car in the basement of my apartment building, on my way to destination unknown. What's worse? I've been through this before, and it's no less scary as an adult.

OUR EXTENDED DRIVING tour of DC before morning traffic is ridiculous, although from past circumstances, it's a standard and necessary precaution. Eventually, we're pulling into another underground parking structure.

I'm led across the dark space into an elevator with a solitary option on the panel. *This can't be good.* When we reach our destination, the doors open to a formal lobby. I see my dad first. His silver hair is perfectly styled as he sits there in khakis and a blue sweater, reading a magazine. Seeing him instantly floods me with relief.

"Oh, Thalia, thank God." Dad stands, and in two quick strides, he's pulling me into his arms, hugging me tightly.

Pressing my face against his cashmere sweater, I squeeze back. I'm holding back the sobs of relief at seeing him alive and well. *Why couldn't the security team just tell me?* There's been this unrealized — until now — fear that the most recent hug I gave him could have been the last. Afraid of what the future holds, I hug even more intensely, sure to make this one count.

When he lets me go, I turn to hug my mother. She's terse and rigid.

The moment we separate, she begins, "Thalia Ann, couldn't you have done something with your hair?"

"Mom, really?" I cringe. It's not like I didn't know it was coming, but there are surely bigger issues at hand. I step back from both of them. "What is going on, they said it wasn't safe? The sun's not even up yet. How can there already be trouble?"

"There have been threats, pumpkin. Someone left, well . . . something not pleasant on our steps. We were worried," my father answers.

He towers over me and kisses the top of my head.

I'm positive there's something he's not telling me. Something is going on, but I'm so glad to see him safe that I don't want to push anything more.

An older woman with a stern face at the reception desk leads us down the halls to a conference room. We're ushered in, with Mom first and Dad following closely behind me, then seated at the table.

My mother turns and fusses with my red curls, just like she would any time before we would be seen by the press. More concerned for my physical state than my mental or emotional well-being. There's some sort of emergency, and all she can think about is appearances. She's still my overly critical mother.

This is one of the many reasons I've purposefully walked away from her politics and this life. She was bearable when we were in Europe for Dad's station as a diplomat; now that it's her turn to be the political force in the family, she's absolutely out of control.

"Mom, what is going on?"

I swat her hand away. It's too early for this fussing. It's impossible to live up to her standards. My coppery-red hair is full of wavy curls that I'm just now kind of learning how to embrace. She constantly cuts me down with reminders that I look just like she did when she was younger. Telling me that my curly hair is only so frazzled because I don't groom it the same way and that my green eyes would look bigger and more attractive if I wore more makeup. I will never be good enough.

With a stern glare, she tucks one last lock of hair behind my ear before dismissively answering the question. "It's like your father said. There have been some threats. We didn't want to worry you unnecessarily, but now it's worth worrying about. We're here for . . ." She pauses, pursing her lips. "A consultation," she continues, "on how to best handle the threat, and until we know it's safe, you're with us."

With a wave of her manicured hand, Mom effectively ends the conversation. Her graying red hair is perfectly coiffed, and she's dressed in a skirt suit. She's impeccably put together, down to a pearl necklace resting on her collarbones. Despite the odd hour of the day, she manages a flawless look. My entire life, I've never seen her looking anything less than annoyingly perfect.

A bald-headed man walks down the hallway and through the conference room door, drawing my attention away from the words 'a consultation,' which implies something more. His suit fits well. It's traditional black with a white linen shirt. He has an air of confidence, not arrogance, that I'm used to seeing with professionals meeting with my parents.

We stand to greet him, and he shakes our hands with a

strong and self-assured grip. Peter Corinth of Corinth Security assures my parents that his best specialist has ended his vacation specifically for this assignment.

Peter tries to be casual when he says, "After speaking more in-depth with you, it seems that you've chosen Corinth Security based on the proven track record of one of my team leads. Based on what my analysts have determined, I believe your request for him is justified. Undoubtedly, he is the only person I could recommend to protect Ms. Clark. However, given your political stance, I feel obligated to disclose that the man you've requested is a shifter. I do, of course, understand if you would like to work with a different team."

"What does the man being a shifter have to do with anything? Will someone please tell me what's going on?" I look to my mom and then to my dad before landing back at Peter, furrowing my brow.

He looks to my parents for an answer. Purposefully avoiding my parents' politics for the last few years may have been a mistake; clearly, they're involved in something awful. Threats don't happen to good people. Do they?

"Thalia Ann, be quiet." My father chastises me, bringing out my middle name, anger dripping in his voice.

I shudder under his harsh gaze. Dad never raises his voice to me. Ever. I'm struck silent by his change in demeanor toward me.

This day, which was abnormal to begin with, is slowly becoming my worst nightmare.

"Bring him in." My mother is curt and bristles in her chair.

Is she scared of them? My parents have never even talked about them in front of me. Shifters have only been public for . . . *has it even been a year?* They're just like other people. How else have they lived hundreds and thousands of years undetected? What would it matter if this person were one?

CHAPTER 2
CADE

SITTING in the great room of the Alloways' pack house, I'm filled with deep melancholy. There is warmth in being with our cousins and their pack for the holidays. Yet, there's this emptiness, knowing I can't cultivate this back at home. Without being the Sovereign, or a Pack Alpha, I cannot host holidays, and it would be considered a hostile act to rebuild a formal pack. *A fucking nightmare.*

So, here I am as an invited guest, along with Deacon and Kathleen — well, she goes by Lena now — to our cousin Judah Alloway's. For the most part, Deacon, Lena, and I are okay. Holidays are a mixed bag of emotions, but our cousins always make us feel welcomed. It's better this way.

Trying to relax with the beer I've been nursing for almost an hour, I listen to Wyatt Thibodeaux play on his guitar and sing along with Lena across the great room by the fireplace.

Judah sitting in the oversized chair next to me, with his feet resting on the coffee table, tries to casually steal glances in their direction. It's a yearnful look. *Puzzling.*

We call the Alloways our cousins despite, by our best

estimations, that we were last blood relatives over a thousand years ago. However, it's always been a general rule that the families with Ardelean gifts refrain from mating. Generally speaking, those of the Ardelean line take mates based on merit and connections through intended arrangements.

I hope, for both of our sakes, he's looking at Wyatt and not Lena. I would never stand in the way between Judah and Lena. Their happiness is important to me. But the high council and other non-Ardelean families would throw a fit over them being together. Just thinking about the potential fallout is exhausting.

Judah's younger sister, Dinah, stretches out on the other end of the sectional sofa with her feet up over the armrest.

She speaks softly to not disturb the sound of playing music. "You could have this, cousin. Well, not *this* this, since it would be preferable if you didn't dethrone Judah and move in here. But this lifestyle? It's yours. You could be home nurturing your rightful pack as Sovereign and cultivating this life."

"It's not all bad," Judah agrees. He nods his head at me with an air of encouragement before narrowing his eyes and flashing a glimpse of his wolf before continuing, "You're seriously going to let Robert make these moves? He has two functioning brain cells. Letting him go head-to-head with that bigoted congresswoman on political issues affecting shifters isn't fair to us. It's bad enough he looks like the idiot he is, but the fact that he now evidently represents all wolves, *all shifters*, across the country is insulting."

Judah has always been the levelheaded one out of our group, so it's out of character for him to be so open in giving his honest opinion of others, especially when it's unsolicited. I try to remember that after his guilt trip.

I try biting the inside of my cheek, but I can't help but remind him there are other options to what he's suggesting.

"See, I've been there, done that, and it was the worst year of my life. You, however, could take over. There's no way he'd beat you in an Alpha challenge. You'd be a hell of a lot better Alpha than Robert is."

Beer almost comes out of Judah's mouth as he chokes on a laugh. "Cade, you'll be a great Alpha. Take back the throne. We've all seen what you and The Leviathan are as a team. I have a home and a pack. Who would step into my shoes here?"

"Fairly certain that would be Dinah." I squint at him, not missing a beat. "Besides, Robert leaves you all mostly alone anyway, right?"

"I mean, except for about two weeks ago. He called and asked if Dinah had any open intentions." Judah arches his eyebrows and cocks his head back and forth before taking a sip of his beer.

I look over at Dinah, who is pretending to be enthralled with the blades of the ceiling fan to avoid looking at us.

"That idiot. After I had to step in to take care of —" Judah's eyes and a sharp flash of his wolf silence me. "Robert has the audacity to call asking for her?" I clench my fist and let it go, shaking my head. I push images from that night from my mind. "Fuck it, never mind. I've got to remember to keep out of pack politics. I shouldn't ask about him. I've told him not to call me, and he doesn't. It's for the best if I keep my nose out of everything."

"Staying out of it is going to make it a whole lot worse than just getting involved," Dinah says coyly, giving me a curious smile.

I open my mouth to inquire what's made her so Cheshire-cat-like, but my phone rings, chirping loudly from my pocket. Eyeing her, I fish it out.

A pit forms in my stomach at seeing my employer's information pop up on the screen.

I answer hesitantly. The music stops. "Hello, Peter. Didn't expect to hear from you —"

"Cade, are you someplace private?" Peter cuts me off.

Judah points down the hallway toward the Alpha's suite, a secluded and private area of the house, and mouths, "Use my bedroom."

Walking briskly down to Judah's bedroom, I close the door behind me before responding, "It's clear."

"I need you in DC in the next twelve hours. I know you're supposed to be on your holiday for two more weeks. If I had any other options, I would call someone else. I need you here first thing in the morning." Peter's words come quickly with urgency.

The way he cuts off all my arguments before I can state them means he expected my pushback. *Something is very wrong.*

"I can't be there tomorrow. I'm in Maine. I can't leave my siblings here, either. I'd have to get them back home first." I inform him politely-ish.

It's not like Peter to even text me on a holiday, let alone call me. I run my hands through my hair and then forward into my face. It's too long, with strands reaching down the center of my nose.

"I'll send a team to escort them home. Flying out of Bangor, right?" Peter presses, unwavering.

"We drove in. Peter, what's going on?" I keep pushing, holding a level tone.

"Do you have your suit with you?" Peter ignores my question.

"Yes. I've got my suit with me. We were at Equinox last night." I push my hair out of my eyes. *I need a haircut; I'm going to look like Deacon at this rate.*

"Bring it. You'll need it." Peter is typing furiously on a

keyboard. "What day were you scheduled to drive back to Wisconsin?"

I pull the phone away from my face looking at it dumbly, like it'll give me some sort of answer that he won't.

I try to be firm without demanding too harshly. "Peter, I don't know what's going on. I'm not dropping everything and coming into the office. I haven't been home in over a month. I drove halfway across the country with my siblings and need this time with my family."

"If I didn't need you, I wouldn't call," Peter snaps. He breathes deeply before continuing, "I'm sorry to pull you away from your family on the holiday, but there's no one else for this job. Once you arrive and see who the client is, I know you'll understand how important this job is to you on a personal level. I can't disclose anything more over the phone. Do you have your Yukon?"

The discussion is over. I'm going to DC regardless of how much I like it or don't. If I worked for anyone else, it would be worth it to pause and debate a career change, but I've worked with Peter for almost six years. He was the first to approach me with a job when I completed my service with the army. I'm afforded a lot of leeway a majority of the time. Four major holidays, extra time off between jobs, and very few questions asked if something comes up or I need a personal day. I doubt I'd ever get a better offer. *Never give an ultimatum you're not willing to walk out on.* I'm not ready to walk out.

"What day should I fly your siblings back?" Peter repeats. The typing continues.

"We were planning to stay until Friday," I answer, hoping Lena will forgive me.

We drove from Wisconsin to Maine on the States' side to get here, and I promised to drive the Canadian side home to stop in her favorite art shop in Toronto.

"I'll book them first class nonstop directly and have the team escort them all the way through the door." Peter is matter-of-fact. "Can you leave now? I need you here as early as possible. It's urgent."

"Yeah. I'm sober. I'll start driving now." I reflect on the half-full warm beer on the coffee table.

I don't give him a chance to say anything else and disconnect the call.

Leaving Judah's suite, I walk back down the hall. Faces fall when they see me, and it's not surprising. I'm not hiding my distaste.

Judah nods, pursing his lips knowingly. "Duty calls?"

Lena glares at me, and Wyatt gently rubs her back, whispering to her. Suddenly I'm not worried if Lena will forgive me. My mind turns gears. I wonder if I need to worry about Wyatt or Judah, or both, asking for my good faith for an intention to mate her. I shake my head, clearing that thought. I can't get wrapped up in this particular mess right now.

Pulling my eyes off the two of them, I look to Judah. "I'm headed to DC. I don't know how long. Can they still stay with you until Friday? Peter's arranging flights out of Bangor and a car once they get home."

"Yeah, it's no problem. They can stay, and I'll get them to the airport," Judah agrees.

"It'll be fun," Dinah chirps. She smiles at me. "DC is going to be very important. You won't want to miss it."

"Scary." It's the only response I can come up with to reply to her remark.

Knowing Dinah has the gift of foresight, you can't ever be certain what's a veiled promise of the future.

I'VE DRIVEN through the night and haven't slept in nearly twenty-three hours. I'm feeling bitter as I pull into the underground parking garage shortly after 6:00 a.m.

I close my eyes for a moment, pinching the bridge of my nose, and take a few deep breaths. Fuck, I'm not twenty anymore, and all the joy I found in working all-night missions has faded. I look down the rows of cars to see Peter's Jaguar already parked in his assigned space. *Was he here all night, or did he try to beat me in?*

Through building security, suit bag in hand, I head up the private, secured elevator directly to our floor. I don't expect to see Alice standing behind her desk, pressing the corded phone firmly against her ear with one hand as she writes a note. She's more than just a receptionist, though, managing more jobs in a single day than I can in a week as the office manager, secretary, and whatever other countless titles Peter decides to toss at her. It's hard not to smile at Alice. She's probably in her sixties and is the nicest woman in the world, yet there's not a person in this building who isn't terrified of her on some level, myself included.

With a curt nod, Alice hangs up her phone and informs me, "Michael called. They're going to be here in twenty minutes. Tell Peter the conference room is set up and ready." She stops and gives me a scornful look. "You look like shit."

"Love you too, Alice," I call over my shoulder before walking through the internal glass doors and down the hall toward Peter's office.

On my walk to his office, I note that our largest conference room is set for five. Peter and I, plus three clients, which doesn't seem abnormal. *So why is he trying to make a good impression?* The clients being so early in the morning is also an interesting development. Something isn't quite right in all of this. A knot forms in my stomach as I ring the doorbell to

Peter's office. Unlike the conference room, which is designed for looks, Peter's office is always completely private. There's soundproofing so impressive that, even with the extra hearing being a wolf grants me, I'm unable to get a clear enough sound to guess if it's occupied.

"Cade, please come in." Peter begins speaking before he pulls the door all the way open. He motions to the suit bag. "You'll need to put your suit on. You brought a tie?"

Exhaustion prevents me from giving him any sort of witty remark. Laying my suit bag over one of the chairs facing his desk, I look him square in the eye and confront him. "Alice said the clients will be here in twenty minutes. What's with the suit and tie? I can't remember the last time you made me dress for a client meeting."

"It's best you don't know just yet." Peter tries and fails miserably to brush off the question as he runs his hand over his bald head and looks away.

He's not one to withhold information from me. At fifty, he's got decades more years in the security game than I do, and we've developed a strong working relationship.

"I don't like the sound of this," I murmur.

After my honorable discharge from the army, I quit blindly accepting orders, and Peter has respected that until now.

I scent the faint smell of fear on Peter. I've never seen him exhibit fear going into a client meeting. Normally one to reserve emotions for those close to him, Peter doesn't get intimidated by clients, only by situations that put his team members at risk.

Unaware of my observation, he tries to downplay the conversation. "It's a very important job, and your skill set is the best I have. For this client, the best is mandatory, and we need to start off on the right foot." His tone mimics a nonchalant attitude as he compliments me.

"Trying to butter me up?" I walk to the window, looking down at the street, crossing my arms in front of my chest.

Commuters on the main road are beginning to start for the day. Other employees enter the building with their morning coffees, unaware of my watchful eyes.

"Is it working?" He sounds hopeful.

"Not especially," I deadpan, not turning to look at him.

Peter's phone buzzes. "Shit, they're early. Put your suit on, and would it kill you to keep your hair neat? I'll buzz you once I get them settled." He's halfway out the door when he pauses with a glance over his shoulder, saying, "And Cade? Just keep in mind, you're their only option."

Ten or so minutes later, I'm in my suit, people watching out Peter's window, when my phone buzzes. The uneasiness that's been incubating for the last twelve hours hatches into a monster of nervous energy.

Under my skin, The Leviathan is on high alert, watching for every possible threat. My wolf and I haven't communicated since I abdicated the throne a decade ago. Despite our differences and the distance we keep from each other, he's proven time and again that he doesn't have a death wish. While he doesn't talk directly to me, I feel his presence and often his displeasure. His attention is generally reserved for true danger. I trust him in that, but I keep control.

I force myself to walk leisurely, especially when coming into view of the glass walls of the conference room, masking any trace of the unsettledness within me. Taking a look at the clients before I enter, it's impossible not to recognize them.

Casual and leisurely are no longer part of my repertoire. My jaw locks tight. The Leviathan bristles. I stifle a snarl. We've found the danger.

I open the glass door to the conference room, my eyes

31

locked on Peter. If I look at *them*, I'm not sure what's going to happen.

"Peter, a moment, please."

Without waiting for Peter to excuse himself, I turn, perfectly composed, but violence brews within me. I stalk away, not waiting for him to follow me. I'm standing outside his office door, breathing, trying to calm down when he rounds the corridor to meet with me.

Peter opens the door, and I follow him in.

Once it closes, I start talking before he can. "I've never turned down a job before. I've done a number of unspeakable things for you. I've done all of those things without question. Take that all into consideration when I say: give these clients to anyone but me."

"I have already told you, Cade, there is no one else with the ability to take this job." Peter gestures back to the conference room. "Shifters are threatening their daughter. I can't trust anyone else to stay loyal like you."

"That shouldn't surprise you, given her mother's political stance on shifters. Senator Clark said in her last meeting with the press, you'll have to forgive me for paraphrasing: shifters exist and are dangerous. Therefore, it is our responsibility to eliminate them systematically." I paraphrase, heavily.

My control is slipping. Peter steps back, his gaze on my eyes. They've shifted from my normal steel blue to the golden yellow color revealing The Leviathan I'm fighting to keep locked inside.

Peter sighs in frustration but takes another small step back from me, nodding. "I'm sure there is a small political conflict for you."

"It's a major conflict of interest! You're not only asking me to put a target on my own head but on Deacon's and Lena's too. If this leaks —" I stop myself from thinking through worst-case scenarios. I scrub my hand down my face. "Anyone but me."

"They need someone who can keep her safe. I'll pay you double for this job and permanently give you extra time off between jobs." Peter tries to barter with me.

I try to stifle the growl pulling from my chest.

Reminding myself that Peter's in an equally fucked up position, I motion to my chest, then hitchhike my way out of the conversation with a thumb pointing out. "The pay isn't good enough for this job. Double, triple, or quadruple. It doesn't matter, money isn't the issue. I'm unavailable. Something has suddenly come up. Anyone but me."

"It's not Thalia's fault that her mother has ridiculous politics." Peter tries another tactic, his voice dropping to a deadly serious tone. He leans forward into my personal space. "If something happens to Thalia in the next nine weeks before the bill passes, and they find a shifter at fault, it further fuels her mother's case. While that may benefit Senator Clark's cause, you don't want that. Ultimately, she is still a mother and doesn't want to see her daughter hurt. Thalia needs a shifter to protect her. One that can't be corrupted or tempted to make a power move or political statement. Senator Clark came here specifically because of our track record, your track record."

Fuck his fucking logic. I'm trapped. This is happening.

I scrub my hand down my face and release a slow exhale. "Let's go talk details with the clients. If they agree for me to be her security detail, I want double and a half for this job, sixteen more paid days off a year, and I want a minimum of one paid week of downtime at home, in Wisconsin, after jobs that are longer than ten days."

"Done." Peter doesn't even balk at the request.

I'm pretty sure he knows I don't need the money, but it's nice to know I'm worth the cost to him.

CHAPTER 3
THALIA

THROUGH THE GLASS walls of the conference room, I watch as a man walks with purposeful, long strides to the door. When he pulls it, the door opens in a loud whoosh of displaced air. The scene is nearly a blur as he demands Peter leave with him.

In mere seconds, the two men are out of sight and once they are, cue the angry bickering. *Mom and Dad are starting early today.*

"Darren, this is a bad idea. Sending her with one of *them*." Mom points at me and then at the table. Her top lip pulls upward into a sneer.

"Marie, we've agreed, whatever it takes to keep Thalia safe," my father urges, holding his hand open, indicating toward me.

Dad's eyes are soft, almost sad?

She huffs in frustration, quickly turning her head away to avoid looking at us.

"I can't believe we're even considering this." She points her finger toward the hallway where the two men went. "They want to be their own legislature. Did you know that? Those are the most recent talks. They want to keep their own kings or whatever."

"Now is not the time for your politics." My father chastises her, then drops to a whisper, trying to lean past me. "Have you forgotten why our daughter is in danger?"

Okay, so they're serious. I'm the one in danger. This isn't about them?!

Purposefully, I've kept myself out of Mom's political career. Engrossing myself in my studies in archival preservation, I've been able to live my life, for the first time ever.

Regret sinks in deeper with each passing minute. *Why am I in danger? I haven't done anything!* Something Mom has been working on is clearly a problem.

I look back to her, opening my mouth to ask all the questions, but I'm cut off.

Her voice is tight as she wags her finger at me. "You need to be careful. He may be your security detail, but you need to be aware. They can't be trusted."

"What are you talking about? Why wouldn't you want me to trust him?" I plead for an answer I know she won't give. "You're being ridiculous. I don't need a security detail. And what does it matter that he's a shifter?"

Movement down the corridor catches my attention, causing my heart to pound.

"Do as I say," Mom hisses before tapping my shoulder.

It's my well-trained command from her to be silent. I'm twenty and being silenced like a petulant child when *my* safety is at risk. *Ridiculous.*

The man who called Peter away returns with him, walking slower and more dedicated. He holds open the door for Peter. At this speed, I'm able to get a better look. Despite the well-tailored black suit, he has an edge of ruggedness about him. Medium-length chocolate hair and a groomed beard, but model-pretty all the same. A man this sexy has no business working private security. His suit fits him just as well as most men in the circles my parents run in. Difference is, whoever he is, he has the confidence and awareness of his own body to make it work. *Peter Corinth must pay well.*

My face heats as I take him in.

Our eyes meet before he turns away to focus on my mother. *Crap! How long was I staring?*

We rise to our feet, ready to greet them, just another trained pomp and circumstance in time for introductions.

"Ambassador and Senator Clark, I would like to introduce you to Cade Al —" Peter quickly cuts off the man's — Cade's — last name after a sharp gaze from him. "Your security specialist. Cade, I would like to introduce you to Ambassador Darren Clark, his wife, Senator Marie Clark, and their daughter, Ms. Thalia Clark." Peter gestures appropriately with a diplomatic open hand.

Well, that was weird.

"Well, Mr. Cade." My mother uses her pretentious and judgmental tone. "You come highly recommended."

Cade gives a cordial nod. "I'm glad my reputation precedes me."

If Cade even recognized the condescension in her remark, he doesn't engage or react in the slightest.

I raise an eyebrow in question of the anomaly. His lack of need for her approval is sexy and not what I'm used to.

His eyes, which had been trained on her, drift past me directly to my father, who has his hand extended for a shake, but Cade declines as his gaze moves back to Peter. "Peter, would you please take Ms. Clark to Adam and have him dissect her phone while I have a word with the ambassador and senator."

The way Cade said 'Ms. Clark' felt like velvet hugging my

skin. I never imagined my name and title could be so alluring. Well, I guess all those historical dramas have some sort of courtship element. So, it probably has more to do with the mouth the words fall from.

"Of course." Peter gives Cade a warning look and then turns to me with a polite smile. "If you'd join me, Ms. Clark."

While leaving, Cade's eyes catch mine for a fraction of a second as I walk by. They flash a brilliant gold color, but it's gone in the same instant. The intensity of his gaze feels nearly scandalous.

My face warms, and as Peter leads me out the door, I fight the urge to fan myself like one of those eighteenth-century British girls in those BBC dramas.

Peter and I walk quietly down another corridor to a room that is, oddly enough, lit by a bunch of mismatched lamps. The room has a warm ambiance, a stark contrast to the fluorescent lights in the hallway. A man sits behind the desk, and his eyes move between the many monitors in front of him.

"Adam, this is Cade's new client. We're needing her phone to go on a vacation. Hook her up with one of the company ones if you would. I'm sure Cade would like it to his specifications. You and Millie up for some time off?" Peter smiles at him, eyes locked on the man sitting behind the computer.

Adam nods but doesn't look up. "Yeah. You can leave her with me. I'll get that underway. Can you tell Millie to pack our bags? I'm betting we're going to the Swiss Alps."

"Absolutely." Peter indicates for me to sit in a chair. "Would it kill you to turn on some proper lights in here?"

"Yes. Yes, it would." Adam laughs as he finishes typing before he turns to look at me with a smile and a cheeky wink.

Peter turns to leave, closing the door behind him and shaking his head in what seems like dismay.

"Alright, uh, Ms. Clark?" Adam smiles. "Let's make sure you're not being cyberstalked."

"I don't think that's necessary." I watch as he opens the little black box that the previous agent had stuffed my phone in. I itch to get it back so I can look into Mom's political platform to understand this situation.

"So, that's not really up to either of us." He puffs his lips up. "How about we delete accounts you don't remember getting, clean up some permissions, and I can promise you that when you get your phone back, it'll be faster and better for streaming videos. I can even get you a setup so you can stream stuff from other countries super easily."

Adam's quirky, nerdy appearance with oversized glasses tells me he's just another pawn in whatever game this is.

It would be nice if I could get better access to the special gallery videos that are only available in their country of origin. *Alright, maybe this isn't awful.*

Two hours later, Adam has gone through every folder on my phone, deleting things. We change passwords to every single account I ever remember signing up for, even some I don't.

"Uh, do you want to look through your photo gallery and delete any, um, confidential photos?" Adam hands me my phone for the first time during this exchange.

"Oh, I don't keep any work documents on my phone." I shrug, handing it back.

"No. Um. Those that perhaps would only stay between you and, uh, your partners of choice." He pushes the phone back toward me.

I don't think my face has ever been as warm as it is listening to him explain. I'm not sure who's more uncomfortable.

"Is that what time it is?" I ask, looking at the cuckoo clock on the wall. *Who has a cuckoo clock?*

"Yes." Adam doesn't look up from his work.

"I wonder if I'm going to make it to school on time," I muse aloud.

"Uh . . ." Adam starts to answer.

The room floods with a harsher, brighter light than the lamps as someone opens the door, and I hear Cade's voice. "Ms. Clark, I've had Peter speak with your school and internship. They've put you on an indefinite leave of absence."

"What?!" I whip my head around to see Cade leaning against the door.

His suit jacket is open, his tie is hanging loose, and his hair is a bit disheveled.

My jaw drops and I let out a startled gasp. Is it possible this look is even more attractive than when he was completely polished?

The anger at his declaration simmers, but heat creeps up my cheeks at my perusal of him. *What is wrong with me? There is no checking out the dude who wants to keep us from the Smithsonian.*

"We're not staying in the city, Ms. Clark," he states firmly. The velvet in his voice is gone. Words he says now are more somber and direct. "It's not safe."

"That's why we're hiring you. To keep me safe, why can't you do that here?" I snap, flying to my feet. I clench my fist. "I'm not giving up my internship over this threat no one will tell me about. I worked hard for this. You're not just taking me away from it. This week we're getting in a series of documents from the . . . No, I'm not missing this. I need to talk to my parents."

"I'll take you to them and would be glad to show you the threats." Cade raises an eyebrow, eyes traveling down my body, focusing on my fist, daring me before stepping out of the doorway.

As we walk, he knots his tie and runs his fingers through his hair, pushing it back out of his silver blue eyes before we arrive back at the conference room. I want to judge him for straightening up his appearance, but I'm fussing with my shirt. Mom has that impact on people.

Cade ushers me in, and although I know it's the same room, it looks vastly different. It's as if in the short time I was with Adam, a paper truck and a photo booth had a collision, spilling their cargo across the table. My parents sit in the same chairs, but Mom's eyes are distant and slightly glossy, and Dad has reclined into his chair, sitting haphazardly, one leg extended before him. They look like they've just heard the most terrible news.

Once we've moved into his field of vision, Dad raises his head, and his gaze falls to me, eyes widening in horror.

Jumping from his seat, he darts between us and the table, positioning himself so I can't see what's contained in the mess on the table. "Cade, she can't see this."

"Ms. Clark is adamant that she wishes to remain in the city. Per our previous discussion, I cannot keep her safe in this city. Seeing as how that is the job you've hired me to do, Ms. Clark would like to evaluate it for herself."

Cade is very formal with his speech. Almost too formal, like one of those emails you send a person grinding on your last gear.

My father gives a reprimanding look to Cade but turns soft when addressing me. "I'm sorry, pumpkin, but the threats are horrible. You shouldn't see this. I don't want you to have this in your head."

"Let her see, Darren. If she insists on questioning the decisions we've made to keep her safe, then let her see," Mom snaps at him, but her eyes refuse to meet mine.

I still don't understand what her problem is. Is this from being in the room with Cade? Because he's a shifter?

Cade steps past my father to the table and picks up various photos before shuffling the rest into a messy pile farther down. He gestures me closer and lays most of them out.

His voice sounds different as he talks, rough and coarse. "Ms. Clark, these were taken by someone who has access to a large part of your life. They were most likely taken by someone you know and believe you can trust."

I recognize the photos. They're all of me, places I've been. All of them are from this week. I remember putting together the outfits as part of my new weekly self-care ritual. My favorite coffee shop, the lobby of my apartment building, and outside the university.

Cade flips over the last one, and I cover my mouth with both hands as I try hard not to react.

The photo in his hand was taken from inside my apartment. It's the view from the hallway into my bedroom, and I'm in bed. You can see my silhouette illuminated by the glow from my phone.

My knees go weak, and I'm lightheaded. Hands steady me before setting me in a chair.

"Ms. Clark, I cannot keep you safe when someone has so easily gained access to you. There isn't a place in this city where I could guarantee your safety. From a bathroom at school to your own home, those targeting you have you completely covered." Cade's voice is softer and closer. "I'm excellent at what I do, but staying in the city is beyond the point of mitigable risk."

His voice rumbles through me. All I can do is sit, nodding in response.

He gives me a moment before continuing, "I can't keep you safe here in the city. The threats are all very centric around you. We've made the decision that it's best if you're removed from the area until the threats lessen to an acceptable range or your mother's bill has gone to vote. It's best if you say goodbye to your parents. This could be the last time you see them for a while."

My world is shattering. The dream I held in my hands four short months ago is slipping through my fingers. All because my mother's politics have ensnared me, despite my best efforts to steer clear of her political games.

CHAPTER 4

CADE

I'VE NEVER SEEN a surveillance photo as disturbing as the one of Thalia in bed. The photo was taken with a cellphone at chest-level height, which means someone was inside her apartment while she was there and awake. She's lucky to be alive.

Maybe I could have shared less with her to get her to agree to come? Maybe just the online comments and the usual stalking photos? Would she have really believed me and understood how real the threat is?

Washington, DC, is not safe for her. Shifters want her dead, or worse, and those on the war path for her have proven they have access to her. Why didn't they kill her when they had her within arm's reach? I don't know. I may never know.

Peter will probably forgive me for striking a deal under the table. It was more than a little reckless to leverage my position — as the only one capable of protecting her daughter — against Senator Marie Clark. However, if she truly can relieve some tension in the conflict she created, there's reason to hope that Thalia could be returned home sooner rather than later.

Then in a few weeks, this whole ordeal will be nothing more than an anecdote to tell at Summer Solstice.

The Leviathan watches Thalia intently as she hugs her mom with a casual 'love you, see you later' and then latches on to her father. Hugging each other tightly, they whisper terms of endearment and a brief but sentimental 'I love you.'

Every time we're in the same room together, my wolf is laser focused on her. Which, seeing as how she's the job, at least we can agree on keeping focused . . . even if his focus is darkly based on the idea of us hunting her.

Peter escorts the senator and ambassador out of the conference room. Thalia and I follow close behind, leaving behind the proof that we just pressed pause on her life. I place my hand between her shoulder blades, gently nudging her down the corridor back toward Adam's office.

"Millie and Adam are going to make you into a whole new person." I pause, seeing her eyes moving back and forth. She can't seem to focus on any one thing. I try to give her more knowledge of what's happening, but I'm not sure it will sink in. "Well, at least on paper. I'm going to grab a few hours of sleep, and then we'll get you out of the city."

We're headed to the lobby and Alice's desk when I spot Millie and Adam approaching. Purposefully congregating in front of Alice's desk, which she hates, I wait for them to reach us.

Millie asks, "So, boss, we need a vacation?"

"Yeah, how do you feel about the Maldives?" I laugh.

"Damn it." Adam groans, pulling a crumpled twenty-dollar bill out of his pocket and handing it to Millie.

"What now?" I shake my head.

It's always something with these two.

"I told him you'd pick someplace tropical, and he bet me

you'd say I should go skiing." Millie snaps the twenty in her fingers before tucking it into her bra, winking at Thalia.

Adam and Millie were the first two people I hired as part of my team with Peter. Millie and I served together overseas, and Adam, well, he's the poor idiot who tried to pickpocket Millie. She nearly ripped him to shreds, but somewhere between then and now, I'm pretty sure they fell in love.

"Adam, you're an idiot. I'm from Wisconsin. I don't voluntarily go somewhere cold unless it's July or August."

It's pointless to try and level with him. Adam's awful in the field, dangerous in the sense of friendly fire when it comes to a firearm, and he sucks at new people. What skills he doesn't have, he makes up for by being completely loyal, making computers seem easy, and having flawless forgeries. We all have our things.

"But you're big and fucking fluffy! You'd think running around in the snow would be fun. I mean, if I had four feet and fur, I'd never come . . ." Adam makes motions like he'd use his hands as front feet to stomp in the snow. He stops, seeing me give him a sideways glance. "Oh shit. Sorry, boss."

Thalia looks at them both and then back at me. For the briefest moment, I think she smiles, but just as quickly, she slips her stony-faced expression back on. She brushes a stray lock of curly red hair out of her face as she looks between the four of us. Her arms rest flat along her sides like she's stuck in neutral. If it weren't for the hammering of her heart and the scent of fear, I'm not sure I'd be able to read her.

"This is my right-hand, Millie, and you've already met her delusional sidekick, Adam. They're going to get you set up and ready to go. I'll catch up with you all later today."

I turn to leave and hear this tiny little huff. I fucking know Millie would never take that attitude with me, Adam is too afraid of me to, and well, Alice wouldn't wait until I had my back turned.

Turning back, I find that Alice has sucked her lips between her teeth, holding back a laugh. Millie and Adam are currently completely absorbed with looking at anything that isn't me. Thalia, however, is looking at me with glassy green eyes like I kicked her puppy; I'm expecting a fight. It's not anger. Maybe fear or uncertainty, which I can empathize with, but I can't coach her through it right now. If we're going to get out of the city today, I need to get at least four hours of sleep before we get on the road. Safety over comfort.

"Ms. Clark, I am sure this is happening very quickly for you, but I assure you, I'd leave my sister with these two. You'll be safe with them."

"High praise. His sister is hot," Adam pipes up.

Millie slaps him on the backside of his head. He winces and rubs the spot.

"I'll see you later this afternoon." I roll my eyes.

This time I let them leave first. The trio heads back down to Adam's and Millie's offices while I wait despite my eagerness to sleep.

Alice and I are left at the desk together. I let out a massive yawn, releasing tension in my shoulders, neck, and jaw. Shaking my shoulders, I start untying my tie again and slipping off my suit jacket. I lean against the counter for support while Alice and I watch them disappear around the corner. Physical tension retreats as I'm left with the familiar circumstances of work.

Once they're gone, Alice cocks one eyebrow at me and leans closer. "I've never seen such a dysfunctional family. I could hear everything they were saying. That poor girl, Cade."

I pinch the bridge of my nose before gesturing after them

down the hall. "This is why I left that life. This. Right here. Fuck."

"Language." Alice scolds, but we both know she's not offended. Ever thinking ahead, she asks, "Do you need me to book accommodations on the way to where you're going?"

"No, I don't know what her tolerance for riding is." Pushing off the desk, I stand, heading in the opposite direction, back toward the conference room. "Thank you, Alice."

"Love you too, Cade."

The Leviathan paces inside, pushing against my control in every direction, reflecting back to Thalia again and again. I try to reason with him: *We'll see her again. I don't know what your problem is, but if you'd fucking talk to me, I'd be able to help.* The Leviathan quits fighting. I'm not surprised. It's been ten and a half years since we've spoken. Why start now?

Peter is shredding documents at the bin when he stops me. "Alice put new clean sheets on your office bed. Millie said they need four hours. I'll come get you when they're done. Don't try to make the whole drive tonight."

"Nothing nice to say right now, Peter." I look at him. "I know you didn't set up a safe house, which means you want me to bring her back to my place."

"I couldn't help but watch the video from when I wasn't in that meeting, and you mentioned she wouldn't truly be safe unless she was in an area where there were no known corruptible shifters."

He's matter-of-fact, which grates the little self-control I have left. He makes strong eye contact holding my gaze.

"One last thing." Peter's voice goes a bit lower, and he tilts his head down, looking at me through his brow. "I would rather you not make any more power plays with our clients in the future. Cutting a deal with me, fine."

"It won't happen again," I assure him, noting how he said *our* clients.

"Thank you."

Taking cues from my mood, The Leviathan stirs again, growling as I start to walk away. Pausing, I turn back. "Remember this day when I tell you that I've got to move and am taking all that shiny new vacation time to do so."

Peter's laugh fades as I walk back to my office. I can't believe my day. I struck two deals in ten minutes. It's drastically more political involvement than I've done in years. Keeping Thalia Clark safe will be the best assignment of my year. Even if it doesn't pan out and Senator Clark doesn't come through with her end of the deal we cut, I've done what I could for my people. I may have abdicated and sworn to stay out of Robert's politics, but there was a golden opportunity, and I took it.

I shuffle my feet, feeling like they're attached to hundred-pound weights. Once I get to the shiny nameplate that simply reads Cade, per my request to leave the last name off, the door is unlocked. I don't bother closing the blinds when I walk in. Tossing my suit jacket down on the chair, I undo my belt and fly. Then I pull off my tie and dress shirt before I nearly pass out lying down. *I love this bed.*

Four hours fly by.

I hear a knock on my office door, followed by Peter's voice. "Rise and shine. It's just after one, and if you want to make it out of the city before rush hour, you'll need to leave now."

Opening my eyes, I squint against the light coming through the window as I sit up.

Peter stands there in my doorway and keeps talking. "Alice

had a set of clothes brought in and washed for you. She said what you were wearing made you look like a ragamuffin."

Feet on the floor, I stretch my arms up. "You got the nice version of her opinion. Thalia ready to go?"

"Usual documents are in the envelope. Gave her a fake name and what you'd need paper-wise to get out of the country, should you need to. Adam set her up with the client-proof phone. It's in her document kit. Obviously, your discretion to give it to her or not. It'll call whomever you program into it with your passcode. I had him put in Lena and Deacon already. Then I had him switch the emergency calls to me directly." Peter gives me the rundown.

Starting to wake up, I'm following along with what he's saying. Peter is nothing if not thorough.

He keeps going, "Your company card has no limit. Get whatever you need and do whatever you need to do but keep it reasonable."

I nod, zipping my fly. As I pull the fresh thermal shirt on, I notice Peter staring at my chest. He's completely silent. I look down and see the jagged scars healing across my chest, arms, back, and sides from the last week of fights. They look red and angry. Good thing Alice bought a long-sleeved shirt.

"Someone brought their pack to my cousins' for the holiday. They wanted to take Lena with them for their pack, and when she declined, they challenged me to try and force my hand in making her go."

"Does this happen a lot?" Peter asks uncharacteristically.

It's not that Peter doesn't care for his employees or my well-being, but he expects us to check our issues at the door.

I shrug, sliding on my fresh shirt. "About twice or so a year."

"Why?"

Peter's original objective in coming in here was Thalia's

safety. Now, he cocks his head at me with his 'I'm thinking' scowl crossing his face.

"Adult female wolves go into heat twice yearly, and some people assume, if they can fight me and beat me, they get to take her." As I finish, our eyes meet.

"I guess I'm not sure what it's like for wolves. But I know from my experience with the fairer sex that cycles are never truly predictable. If you're ever not home when you need to be, I'll make it happen." Peter rubs his hand over his bald head.

It's another few moments of silence as I move my belt and wallet into the new jeans. I would love to say I'm shocked that Alice knew exactly what size to buy, but Alice knows everything.

Once I'm dressed, Peter ushers me out of my own office.

I find Thalia with Millie and Adam in our team's lounge, laughing at the mission table. Millie is in the midst of one of her stories from when we did an op in the Sahara. She sees me and tosses me a wink as she finishes up the story. Adam is too engrossed with her to notice; it's the sweetest form of intense.

Thalia's laughter seems to have shaken off some of her nervous energy. Seeing a threat, especially one on your life, is enough to make anyone nervous. But she's safe now, and the sooner she settles in with that realization, the sooner she can move forward and try to enjoy the new normal of her life. Even if it's temporary, life's better when you don't hate your surroundings.

I've been captivated by her since I saw her from the hallway. Thalia is a knockout. Gorgeous curves and soft pale skin with delicate freckles across her face. Her curls and stray locks bounce as she laughs, which she brushes out of her face. She must have to beat boys off with sticks. That would explain why no serious relationships came up when our teams ran searches. It seems suspicious that she doesn't date, but it rules out the usual suspect types for the home invasion. Not that it matters, so why do I care if she's dated?

The Leviathan pushes the idea of a literal manhunt and the fun it would be to stalk her stalkers, which is wrong on so many levels. The weirdest part in all of this is that he's thinking of anyone other than himself.

Thalia Clark may be my ideal woman, but there's no way I'll betray my people like that. It's one thing for me to stow her away. It's a passive act in casually preventing idiots from killing her and making things worse. And mating with the daughter of the enemy of all shifters would only end in bloodshed. The exact bloodshed I swore to avoid. The Leviathan will have to get over it and resist the little temptress with green eyes, vibrant red hair, and curves for days because there is more to life. There will be other women and potential mates.

The Leviathan growls in argument.

If you want to talk about it, asshole, you're more than welcome to talk back, but I don't see any way for this to work. You'll have to pick anyone but her. She's trouble, the kind that puts us back in the line of fire. I'm not going back to that life. Not over some woman. No matter how beautiful she is.

Millie finishes up the story, popping a quick, "Oh, shit. He heard us," that causes Thalia to giggle, her shoulders shrugging with the noise, and Adam to jump back, startled that I was so close to him all this time.

"Warn a guy, Cade. Would it kill you to make a sound?"

I can hear Adam's heart beating faster. He clutches his chest, taking deep breaths to regulate his heart rate.

"Predators don't make sounds." I smile, patting him on the shoulder. I turn my attention to Thalia, who is now my sole responsibility. "Ready to hit the road?"

"Where are we going?" she asks with a heavy waver in her voice. "Do we need to go by my place and pack things?"

"I can't tell you where we're going just yet. And I've got a list of things we'll pick up or have ordered when we get there. As for your apartment, it's not safe to go back."

Her face falls, and the stoic political-figure's-child mask she wore this morning returns. If she doesn't open up and trust me, we're going to have issues.

"Come on, let's chat in the car."

Thalia's shoulders stiffen, her eyes shifting from me to Millie and back again. I see the same stubborn defiance in her as I do in Lena, so I try the same trick that works on my little sister: walk away at an unhurried pace, silently inviting her to follow.

"It's okay, go." Millie's voice is soft as she assures her, and soon, I hear Thalia's footfalls behind me.

She's quiet as we make our way to the SUV, her arms folded across her chest. I pull out my good manners and open the passenger door for her.

"Thank you," she whispers, the silence between us finally breaking.

"You're welcome," I answer quickly and close the door behind her.

It's awful having your world obliterated because of what your parents have done — I would know. All the emotions she's experiencing are familiar, and quickly processing them is in her best interest. Hopefully, I'll have time to get her home and settled in before Deacon and Lena get back from Judah's.

So, I'll just drive and wait for her to be ready to talk to me. With any luck, the nearly twenty hours in the car will help her adjust.

WE'RE out of the city and have been on the freeway for an hour before she speaks again. "Where are we going? Or am I still not allowed to know yet?"

I can feel her frustration rolling off her in waves.

"Wisconsin." The first is a valid question, but I let the second pointed question fall off without an answer. She's going to get bored of verbally chastising me very quickly. "I've got a home there that will be safer than any of the safe houses Peter owns."

"Your people won't mind you bringing your work home with you? Don't you need to clear it with your pack leader?"

Thalia's questions drip with less venom, but she's still quite confident in her condescending words. I can't figure her out.

Pulling my eyes off the road, I look at her. "Thalia, do you have any idea who I am?"

"Should I? Are you going to tell me you're some sort of shifter royalty or something?" Her question is laced with frustration but also genuine curiosity.

So many questions form in my head. *How could she not know who I am?* Her mother knew immediately. They did say Thalia has removed herself from politics; could she be that far out of it? Problem-solving. When faced with many questions, it's best to keep things simple.

"Do you know what your mother's politics are?"

From my peripheral, I see her push her hands to her cheeks as her face grows red.

It's a brief moment before she answers. "I stay clear of Mom and Dad's politics as best I can. They're good people and fairly decent parents. They mean well. I'm just so sick of the doom and gloom all the time. I don't let them talk to me about it. I keep my head clear of all their drama. Which, I know, isn't a good way to live your life. I probably should have some political opinions. It's just..."

"That's all your life has been about." I offer when her sentence dies out.

"Yeah. That." Thalia slumps down into her seat.

Is it my place to tell her? How can I live the next nine weeks with her and keep her in the dark? If it were just the two of us, there wouldn't be an issue. Lena is probably trustworthy enough not to bring up the political issue, maybe. But depending on how strung-out Deacon is, well . . . I let the silence hang for a little bit longer, trying to choose my words. How do I not scare her any further but also provide her with information?

Before I can find words, she does. "What Mom's involved in is really bad, isn't it?"

"I can't answer that objectively." It's honest, and like most truths, it's hard to admit. "The bill your mother is spearheading is extremely controversial and has divided the nation. A majority of the world is holding its breath, watching as we figure out how to navigate this issue."

"What issue? What is she legislating?" Thalia asks, throwing her hands up, frustration growing.

I don't know how to sugarcoat this, so I don't. "Thalia, your mother is legislating for shifters to register, be sterilized, and executed without a trial if any sort of conflict escalates where law enforcement may be called, regardless of fault."

Thalia's hands drop to her lap, and she goes so still that I have to focus intensely, listening hard over the white noise of the tires on the road. Minutes tick by, and I finally hear signs of life.

"You must hate me," Thalia whispers after a few more minutes of silence. Her hand covers her mouth. "I mean, how can you not hate me? Why are you helping me?"

"I don't hate you. I don't hate your mother." I try to explain, lifting a hand off the steering wheel and offering her my opinion. "I don't know what has caused your mother to take this political stance. If it's out of fear because we're new and different or if there's something else at play. But spending my time hating her or anyone else makes *me* a hateful person. Nothing worth having comes from that much anger."

Thalia starts talking quickly. "Your leader is going to kill me. I can't imagine that anyone will allow the enemy's daughter into their camp."

I scent her fear again and grip the steering wheel. This isn't a position I've been in before. Sure, some clients aren't angels, but at least they had a niggling idea that their loved one wasn't squeaky clean. Does Thalia share her mother's politics? This could be a long fucking spring if that's the case.

She doesn't say anything else. I look over, and she's not moving. Her survival instinct seems to be freeze.

I try feeding her more facts, hoping information will help ease her out of this quiet state and back toward building trust. "At home, it's just three of us. With you, that makes four, and it'll be safe. There's no Alpha to worry about."

"Easy for you to say." She shuffles in her seat. "Until one of them turns on you and decides to get rid of me."

We've got miles and hours ahead of us, and the longer this festers, the more she won't believe me.

"You're safe, Thalia. The very few people I keep in my life are loyal above all else."

CHAPTER 5
THALIA

THE CITY SCENERY HAS PASSED. Buildings have given way to housing developments, and now the countryside is dotted with houses in the distance. Is this day even real? Is this happening? I'm driving to Wisconsin with a shifter — who my mom says I can't trust — because there's a picture of me in my apartment. *There is a picture of me in my apartment at night when I was alone.*

My chest is tight, and my pulse throbs in my head. I can't breathe. I gasp, trying to get air. I struggle in my seat, pulling the seat belt. I need more air. I barely notice the SUV pulling off the side of the road. When I look over at Cade, he's gone. How? Where?

There's no air.

My door opens. Cade is leaning over me, unbuckling my seat belt, and pulling me from the vehicle. Is the SUV okay? What's going on? I still can't breathe. The dizziness is creeping in.

I'm pushed against the SUV. Cade's lips are moving, but there's no noise. Why can't I hear anything?

I close my eyes, squeezing them as tight as possible until tears leak from the corners. *Breathe. I don't want to die. Breathe.*

The world roars back, full sound.

I gasp, my throat burning with air. My lungs flutter open, banging against my ribs. Cade's voice is strong and demanding. It's nothing like how I've heard other men speak. It takes a few more breaths before his voice forms words.

"Fuck, I didn't know I had to worry about you killing yourself. What kind of response is that? Stopping breathing?"

He's so close to me that his nose brushes against my ear. His hands rest on my waist. They're big and warm. *Safe.*

He's speaking low, close to my ear, velvet smooth as he coaxes, keeping a perfect rhythm while coaching me. "Count your breaths. Time them. Breathe in: two, three, four. Hold it: two, three, four. Let it out: two, three, four. Be empty: two, three, four."

He repeats it, breathing with me as I sag against the SUV and brace my hands on his forearms. I lose count of how many times we go through the cycle. His breath mixes with mine. He's standing so close. Each breath smells like him, warm and woodsy. And for a moment, I'm caught up in his warmth.

I must meet whatever criteria he uses to deem I'm okay to move because he steps back, eyes locking with mine. They're soft, yellow gold, the irises wide, watching and analyzing me.

Nodding, he smiles. "You good?"

I take a self-inventory, focusing on what my body is doing. My heart is still pounding heavily in my chest. I'm exhausted, but that always happens after a panic attack. There's never been one this big though.

"How long have you been having panic attacks?" he asks softly before ushering me back into my seat.

It doesn't come with the undercutting judgmental tone others have used when asking about them. Instead, Cade's question sounds pure with genuine curiosity, as if he's trying to understand me.

"Four years, but Mom and Dad don't know. I don't have my meds." I bite my bottom lip, tears welling in my eyes. "I'm mostly okay without them. It'll be fine. Today's just been a weird day. It's normally nothing like this. Work induced mostly. It's fine. I'm fine."

"Okay." He leans across, buckling my seat belt for me, lingering for a moment, slowly checking that I'm completely tucked into the vehicle.

My stomach flips, and I don't know if it's from the remnants of my panic attack or Cade's nearness and care.

Cade jogs across the front of the SUV, watching for traffic before climbing in on his side.

Cade pulls his phone out of the center console and hands it to me before instructing, "It's not locked. Go to Dinah Alloway and text her what meds you're taking. Ask her for a three-month fill. Every drug you take that's a prescription. I don't care if it's a med you take on occasion for migraines, general birth control, or seasonal allergies. Anything you take."

"Isn't that illegal? She's never met me." I try to make him understand. "I don't want someone to get in trouble. I'll be okay, really, they're not that frequent."

"She won't get in trouble. Tell her the name to put it under is Emily Elizabeth Miller." He motions to the phone again, insisting, "Please."

"You keep your phone unlocked? Is that a good idea?" I question but do as he requests.

It's weird enough opening the messaging app on someone else's phone. I don't know Cade that well; what am I going to learn? Scrolling, I find Dinah a few contacts down. It's impossible to avoid reading the last thing they messaged each other. It seems intimate:

> Cade: You know what they say, life's a bitch until you make it yours.

> Dinah: It may be a bitch but at least I've got you to make it better. Can't wait for tonight. *smirking face* you are still... coming?

> Cade: Wouldn't miss it for the world.

This must be his girlfriend. A deep pang of disappointment accompanies that thought. Why? I don't know.

Shaking it off, I read the start of the message out loud as I type. "Hey Dinah, I need to get the following prescriptions for my client. The name they're under should be Emily Elizabeth Miller."

"Sounds good, then send what you need. She'll probably ask what pharmacy. I'll figure out where we're close to." Cade's focus is on the road ahead.

My fingers shake as I try to type the drug names. *Do I get my birth control? Crap, that could be awkward. What's more awkward, periods or pills? Get it and skip my periods? Yes.*

"So embarrassing," I say under my breath after sending the message.

Putting his phone down, I divert my attention out the window.

"What's embarrassing?" Cade asks earnestly.

"Everything. I feel like a complete mess. You knew what you were signing up for since you're aware of my mother's politics. But my emotional and psychological turmoil? That's the cherry you didn't even ask for on top of this crap sundae." I wipe my face as more tears form.

I'm such a disaster. Maybe I'm not worth this much trouble to Cade. I'm sure he sees me that way: trouble. How could I be anything else to him?

My hands twist in my lap as my leg bounces up and down. He gently rests his hand just above the knee on my bouncing thigh. Instantly I still, waiting for him to chastise me, that it's annoying, a bad habit, just like Mom does, but when he speaks, it's with kindness.

"We've all got our things. No one is perfect. Would have been nice to know about in advance, but now I know what happens and how to fix it. We'll get your meds. Everything will be okay."

"Why are you so chill about everything?" I blurt out before I can think twice. Mentally smacking myself, I backtrack. "You don't have to answer that."

Cade shrugs. "Until there's a reason to get upset, I try to keep a level perspective the best as I can."

That's it? Eyeing him, I wait for him to continue, but he doesn't. Instead, he flips on his blinker, merges lanes, and proceeds to take the next exit. All the while, his right hand remains fixed on my thigh.

I can't help the scientist within me from studying him. Cade is, by every definition, highly attractive. From his strong jawline, with good cheekbones, to his broad shoulders, not an ounce of tension is in his muscles. He's self-assured when he speaks. In the little I've heard about him, anecdotes from Millie and Adam, he's painted as a natural leader with a light heart. Now this, effortlessly moving on. I wish I was able to be calm and collected like him.

Before I realize it, the car has stopped, and we're sitting outside a pharmacy.

Removing his hand, Cade grabs his phone and sends off a message.

Wonder what his girlfriend is going to think about this?

It pings with a new message almost immediately.

Cade groans, but it's muffled by the giant yawn that comes

from him. "Meds are going to be a bit. She's got some strings to pull. Let's grab some food and a place to crash. I'm sorry you'll be cooped up in a hotel room tonight, but I can't drive much longer."

At the mention of food, my stomach growls. "Food sounds good."

He lets out the softest little laugh before pulling back onto the road. Cade yawns again, and it's none of my business, but I ask anyway, "Dinah keep you up late last night?"

The corner of his lip curls back into a smirk, but he keeps his eyes on the road. "No, that was all you."

"What? Me?" I raise an eyebrow. "I think I'd remember that." *Oh my god, did I just say that out loud?*

I freeze, unsure how he'll respond. I just know my cheeks are bright red.

He chuckles and shakes his head. "I left my cousin Judah's at like seven last night. Drove straight through to get to DC this morning to take your meeting. While you were with my team, I grabbed four hours of sleep and ta-da." He takes his hand off the wheel, shaking it like the jazz hands you see cheerleaders do.

Cade gives me a coy smile. "Besides, it would be a little awkward fucking my cousin."

My face heats again. I press the back of my hand to my cheeks as I whimper out a pathetic, "Oh."

Of course, it wasn't his girlfriend. Why did I jump to that conclusion?

It's like he has some sort of internal GPS because he navigates through the town without consulting a map or search engine.

Cade is truly an enigma, and I'd like to dissect how his thought processes work, in the nicest way possible.

We settle on the cutest mom-and-pop diner with signs outside boasting about their all-day breakfast menu. Stepping inside is like being transported to the realm of the Americana movement. Shelves full of knickknacks are all over the place. The entire establishment is decorated around the American flag with pigs and pitchforks.

As we wait for the hostess to seat us, I become increasingly conscious of the size difference between Cade and me. He's a lot taller than my five-foot-two frame. Broad shoulders stretch his Henley and then fall to a proportionate taper at his waist. He's well-built but not obscenely stacked like those gym rats who are all upper body. I'm fixated, watching his thighs move against the denim. Are those muscular too? They must be, right?

Casually, I take a step back, making it look like I'm checking out the stand of tourist flyers behind us, not my security detail. From the corner of my eye, I glance at his butt. *Who knew security could look this good?*

I catch myself biting my bottom lip and gripping the flyer in my hand a little too tightly. *Did someone crank the heater up in here?*

Once the hostess appears and leads us from the host station to a booth, Cade ushers me in front of him, destroying my view of his ass. I'm definitely out of my league between his good looks and the hostess that takes the longest possible route through the restaurant to our table.

"So, do you live in the area?"

Her attention is completely on Cade. I'm fairly certain she actually bats her eyelashes. *Who does that?*

"Just passing through." Cade smiles. He waits for me to be seated before sitting himself. The hostess stands there swaying back and forth until he prompts her, "But, I could really use a glass of water."

"Someone's thirsty," she says coyly.

Did she just wink at him? *Barf.*

She and I are about the same age. At least, the tattoos peeking out from under her shirt sleeve indicate that she is, in fact, older than jailbait. She's well blessed in the beauty department. The one-size-too-small T-shirt stretches across her boobs and clings tightly to her slim waist, and I'm not sure if she painted on those pants or if she'll have to cut them off later.

Cade's attention zones down onto the menu, but her sashay as she walked away was clearly intended to captivate his eyes, and it's obnoxious.

"I thought she was never going to leave," Cade whispers.

I'm not sure if he's talking to himself or me as he scrubs his hand down his face.

"You must have your fair pick of women. Is she not your type? More of an ass man?" I've said it. Now, there's no taking it back.

I resist the urge to slap my hands over my mouth. *Can I blame my bitchy attitude on lack of sleep?* This behavior isn't normal for me. That has to be the answer.

Cade looks at me and then back down at his menu, shaking his head. "I'm not big on using your physical appearance as your only redeeming quality."

If the scowl is any indication, he's just being polite now.

Keeping with my trend of being so awkward it hurts, I try to change the conversation, gesturing about the dining room. "It's a bit . . . odd. The restaurant sure has a unique . . . vibe."

Cade looks up at me again. "I can't tell if you're trying to be funny or offensive."

Could I stuff both feet farther into my mouth? I'm tense and out of place, saying things I normally wouldn't. Now, based on Cade's tone, it seems I've pissed off the only human I know in probably a hundred miles. Mom would want me to note that he's not even really human. I can't imagine how he sees me. Best guess is that to him, I'm probably an evil bitch who is rude about everything and super entitled.

My vision gets blurry looking at him. I blink quickly, stopping what could be a catastrophic failure of a lifetime of grooming from my parents.

I plaster on my best 'stick to it' smile and answer him, trying to sound earnest. "I've never eaten in such a unique place."

CHAPTER 6
CADE

THE HOSTESS RETURNS with our waters. Luckily, our server comes over and chases her off. Between trying to politely dismiss her without drawing attention to myself, and watching Thalia process all the emotions flitting within her eyes, I'm in over my head.

"You just passing through, beautiful?" our server asks Thalia as he puts on a creepy smile, flirting with her.

I groan inwardly. And here I thought he and I were going to be friends.

"Yes." Thalia is polite in answering him, giving a smile.

"Well, that's fantastic." He gets closer to her side of the table, tilting his body so he's more parallel with her. "Did you need any suggestions off the menu?"

The Leviathan snarls inside, and I stifle him back. *The fuck is your problem? He's allowed to get close to her.* The Leviathan doesn't answer but stays focused on the server. He's nearly bloodthirsty. *Seriously, the fuck do you even care? You're never interested in anything that has to do with my life.*

He's about her age; my guess is a bit older. If I make a big deal out of it, all I'm doing is drawing attention to us. I watch him smile and her return it. When he tells a joke, she laughs. His attention to her is harmless.

Was harmless. The server steps over to her side of the booth a bit farther. Getting closer, he brushes his hand against her arm. When she looks up at him, he gives her a weasel smile. That smile. If I've seen it once, I've seen it a thousand times in boys barking around Lena's tree. I'm not having it today.

I clench my fists, crumbling the edges of the menu still in my hands.

"I think I'll have the American platter." I interrupt them through clenched teeth, picking the first thing on the menu that has pancakes.

The server seems to remember his place, or at the very least my existence, while he takes my order. Thalia, taking her cue from me, places an order and gives him a smile shrugging her shoulders, blushing when he calls her sugar.

The Leviathan pushes on me, bristling against my skin, daring the waiter to cross him further as the guy walks past us.

We don't get to be pissy over her flirting. She's not fucking ours. I urge The Leviathan to let it go. He doesn't care. His growing presence in my headspace is a constant reminder of how things should be. The usual feeling of emptiness is lacking, but his presence is uncomfortable as he focuses on her. His involvement distracts me from the task at hand. It's not that we're unaware of our surroundings, it's that we're more aware of male threats than female ones.

I've spent so much time in my head, it seems like only seconds, and our food is before us. The server checks in so regularly I'm not sure Thalia's even gotten to eat anything between his first and second trip by the table. I would have liked a refill on my water, but rather than give him a reason to come back to the table, I decided to go thirsty.

Each time he circles back, he gets more comfortable with her. He gets closer to touching her when telling a quick little joke. It makes her laugh. I'm struggling with my composure, stuck between wanting to fly under the radar and telling him to fuck off. Ultimately, her not getting to eat dinner superfast isn't the worst thing in the world. That's nothing. *She's a client, a job, and none of our damn business outside of that.* It shouldn't matter that he's flirting with her. He hasn't crossed any lines.

The Leviathan doesn't settle with his thought. He continues watching her and nearly growling.

Thirty minutes later, Thalia has finished the food on her plate, and I'm ready to go. When the waiter brings the check, he flirts for the last time. This time, his hand brushes against her shoulder and the beautiful red curls of her hair.

It's not even a debate. Not wanting to be here any longer than necessary, I pull cash from my wallet and put it on the table with more than enough to cover the tip. Fuck billing Peter. I casually walk out with Thalia close to me. I try not to smother her.

"You've been quiet." Thalia observes. "Everything okay?"

"I didn't want to interrupt the two of you." So much for not caring, staying neutral, and minding my own damn business. That was beyond inappropriate.

Thalia tilts her head up to look at me, a variety of emotions dancing across her face, reflected in her eyes.

"I guess we'll have to call it even for you flirting with the hostess." She cocks a brow at me and shrugs her shoulders, hands landing on the curve of her hips as she walks to the SUV.

She thought that was flirting? I bite my bottom lip and clench my fists at my sides. Her possessive nature pairs so well with the irrational idea of pushing her up against my SUV and kissing her. *I could show her the real meaning of flirting.* My cock twitches at the thought.

The Leviathan agrees, urging me forward. He's just beneath my skin, salivating at the idea as we stalk after her.

Then there's the levelheaded, responsible realization: I'm required to keep control. Betraying my dick, and apparently my wolf, I have to maintain the little bit of professionalism I've got left. It's been less than a day, and I'm, for the first time in my career, finding myself struggling to stay objective. Saying nothing and letting it go is the right path. She's a job.

I hold the front passenger door open for her, making sure she climbs in before I slowly walk behind the SUV to my side of the car.

Where the fuck did the idea of kissing her come from? The Leviathan flashes across the back of my mind. *Fucking predator.* He would be on the do-awful-things-to-Thalia-Clark bandwagon. Dirty, awful, up-all-night, toe-curling, terrible things. It all rolls about in my brain.

I shake my head and take a deep breath, then take my place behind the wheel in the SUV. Looking at her, I start, "I'm —"

"I was —"

We start at the same time. I extend my hand out, offering for her to go first.

"I'm sorry. It's been an incredibly long day, and I shouldn't say anything. Your personal life is not my business."

Her tone is harsh, almost as though she's scolding or chastising herself, as she puts her hand on her chest just above her perfect tits.

She continues, motioning to me, "You've been very kind in derailing your last few days for me, and I should be more grateful for you. It was inappropriate for me to attract his attention. I'll follow protocols better in the future."

I furrow my brow. *It was inappropriate for her to attract his attention?* Unless she wears a paper sack over her head, she wouldn't be able to keep someone from noticing her good looks.

She's trying to disarm me, by stating what she thought I'd be upset about before I could bring it up. It's none of what I wanted to address, but it's another glimpse into her stress response, which is how she's been conditioned her whole life. It's heart crushing to see her so hard on herself. Giving her more negative feedback won't help our working relationship.

She didn't create any security risks, so I let it go, starting the SUV.

"Let's get your meds and grab a hotel for the night. We're both tired, and I think we've had enough for the day."

THALIA IS stiff beside me as she presents the fake ID to the unenthusiastic pharmacy technician at the counter. The tech does their job and brings the bottles of pills. The whole exchange goes off without a hitch. It's not until we're in the car and she checks them that Thalia's shoulders relax, and she lets out a long breath.

I'm about to start the vehicle when I hear her heart rate pick up. Warning bells go off in my head, but I keep my cool and, with a casual sideways glance, ask, "What's wrong?"

"Did I break the law? Is this a felony? This feels like a felony." She squirms and checks the rearview mirror before hurriedly tucking the medications under her seat.

I check in with her breathing to make sure there isn't an impending panic attack. Her response now doesn't match the ragged breaths before the last attack, when she stopped breathing altogether. I'm guessing she's fine and direct us back onto the road.

This kinda seems like one of the very few times it's okay to flat-out lie. Yet, I can't bring myself to do it. "Technically, yes, it's fraudulent. From my understanding, it's only illegal if you get caught. We won't."

Thalia nods slightly. I'm not sure I've reassured her enough, but she doesn't argue.

THALIA WOBBLES while we're checking in at the front desk of our hotel. Glancing over at her, I see the culprit: closed eyes.

Carefully wrapping my arm around her waist, I steady her while I finish.

Pulling her close, I whisper against the top of her head, "Hang in there a little longer. We'll get you to bed."

We slowly and quietly make our way to the third floor and our room. The Leviathan and I listen as we walk past doors. We're in tune, checking for different occupants. The rooms closest to us are filled with children. Children are excellent deterrents for would-be criminals.

Opening our door starts the natural instincts of the job: checking the hotel room and keeping Thalia close to me.

She shuffles over to the bed farthest from the door. I'm surprised, but then she reminds me this isn't her first security detail. "Standard protocol, right?"

"You're going to crash pretty quickly; I'd recommend you change and do your nighttime routine now." I motion to the bathroom with my hand.

Within thirty minutes, Thalia is sleeping softly. It's barely after seven, and from years of experience, if the client has had this kind of day, they're not waking back up until morning once they go down. Typically, I wouldn't bother moving the SUV and leaving a client alone. But the security threat in this situation isn't high.

Locking the door, I head back to the Yukon. The farther I get from her, the more The Leviathan becomes restless and desires to be unleashed. *Asshole predator.* I pull hard on my control, moving us on from thinking about her.

Reparking the Yukon quickly to the side door closest to our room, I find myself moving with urgency. Once I'm back in the room with Thalia, The Leviathan settles down and quits pushing under my skin. *Dramatic asshole.*

THE ALARM GOES OFF FAR TOO EARLY for my liking. In a well-trained habit, my feet find the floor, and I stand up. Thalia grumbles and rolls over but isn't in a functioning awake state. Pulling my duffel into the bathroom, I close the door, turn on the light, and open my bag to find a handwritten note:

> SNOOTY BELLEND,
> I KNOW WHY YOU HAD TO GO. I ALSO KNOW THAT BY THE TIME YOU GET THIS, YOU'VE NOW MADE A DEAL WITH THE LITERAL DEVIL TO KEEP HER KID SAFE. I TRIED TO PICK SOMETHING CLOSE TO HER SIZE FOR HER. BUT VISIONS DON'T COME WITH CLOTHING SIZES. HAVE FUN AT ANSEL'S. TELL EZRA I MISS HIM.
> SEE YOU AT SOLSTICE.
> - DINAH

Sure enough, wrapped and folded together is a pair of leggings, a tank top, and a sweater. There are also feminine toiletries.

What the fuck does she mean by Ansel's?

I pull my phone off the counter to text her but see twelve text messages from the one woman I want nothing to do with in my life: *Isabel LeFleur*. With my phone's security mode on, it's safe to open them because she won't get any sort of receipt or visibility of me reading them, so I do. I'll have to text her back, but at least this way, I can formulate a solid response before I do.

> Isabel: Hey, where are you for the holiday? We should meet.

> Isabel: Should I come over? We could kick your siblings out and fuck on every flat surface. Call me back.

> Isabel: What are you wearing? Should I come visit, wear nothing but my parka? Remember that time I went commando under my skirt at Summer Solstice? You broke his hand like it was nothing just for looking like he was going to try and cop a feel. I wonder what happened to him. Hope it was the one he used to jerk off.

She brought out the worst in me. I can't remember that guy's name or I would apologize for how big of a dick I was. I was a loaded gun with her in my life. Everyone was a potential target. The Leviathan was her own personal henchman and I was too young and dumb to see it.

> Isabel: You know what gets me hot? Thinking of that time at Winter Solstice when that wolf sat too close to me. The way you threw that punch? He didn't have a chance. I love your violence.

I don't miss being that way. Though, I wouldn't apologize to him. He was an asshole then and he's a bigger asshole now. Mated with two brats, and both are spoiled little jerks too. I shouldn't have done that to him. There was no controlling myself or The Leviathan.

> Isabel: Why aren't you saying anything back?
> Are you fucking around with some bitch?

Why does she have to be this way?

I stop reading the flurry of her texts to another notification. It's my driveway sensor. *No. She wouldn't have.*

I open the feed, and my jaw drops as three white SUVs pull up my driveway. That fucking bitch and her timing. Of course, she would come snooping around, hoping I was home for the holiday. It's an hour earlier back home. Meaning she left home in the middle of the night to get there before the sun rose. We're over an hour from the cities, for fuck's sake.

Leaning against the wall in the bathroom, I flip through camera feeds to monitor her as she snoops around, peeking in doors and windows. She tries the doorknob and looks in usual places for hide-a-keys. She won't find any. There isn't any key to be found. Her pack of 'friends' linger around out by the car. No decent company arrives at someone's house early in the morning without looking for trouble. The camera shows her pulling out her phone. A half second later, I get the call notification.

The phone call pulls back up her trail of messages. They're more comical with each one.

> Isabel: Look, I'll forgive you for being with other girls. I love you, and I know deep down you love me. We belong together.

Love is not a word I would use to describe my feelings toward Isabel.

Isabel: Oh, I just remembered that time that we snuck out of your dad's house and went to that human bonfire. The look on that dude's face when you dropped his friend for saying I had a fat ass. I love when you go alpha on people.

Isabel: Seriously Cade? Fucking answer me. Man up.

Isabel: I'm sorry, Alpha, you know how I get. I just want to talk. Please, baby, answer me.

Mood swings, instability, and the oddest memory about how things were and how they are now. What the fuck did I see in her?

Isabel: I miss you. We were so good together. Think about it. I'll wear something sexy if nothing doesn't do the trick for you.

Isabel: We'd make great Alphas together. I can catch you up on all of the pack drama you've missed. Keep you in the loop on who is fucking who.

Isabel: You haven't answered me. I miss you. I think I'll just drive out there to see if you're home. We can spend the weekend reconnecting. Love you, Cade. Text me, I'll just be driving.

I go back to the feed with my security cameras. I need to know exactly what she's up to. Where she's standing, my best view is the trail cam from the large pine near the driveway. I watch her have one of her temper tantrums. She still behaves like this, stomping, yelling, and huffing about. She hated when I left and swore I'd live to see the day I regretted leaving her.

Well, it's been ten years, and it hasn't happened. I'm not hanging any hopes on the words she speaks coming to life.

The Leviathan is snarling. I'm positive my eyes are golden right now, no need to check the mirror. We're both upset with the violation of our territory. The balls of this bitch to show up at my house at this hour, me being there or not. How fucking dare she?

My chest rattles with a growl. Forcing it down, I try to keep quiet. Thalia can't wake up to me growling. Thoughts of Thalia deescalate the intensity of The Leviathan's fury. He's not happy with the invasion of his territory but he's more manageable. Maybe letting him live in a fantasy of interest in Thalia isn't awful. Maybe.

My phone rings again, and I let it roll through voicemail. I get a ping that she's left a message and another group of new text messages. All saying she knows I'm not home and that she'll come to wherever I am to see me. The more she pleads, the sadder it becomes. How do I get it through to her that we're done? It's been a decade.

My jaw is locked tight. I grind my teeth, shaking my head. This is why Dinah told me I'm going to Ansel's. She had a vision of that bitch. Well, Isabel can sit at my house as long as she wants or until Deacon's antics run her off. Whichever happens first is fine by me.

Closing out my live feed on my cameras, I try to leave my rage with the view. It's problem-solving time. Pulling up the GPS to figure out where we are, I start doing the math on how long we need to be in the car before we get to Ansel's. It's going to be a massive drive. Rolling with the punches, I accept the new route and, finally, hop in the shower.

While toweling off, I check the cameras again. Isabel and her friends have claimed seats on the covered part of the deck. I asked Deacon to put those away before we left. This, this right here, is why one doesn't leave outside furniture accessible to people. They think it's acceptable to sit and wait for you to return.

I flick off the live feed, head back to my messages, and open my conversation with the cousin everyone loves.

> Me: Hey cousin, call me when you get up. Please.

I check the cameras at home again. The sun's rising, and they're still sitting there, chatting and laughing. The Leviathan growls, seeing them invading the sanctity of what is ours. He's not wrong. The tenacity to stay is impressive, but I'd expect nothing less from Isabel. She's proven time and time again that she's still very serious about wanting the Ardelean bloodline. Well, I'm a dead end. She'll have to find another option.

CHAPTER 7

THALIA

THE SOUND of running water wakes me. I jolt up in bed. Looking for where the leak would come from in my apartment, I'm hit with the sullen reminder that I'm not home. Falling back to the mattress, I want to snooze until he's done in the bathroom. Without the promise of my morning coffee, there's not really a motivator to get out of bed.

My anxiety has other plans. Staring up at the textured hotel ceiling, I'm forced to examine the last day's events chronologically.

I'm in danger because, apparently, Mom's a crummy, polarizing politician and made enemies of shifters. My parents would rather I go on a cross-country road trip with a shifter, who is ultimately a victim of Mom's legislation. The irony isn't lost on me. I've worked for years to secure my dream internship at the country's most prestigious archive and museum, and it's been ripped away from me. I'm allegedly on some sort of leave of absence, but until I go back, there's no way to know for sure. Those things, on their own, feel like the deep intrinsic loss of The Library of Alexandria. But it's so much more personal.

While I consider myself smart and passionate about topics I'm intrigued by, I'm still a senator's daughter with wild, untamable hair and a never-been-perfect figure. I have soft spots and curves that don't flow perfectly. I'm, at best, a generalized ball of anxiety that seemingly can't keep my wits about me for even one day. Is this all I am, really? It can't be?

But Cade? Nothing, not even my panic attack, made him break that cool facade. Keeping me alive is his job. He has very limited concerns about what happens to me. And why should he care beyond his job? It looks bad if I die. Hell, it looks bad if we're seen together in public; probably part of the whole reason why I can't live my life in DC. If shifters recognize each other somehow, it wouldn't look good for him.

My brain pulls the compilation video of Cade it stored: walking, talking, nodding, a half smile, and the warm weight of his hand on my thigh. The visit down memory lane brings warmth to my cheeks. I'm now wide awake and vehemently aware that in the bathroom, on the other side of a paper-thin wall, is a naked Cade.

It's not that I've never seen a naked man. There's a significant difference between the guys I kissed in high school and college, the few guys I've been on dates with, and a man like Cade. Shifters truly are different. The way he fills out jeans makes a girl, me, want to do dirty things.

I'm lying here, thinking dirty thoughts about him, when the bathroom door pops open. *Crap.* I'm sure my cheeks are scarlet at this point.

Taking that as my cue, I roll out of bed. When I try to put my feet on the floor, I get caught in the blanket and barely catch myself before I face-plant on the floor.

"You okay, Thalia?" His voice comes with a laugh disguised as clearing his throat.

I pull my eyes up his frame. Once I pass the denim covering

his legs, it's just lickable skin. Various scars cover Cade's torso. An intricate, segmented linework tattoo decorates his left pec and shoulder. Surprised, I get a full look at the muscles I've been dreaming of. The *Self-Made Man* had better finish carving himself from bronze, if he wants to give Cade a run for his money.

Trying to pull it together, blinking back tears of embarrassment, I settle on his face until he smirks and cocks his eyebrow. Dropping my face to the floor so he can't see my pinkened cheeks, I scramble past him as quickly as possible to the bathroom door and slam it. I turn on the shower and relive the mortification again.

He's obviously used to it. You don't walk around looking that hot and not know you're attractive. This happens to him all the time. Nothing to be embarrassed about.

This is the worst pep talk in the world. *Ugh.* I'm going to blush a few more times today, and it'll be fine.

Drying off, I fuss over my wavy red hair for a few minutes. Then I see a pile of clothes on the counter. Leggings, a tank top, and a cozy knit sweater. They're clean. *Where did he get these?* Dressing, I allow myself three times to adjust my leggings and oversized sweater to look cute. *How did he know my size?*

When I step out of the bathroom with my dirty clothes tucked into a little ball, Cade has stripped both beds and is sitting on the edge of his, typing a message on his cell phone. He doesn't look up, which honestly, is probably for the best.

"You can put your dirty laundry in my duffle," he says before he's finished with his phone.

When he looks at me, I can almost feel his eyes raking up my body.

He clears his throat. His voice is still thick and gravelly. "Um, there's been a bit of a change of plans. We've got about ten hours in the car today before we get to the next leg of where we're going. Don't hesitate to tell me if you're uncomfortable, need to stretch, or anything. This isn't a race anywhere."

"Okay." I drag out the last half of the word. Suspicious.

Mom said not to trust him, but Mom's not here. I don't have a lot of options. Change of plans doesn't necessarily mean something nefarious. But after what I've learned, maybe Mom is the one I should be worried about.

Over the last day, Cade hasn't given me a reason not to trust him, so I give him the benefit of the doubt.

Cade doesn't rush me through the hotel. Despite our stride difference, he walks at my pace. In the hallways, Cade smiles and interacts courteously. It's like he's naturally charismatic with everyone. If that's true, how will I know what's real between us?

Do I want something to be real between us? Why am I even thinking this?

Outside, the SUV is closer to these stairs than the front desk, where I remember it being last night. He must have moved the car when I was sleeping. Should I be concerned or relieved that he felt comfortable enough to leave me alone while he moved it? Pushing that thought aside, I focus back on what he mentioned in the hotel room.

"Cade?" I ask, and my voice wavers. "Why is there a change in plans?"

He stops partway to opening the door for me. The keys jingle in his hand when he turns back to look at me.

With a shrug, he answers, "There's an issue with our original destination, and I'm having someone from Corinth Security handle it before we can get there. But I'm not sure how long it will take, so we're heading somewhere that's mostly safe. I can't live in hotels for that long."

His answer seems logical. The honesty is nice. But I don't miss that he says *mostly* safe. Although, at this point, I suppose he can't guarantee absolute safety unless he takes me away from all civilization.

"Oh. Okay."

I let him open the door to the SUV and climb in willingly.

Before closing the door, Cade looks like he's about to say something but decides against it.

Climbing into the vehicle, he smiles. "Breakfast?"

"Please and coffee?"

I can imagine the incredible sensation of coffee invading my system. The promise of coffee is enough to push some of the worry from my mind. There's no reason not to trust him.

"Suggestions for places? Fast food? Sit down? Fancy coffee? Black?" Cade asks as we follow the morning traffic through town.

"I'm okay with fast food, but I love frilly coffee drinks." I cannot wait to make him order something girly.

Much to my disappointment, Cade doesn't even flinch when relaying my coffee order to the barista through the speakers. Adam mentioned he had a hot sister. She must have already broken in the coffee-order shock. Without complaint, Cade drives through a fast-food drive-through to accommodate my breakfast request. It goes against his strong-silent-guy vibe. Breakfast obtained, he drives to a park we had driven past earlier and backs us into a spot.

"I'm going to fold down the back and eat in the sun. I'd like you to join if you're up for it." He invites me but doesn't wait for me to answer before getting out of the car, taking all the food with him.

If I want to eat, I have to follow.

The hatch opens on the SUV. Even with his massive frame sitting in half the space, I have plenty of room to sit next to him. He hands me my sandwiches, and I see the massive amount of food he ordered himself. *Do shifters eat more? Or is it a hot dude thing?*

I unwrap my sandwich, but my eyes keep darting back to him. I'm sitting with my leg touching a shifter. I've driven a whole day in a car with a shifter. I've slept in the room with a shifter. Why isn't my mother more freaked out about this? Why am I freaking out now? *It didn't matter before. Does it now?*

"Thalia, breathe, please." Cade's voice is strong and commanding as he watches me.

I gasp for air while he takes the sandwich from my hands. He slowly sets it down while holding one of my hands with his free one. His steely-blue eyes are laser focused on me, observing every bit of me.

A low grumbling noise penetrates the air, soft and almost calming.

Cade addresses me again, "Thalia, I want to fix this, but I can't if you don't talk to me."

Shaking my head, I banish the idea of him fixing it. I can't possibly tell him what I'm feeling. How insulting would that be? He's been nothing but well-behaved. He waved to kids in the hotel hallway. For me to tell him what's happening will make this situation that much more awkward. It's so insensitive.

"You smell like fear. Thalia, I know something's going on. It takes a lot to offend me, just tell me what it is. Let's not repeat yesterday. Did you take your meds?"

He's being so patient with me. Cade's questions about my care seem so genuine. Do I trust him? *What choice do I have?* It's time to just let go of what Mom said. I can't keep doing this to myself.

"What are you?"

That comes out awful. Oh, no.

Trying to recover, I rephrase it. "I mean, when you're not human, that is. Like, animal."

Arguably, that sounds worse. I cover my face with my hands, hiding from what I'm assuming is some sort of death glare.

There's a small chuckle, and then the SUV shakes as he stands up. This is probably when I die. If he doesn't kill me, then I'm dying from the embarrassment of shoving my foot so far in my mouth I choke. The SUV moves again, and he must have sat back down.

The warmth of his hands on mine as he pulls them from my face is reassuring. I try to look down away from him to avoid confronting the offense I've caused. Cade apparently has other ideas. He hooks his finger under my chin and drags my gaze up. An unexpected smile crosses his entire face, and his eyes glisten that bright yellow-gold color from yesterday.

"Thalia, you had me terrified that something was actually wrong. Don't hesitate to ask questions. You're in for a massive culture shock. Questions are important."

He's studying me, and his thumb brushes against my cheek. It's so comforting.

I close my eyes, leaning against his hand. I can't even bring myself to worry that it's weird. *Why is he so familiar?*

Cade's voice is soft. "I'm a wolf. My second skin is a massive wolf, and to quote Adam, I'm fucking fluffy."

I open my eyes to find him with a goofy grin.

"Yeah, I said it. I'm fucking fluffy."

Laughter erupts. I don't recognize it as my own until I'm gasping for air. Cade starts laughing too. I'm wiping tears from my face.

He pulls out his phone. "Would you want to see?"

"Uhhhh." It's a hard decision. Is it okay to be curious? "Yeah. If that's okay?"

He pulls out a sandwich from the bag before he slides a bag of food back to me. "Eat. I'll pull up photos from the Equinox."

He tilts his phone for me to see as he flips through his gallery. I examine pictures of people in various groups. Laughing, drinking, telling stories; there's so much life in each photo. Most people appear to be making gestures when talking. Then the photos show people and massive wolves.

Between bites in his sandwich, he points. "That's my sister, Lena, and that's my brother Deacon in his wolf. He had stolen her steak off her plate."

Lena has fire-engine red highlights in her dark brown hair, but there's still somewhat of a family resemblance.

He flips to the next one, it's still them, and then a new set of people come up.

"That's my cousin Judah and his sister Dinah. You'll get to meet Judah's twin, Ezra, tomorrow or the next day."

More wolves are mixed in with people in the next photo. It's so strange seeing these massive animals next to incredibly attractive people. Each photo could be a print ad for any number of products. The people mixed in with larger-than-life wolves make everything desirable.

Cade flicks to the next one and looks at me for a reaction, watching before hesitatingly saying, "That's me."

I try to memorize the image. The wolf on the screen is not what I expected — he's so much more. There's nothing for scale, but I assume he's massive. His muzzle is light, nearly white, blending to a light tan, then bronze and russet brown. Round, cupped ears sit facing slightly outward across a wide brow, above haunting light-yellow eyes, looking at something above where the camera would be. I'm fixated on it until he crinkles his sandwich paper.

My mouth speaks sans brain again. "You're beautiful."

He chuckles. "Thank you."

"That probably sounded really stupid." I purse my lips. I need lessons on shifter societal norms to learn to fit in. "How does one normally compliment someone on their wolf? Or is that just a human thing?"

"Beautiful works fine." He turns the screen on his phone off.

His smile alleviates some of my embarrassment while also making me wonder how many panties he's melted off with it.

"Confession." I wince while ducking my head.

"Oh?" He looks at me, concerned but not completely alarmed. "What's that?"

"I pictured you much fluffier. I'm moderately disappointed." I bite my lips together, hoping he senses the joke.

I hear more of the genuine laughter from before. It continues, and a minute later, he's wiping his eyes.

Cade nods before recovering. "Fair. I maybe oversold the fucking fluffy. But it's the only fluffy thing about me."

CHAPTER 8
CADE

WATCHING Thalia's eyes dilate to the size of saucers when I flirted with her was priceless. From the way her skin pinked when she blushed to the look in her eyes, she's a level of beauty I'm not used to having in my life.

After Thalia is safe in the vehicle, I walk around to the back of the SUV to pick up the trash and dispose of it. I smile, thinking about sitting so close to her and how quickly she warmed up about shifters. Her desire to learn and know is strong. Maybe it won't be so hard to send her home with a glowing review.

Anyone not draga mea, hmmm? The Leviathan's voice echoes in my brain.

I freeze in my spot for a moment and nearly climb out of my skin, looking around me. Almost eleven fucking years, and now he decides to actually talk to me?

He keeps talking. *You don't want? Draga mea, perfect mate. Resilient, knows wrong then makes right. Wants new life. Perfect Alpha Female.*

I'm not even sure what's happening in my life anymore.

Now? Now you decide to have an opinion worth discussing? A human woman?

The wolf relaxes within me. His holier-than-thou attitude is just as annoying verbally as non-verbally.

Have found mate many times. Many lives. Our mate.

I shake my head, running my hand down my face and looking up at the sky. At least I don't have an audience, witnessing my reaction to hearing a voice I never thought I'd hear again. This in addition to the sensitive issue of keeping Thalia Clark alive. I'm out of touch, talking to my wolf. Plus, he's still a dick. I feel the shake of his head as he once again backs out of the conversation.

Thalia points to my phone before I even climb behind the wheel. The lighthearted and laughing Thalia is gone again.

With a prickly undertone, she says, "Your phone keeps lighting up. Apparently, Isabel needs to talk to you."

"Oh, we've got nothing to say to each other." I smile at her, hoping to push this dark mood off. "Ansel didn't happen to call, did he?"

Angry. Possessive draga mea. Wants us for only her. The Leviathan pushes. *Draga mea wants to show others we are hers.*

That's not what's happening. I try to shut The Leviathan down. *Thalia's frustrated with us not doing our job and keeping our focus on her. It's not professional.* It's fucking hot though. There's something about her, specifically, being jealous that's got my attention. It can't fucking happen. We'll have to admire from a distance.

She shrugs her shoulders and looks out the passenger window.

I slide up to open the screen and look at the call history. In the few minutes it's taken to get moving, I've missed three calls from Isabel and a single call from Ansel. Normally, I'd take the call to Ansel outside, but I want to get on the road. Driving math says it's going to be a miserable couple of days. My skin itches with the need to shift at the thought of being cooped up that long.

I scroll back to Ansel's phone number and hit the call button. It rings a few times while I put the phone through the Bluetooth on my SUV. Thalia looks at me, suspicious of me letting her in on what I'm guessing she thinks is a private phone call. It concerns her, so why shouldn't she hear?

The fifth or so ring, there's scuffling and then a muffled shout from Ansel, "Ripley! I said no."

Another second later and Ansel is intentionally talking to us. His voice is the pure cheer and happy-go-lucky vibe you learn to love. "Hey, Cade, how's it going?"

"It's going, that's for sure. Did I catch you at a bad time?" I know the answer before he even has to say it.

"Never a bad time."

I can practically hear the smile in his voice.

He continues, "You don't ask me to call you out of the blue to catch up. Someone in trouble or somethin' else?"

"I'm a shitty cousin. I know it." I wince, scrunching my face a bit. I catch Thalia keeping her eyes locked on me while I drive. Ansel's not wrong. The commotion in the background on his end gets louder. I keep talking, "Worse. I call asking for a favor. Do you have any cabins available?"

"Wait. What?!" Ansel walks away from the noise, and I hear a door slam. Ansel is much more serious sounding. It's not sharp, but very focused as he presses, "What's goin' on, Cade? Is Deacon okay?"

"It's not that. I don't need your gift or station. I would handle anything like that. I just need a place for me and a client to lay low for a few days."

It's a fine balance keeping this conversation vague while settling his mind about what's going on. Thalia is going to find out everything, and so is he, eventually. I don't want anyone upset until it's absolutely necessary.

The line goes eerily quiet. Thalia tries to listen harder by leaning toward me in her seat. She's not alone. Tapping the screen, I check to see if he's hung up on me. It's quiet for another moment.

I take the phone off speaker and put it to my ear. "Ansel?"

"Cousin, what did you get wrapped up in?" Ansel pauses. His joyful tone that had turned focused dies into one laced with morbidity and mysticism. I can hear the judgment of me, and best guess, it's from what his gift has shown him. "Huh. There's a redhead who is very new. Any chance the client you need to lay low with is a redhead?"

My breath stalls in my chest at that, and I don't respond. I glance over at Thalia. She's leaning forward in her seat with her head turned to catch a better look at my face, furrowing her eyebrows and examining me thoroughly.

How am I going to explain this?

Ansel has perhaps the most morbid gift of us all. He lives with the dark knowledge of how people die. While he won't tell you unless you ask directly, Ansel knows when your days become numbered. I asked Ansel for mine just before I enlisted. My death has always been at home in my old age, surrounded by family. I don't go out of my way to tempt the fates, but it's allowed me to be a little less cautious. I've asked Ansel to keep me up to date on any changes in my death. And apparently, now, there's a redhead.

Tense that I might need to come up with a new location to divert to again, I keep my hand on the wheel near the blinker, ready to take any of the next few exits. Out of hope, and not wanting to be in the car longer than I have to, I fight his Ardelean gift with another.

"Dinah said that you'd be glad to see us."

"I'm always glad to see you." Ansel cuts his words sharply, offended by my inference.

He takes a breath and exhales it harshly.

"Well, she's new, but in general, it hasn't changed. It all works out in the end." Ansel pulls himself back to carefree and continues, "I don't have a cabin available, but I've got extra beds in the loft. You and I guess yours are welcome to 'em."

I guess my silence was the confirmation he needed to connect the dots. Relaxing back into my seat, I pull my hand away from the indicator switch. Ansel's idea of it working out in the end is that you get to die old and gray.

"And you're sure, it all works out in the end?" I don't know why I'm asking. This, between Thalia and I, shouldn't happen.

She ours to death. The Leviathan interjects. The snarky tone is implied, but I'm not ready to even fully consider what this would truly mean.

Ansel's visions of death can be ever changing. What he sees right now may only be a reflection of the future truth. The Leviathan's opinion is just that, an opinion.

"That's what I said. When should I expect you?"

I hear hinges squeaking, presumably from the door he slammed earlier.

I risk a glance at Thalia and find her looking out the window, bouncing her leg up and down. I take the transition to put the phone back on speaker while tossing it on the console.

"I'm in Pennsylvania. That's what? Twenty-seven hours, no stops?"

Heaviness sets in at the thought of driving that much. I scrub a hand down my face before reaching over and placing my hand on her thigh.

"You're gonna drive three days here and stay for a day or two, then drive two days home?" Ansel says those words slowly, working out the puzzle.

"Yup." Driving doesn't seem too daunting once I remember the alternative. With a heavy-handed amount of attitude, I grit my teeth. "Crazy."

"Crazy, as in Isabel?" Ansel asks.

I don't answer. It's not worth spelling it out.

Ansel laughs. "Oh, cousin. Take a night on the river, I'll have a couple of the guys come out to meet you at that Spaceship Water Tower in Nebraska. It's kinda nifty to look at. One of 'em can drive you back here through the night. That way, you get here faster and give The Leviathan some rest. It'll be a good time, Cade."

"You don't have to send someone; we'll take an extra night."

I don't want more people involved than necessary. Also, is it selfish to want to spend another night with Thalia alone before the craziness of pack life? Probably.

I squeeze her leg gently. When it draws her attention to me, I give her a soft smile. It seems to reassure her, and the bouncing stops.

The Leviathan pictures us close together. Implying all sorts of connections. None of which I'm willing to let happen.

Ansel keeps laughing through a trail of rhetorical questions. "Because what, your client is someone close to you? I'm assumin', like most of your clients, it's classified. And that hair and bone structure lead me to believe I've been seein' her mom in the papers."

Ansel's quick to begin piecing things together: traveling from DC, a vision of my death with a woman who has red hair, and whatever press may have hit the papers. It's not a lot to go on, but Ansel's sharp. Most people underestimate him because of the slight twang and shortened words in his speech. I just did.

He scolds me, "Have you forgot who you are? The lengths

he'd go to protect his? Take the hospitality. I wouldn't put anyone in danger."

"You're right. See you in thirty-eight-ish hours."

The phone clicks. Ansel hung up on me.

Knows draga mea as ours. You accept now. The Leviathan huffs, apparently also now concerning himself with phone calls. Last week, he didn't care about anything.

"I didn't understand any of that." Thalia sighs before grumbling. It's this perfect almost growl. "I'm going to feel lost a lot, aren't I?"

"I'll do whatever I can to make you feel less lost." It's honest, but there's no sense in denying it: wolves are different from humans. Ardelean wolves, my family and I, are even more complicated. I start by explaining the phone call, well, most of it. "So, maybe fifteen years ago? I was under intention with an Alpha Female. We were good together, until we weren't."

"Wait, what is 'intention'?" Thalia interjects while holding up a finger to interrupt.

"Uhhh." *The fuck would humans call this?* I've gotta make it a point to learn more about their customs, not just the bare minimum to keep them alive. I try to pick universal words. "So, my parents were kinda a big deal, and her parents are kinda a big deal, so they agreed that we'd be mates."

"Oh! Like an arranged marriage." Thalia makes the connection, bouncing in her seat with excitement before stopping still. "Wait, how old were you?"

"Arrangements generally take place when you're thirteen or fourteen. It's when you start finding out the true temperament of wolves. You can shift from birth, but you grow a lot as a human, and generally, the wolf's personality starts to develop at about adolescence. Obviously, it's not set in stone, but it's accurate enough." I wobble my hand, trying to indicate the balance.

The Leviathan snorts. *Not right. False mate not worthy. Draga mea worthy, yes. Thalia our mate. She best fit. We give wolf now, she flawless.*

Regardless of his opinions, and apparently, his new desire to go around gifting wolves to humans we've just met, I continue, "Well, something big happened. I didn't become who Isabel wanted me to be. When I left, I thought she'd get the hint and move on. There's plenty of people interested in her."

"She's hung up on you?" Thalia gives me side-eye, choosing her words carefully. "But you're not interested?"

I snort. It's rude, involuntary, but rude nonetheless.

Shaking my head, I assure her the idea of going back to Isabel turns my stomach. "I don't want to be the man she wants. She shows up once every year or so and tries to convince me. I figured I'd be good for another eight months since she was over at Lunar New Year banging down my door."

"You don't want what she does. Seems like a good enough reason to find someone else."

Thalia uses logic, which . . . I absolutely agree with, but we're wolves; bloodlines and legacies don't care about logic. A whole other reason why The Leviathan cannot have a human mate. As perfect, smart, and accepting as she may be, Thalia is a human. She's off-limits to me.

"One would think it would be that easy." I draw a deep breath and try to sum up the rest of the call. "It's all good. As Ansel said, we'll divert to his place in Utah, spend a couple of days out there. Deacon will come home and scare off Isabel, and it'll be safe for us to head back."

"Cool. We can cross off states I haven't been to."

Thalia surprises me by being ready to make the most of what could have been a lousy trip.

The Leviathan huffs. *Our mate strong. Tell draga mea we are hers. She will be yes.*

Hearing him is still jarring. It's foreign to have his input. I find myself shaking my head in response. I have to keep it together better.

Looking at the road ahead, we sit in comfortable silence for a bit.

"So, how is it you seem to know where we're going all the time? You never consult a map, is that a wolf thing?"

Her curiosity is genuine. Really adorable, actually. I can't help but smile. That, I don't try to hide.

"Nothing so magical as that. I drive into DC regularly for work. I get restless on planes. If I'm driving, I'm in control and can get out of the car if I need to. Generally, I get enough notice to allow a full day or two of driving. Speaking of which, do you want to pop on some tunes, podcasts, audiobooks, anything? I'm good with silence. I'll need to put on some directions at some point, but in between them, any requests?"

"Uhhh. What do you have for audiobooks?"

The end of that sentence holds a hopeful lift that it'll be something she's interested in.

"Whatever your heart desires. The phone's in client mode, so company card is on file in the app. My one request is that if it's high fantasy or super involved, start at book one or be ready to explain." I smile.

She's so fucking easy to be around. Making her happy and distracting her from the bad shit feels so good.

Pick someone else, hmmm? The Leviathan gets snooty in my head. *Draga mea ours. Perfect once wolf.*

You know, maybe you not talking to me wasn't so bad after all, I clip back. He grumbles, leaving me alone.

Pressure sits heavy in my chest that he's right, and I could do this with her. It doesn't change the fact that I've given my word. The deal has to be upheld. Thalia Clark might be the devil's daughter, and the deal I cut might not have been the smartest move, but it's done. Keeping up my end is crucial.

Thalia chooses some sort of murder mystery with fantastical elements relating to secret societies. It's really easy to get wrapped up in. As promised, without hesitating, I find the next exit, and we get snacks and use the bathroom. She's amazing with protocol and staying in my line of sight when possible. It's evident that she's an ambassador's kid and has been through the trainings on security protocols.

After yesterday's episode, I anticipated more struggles: anxiety or social class based. I'm not ruling out more issues, but I'll take a page from Ansel's book and be happy about the good things as they come.

CHAPTER 9
THALIA

I'VE SEEN and heard road trip horror stories, but I've never been on a road trip personally. From what I can tell, they're nice. Though, it might just be the company. Cade and I have hit our groove. The day in the car isn't bad at all. True to his word, anytime I ask, he pulls off. The audiobook I found is a little more risqué than I anticipated, but Cade doesn't make it weird.

Maybe it's in my head, or he's just good at his job, but it feels like he enjoys spending time with me. I could see myself hanging with Cade for the rest of my life. *What is wrong with me?* There's no way this can be anything more than a work exchange. He's being nice because it's his job, and being a jerk about us stuck together would make things uncomfortable. No one wants to spend time with someone you can't stand.

JUST BEFORE DINNER TIME, we stop for the night in some sort of metropolis that sprawls on both sides of the Mississippi River.

105

Cade handles checking us in while I look around the warm and cozy lobby.

"Alright, and for the happy couple, I've luckily got one room left, and it's a single king."

Single king grabs my attention as the man at the front desk slides the keys across.

Cade hesitates. His hand hovers over the key. "It's the last one left? I snore, and she sometimes needs her own space."

"I'm sorry, sir, it's all we have." The man at the front desk frowns.

Something causes him to take a small step back. The man's reaction makes me turn to Cade. His body is rigid, his shoulders back, and he's standing tall. It's like he's frozen.

Something is wrong, very wrong.

Without hesitation, I reach forward, picking the keys up. "It's alright." I try to diffuse and smile at the man behind the desk. I turn back to Cade. "That means that every time you wake me up snoring, you're buying me an extra piece of bacon for breakfast."

It isn't until he squeezes my hand that I realize my hand has looped into Cade's. It feels natural, and the butterflies in my stomach take flight.

I don't pull away but step into him, selling the happy couple act, or at least trying to. He lets me lead the way to the elevator bank.

Cade's silence is deafening and puts me on edge. He's not only distant but nearly mechanical, all the while holding my hand on the way to our room. Inside there is, in fact, one single solitary king-sized bed.

Cade puts the duffle bag on the bed and sits down on it. Breathing slowly and focusing on each breath like he had me do.

"Are you having a panic attack?" I whisper.

He shakes his head and whispers back, "No, disagreement."

"Oh." I keep my mouth in the O shape, hoping to gather more insight.

I assume that would mean something to someone who is also a shifter, but it's like that comic, *Non Sequitur*, you need some context to understand it. *Do I ask? That seems rude.*

Giving him more time, I rock back and forth, hoping for an idea of what to say or do to help. My stomach growls, and I put my hand over it to try and silence it.

Slowly Cade stands, and when he does, it's like the negative energy has separated from him. He gently rests his hand on my shoulder and quirks a soft smile.

"Let's get you some food and a few days of clothes."

CADE HAS a list of everything to replace whatever I would have packed from home. Walking around the store, checking the note on his phone, he efficiently informs me of what I will need for the next few weeks. It's a lot of different things, but he assures me it's fine. He instructs on the type of clothing I'll likely need but doesn't comment on colors or patterns, even when I intentionally tried picking up a hideous sweater. All he mustered was a noncommittal shrug. For half an instant, I could see a glimpse of Cade from earlier today, it came as a small smile when I put the grotesque sweater back.

Wherever we're going must have unpredictable weather because there are base layers, over layers, a jacket, and three different kinds of socks. Nothing phases him: feminine products, bras, and underwear. He even double-checks on feminine products. He seems very well-adjusted to having a woman around. I suppose I can thank the hot sister for that? At the checkout, it's a few hundred dollars, but Cade doesn't even flinch.

AFTER SHOPPING, he pulls us up in front of a steakhouse. Once seated inside, the waitress brings us amazing smelling rolls and fancy sweet butter.

After ordering, Cade makes eye contact with me. "I'm sorry."

"What?" I answer dumbly to his apology.

There's genuine sincerity. I can tell it means a lot for him to do this.

"You shouldn't have seen me crack today. You sure as hell shouldn't have had to cover for me at the front desk. I'm sorry. I'll do my best to make sure it doesn't happen again."

His words are so heavy. Cade's eyes are still blue, but they hold the same focus as when they're golden.

It's uncomfortable to receive such an intense apology. I squirm under his gaze, but I ask anyway, "Was I in danger?"

"No," he answers firmly.

"Was the man at the front desk in danger?" I pry.

"No." His answer is less firm but believable, mostly.

He moves, buttering a roll for himself.

"Does this have to do with what Ansel said about The Leviathan?" I hit a nerve. His eyes snap to me.

"Yes." He nods ever so slightly. "I can explain some, but later, not here. No one is in danger, least of all you."

What is The Leviathan? Why would it need a break? I'm wrapped up in my head until Cade's hand touches mine.

I raise my eyes from my plate back to his.

"You'll get your answers. It's going to be okay."

His voice is calm, softer, like it's only for me. His hand lingers on mine. My heart flutters with the intimacy. I'm probably enjoying the contact more than I should. *I'm just a job.*

The harsh concern leaves his face before he casually tilts his head to the side. "Tell me more, what are you studying?"

CHAPTER 10

CADE

THE LEVIATHAN SLAMS against my control at every turn. He's back to pacing, thinking about how close we could be to Thalia. *Back to sleep space. One bed, now. We take our mate. Bite her. Claim her. Make her ours. Our draga mea.* With over a decade of no formal communication, he's loud and demanding in my head. Visions of standing behind Thalia with my nose buried in her neck assault my brain, paired with devious thoughts of wondering how it would sound when she screams my name. The Leviathan pushes the thoughts harder.

It's enticing, and my cock throbs in my pants. The Leviathan isn't alone in temptation. I want her. Desperately. She's the most beautiful woman I've ever met, and I don't know that . . . *Fuck. No. I can't do this. We can't do this.*

Show her how special. How we need only her. The Leviathan urges. Not pacified simply by envisioning her. *Mate likes us.*

Thalia explains her internship at the museum and how she's part historian, educator, and archivist. When talking about her academics, she beams with pride. There's a dip as she downplays her original dream to work in the field. Digs in her freshman-year classes weren't as 'interesting' as she had hoped. There's something she isn't saying. Her entire body language changes, making me want to dig more into her past. Is there a threat we missed in the assessment? Maybe I should message Adam and have him look? No, it doesn't matter. DC is almost a thousand miles away.

As I eat, she tells me how she loves the analysis of all sorts of things I had no idea could be analyzed, such as paint compositions in older paintings. The way she rattles off documents, paintings, statues, and other historical events related to each of them is impressive, and I'm at a huge disadvantage in the book smart category.

This conversation eventually leads to hearing about how she wants to work with children more regularly. The passion is written on her face in big strokes. Her eyes sparkle, her cheeks are high, and her smile is nonstop when she talks about encouraging children, especially girls, into the STEM field. The vibrancy she lives her life with leaves me in fucking awe. She's brilliant.

She's making it increasingly difficult to see her as just my job.

Our mate wants pups. Good for pack. The Leviathan imagines sitting on the lawn with a puppy running around in the yard.

"You've a bachelor's? What was your field of study?"

She turns the subject back to me while I remind The Leviathan that liking children is not the same as wanting to parent. He disagrees, naturally.

I shake my head. "No. I have a GED and an honorable discharge from the US Army."

The surprise on her face isn't the first time someone's reacted that way. She sits with raised eyebrows, biting her tongue. It's nice to see that I've surprised her. Even if it isn't the good kind.

"Thank you for your service." She's polite with the obviously regimented, politically correct response to military service. Thalia moves on quickly. "I guessed a military background. I assumed you'd have attended school more traditionally through the GI Bill."

"For most wolves, traditional school is out of the question on some levels. Especially in the late teens. Hormones are all over the place, females going into heat for the first time, males trying to handle animals coming into their full strength. I managed to scrape my GED together by eighteen and then enlisted shortly after I turned nineteen. For me, surviving in the army happened because my superior officer was a bear, literally. I served four years, and I've been working for Peter for the last six." I try not to focus on the negatives. I need to make certain the senator's daughter hears good things about shifters. "My cousin Judah and his brother, Ezra, who you'll meet tomorrow or the next day, both hold bachelor's degrees, and their sister Dinah finishes up her master's soon. My little sister Lena is working on her master's as well."

"Why did you enlist?" She pauses, and I wait for her second question.

She scrunches her face while she thinks. She's been asking questions in pairs. It's a cute quirk I'm really starting to appreciate about her.

The next one comes more slowly. "That seems dangerous. What if someone found out you were a shifter?"

"It's complicated. I didn't have many options. So, I chose the one I felt I could live with." I try to move on before talks of lineage and abdicating thrones arrive at the dinner table.

Coward. Our mate will know. You betrayed our people. Robert has what is ours. Ran away to play warrior for them not ours. Not champion for us. The Leviathan growls when he thinks of

113

Robert, imagining him as a bloody corpse. *End him. Take back ours with draga mea at side.* His insistence is growing old.

Wanting Thalia and keeping her are two very different things. The Leviathan doesn't hear how much her job means to her. If we were to have a relationship with her, it would have to be from a distance.

"I can respect that." Thalia's face falls.

She pulls at loose strands of hair around her face. Guilt?

Her voice is quieter. "Until last semester, I let Mom believe I was studying poli-sci. It's why she let me take summer and winter break classes. She thought my study abroad in Italy was to learn about the politics of Rome. I had just started talking to a therapist who agreed avoiding politics was in my own best interest. So, I went abroad. When she found out I was museum hopping and taking classes on painting restorations and the handling of fragile documents . . . she was livid. Dad convinced her that since I was only a semester away from graduating, it was better to get my bachelor's in history. I could get a master's in poli-sci. Though, I think he knows that's never going to happen."

Her experiences strike an all too familiar chord. I'd bet no one particularly enjoys disappointing their parents. I certainly didn't. Even if I disliked them, they were still mine, and there's a basic want for approval from them.

While waiting for the check, I open my phone to view my security camera streams. Isabel's SUV sits in the driveway. Her companions' vehicles are gone. I know she's with them, leaving the SUV in my driveway as a calling card. *She'll be back.* Having seen enough, I close it.

False mate, must die. The Leviathan says. I internally roll my eyes at him. Death seems a bit harsh for trespass, but she needs to go the fuck away.

I USHER Thalia into the hotel room, and she turns, squaring up to me. Brow furrowed, hands resting on her hips, she looks angry.

The Leviathan takes notice. *Bitey little mate. Wants us to obey her. Hear her demands.* The Leviathan shuffles with the excitement of playing a game, flicking his tail, ready for a move.

I let the door fall closed, locking behind me. *We will listen to her request and decide how to best accommodate. We're not here to obey or demand.* I echo, correcting him the best I can.

"Listen, I know you're going to do the whole caveman macho routine: 'I man. I sleep floor. You sleep bed.' And make a big deal about how chivalrous you are. Which is fine and all, but since this bed is massive, I propose we put up a pillow wall. You sleep on one side and I on the other. Puritan style."

Her face slowly falls, cheeks turning that adorable shade of pink. Moving one hand from her hip to shield her eyes from me, she plays the most adorable version of 'if I can't see you, you can't see me.'

The Leviathan's head cocks, watching her. *Why does our mate hide? Draga mea offers good things. Trust is good. Why hide?*

Shame. She feels bad commanding an Alpha. Hiding from authority that you may have caused upset to lessen punishment. I try to explain to him quickly, using ideas he'll understand. It's hard when he's so set in the old ways.

The problem we have now is that we both see her true feelings, but we interpret them slightly differently. That shame isn't just from making a demand of us. It's from humans having closed doors about sex. Thalia's nervous about the idea of sharing a bed, and if her reaction from the diner with the hostess is any indication, she's likely ashamed of her attraction.

I wet my lips thinking about *having* her in bed. She wants to be near us. That's how it smells anyway. Oh, what would it be like to be buried deep in Thalia?

The Leviathan accepts that thought as an answer, also seeing the idea of her pressed into the bed. I'm hot and shake the collar on my shirt to cool down.

I try to divert my thoughts, begrudgingly, because if I'm going to throw away my quiet life for the senator's daughter, it'll be in my own bed. I don't wait for her to open her eyes before I walk past her.

I draw another breath of the delicious arousal in her scent and torture myself in exhale. I clear my throat. "Do you prefer the left or the right?"

THE LEVIATHAN DOESN'T CARE that she's fluffed the pillows between us seventeen times and tried to build it as vertical as possible. We agree. As soon as she's asleep, those pillows are going on the floor.

Soft sleeping sounds that I recognize from last night come from Thalia. Gently, moving with as much tact as I can, I toss the barrier aside. I tuck my hand and forearm gently between us, forming a physical connection. I want to pull her into my arms, but for fear of waking her up, I settle with just the touch.

The Leviathan lets out a contented groan, and together we relax. The comfort of our skin against hers is otherworldly. For the first time in over a week, drifting into sleep is luxurious.

WHEN MY 7:00 a.m. alarm pings softly, I reach for my phone, feeling a weight on my shoulder. Thalia is curled into the crook of my arm, her head resting on my shoulder and her hand draped across my chest.

The Leviathan, resting peacefully, grumbles in approval of our touch. I silence my alarm, but only get to enjoy a few quick seconds of bliss before Thalia wakes, becomes aware, and quickly scoots away.

Opting to say nothing, I smile.

Thalia grumbles incoherently and slides out of bed, her hair and clothing disheveled. This reality brings a desire to see her walking naked to the bathroom after a night of lust.

Should I feel guilty for moving the pillows? Probably, but I don't — and The Leviathan approves.

CHAPTER 11
THALIA

"I woke up in Cade's arms," I seethe to myself against the thunderous pounding sound of the shower as it warms up. "And I loved it." Shame rolls around in my stomach, making me feel sick.

What if he's married? A girlfriend? Did I ogle someone else's partner?!

I don't know for sure that he isn't attached to someone else. No, not attached. What is the right word? Indisposed, attended, intended. Intended. That's the right term. I might have spent the night cuddling with a man intended, or more, for someone else. It's a dirty, terrible feeling.

There's no way Cade isn't with someone. Somehow, I'm sure they're going to know. And they'll be so mad when they find out what I've done. A shifter seems like the last person you want to make angry.

I was far too close with someone I shouldn't have been. I ball my hands into fists, bringing them to my forehead. Leaning against the wall, I sink to the floor and pull my knees to my chest. I want to crawl out of my skin. This is awful.

Well, no. He can't be married. I draw a deep breath. Let's think this through. He's most certainly the dedicated type that would wear a ring. Wait. Do shifters do that? I know nothing. *Stupid tabloids.* Nothing really in-depth or meaningful is printed in those.

There's a limited amount of time I can spend in the bathroom before he gets worried that I've tripped and died. That would be worse. I can only imagine him barging in having to save me from myself.

So I push aside my freak-out and focus on finishing my shower and getting ready.

Once I'm presentable again, I emerge from the bathroom to see Cade sitting, scrolling on his phone. He instantly puts it down on the bed and looks at me. Worry quickly paints his face, eyebrows drawn together and lips pursed; he's assessing everything. His eyes, scanning me methodically, look for answers. Moments of silence tick by. Is he waiting for me to offer information?

Finally, he asks, "Thalia, what's wrong?"

Swallowing is hard. My throat is thick and unresponsive. I blurt out, "Are you intended? Do you have a mate?"

Much to my relief, Cade shakes his head, but his face remains drawn together, crossed with concern. "No. I'm not currently intended or mated. I don't date. Everyone in my recent sex life has been well informed and explicitly made aware that our connection is temporary."

Cade offers more information than I asked for. Guilt is replaced but not with relief. Green, ugly, and uncharacteristic jealousy creeps in from nowhere. Intrusive, angry thoughts of him in bed with someone else bubble into my mind. It simmers with distaste. I nod dumbly and step out of the way, gesturing to the bathroom with one arm, signaling it's all his.

What is this? Why am I feeling like this? I've no claim on

Cade. We just met. We are entirely different. Even if he's attracted to me, which I'm sure he's not, we could never work. I'm a client. He's my security detail. He's a wolf. I'm human. He's nearly thirty. I think back to our conversation last night, running the numbers. Yeah. He's nearly thirty, and I'm not even legal to drink until May. Plain and simple, there's no common ground. We're two people in close proximity who happened to spend the night sleeping, platonically, in the same bed. It wasn't sexual. No matter how enticing Cade is, I've got to remember that we can't happen.

While he showers, I become increasingly aware of his phone sitting on the bed. I have this uncontrollable desire to rifle through its contents. If I could just look around and figure out if there's someone in his life. Someone that I would have just severely offended. *I want to know.* Minutes tick by. If I look now . . . He said it's in client mode, so it's not like I'd find anything anyway. It'd make sense that he'd safeguard against his personal life colliding with his clients. But why on earth do I care? We're nothing. I'm his job. We cuddled a little. People crave connection, so it's not that abnormal, right? *Right?!*

Frozen in indecision, I haven't moved toward his phone by the time the bathroom door opens. I gasp, trying to breathe through my own tense emotions and the startle of the opening door.

Cade comes out, rolling up the sleeves on his buffalo plaid flannel button-down that hangs open to a gray T-shirt, clinging to his frame.

"You okay?" he asks, looking at me from the corner of his eye while packing his bag.

I nod and shrug. It's pretty much the most noncommittal answer I can give. The actuality of it all is I'm overwhelmed. I keep trying to draw air deep into my lungs, but the more I think, the more I become confused. There isn't enough air in this room for me to breathe.

Cade picks his bag up off the bed, looking at me, on the verge of motioning me out the door. He puts it back down. His shoes on the floor make soft thuds as he approaches. In an instant, I'm wrapped in his embrace.

The touch startles me. I shrink away, but Cade's arms are steady. In a few seconds, I wilt into him, and I can't stop the tears.

He's a silent calm. I hug him back, pressing my ear against Cade's chest. I hear the steady beat of his heart.

"I'm getting you wet." I try to unbury myself from in his shirt, but he keeps holding me tight.

"Don't worry about it," Cade assures me.

He doesn't let go.

"Okay, but there's snot, and I can't breathe," I argue, squirming harder.

There's the telltale movement of Cade suppressing a laugh. This time, when I pull away. Cade lets me.

He grabs tissues from the box on the dresser and hands them to me. Wiping at my face, I try to put myself back together.

I freeze when his hands gently corral wayward strands of hair from my face, tucking them behind my ears.

The way he behaves gives the impression that he cares. Unless that's maybe not true, and keeping me held together is easier than dealing with me falling apart?

"I'm ready. I'm sorry. It won't happen again." The words bring more tears to my eyes, but I blink them away and draw another deep breath into my lungs.

"What won't?" He tilts his head, looking at me.

With his eyebrows pulled up, Cade looks concerned but not agitated. *That's unexpected.*

"Falling apart constantly, we've barely known each other for three days. This isn't fair to you." I gesture to the door.

"You're allowed to have emotions. They're not something to apologize for. What you see as a failure, I see as awe-inspiring. I read somewhere: hard is hard. There's no comparing things that are difficult because we all experience things differently. But I can tell you, I don't know if I'd be able to deal with having my life turned upside down like this so gracefully." Cade raises his arms and drops them again. It almost seems like he wants to hug me again, but he's fighting it. His voice is sweet with that velvety tone from the first day. "I'm really enjoying getting to know you. And hands down, you're the best non-family road trip partner I've had."

CHAPTER 12

CADE

BEING the reason Thalia shed tears from those beautiful green eyes guts me.

You tell her mate. Draga mea will understand. The Leviathan pushes.

I don't want The Leviathan to be right. The truth is unavoidable. She's easy to be around, makes me laugh, and I thoroughly enjoy talking with her. It's not that I'm a recluse, I tend to make friends wherever I go, but Thalia's different. Talking with her feels like being with anyone from one of my closest inner circles.

We woke up in bed together, and she darted to the bathroom. I could scent her fear and hear how her heartbeat picked up. Her fear held even when I came back into the room. Then she cried when she saw me again after I answered her question truthfully. *Was I too honest with her?*

Not enough honest. The Leviathan growls at me. *She feels us. Why no tell draga mea ours? We are hers.*

I used to think that The Leviathan making no effort to work with me beyond the most primal levels was frustrating. Useful, but frustrating. I was mistaken. Our constant disagreement over a woman, that we can't have, is downright aggravating.

Draga mea ours. You know. The Leviathan huffs, ordering me around. *You fight me. You more wrong, you puppy brain. Take mate. Make ours. Claim territory. Be Alpha. Kill enemies for future. Draga mea ours. You make good.*

Despite my reassurance that everything is alright, I've found myself on the cold side of the booth at the diner I found us for breakfast. Thalia is distant and terse; each conversation grows shorter and shorter. When the food is served, Thalia takes a few meaningful bites before it devolves into simply pushing food around her plate.

The Leviathan agonizes over why she isn't eating and how we should fix it. *Make mate better. Food not good. She needs black stuff we dislike.*

Appeasing him, I ask about her food and am dismissed. Further fueling my certainty that it isn't a food problem. Rather, it's a problem with me. I fucked up moving her stupid pillows and cuddling with her for my own benefit.

I've got nine hours, before pitstops, in the car with her before we meet up with other wolves. Will it be enough time to fix the tenuous bond I broke?

MEAL PAID for and out the door, I walk slightly behind her to stop myself from wrapping an arm around her shoulder. After closing her door on the SUV, I make my way around and climb in behind the wheel.

In the relative privacy of the Yukon, I carefully try to broach the subject. "Thalia, what's going on in that head of yours?"

"It's nothing. I'm fine," she snaps.

Her sharp tone is followed by the click of her seat belt.

Not fine. The Leviathan growls, angry that she takes that attitude with us. *Mate or no she no disrespect.*

Starting the vehicle and beginning to drive, I push him back, checking my emotions and apparently now his, before proceeding, "Are you upset that we woke up together?"

"No," Thalia answers. The *o* is elongated and drawn out.

When I check my mirrors, I watch her for a brief moment as she fidgets.

The best way to get information is to wait. So, that's what I do, slowly getting back onto the freeway.

It's not long before she breaks. "I don't know what's going on." She pauses again, and I wait even less time before she begins, "Cade, did . . . was last night . . . this morning . . . Can we forget it happened?"

Fuck this fucking road trip. Hearing her words and the shame in her voice rocks my resolve. I want to pull the vehicle over and hold her until she understands everything I haven't had a chance to explain to her. That sounds so sappy, but it's the truth. Let Lena mock me later when she finds out I'm going soft. *How am I supposed to forget how I feel? Especially about her.*

The Leviathan agrees with every single thought. I'm fucked. The most harmony we've ever had, a woman we've no business wanting, craving, needing. Most importantly, no business claiming as our own, even if part of me is ready to admit . . .

Pulling over isn't an option. I reach over and pick up her hand, holding it. I run my thumb over the soft skin on the back of her knuckles. There are so many different options as to how to answer her.

I pick honesty, and even The Leviathan agrees with this answer. "I don't want to forget what happened last night."

Thalia doesn't recoil from my touch. She keeps her hand in

mine. But she offers no response and instead withdraws back into silence.

WE DRIVE for at least an hour before I need my hand for the steering wheel. I begrudgingly pull it from hers. It's hollow without hers nestled within it. When I no longer need my hand to drive, I gently offer it back to her, waiting to be accepted.

From what I know, humans don't connect as quickly as wolves. When they pair up, it's an emotional love that grows over time, and they can differentiate it from familial love, but it's not all-consuming, like finding a mate. Some of their movies show quick, whirlwind romances, but it's less intense than it is with shifters and not common. A plethora of videos exist on the internet of little old people saying, 'I knew from the first minute I laid eyes on her,' but unfortunately, many of those videos are of wolves.

I wish I could get years of my life back to learn more about humans, but pack life, the army, and working crazy hours for Corinth Security didn't leave a ton of time for studying human mating rituals. Not to mention, I didn't consider it necessary.

Seconds tick by, and she hasn't accepted my hand.

The Leviathan scoffs at the notion of Thalia not feeling what's between us. *Our mate will understand. She is brilliant. You've said: school science special. Draga mea learns quickly.*

Fighting The Leviathan is impossible because the longer this goes on, the more I wonder if he's not wrong. What if she's ours? What happens if I need her?

Our lives aren't simple. Needing her, wanting her, doesn't mean we can have her. Even if it's fate, with the way things are now, I can't take Senator Clark's daughter as my mate. It's a sinking feeling in my stomach.

Thalia, as my mate, means I would have to find a way to make a life with her. For now, I pick up her hand with my own, wrapping my fingers around her and brushing my thumb across her skin. I'll take every moment and every touch that I can. *Fuck it, I'll figure the rest out as I go along.*

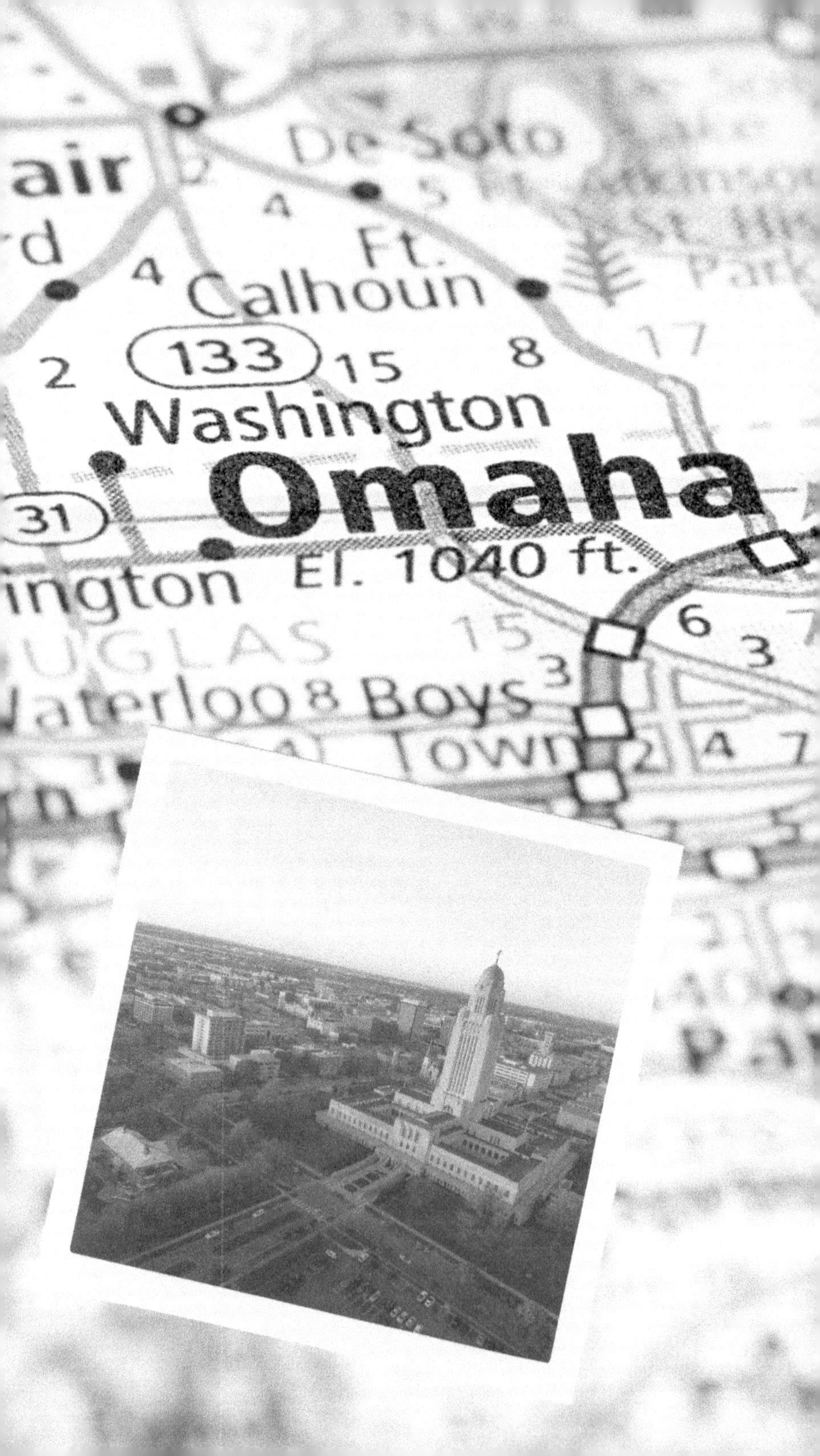
De Soto
Ft.
Calhoun
133
Washington
Omaha
El. 1040 ft.
31
Boys

CHAPTER 13

THALIA

I DON'T WANT to forget what happened last night. His voice repeats in my brain as I ride shotgun across miles of barren crop fields, too soon in the year for anything to grow. A solitary thought ruminates, different from the thoughts that trigger panic attacks, maybe like hope? Hope of seeing more of Cade's gorgeous half-naked body? My imagination is wild, assuming everything from the waist down is as proportional as the upper half.

His casual confidence isn't forced. It's clear Cade knows how to command the attention of others around him. Millie and Adam both sang his praises, encouraging me to trust him. He has a silent intensity that any girl, or guy, if that's how he plays, would be lucky to get lost in.

I'm the opposite. It's not difficult to see that. My curves are soft, and while I spend some time on the treadmill and in yoga classes, I'm happy to accept that my shape is more full-figured. I like my curves, somedays. I've tried to focus more on what my body can do than what it looks like. It's just not easy.

Beyond that, setting the physicality of it all aside, I'm not confident. I have my niche of things I like and know. There's a reason I'm in academics. I'm book smart, not people smart. No one in my life is going to sing my praises outside of academia. Only one person has ever really shown a ton of interest in being anything more than a one-off fling. And it's so inappropriate that I could never consider it.

I don't want to forget what happened last night. That's the kind of talk a woman wants to hear. That I want to hear. It's that promise of tomorrow and the next day. The world you dream about where you're celebrating your fiftieth wedding anniversary, dancing to 'the oldies' and eating cake surrounded by your grandchildren. My whole body shivers. Could I have that? *Could I have that with Cade?*

This isn't plausible. I don't even know enough about his culture to tell you if weddings and anniversaries are something shifters do.

I don't want to forget what happened last night.

It takes me a moment to realize Cade is talking. I look over at him. "I'm sorry, what?"

"Well, Miss Bladder Of Steel, I've gotta make a pit stop." Cade turns to look at me. "Can you look up somewhere in the next twenty minutes to pee and eat?"

His hand leaves mine to reach for his phone. We've been holding hands for hours, and I've been too lost in my head to just enjoy it.

I've heard the terms 'fly-over states' and 'the great plains.' Now, I get it. Iowa runs into Nebraska, and watching out the window is absolutely mind-numbing. Cross-country road trips always seem more exciting in movies. They lie. According to the GPS, it's a bit more than twenty minutes before we find anything at all. It's flat nothingness. Then, in the middle of nowhere, civilization springs up.

At the fuel station, I wait in the SUV while he pumps our

fuel, per the protocol. But when he opens my door, Cade blocks my path instead of letting me out. He's different at this stop. I can't put my finger on it. It's almost regimented. His eyes are that bright gold color. Something is very wrong.

"We're not *alone* here." Cade hints heavily. His eyes and the word strongly imply other shifters. "If someone says they recognize either of us, stick to our aliases. We get confused for whoever they think we are all the time. It's frustrating. We don't see the resemblances." He nods, encouraging me. "Try not to engage beyond that. Defer to me. Let them assume we're mates. It's common for wolves to let the male do the talking and for the female to shy away from others, especially shifters." Cade instructs briefly. His words are quick before offering me a hand out of the SUV.

Between his tone and the depth of his instructions, I'm lost in fear. My heart pounds hard in my chest, and I draw small shallow breaths. Focus on the easiest instructions. I keep my mouth closed and nod. If you don't say anything, you can't get yourself in trouble.

His eyes slowly fade back to a steel gray. He gives me a small smile and keeps me much closer to him than at any stop before. He wraps his arm around my shoulder, and once inside, he's more obvious when checking our surroundings. Careful-but-carefree Cade is absent. This Cade is completely calculated. He isn't his usual friendly self with the man at the counter. There's no small talk.

The man at the counter bounces his eyes back and forth between us. It feels like we're just one question away from being in trouble. *What happens if we run into other shifters? What's the worst — no — don't go there.* I take a deep breath, shoving those thoughts away.

When Cade leads me out toward the vehicle, he quickly steps in front of me, handing me the bag. But then, he stops, standing perfectly still in the middle of the lot. The strangest noise comes from him. Loud but not deafening.

Is that, is it a growl? It's kind of like a growl.

I lean around Cade, taking a curious peek, but dart back after catching a glimpse of a man leaning against the grill of the Yukon. My toes curl in my shoes, and I tightly squeeze the bag's handles. I try to focus on anything other than the fact that Cade is, I'm pretty sure, growling.

Cade leads me over to the vehicle, walking slowly with his shoulders back. We skirt along the side. I follow as closely as I can, letting him shield me from the man leaning against the hood.

"This must be yours?" A southern drawl rolls out.

Cade gets me to my door, hurrying me inside. I scurry into the safety of the vehicle. Cade hands me the keys and flicks down the button to lock all the doors. My heart beats a million miles a minute, thumping through my bones. I swear I feel it while resting my hand on my chest.

The glass and metal of the SUV muffle the conversation, but I make out enough.

Cade raises one shoulder, just now responding to the first question. "Yeah. Just passing through."

"Must be a big road trip for you to be down here from Wisconsin. Where are you headed?" the man asks, pressing off the hood and blocking Cade's path to the driver's seat.

Cade isn't small. Yet this man dwarfs Cade by at least six inches in height and maybe twelve inches wider across the shoulders. The large man crosses his arms over his chest.

"West. Visiting some family late for the holiday. Like I said, passing through, nothing more. Didn't know we were in a territory. Certainly not looking for any trouble."

Cade shrugs, then casually motions, I'm guessing west, with his hand.

The other man steps into Cade's personal space, barely two feet from him. Cade doesn't back up. I fight the urge to cover my eyes.

No. Get away from him. Please. Don't hurt Cade. Get away. We don't want trouble.

As an ambassador's daughter, you're trained on what to do if your security gets taken down. But the training against those threats seems significantly subpar when the threat is a shifter and you're the daughter of the senator who wants to destroy them.

"Headed to Ardelean country then?" the man asks.

He doesn't hear my mental pleas. He doesn't step away from Cade.

What does that mean? I've never heard of a part of the country referred to as Ardelean. It's not an area of the United States. I'm positive.

"We'll pass through. They're expecting us. Not looking to aggravate anyone's people. Honest mistake, outta fuel and had to pee. We won't make the same mistake again." Cade keeps a level tone but squares himself up with the man. Shoulders back and chin high, he stands his ground.

Apparently, the man likes Cade's answer. He sidesteps out of Cade's way.

Walking past the stranger, Cade rotates, not taking eyes from him until the monstrous man turns and walks away. After a few more seconds, Cade indicates for me to unlock the door. I climb over his seat to unlock only his door. Even inside the vehicle, Cade watches the man until he goes into the fuel station. Then Cade quickly pulls the SUV away from our spot beside the pump. A massive weight is lifted from my chest as the Yukon's wheels roll us back onto the road.

I heave out a sigh of relief.

Uncharacteristically, Cade opens his phone and turns on an

app leaving the screen up. Normally, the man doesn't even eat and drive. I've used his phone more than he has in the last few days. He switches to another screen, starts a call, and goes back to the app. Cade's driving is more aggressive and over the speed limit. We're back on the freeway and nearly flying by the time a familiar voice comes through the car speakers.

"Code?" Peter asks.

"1919," Cade answers. "I need a clear path from my location to the other side of Nebraska."

"Working. You're on the eighty?" Peter sounds skeptical as he questions Cade. "Nebraska and Wisconsin move closer together? I didn't hear about it."

"It's a long story."

I note how Cade doesn't give him a full answer or explanation. Cade's eyes are constantly scanning the mirrors behind us. I try to look back too. That sensation of being watched creeps through me. His paranoia fuels mine. I squirm. I thought we were okay when we left the fuel station, but Cade's behavior has me questioning that.

"Alright. You're clear for the next 150 miles. Check back in if you need more distance." Peter pauses. "I'll run tailing software to be safe. You'll get notice anytime someone follows you too closely for too long. Be careful."

Peter must hang up. Cade puts his phone in the cupholder and scrubs a hand down his face, going back to weaving in and out of traffic. We're flying close to ninety miles an hour.

My fingers clench around the door handle. I'm terrified of the weaving. Everything feels so big. Tears well in my eyes, and I don't know if I'm more afraid it happened or glad it's over.

"Leave the app that's running open but call Ansel," Cade instructs.

My fingers are still shaking when the newly familiar voice of Ansel picks up on the second ring. "Hello."

"We're going to be early. I didn't realize Nebraska had bears."

Cade is short with him; the tone is less polite than with Peter. It has an edge to it.

Is he growling? Wait. BEARS?!

"Oh. Shit. Yeah. After Omaha, the sleuth popped up a few years back. I've never had any issues with 'em. Smells but never seen any." Ansel doesn't engage in the same tone. "Guessin', with how grumpy you are, that wasn't your experience?"

Bear shifters, okay, I knew there were more than wolf shifters. The media talks about lions and mountain lion shifters. They're not as open to talking with the press as the wolves. But bears? I had no idea. But also, how did Cade know he was a bear? Size maybe? Can he smell them? I mean, wolves are known for having excellent senses of smell but would bears smell differently than lions and wolves?

"No. One of them wanted to intimidate me. He asked if I was headed toward Ardelean country."

Cade makes the sound again. It's absolutely a growl.

"Alright. I'll call the guys. Ezra is with 'em. You send your vehicle with the two of 'em and ride back in Ezra's truck. Let 'em drive your SUV around Colorado. I'll let the Alpha in Colorado know about the incident, and he'll buffer any questions. Did the bear know who you were?" Ansel keeps the same level tone.

"He specifically chose Ardelean," Cade says coolly. He pauses, drumming his fingers on the steering wheel. "Ezra doesn't ride ever. He only drives, after, well . . ."

I place my hand on Cade's thigh, resting it there. His touch makes me feel better when I'm upset. Maybe it's a wolf thing? Maybe it'll work for him? Also, what happened to Ezra? Cade drops a hand from the steering wheel and places it over mine. He gives it a soft squeeze.

A smile crosses my face. *I'm making a difference.*

"Well, I drive through there from time to time. He probably only knows about me. Maybe he's tryin' to intimidate you by makin' you think we're close. Let's not worry about it 'til we're sure it's worth worrying about. There's a massive pack and then my territory. They'd have to be stupid to chase you this far." Ansel must raspberry his lips with an exhale.

I stifle a giggle hearing the funny noise.

"Alright. I'll make calls. You do what you've gotta do out there. See you soon, cousin." Ansel hangs up the phone.

Watching Cade weave around traffic is still terrifying. Holding hands together in his lap is comforting despite what seems like certain death driving this fast down the road. I try to think about how this is just a roller coaster. It's perfectly safe. Just a roller coaster.

The next hour is an eternity, but soon Cade slows down and blends in with normal traffic. He leans back in his seat, but there's still nervous energy floating between us.

"Cade?" I ask softly. It seems safe to speak now. Maybe.

"Yeah." He turns his head to look at me. "You okay?"

I shake my head. I don't want to upset him. I'm not okay, but maybe knowing more will help. "What's going on?"

De Soto
Ft.
Calhoun
133
Washington
Omaha
31
El. 1040 ft.
Waterloo
Boys

CHAPTER 14
CADE

How am I supposed to answer that? Drawing a deep breath, I hold it. Thinking.

I've purposefully not given her my last name. Doing so would have let her in on the fact that I'm very closely tied to her mother's politics by way of bloodlines. She already admitted to not knowing anything about what was going on.

Par for the course, The Leviathan decides that he needs to vocalize an opinion: *she learns truth. Good.*

"Cade," she prompts.

"Yeah. I'm . . ." I let out the air trapped in my lungs, explaining, "It's not simple. It's not objective for me to tell you. You admitted to not knowing. I've told you mostly objective information so far. If I start telling you things, what you learn could drive a wedge between us. It's more professional to keep it non-political."

"And me in the dark. I just found out, well, I'm pretty sure I found out, that there are bear shifters. Bears, Cade," she snaps, pulling her hand from my lap.

Shuffling in her seat she looks out the window, not saying anything.

Uncomfortable silence fills the cab. Her disappointment simmers in the tension between us.

"Yes, there are bear shifters," I confirm.

Black and brown bears, lions, mountain lions, and I've heard rumors of polar bears. I opt to not tell her about those.

Coward. The Leviathan huffs. *Draga mea strong. You treat her as puppy. Smart mate.*

Is it self-loathing if it's your wolf that actually hates you? We're supposed to be a team. Being divided is another bone of contention piled on the shit I'm dealing with. What happened to having a simple, quiet life? What was wrong with that?

Formulating words, I try to find the best way to tell Thalia enough to make sense without scaring her. When building trust, it's from the ground up, right?

"What do you know about shifters?" I question.

Thalia seems surprised by my question.

"Uhm. Okay, so," she stammers, which is unlike her.

Now that we're driving at a normal speed, I steal a glance at her.

The motion prompts her, and she continues, "Tabloids most recently." Her voice drops to what's best described as an embarrassed half mumble, half speech. "Fiction books, romance novels, fantasy pieces, and classic mythology I read before shifters were outed to the public, which I'm going to guess don't count because they're housed in the library's fiction section." Her tone changes to more defensive. "But they were always so cool with this, superpower, if you will, changing shapes, being more than one thing." She lets out a big sigh and gives me the last tidbit I had been expecting all along. "And, like, the very little I finally heard Mom say before we left when you weren't in the room, about how shifters want their own governments and that . . ."

Her voice trails off, and she looks out the passenger window away from me.

I finish her sentence for her. I offer her the words her mother chose in a press conference, "We're dangerous, secretive, and can't be trusted?"

"Yeah." The end of her answer deflates.

Thalia's response wrenches my heart. I don't know that Thalia wants to share her mother's beliefs. *Maybe she just doesn't know anything else?*

Draga mea wants to be wolf. That is all we need. Make her ours in all ways. The Leviathan, of course, would latch onto that fact.

He's delusional. *Is this what it's like for everyone else?*

No, too stubborn. The wolf right. The Leviathan quips. Clearly disapproving of my distaste for his commentary.

"So, Ardelean is a bloodline. I guess, it's kinda similar to royal families in humans. It's about succession through genetics and power. In some cases, power is more literal than others." I try to explain, stumbling with my words.

"So, you and Ansel are of Ardelean bloodline?" Thalia helps me explain by quickly putting together the pieces.

"Yes," I firmly answer.

I may deny my association with Robert and the calls for me to take the throne, but there's no way I will ever deny the bloodline and those who share it.

"That's very impressive that people know about your bloodline." She's not asking nor being condescending.

Odd statement.

"I don't find it impressive, but, yeah. You're essentially royalty in your world, and I'm royal court in my own." I grip the steering wheel with both hands now.

Without her hand to hold, I'm left trying to play it cool. I'm hoping she doesn't make the parallel between Robert and me, but The Leviathan's right. Thalia is very smart. With every passing second of silence, I can practically hear her brain running through the information. It won't be long.

"You're related to Robert Alden?"

Like clockwork, she figures it out. My nod triggers her next question. It's slow with hesitation.

"Which is something my mom knew?"

"Yes, she knows my relationship to Robert."

Should I specify he's my brother? What purpose would telling her serve? Another panic attack? I'm willing to do anything to stop her from suffering that way.

Tell our mate we are better than Robert and how special we are. The Leviathan has other opinions.

"Cade, am I safe with you?" Thalia asks the easiest question in the world.

"You will never be safer than standing next to me." Can she hear how much I mean what I've said?

Thalia falls silent again. I'm wondering if that'll be the end of the questioning. I doubt it, but for now, she seems content. Her hands stay tucked under her butt as we drive farther down the road. There's no opportunity for me to try and hold one. It crosses my mind more than once to put my hand on her thigh, but she's clearly communicating not to touch her. I respect it.

An hour later, we pull off for a bathroom break and snacks.

Once we're back on the road, Thalia munches on her snacks. I break down and, against my cardinal rule, munch while driving. The Leviathan, unimpressed with my trail mix dining option, grumbles. He wants more substantial food, but it's fuel. He'll have to be satisfied later.

"Alright, you've mentioned culture shock. I've got questions," Thalia says between bites of her funny smelling sour candies.

The change in her comfort level to more responsive and open is puzzling, but I'm thankful for the shift.

"Shoot," I answer, trying not to look a gift horse in the mouth.

"So, from a sociology standpoint. Nonverbals are really big." Thalia explains her point, "What are some nonverbal things I need to know? Like flipping someone the bird isn't universal, any faux pas I've already messed up?"

"Nonverbal cues, body language, and lack thereof are everything." I barely stifle a laugh before I reassure her, "You're pretty quiet, nonverbally speaking. You're decent with being vocal about your wants, but wolves move a lot more. I do a lot of wondering what you're thinking. There are various things, from posturing to body blocking to submission and dominance. It's not full silent conversations in the traditional sense, but there's a whole element of what we *don't* say, like subtext, I guess?"

"You were posturing with the man at the fuel station? Do all shifters communicate nonverbally?" Thalia asks in what I'm sure is meant to be in the most innocent sense.

The laugh I stopped before escapes now. "When you say it that way, it sounds dirty."

Thalia snorts, and I sense an eye roll. "That's so not what I meant."

"I know. It doesn't make it less funny." I roll my head to look at her, giving her a smile. "Yes, he was trying to intimidate me. From what I know, body language is pretty universal among shifters."

"Did it work?" Thalia asks, a small squeak in her voice. "Did you —"

"No." I shake my head; I don't want to know what that second question is.

Whatever it is, the answer will probably scare her. I'm

trying to find a subject to change the conversation to when my cell phone rings. Ansel's name pops up.

She nods an acknowledgment while I answer the phone, "Ansel, what do you know?"

"Yes, hello. The weather's fine, thanks for askin'. Oh, right. Yeah. Zero and Ripley said they're almost to the meeting point. They can meet you early. Ezra's groggy but waking up. He'll be ready for the blitz back." Ansel's voice isn't his normally chipper tone. He's uncharacteristically gruff.

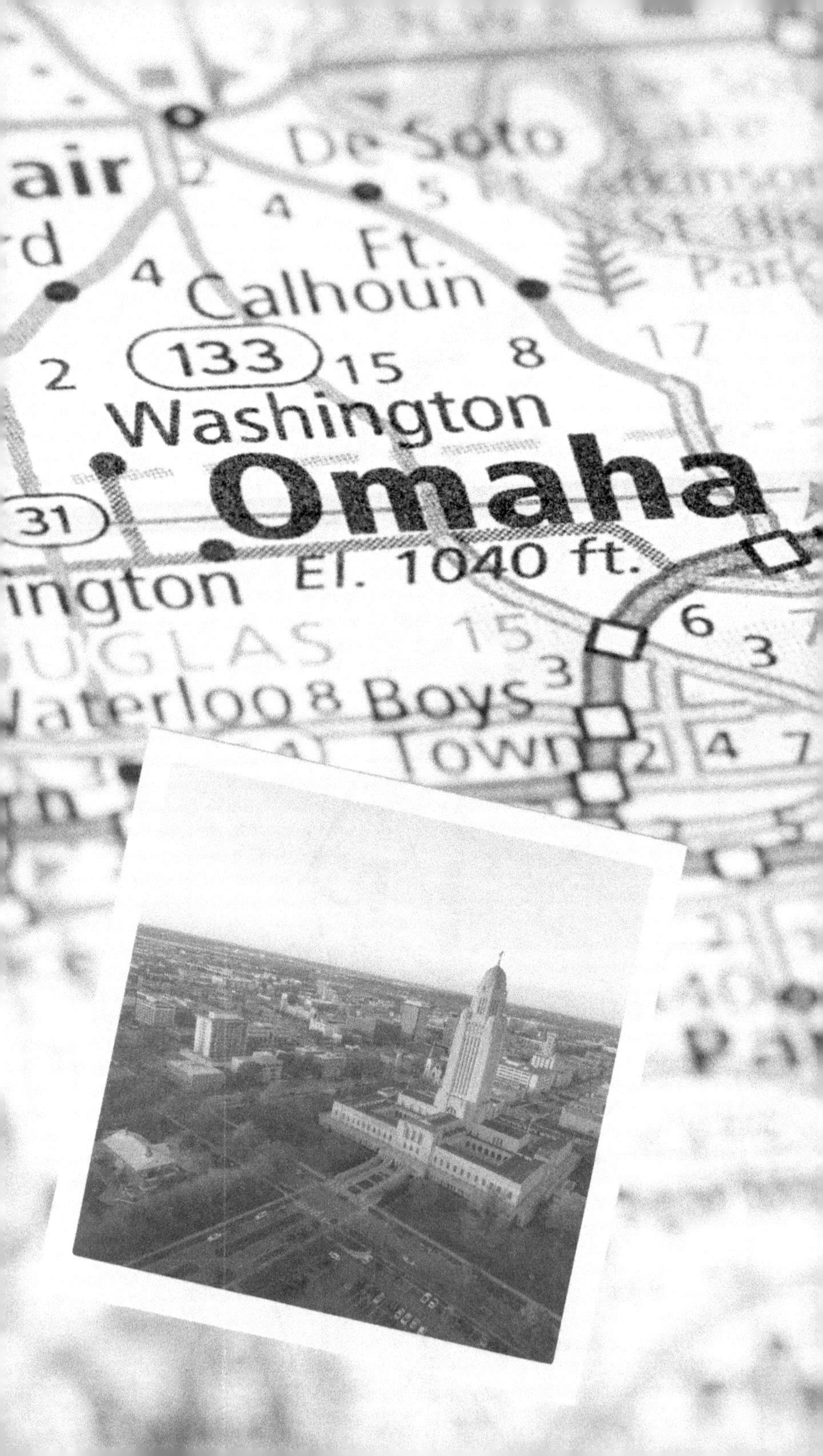
De Soto
Ft.
Calhoun
133
Washington
Omaha
31
El. 1040 ft.
Boys

CHAPTER 15
THALIA

CADE PUSHES a button and picks up his phone, pulling it to his ear. "Ansel, you're not on speaker anymore. What's wrong?"

I can't hear anything on the other end of the line. A hollow feeling fills my chest, listening, trying to figure out what's going on. Cade doesn't stiffen like at the fuel stop. Maybe more concerned? It's admirable how much he cares, apparently, for everyone. He has a big heart.

"I'm so sorry, Ansel. Don't worry about that. I'll do it," he responds to whatever Ansel explains.

There's this genuine sincerity there, but it fuels my uneasiness.

Do what? Sorry why? Did someone die? Are we still going someplace safe? I grip hard on the seat of the SUV. All these questions swarm my brain. I try to breathe through it and calm down like Cade showed me. It's not as easy without him guiding me. How does he make panic attacks easier? Why is it easier to breathe when he's next to me?

"You didn't ask, I offered. I'm capable and willing. It

doesn't have to be you this time. I'm almost there." Cade's voice is softer at the end.

He looks at me over the side of the phone and demonstrates a deep breath.

"Well, about that. I'll explain later. You unwind. Have an after-work drink for me and chill for a bit. We'll handle it tomorrow."

Those last words seem very vow filled. Ansel must answer again because he speaks with strong reassurances.

Cade sets the phone down. "Sorry. I don't want you to feel excluded, but that's not something you want to know about right this second."

"I understand." I lie.

"Thanks for saying that. But you can stick to telling me the truth."

Cade's hand rests on the console between us, inviting me in.

I make a small move toward his hand. I hesitate until Cade looks at me and then picks his hand up. I slide mine under his. When he sets his hand on mine and his long fingers wrap around my hand, the connection radiates through my body. He squeezes gently, and warmth travels through me. I'm so comfortable with him; does he feel this way too? It has to be just a me thing, right? There's this happy feeling in my heart, and I'm left wondering what it means.

I debate asking but already thoroughly embarrassed myself once. How awkward would it be if I asked him if he had feelings? No, that's quite enough for today. Having Cade think I'm reading way too far into all the small gestures for my comfort could ruin it all.

Cade's voice is soft. "Touch is big for wolves. The army was especially hard for that. I was the only wolf anywhere we went. Human men aren't very secure in their bodies. General touches to the shoulder are okay, but it's not enough for wolves. It wasn't until I met Millie that I had enough touch."

Am I sure Cade can't read my mind?

Judgmental Thalia sulks out before I can stop her. "You and Millie? Really?"

Biting my lips together, I hope he understands I didn't mean that how it came out. I don't mean to judge him or his past. *Why does it bother me to think about him with someone else?* A few days in the car together and a tiny cuddling session does not a relationship make. I want it to though. Has it only been a few days? *What is wrong with me?*

I feel Cade cringe as he shakes his head. "No, Millie and I never had an intimate relationship. That'd be weird. It's that Millie has exactly zero sense of personal space. Guys in the unit kept thinking she was coming onto them when, in all reality, she simply has no boundaries."

"Oh, so, it happened to work out. You and she buddied up both needing physical closeness." I'm starting to understand.

The green monster I've been trying to use logic on disappears, sated by his reassurance.

"Yeah."

A memory hits Cade, his eyes are distant. Just watching traffic, he's quiet for a moment.

When it passes, he shakes his head, brushing it off. "The thing that's pretty universal between wolves and men is that there's almost always a bigger predator. Some guys started harassing her, and one got handsy. The unit chief said his hands were tied. So, I stepped in. Asshole wouldn't even stay in the same room with her unless he was ordered to . . . after our . . . discussion. I didn't leave Millie's side unless absolutely necessary after that."

The way Cade talks tells me he's leaving things out. Is he protecting me? Himself? Millie? I can't tell. The answers I get from him give me a sense that I'm starting to get to know him, but I want to know more. Yet, I don't want to be creepy.

"What does touch normally look like for wolves? Is it all touch? Certain things?"

"We sit next to each other, probably closer than usual for humans. Most of us will lean against each other somehow. Sentences are sometimes punctuated by a touch, pat on a shoulder, hug, or a shake. It's a personal and situational preference."

His thumb runs against the side of my fingers again as he says this.

Is he touching me because of his culture or because he wants to? What Cade says leads me to believe I'm reading into his touch. That hurts my heart a little bit. *Why do I want to be special?*

"If something doesn't feel right, or you don't like something or how close someone is to you, myself included, then it isn't right." Cade pauses, his voice firmer, choppy, like he's trying not to command me but make me wary. "If you don't like something, say something. If someone doesn't respect it, then tell me." Cade pauses, longer this time. A soft rumble like distant thunder comes from him again. "I assure you, no one is willing to risk pissing me off."

The GPS tells us we're close, indicating that we're nearing an exit. His phone lights up with a text message.

"Would you check that for me, please?" Cade asks, slow to move his hand from mine.

I fumble for a moment before turning on his phone, reading the message aloud. "Ezra says, 'This water tower is giving me the creeps. Can you get here faster? Don't stop for gas, let the assholes fill your rig.'"

He shakes his head and sighs, one hand running up and down the bridge of his nose. "He's such an ass."

"He's your cousin?"

I try to remember; Cade mentioned him and Judah, and was it Deena? Dana? Dinah? Maybe they'll mention her again so I can remember.

"Yeah, Ezra is my cousin. His brother's house is where my siblings are celebrating the holiday."

"Holiday?"

We pull up, parking behind a big black truck.

Off to the left is a pretty standard-looking water tower shape. It's painted white with a green stripe and black figures. I guess they probably do look a little like aliens, poking their heads out of windows. It's reminiscent of a spaceship, but Ezra isn't wrong. It's creepy. When I look back at the truck, three men are standing there at the tailgate, waiting.

The thunder sound is louder as it comes from Cade. He clears his throat, maybe trying to stop it?

He commands, "Stay in the SUV. Let me talk to them first."

The men look menacing. The one on the left has a slender build, kind of the epitome of a string-bean type character. The middle one is buff, gym-rat style, with a bald head making him look tougher. Then the one on the right, yawning, has a similar build to Cade. I assume he must be Ezra.

Watching Cade watch them is interesting. He doesn't close the SUV door before slowly making his way toward the front of the SUV. *Odd. Why wouldn't he close it?* The buff, bald man in the middle steps toward Cade before he's in front of the Yukon. Cade pushes forward almost in a lunge. The man steps back, bumping into the truck behind him, causing it to rock. He puts his hands up in surrender and tips his head to the side, refusing to look at Cade. The string bean man hunches a bit. But the one I'm guessing is Ezra is completely unfazed, rubbing sleep out of his eyes.

The man on the end most definitely is Ezra.

Through the open truck door, I make out what he says, "Cousin, don't be so dramatic. No one's making any moves. We all want to go home. Let's load luggage and get on the road."

"Luggage is in the back. I'll move Emily."

Cade walks back to his side of the SUV, closing the door. He then walks around the SUV before arriving at my door. When he reaches me, the other two not-Ezras walk along the other side, seemingly intentionally not looking at me. Ezra walks back toward the driver's door of the pickup and climbs in.

Cade positions himself strangely while opening my door. His body constantly stands between me and the back of the vehicle. This must be an example of blocking? Or would this be posturing? I try to remember the root differences of words. The sociology of Cade interacting with other wolves is interesting.

I let him usher me quickly into the backseat of the big black truck. It takes me a minute to hop up the rail thingy and into the back seat. Cade's biting his bottom lip like he wants to say something but refrains from doing so, waiting for me to buckle before closing the back door. I hear noise behind me.

I jump but refrain from looking to see. *Be brave, they're just people. Cade wouldn't put me in danger. Right?* It must be our bags being loaded.

"You won't touch her," Cade says sharply at Ezra while pulling the truck door closed.

That's a weird order. I thought I determined who I was comfortable with touching me?

"Wouldn't dream of it. I assure you," he answers softly. He looks at me through the rearview mirror. "Emily, it's a pleasure to meet you. And yes, Cade. I can still hear you. Secret is safe with me."

"What?" I ask Ezra.

Why would he say that?

154

Ezra laughs. "Ahhh, someone didn't explain the Ardelean gifts."

"How do I even explain that?" Cade runs his hand through his hair. I see his hand moving above his head.

Apprehension builds not being able to see his facial expressions.

"So, nice to meet you. I'm Ezra. Don't touch me. I can hear your thoughts if you do. I'd shake your hand, but we just covered that." Ezra looks over his shoulder with a big grin and a wink before pulling the truck away from the curb.

He rolls down the window and talks to the wolves in Cade's SUV. The string bean is driving. "You know the assignment. Don't run it out of gas, treat it right, and explore the Rockies."

"Aye, aye." The string bean salutes.

Cade laughs, and Ezra pulls away, driving quickly back out of the quiet town and away from their weird water tower.

Cade pauses. "Ez, you're sure you're good to drive?"

"Yeah. Little groggy, but it's evaporating quickly," Ezra says cryptically.

"Are we going to brush past the part where you said you can read minds?" I'm fairly certain my jaw is hanging open at the prospect.

"Oh yeah." Cade's voice comes with what sounds like apprehension. "Was hoping you'd just move right past that."

"It's not as cool as it sounds. Most people have really dumb and boring inner voices. And they're super critical of themselves. It's only helpful if I need or want something," Ezra prattles. His hands rise and fall off the steering wheel as he talks. "Most of the time, it's exhausting, and you always get people wondering if I'm listening to them. And, really, how do you politely explain that they're not as interesting as the voices inside my own head to start with?"

How do you respond to that? There's a person in this

vehicle that can hear other people's thoughts. What on earth is the world coming to? Can all wolves do this? Has Cade been hearing my thoughts? That would explain so much. Is this usual? It can't be because why would they be big on body language if you can always read what someone else is thinking?

My internal debate lapses time, and soon, Cade and Ezra are speaking quietly between themselves. I try to listen, but they're talking too softly. It's hard to make out enough of the conversation when you're only getting about every fourth word. While I'm sure they're not trying to be rude, it's obvious that they don't want my involvement. The freeway here is very much the same; this part of Colorado is no more interesting than Nebraska.

Fall River
Pass
3713

Greele

Boulder

Longmon

3449

Denver

Aurora

Castle Roc

RAD

4301

Colorado
Springs

Pueblo

CHAPTER 16
CADE

EZRA GOOD. Less troubled. Will keep mate safe. Loyal. The Leviathan assesses Ezra, watching him with constant focus. I try to remind him that just because Ezra appears stable doesn't mean anything. The last I'd talked to Judah, he was very worried over Ezra's control issues. Ansel wouldn't have sent him, though, had he thought he wasn't safe for the drive or for Thalia. *Pretty sure.*

We fall into a comfortable rhythm of communicating. When we hit the more populated areas of Colorado, I look over my shoulder to ask Thalia if she wants something to eat, but she's asleep, head resting against the headrest. Lips slightly parted. The thought of kissing them crosses my mind and lingers there slowly.

Ezra clears his throat, giving me side-eye. "Let her sleep."

"I thought you weren't listening to people because they're not interesting, and it isn't self-serving." I turn back, facing forward. My eyes are so heavy after the day of driving.

"You're enjoyable." Ezra snorts. I can hear his smile as he

prattles, "You're smitten. The Leviathan clearly made his choice. Nice to hear his voice in your head again. How long will you remain delusional about your place in the world?"

"The Fates chose wrong by giving me The Leviathan. Judah was the better choice. I abdicated once. I can't find any reason to resume my reign." It's a half-truth.

As always, Ezra knows. I crack open an eye to see him shaking his head. It takes him another few moments.

"If you have the opportunity to be happy, chase it. Even if it's uncomfortable initially, you should take it. We grow when we're the least comfortable."

"That's why you're roughing it with Ansel and not home with Judah and Dinah?" I poke back with my agitation.

That's enough to silence him for a while.

Thirty minutes later, I've nearly dozed off when he starts speaking. "Thank you for coming, for Dinah. I know you stay out of pack drama because Robert could try to have you executed, or the council could try to force you back into power. But Judah and I couldn't have handled it without you, Deacon, and Ansel. Dinah might not be alive if it weren't for you."

"You would have come if something had happened to Lena. We've chosen our family. It's always been us together." I assure him. "Let Robert come for me. Let the council try. If I take back the throne, it'll be on my terms. None of them will like it."

Ezra nods.

I try so hard not to think about what happened to Dinah. Yet, my brain drifts to her, physically beaten and destroyed mentally. The life drained out of her. No snark and veiled cryptic messages, only hollowness. She's on the mend, but still not the same. Although, I don't suppose she ever will be. It's sickening to know a whole pack was willing to look away from her mate's abuse. Bile rises in my throat. *Was this something I could have stopped?* I've always openly accepted my blame when it's come to Deacon and Lena. I failed them both. *How many others am I failing?*

"Do you want any answers to those self-loathing questions or . . ." Ezra's voice trails off.

"What do you know, Ezra?" I'm not sure I'm ready to hear what he has to say. I trace the seam along the side of my jeans.

"You absolutely did not hear this from me." Ezra is cautious and punctuates his word, running his hand across the back of his neck. "Judah and Wyatt are together. Judah has always struggled with it. He doesn't want to be different. Now he's afraid to even consider coming out, ever, because of Robert's stupid 'build our people stronger' platform. Would other Alphas come for Judah's pack? How many fights would it take for Judah to prove himself worthy of his last name and pack? The two of them sneak around in the night. When we get visitors, like at Equinox or Solstice, they'll both make a point of being with a woman or, in Wyatt's case, two or three. Wyatt keeps thinking of leaving. He's struggling with not having a place. Being there with his mate and not sealing the bond is hurting him. Judah's fear, while valid, will ruin the two of them being happy together."

I blow out a harsh breath. *I had no idea.*

"Now," Ezra continues after another moment, his fingers drumming across the steering wheel, back and forth, "with your mate's mother's talk of potential sterilization, there's this pressure on everyone to breed. And not in the fun, sexy way. No one's willing to say it, but there's definitely fear that in the dead of night, police will show up, and it'll be over. There are active contemplations of orchestrating their own deaths so they have some control in the matter." Ezra stops, clearly having awful thoughts creep in with what he's saying.

All I have ever wanted is the opposite of this.

"It's not your fault. When you abdicated, you were a different person than you are now."

Ezra's statement gives me the slightest bit of hope.

He affirms, "There's a lot of people thinking that you would be better at dealing with the media. Robert is combative and unstable. You've always been cool under pressure. I don't want to guilt-trip you, but we're all losing hope. Wolves, cats, bears, everyone is consumed by fear. We're raised with it: don't tell the humans. They'll kill us. Experiencing it, is so much more terrifying."

Everything Ezra says he means, including that it's not my fault. Ezra isn't one to flourish. Judah is the diplomat. Ezra is, well, just not. Despite his best intentions, the assessment hurts, nonetheless. I just don't think I can fix this. I may do better under pressure, but I haven't found a solution to the new way of the world.

The Leviathan huffs. *No faith. No trust. We are Sovereign, humans no scary. Make them see. Take back ours. Fix wolves. Not let false ruler play king.*

"I've cut a deal with the devil." I pause.

Ezra looks at me. I recall the scenario from the conference room, knowing he'll be listening.

Ezra shakes his head before letting it fall back against the headrest. He sighs. "I would have never guessed she could be persuaded."

"Thalia was in the kind of nightmares I'd never wish on anyone." I try to explain, but a yawn hitches my words.

"Fuck," Ezra huffs, clearly having listened to my thoughts about it. "That is terrifying."

A few more minutes, and my eyelids are heavy. I fight to stay awake.

"Get some rest," Ezra suggests. "As long as I'm driving, I'm good."

THE VEHICLE STOPPED MOVING. Blinking against the bright morning sky, I squint to see Ansel's cabin. The main house sits atop a small hill, and we've got a good view over the yard and, subsequently, out over the scrub brush and wooded areas.

Ezra yawns as he's halfway out of the truck. "She slept the entire way home. I need food and sleep. So, good night. I don't know where boss is, but he'll show up."

Thalia is still sleeping peacefully in the back. Opening my door, I hear distant sounds of inhabitation from down the hill where Ansel's pack cabins are. Someone's splitting wood, and another yells for them to shut up and go back to bed. Hearing the normalcy of pack life stings. Tossed in with the truth from Ezra, reflecting on what it was like at Equinox at Judah's, and the disappointment from The Leviathan, it's a homesick feeling.

How can you be homesick for a life you never lived?

Movement from the brush line draws my attention, and I move in front of Thalia's door. Ansel walks up the steep embankment of the scrub brush. His brown hair, a little shaggy, rests on his shoulders.

Hands tucked into his pockets, he motions to the truck with just his shoulders. "Dangerous game you're playing, cousin."

"She's worth it." I can't explain how deep these feelings are for her. There's no frame of reference to leverage it.

His head cocks back and forth a few times. Then his green eyes darken, overtaken by a warm brown before nearly turning entirely bright white. Then with a slow blink, they return to their natural state.

He smiles a shit-eating grin. "Let's get you settled. Lena called about an hour ago. I lied. Told her you were already here, sleepin'. She didn't seem too upset. Also, didn't ask about who was with you."

Ansel's voice trails off, looking over my shoulder at something. I don't turn to look, showing my trust in him.

"You'll be stayin' in the main house with me. I've got two bedrooms upstairs. You can share that bathroom. Kennels are empty, for now. Might not be tomorrow. We'll do what we have to. Ripley and Zero are driving your SUV around. I'm headed into town later today if you need anything."

He's walking off toward his garage, keeping on with his day before calling over his shoulder, "Keys are on the counter. Lock up when she's in the house alone. She shouldn't go outside alone, for their sake, not hers."

Before waking up Thalia, I stretch myself out. For a moment, we're safe, and it's a good feeling.

The Leviathan is restless, pushing at me to let him out. And he's not alone; it would be great to get a run in. With as much difficulty I've had in the last few days reacclimating with The Leviathan, I need to cement us back together.

I open the door to see Thalia sleeping as peacefully as one can in the backseat of a pickup truck.

Carefully, to not startle her, I place my hand on her thigh. "Thalia, we're here."

She scrubs her eyes with her hands and groans. Wincing, she tries to move her neck to face me.

With slow blinks, squinting, shielding her eyes with her hand against the sun, she asks, "Where is here? What time is it?"

"We're in the mountains of Utah. I honestly don't

remember the name of the nearest town. For all intents and purposes, we're in the middle of nowhere." I pause. "The local time is 7:35 a.m. with partially cloudy skies and a chance of weird happenings."

She groans. "An airline joke? Do I at least get free peanuts?"

"I'll see if Ansel has some."

I help her down out of Ezra's lifted rig. With stiff legs, we make our way to the house.

CHAPTER 17

THALIA

THE SCENERY IS BEAUTIFUL. We're in some desert elevation. Birds are making noises in the brush, and the smell of burning wood is in the air. It's this perfect mountain lodge experience if I've ever seen one. They could film one of those sappy television love stories here. My legs are stiff and object to walking, but Cade is patient, almost hovering around me, as we walk to the beautiful house.

It's a two-story home with brown siding. Cade opens the back door without knocking and ushers me across the threshold into a small mudroom. There's a stacked washer and dryer, a bench for shoes, and hooks for coats. Putting our shoes away, he leads me down the hallway, pointing out the main bathroom on the right and a door that he indicates as Ansel's room off to the left. At the end of the hallway, a staircase goes down, and then the whole house opens into a great room. In the main living area, I find a kitchen with laminate countertops and mismatched appliances mixed in. The living room has a long couch and a reclining chair around a medium-sized television. A rectangle table and chairs to seat six are off to the side. A door leading to what looks like another semi-outdoor dining space is to the right of the kitchen.

What catches my eye, and holds my focus, is the far wall of the house. It's nearly all windows, looking out first to a deck and then a small clearing flocked by scrub-brushy-mountains scenery. It's not your traditional mountain view. It's not cinematic or postcard-perfect, but I feel immersed in the wild nature of it all.

I'm looking out in awe when I feel Cade's hand between my shoulder blades, gently pushing me past the stairwell leading down and farther into the house. I see him indicate in my peripheral to head to the left, another staircase. Walking past the loved, but not dingy, living room furniture, I find myself climbing stairs to the loft space.

At the landing, he finally says, "Your room on the left, bathroom in the middle, and I'll be on the right."

"How long will we be here? Where will we go next?" I try to remember what he said before.

My stomach growls in protest of thinking, opting for breakfast and my morning coffee craving.

"Let's get you fed. We'll always stay in a place that keeps you the most safe." He smiles but doesn't answer my question before heading back down the stairs.

After a trip to the restroom, I find Cade downstairs in the kitchen. He's rooting through the cupboards and heading to the fridge. I pull out one of the stools at the island and sit, resting my elbows on the laminate top.

"Won't he be angry you're rooting around?"

"Nah, Ansel isn't that kind of guy." Cade turns his head to look at me from where he's at in the fridge. "He's unique. I don't really have a way to explain it. It's one of those things where you just have to meet him. Other than his bedroom and the basement, the house is fair game."

Satisfied with his ransacking, Cade turns on the stove in front of me and keeps talking. "So, this isn't where I'd like to have brought the senator's daughter to make a good first impression. Things are different here. You're mostly safe. I mostly won't be far from your side. If we are apart, there are some different rules here: leave the doors and windows locked. Don't go outside without Ansel."

Cade oddly stops talking, looking past me.

Turning, I see a wolf standing on the deck. It's wild looking and narrower than I imagined wolves. While it sniffs the bottom of the deck door, I watch the fur arch in tufts along its neck, looking sickly as it does so, before going back to staring at us. The haunting yellow eyes rest above two fluffy white cheeks.

My voice, unrecognizable, comes out as a squeak. "Cade?"

"It's okay, don't make any sudden movements." Cade's voice is calm. "Turn slowly back to face me. He'll go away."

I slowly turn to face Cade again, taking as deep a breath as I can and gripping the counter in front of me.

Despite his reassurance, nothing seems fine. Cade's different, and then there's the overwhelming feeling of being watched. I'm anxious? No, this is fear. I think back to the photos on the table, photos of me that someone took and I didn't know. I was being watched then, much like I am now. I close my eyes, trying to push it all out of my memory. My body starts shaking. I fight to try and stay still.

My shaking is made worse when I hear a click. My eyes flash open, and Cade has turned off the gas stovetop. I try to figure out what his body language might be saying, distracting myself with the science of the situation. He's not quite turned toward the door. His head is held high, and his torso is tilted in that direction.

Another minute? I can't breathe. Two minutes? Ten?

Thudding sounds come from outside. Cade turns back toward me and ignites the stove. The sound must have been footfalls on the wood as the wolf left his spot at the door.

Cade's eyes lock on me. I meet them. The golden color drifts from his eyes.

There's that strength behind his voice. "Breathe, draga mea. It's okay."

A breath is drawn into my lungs. I'm slightly calmer. *What's a draga mea?*

There's an urgency in Cade's voice as he moves us along after the experience.

"Don't go outside. Under no circumstances do you go outside without me or Ansel next to you. Don't go to the basement. If you can't find me, Ansel is your only friend. No matter how nice someone is. Never tell anyone who you are, stick to the name Adam and Millie gave you: Emily Elizabeth Miller. What would you like me to call you? I guess there are a few options for nicknames."

"Uh, Emily? I guess?"

What he's saying doesn't set my mind at ease. I shudder, feeling cold. I run my hand up and down my arm trying to warm myself. Security details usually at least try to convince you that you're safe. Cade instructs but gives me no false pretenses. We're someplace slightly dangerous but whatever dangers are here are less threatening than at his home in Wisconsin.

Calm becomes more and more difficult. The back door opens, and another man walks into the house.

I jump up, trying to flee, but my foot gets caught in the barstool, and I fall with a girly shriek. My fluffy butt takes the worst of the fall.

Cade hurries to my side. A man laughs while Cade lifts me to my feet.

The man who came in the door is laughing. His long hair, hanging about his shoulders, bounces while he laughs with one hand resting on his belly.

Finally able to bring his laughter under control, he smiles wide. "Are you okay? I've never seen someone actually fall off a bar stool who wasn't drunk. You're not drunk, right?"

Dusting my butt off, I wish, desperately, that I could dust that fall off the record books. And that shriek, *how embarrassing.* It feels rude not to answer, but I don't understand why being drunk would be logical at this hour.

I sigh. "I'm not drunk. Why would I be drunk? Isn't it super early in the morning?"

Leaving my side, Cade goes back to the stove. Before, the man on the deck had Cade on edge. He's comfortable with this one. I take my cue from him.

The man extends his hand. "Ansel Abbot."

"It's nice to meet you Ansel, I'm Emily."

The fake name feels awkward. Hesitantly recalling the don't-touch-Ezra policy, I shake his hand.

Ansel's smile and personality match the voice I've heard on the phone. However, his appearance is different than I expected. He's oddly untamed.

"No, you're Thalia Clark, the senator's daughter. I'm assuming that's the cover you're supposed to tell everyone you come across. Until you lie better, you should tell people they can call you Emily."

He walks past me around the counter to the fridge, leaving me at a loss of how he knows that. Between him and Cade, it's like I live in the land of a polygraph.

"So, what? You're all ex-special forces and can hear lies?"

"No, I'm the only ex-military in the family, and it's just a shifter thing. Not saying lying to us can't happen, but most people struggle to do it well," Cade answers.

There's less family resemblance between Cade and Ansel than between Cade and Ezra. Ansel is equally as attractive. His long hair and plaid shirt go well with the scenery. Like he belongs here, which, it's his house, so I guess he does.

"Beer?" Ansel offers a bottle to me.

I now understand the drunk question. Mimosas and margaritas with breakfast occasionally, sure, but who drinks a beer at 8:00 a.m.?

"No, thank you." I wave my hands in front of me.

"So, you want a beer or somethin' stronger?" He turns back to look at Cade.

There's still an emotion I can't put my finger on as Cade turns back to the food, articulating dryly, "On duty. Can't."

"Right, because The Leviathan would ever let anyone hurt his mate?" Ansel rolls his eyes, making a face at me while mocking Cade's response and rigid frame in a goofy wobble.

Cade, having seen the whole exchange, shakes his head in what seems like amusement?

Mate? I thought Cade said there wasn't anyone in the picture? Who is he talking about?

Carrying our two plates to the table, he leaves one for Ansel on the counter. Back and forth from the kitchen to the dining space, they bring water glasses and a pitcher from the fridge. Plus, forks and then syrup, peanut butter, and jam.

Taking a bite, I'm pleasantly surprised. Cade can cook. He made French toast, and with all these options, it's impossible to decide. I divide things on my plate, trying everything.

It's a few minutes of the sounds of utensils on plates before Ansel asks, "Why the fuck won't Isabel take the hint? It's been what? Eleven? Twelve years? You left her, and she still can't get over herself to mate some other poor bastard?"

"Problem is the poor part." Cade points his fork at Ansel

before his next bite. "She wants the bloodline and the opportunity."

"Opportunity for what?" I ask quickly. "Why?"

"An Ardelean gift," Cade answers. "Our gifts come from our wolves and put us in an exclusive class among our people. Most of our family has them."

"Ezra showed her his?" Ansel asks, turning his head slightly to look at me.

"No, he and I have an agreement," Cade answers.

Ansel nods at me with a bright smile. "That's okay. I can show you mine."

"No," Cade snaps at Ansel.

I think I heard the sound of Cade's teeth clicking together.

Entirely unfazed, Ansel huffs and takes another bite.

Is Cade not scary to wolves? Is Ansel just weird? The ones when we switched trucks were plenty scared of him.

"I get it. Don't tell the human. It's cool. I don't even want to know." I shrug, brushing them off, hoping my reverse psychology works.

"You'll know soon. I don't think today is the right day to spring more on you. I'm already concerned with how well you've adapted," Cade concedes.

Ansel takes a sip of his beer, raising it in a small toast to victory with a smile.

"So, what's the trick? Is that a yes, I get to know?"

I push my luck, all this new knowledge bumping around in my brain. It feels so normal, like research. It's a nice break in thinking about all the randomness that's led me here, but how do I explain that to them? Without them feeling like science experiments instead of people?

Cade examines me. I watch his eyes dart back and forth. I nod a bit, encouraging him to tell me. He comes to a compromise.

"Once you've heard what Ansel can do, and have processed it for more than twenty minutes, maybe more than twenty-four hours, then yes. If you still want to see the party trick, I'll let him show you."

The smile on Ansel's face softens for a minute. "He's right. It's not to be taken lightly. Cade's a good judge of that."

It's acceptable to hear a consensus between them. I wait for my answer.

Ansel obliges, "I see death."

My fork freezes halfway to my mouth.

I understand those three words separately, but I don't have any idea what they mean together based on context. Ezra reads minds? Ansel sees death? How? What does Cade do? I promised to process the information for more than twenty minutes. So, I'm going to, despite a burning desire to know more.

Bringing the fork back to my plate, I push the last bit of French toast around and ask, "Is no one going to talk about the wolf on the deck? Who just stood there?"

"She always ask two questions at once?" Ansel looks at Cade, then moves past his own question and answers mine. He sets his fork down. "Nah, doesn't matter. What'd he look like?"

"That's an odd observation." The words come out before I can think about how they sound. Ansel waits, watching me, his head cocked to the side. His field-green eyes keep watching. I feel thoroughly analyzed before I can continue speaking. "Uh, wolf? Gray, with white cheeks and yellow eyes."

Ansel points at me, knowing who I'm talking about. He returns to holding his fork.

"Sherman. Good guy, he's got time. He was probably looking for me. I told him he could build a chicken hut so long as he promised to take care of 'em."

Cade is still eating, looking at me from time to time.

Between the two of them watching me, I'm starting to feel like *I'm* some sort of specimen.

After a bit, Cade pushes his plate aside, turning his attention to Ansel, who shoves a giant bite in his mouth at the same time. "You've a pack meeting tonight?"

Ansel is unhurried, despite Cade's commanding tone. "Wasn't plannin' on it but probably for the best. The Leviathan feels huge. It might help the issues we've got. It's been touch and go for the past couple days. When was the last time you spent time with The Leviathan and a pack? At Judah's?"

"Not since I left home; put a run in with Lena and Deacon, but it's been a while since it was more than just the three of us," Cade answers. "Issues over Lena, then I got called in."

The sip of beer that Ansel was taking garbles and nearly comes out. He uses the back of his wrist to bring it back into his mouth.

"What? You're saying someone was stupid enough to fight you . . . for Lena?"

The air in the room feels different, so thick you *couldn't* cut the tension with a knife. Cade doesn't answer him. Ansel shakes his head, muttering under his breath. I think I make out something about people having all gone crazy.

I'm not wasting an opportunity. Ansel likes to answer questions. I debate between asking about Lena and the pack run. Cade seemed even more tense talking about Lena. I take my chance with the safer option.

"What's a pack run? Why can Cade help?"

"Uh."

Ansel seems startled at my interjection.

He thinks for a moment, hand running over the top of his head. His long brown hair runs through his fingers to the other side.

"It's like . . . Gah, you know who's good at explaining shit is Ezra."

Cade sits back in his chair, watching Ansel flounder. He offers, "Just explain pack dynamics."

"Ooo. Excellent." Ansel's eyes brighten, and he nods. "There's that dude from, like, forever ago who said that wolves in the wild form a hierarchy based on dominance."

"Yeah." I interrupt him. "But, he was studying wolves in captivity, and he's spent practically his entire career trying to tell people he was wrong."

Ansel laughs. "Well, he's an idiot. But what he published about wolves is kinda right with shifters. You've an alpha male or alpha female who's in charge. They're the most dominant wolf, and for the most part, they've this natural ability to simply . . ." Ansel's hand snarls in his hair as he pulls at it, gently straightening the strands. "Tell others what to do. And they kinda have to. But not really."

I nod along in understanding, coaxing Ansel to continue.

"It's not absolute, more like a very firm suggestion." Ansel shrugs. "Most wolves think it's a lot more effective than it is. It's an honor system, their wolf recognizes the alpha wolf's dominance and the protective nature that goes along with it. In exchange for sanctuary and a place to call home, wolves give their alphas loyalty and obedience."

He's trying to make the metaphor work.

"Cade's wolf is special. Part of his gift, completely unique, is that he's everyone's Alpha — kinda. The Leviathan rules almost completely. If Cade were to order someone to do somethin', it's a nearly perfect response. There're limitations to it. Like, if he were to go any crazier."

Cade clears his throat, cutting Ansel off. "I'm right here. I'm not crazy."

"I'm not blind and debatable," Ansel answers his statement

with a dramatic dismissal wave of his hand. "See, he's really touchy. Has he been this touchy with you?"

Trying not to laugh, I bite my bottom lip. "He's been much better than my other security details. I guess I don't have much to compare his personality to. I've never spent time with wolves."

"I don't know how to explain this to her without telling her," Ansel whisper-yells at Cade.

"That's because you don't know how to shut up." Cade scrubs his hand down his face.

Ansel chuckles, grinning wide. "You live here for months without someone new to talk to, you'd get chatty too."

The banter between Cade and Ansel brings some levity to a complicated topic, loosening my shoulders a bit.

Cade sighs but explains further, "My gift is complicated. Unlike most wolves, who are new souls or wiped clean, or whatever version of religion you want to believe, The Leviathan, my wolf, is reincarnated. But, he doesn't just happen all the time because his gift is so powerful it can be easily abused."

"Some people say that The Leviathan is only incarnated, reincarnated, carnated? Which one is right? Oh. Never mind. He comes around when he's needed. So, the fact that Cade has 'em, is highly important," Ansel rambles. He pulls back a little bit. "All alpha wolves can tell other uh, regular, I guess, wolves what to do. And it works, mostly-ish. It's limited 'cause if someone gets an idea really rooted inside, you can't talk 'em out of it. Cade's special 'cause he can command other alphas. Where if I tried to command another alpha, it wouldn't work out so good."

"And it only works on wolves and alpha wolves?" I ask, watching the two of them. "You can't do this to humans?"

Cade's eyes lock on mine, and he moves his head from side

to side. "I avoid using my gift on humans for several reasons, but it will work on them if I need it to. It's not mind control. It's an order or an interjection. But it's uncomfortable and unethical to use it on people who wouldn't have any way of knowing."

I dislike his answer. It's scary. I feel my eyebrows shoot up and try to pull them back down. The idea that he could just make people do things. The weird thing is that Cade doesn't really seem like the type to force someone to do something. I mean, he's been nothing but kind and gentle with me. Millie and Adam like him.

"So, when Cade comes and hangs out with a pack like my own, it brings balance. We quite literally run, like we would if we were huntin'. With him here, there's this extra dominant force that makes wolves want to listen. They feel this presence of an Alpha, one with experience, and it levels 'em." Ansel shrugs and looks at Cade. "I don't know if it'll work or if it's too late, but since he's here, he might as well run with the pack and see if he can't sort out the issues."

Standing up and leaving the table, Ansel clears his plate to the sink. "Anyway, pack meeting tonight and then a run. Humans must stay secure in the house. Doors and windows locked. No exceptions."

Fort Hall
River
Franklin
Bear Lake
W Y
River
Green River City
Corinne
Brigham City
Echo City
GREAT
SALT LAKE
Ogden City
Green
Evanston
Salt Lake City
Bingham Canon
Alta
UINTAH MTS.
Stockton
Forest Cy.
Chapin Spr.
York
Mt. Pleasant
Ft. Ro
U T A H
River
Manti
Richfield
Green
Grand River
Frisco
ullion City
WAHSATCH MTS.
ELK MTS
arowan
querville
Rio San
River

CHAPTER 18
CADE

After our quick meal, Ansel flees out the back door. Of course, bolting right after stirring up possible questions that I'm not sure Thalia will ask or not. After clearing the table and wiping my hands, I realize there's absolutely nothing we can do to occupy ourselves. At least while driving, there was a task to keep me busy. Now, with idle hands, all I can think about is her and I being alone together.

Tell draga mea is mate. Claim her. Make her ours. Safe covered in our scent. Wolf be beautiful. The Leviathan unsurprisingly has his own opinion of how to spend the time. And I can't fault him. I'm drawn to touch, taste, and see every inch of her.

Every passing moment we're left alone together solidifies how I feel. She's exactly what and who I want in a mate. My 'anyone but her' stance is gone. There's no one else. I'm sick of pretending that I can walk away. She's not just a job anymore.

"Well, the TV gets two channels, but I know Ansel's got a decent DVD collection. We can sit on the deck and get some sunshine? We can go back to bed. I can give you some space alone in the house if you want. What would you like to do today?"

I try to come up with new options. I sneak going back to bed in there. I'm grateful for Ezra coming to pick us up, but missing the opportunity to spend the night with Thalia leaves me wanting to make it up.

"Is it really going to be that simple?" she asks, wrapping her arms around herself. She holds her head high.

Guarded? The Leviathan is confused. Together we tilt our head, watching her.

"It is that simple for me." I pause.

It's too soon to tell her how I feel. But I want her in every way. So maybe it's time to start dropping some hints.

What is she thinking about? Is it what we talked about with Ansel or something more? I step closer, testing her guarded nature.

"Country life is dull. I don't exactly work here, which means I'm pretty much stuck to whatever chores Ansel's left around the house, and you're left to whatever sanity-keeping activities you can find. I guess if you're feeling adventurous . . ." I shrug. "Have you ever been to Arches?"

"No, I've heard it's beautiful, but this is my first time in Utah."

Thalia's eyes light up, and I know the answer.

"Would you like to go today?" I ask slowly.

Thalia starts nodding.

I smile, seeing her excitement. "Ansel's right, it's been too long since I've given The Leviathan a little bit of time to run. Plus, I think it would be beneficial for you to meet a wolf, in a positive environment, with someone who's in control before someone else can further taint the experience. I know Sherman was a little upsetting for you. I can ask Ansel or Ezra, but their wolves are pretty scary looking if you're not used to looking at wolves." I pause and give her a smirk, licking my bottom lip before sighing. "They're also not really fucking fluffy."

"Did you just ask me to take your wolf on a walk?" she returns with a sly smile, raising an eyebrow.

Her comment catches me off guard, and my face heats. There are so many different ways I could answer. But she started it. Thalia was comfortable enough with me to crack a joke. I shrug and release my bottom lip from between my teeth.

Tell our mate. The Leviathan encourages with the image of a ceremonial collar wrapping around Thalia's neck. I feel him brush and know my eyes just went gold.

My version is dirtier. "Not quite. I'm not following any of the leash laws. And if anyone will be doing any collaring, it'll be me clasping one around your neck. If there's going to be any tying, it'll be you to the bed, while I show you all the ways I can make you scream my name."

A chill rips through Thalia's body, and she shudders, her whole body standing taller. I step into her personal space. Thalia wobbles, looking up at me. I watch her wet her bottom lip with her tongue. Drawing a deep breath, I catch the scent of her arousal.

The Leviathan paces. *Give mate wolf, we run together.*

"Easy, draga mea."

I kiss her forehead. When I step back, I see her trying to figure out the cute nickname The Leviathan's given her. Only having the briefest memory of Romanian spoken in the home growing up, even I had to look it up. 'My darling.' I could tell her, but I'm not sure she's ready.

A backpack, snacks, water, and a trip to the restroom later, I walk Thalia out of the house and to the garage. The classic pickup truck Ansel loves so much is right where it always is. Thalia seems impressed when the old Ford roars to life. I just smile. Ansel's love for this truck runs deep, and I'd be surprised if it didn't turn over.

We're somewhere farther onto Ansel's property and close to the border with the national park. It's a gamble that we may come across someone. It's not common for tourists to make it out this far, but we'll have to be in the national park to see some cool rock formations. It's selfish and maybe a bit cocky to risk bringing her into public like this, but I want her to have a positive experience. I know The Leviathan is set on wanting to give her a wolf, but not so badly that he would sabotage all the progress we're making in having her accept wolves and what this life looks like.

We find Ansel's secret entrance to Arches National Park. It's denoted by an old wooden trunk tucked off the side of the gravel trail behind some scrub brush.

Putting the old Ford in park, I turn in my seat to look at her. "Two rules."

Thalia's eyes go wide, and there's the smallest hint of fear.

"Okay . . ." She draws out the last syllable.

"Don't run. The Leviathan will chase. I'm worried he'll push you down and you'll get hurt. Humans are breakable compared to wolves, and even a friendly little shove could hurt you," I caution.

Thalia nods. "The second one?"

"Breathe." I lock eyes with her. "Enjoy this and know I'm here."

Thalia shakes her head with a huge smile. "I can manage that. I don't run. I'm an excellent amateur cellphone photographer. Only half the photos come out blurry. So I'm excited to capture some of the formations."

The Leviathan paws desperately to put his feet on the ground and bond with her. *Walk mate. No turn. Move.* It's the closest thing to a promise I'm going to get from him.

I open the door and slide out. Thalia hesitates but does the same. I thought I might have heard her say 'uhm,' but nothing further came out. If she weren't nervous, I'd be more worried.

I'm forced to shudder as The Leviathan keeps pushing. *Cool it. I don't have any spare clothes.*

Fishing the backpack out of the truck bed on my way around to her side of the truck, I pull the phone I had Adam make up for her out of the front pocket.

Handing it to her, I say, "This is yours. It'll only call people I trust and gets no internet service, but the camera on it is pretty good. All pictures you take can be transferred to yours when we get you home." I push down the reminder that her home isn't with me. "Here, I'll go around the far side of the truck and fold my clothes. You'll have to put them in the bag though. It's not too heavy for you to carry, is it?"

"Um." Thalia takes the bag hesitantly. A devious smile crosses her face. "Listen, I understand you're not a dog, but what if we get you one of those cool doggy backpacks to wear."

"I don't think they make one in my size, and besides, the only strappy things I want in my life are the ones holding you down or holding your beautiful tits in place," I say with a grin and watch as her jaw falls open.

She's so much fun to fluster. Her cheeks turn bright red. I pull my shirt off over the top of my head.

Mate stays. Yes. The Leviathan assures me.

CHAPTER 19
THALIA

I'M GOING to see a wolf. Up close and in person, a wolf and I are going on a hike. There isn't panic with this cemented revelation. *Should I be afraid? Is this something to worry about?* Cade wouldn't put me in danger. I just know it.

Cade walks around the truck and gives me one last smile before I turn around. This feels like it should be personal. I wait, trying to listen to what is going on. I hear what sounds like a bunch of knuckles cracking. It quickly passes. The sound of feet walking on the ground soon follow.

I can't. I can't even turn to look. I tightly clench my eyes together. Shifters are just bigger versions of regular animals, right? Cade showed me a picture. I know what to expect when I see him. Right? *Why can't I open my eyes?* Something cold brushes my hand.

I pull my hand to my chest. A huff of warm air hits my leg. Then I'm almost pushed over by something big. My eyes fly open as I try to steady myself, taking a step away before I fall over. There before me is the massive wolf from the pictures on Cade's phone.

The air is sucked out of my lungs, and I can't breathe. The wolf cocks his head, takes a few steps closer to me, and sits down. Brilliant gold eyes watch me. I've seen Cade's eyes turn this color before. It makes so much sense now. They're one and the same.

His head is up to my chest, even sitting. He whines, tossing his head a bit. We're looking eye to eye. His muzzle reaches forward and pushes against my stomach in a quick poke, then he sits back, looking at me.

I gasp at the sudden touch.

"Holy crap."

I look him over, bending at the waist, to see more of his size. He's huge. I know wolves in the wild are huge. I've seen some at the zoo. But he's so much bigger. Is that because he's so close? Because shifters are bigger? Much bigger.

The wolf stands up and turns sideways, then turns around in a small circle, almost taking part in my examination of him. He stretches out, shoulders up, feet extending behind him.

"Oh, big stretch!" I say before slapping my hands over my mouth.

Oh, no. Did I just . . .? Well, too late.

"It's nice to meet you, The Leviathan," I say quietly.

Can The Leviathan understand me?

The red and tan fur shakes, and his head tilts, looking at me in what I assume is the wolf equivalent of Cade's raised eyebrow look.

When he steps closer to me, this time, I don't back away. He pushes against me a bit, and I run my hand into his fur. It's dense and coarse, and while fluffy, it's not as soft as I anticipated. I sink my hand deep into his neck fur, and when I reach the skin, I scratch a little bit. He lets out a satisfied groan and leans into it.

I'm laughing, bringing my other hand up to pet next to his

ear. "I suppose you want to take your pet human on a walk now?"

The Leviathan makes a big huff and pushes me gently around the truck. I find Cade's shoes and clothes all folded, neatly tucked together. They fit nicely in the backpack. Once it's on, The Leviathan walks slowly next to me, nudging me with his nose toward a path. Before turning back, I witness perhaps the most boy thing ever. The Leviathan lifts his leg and marks a scrub brush at the front of the truck.

Turning around quickly to not watch him finish, I call over my shoulder, "Indecent exposure!"

Once he finishes his business, we take off on a path.

With The Leviathan, I feel the same patience Cade exhibits with me. As The Leviathan lopes about gracefully in and out among the scrub bushes, he loops back every few minutes. It feels like constant reassurance as he checks in and nuzzles my hands. If I stop and crouch to look at something or take a picture, The Leviathan comes over, wagging his tail slightly, and crouches down, nearly lying down on the ground, to look too. As comfortable as I was on the road with Cade, I'm at ease with the silence, mostly.

Despite not knowing how much is Cade and how much is The Leviathan, it's beautiful the way they seem to work so well together. It's this ordinary daily thing for them. This is normal, and it feels normal. Yet, they're in trouble, and it's my mom's fault. Why would anyone want to stop this? Why is my mother against shifters?

I don't even know why she's targeting them. Not once have they ever come up. Does she even have a reason? How can I make this right? Is there a way to help?

It's been a few hours, and on this pass back to me, The Leviathan stops in front of me. He angles his body, blocking me from walking past him. Ahead there are people just cresting over the hillside. I try to push him forward to keep walking. The Leviathan doesn't budge. Instead, he steps back into me, pushing me off the trail.

The hikers, two men, are laughing as they approach. I can't hear what they're talking about, but The Leviathan begins growling. Fur all along his spine stands on end.

One of the men locks eyes with me while the other directs his attention to The Leviathan.

"Hey, what's a pretty little woman like you out here walking alone for?" The man with brown hair says while leering at me.

It's slimy, being hit on in the middle of nowhere.

"I'm not alone. I'm with The Leviathan," I answer while wrapping my fingers into The Leviathan's thick fur, trying to disguise holding him close to me as affection.

I'm fairly certain he outweighs me by at least a hundred pounds. What happens if these two get too close?

"The Leviathan," the blond one repeats in a patronizing tone, scoffing. "That's a big name."

I've nothing intelligent to say to that. Well, nothing that won't escalate the situation further.

Playing dumb with a smile and a slight tone of condescension, I plaster on the same voice I use in the bar when someone flirts with me. "He *is* big."

I'm petting The Leviathan on the head, trying to stop him from growling. I don't know how to make The Leviathan understand his aggression isn't helping. My only hope is that this idiot can see the literal wolf, wolf shifter, standing between us would eat him for lunch and have room to eat his friend for dessert.

The unironically idiot blond steps forward. "Can I pet him?"

"No." I hold on tighter to the fur wrapped in my fingers, pulling back. "No, no. He's not friendly."

"All dogs love me." The man steps closer again with the most dismissive tone possible.

This is starting to seem like it's going to become deadly very quickly. Cade doesn't seem like the violent type, but something tells me The Leviathan wouldn't have any issues with defending me.

I try to caution him away. "Seriously, he's not friendly. Stay back."

I pull harder on The Leviathan's fur, trying to get him to take a step back to drag him with me, which, of course, is useless.

The growl coming from The Leviathan intensifies. It's so loud. This dude obviously has a death wish. *Honestly, this jerk deserves anything The Leviathan does at this point.*

"Aww, it's okay, boy. I just want to say hi. Your mommy seems really nice." He sticks his hand out toward The Leviathan as one would a dog wanting it to smell your hand.

Growls from The Leviathan turn to a snarl.

The blond keeps coming closer. I don't know what to do. I release the grasp I have on The Leviathan's neck. Time moves in slow motion as The Leviathan lunges forward, snapping, nearly biting the blond's arm.

The blond falls backward, scrambling away from us. The Leviathan barks and snarls, lunging at his legs but never touching the man. The brunette grabs his friend's arm and tugs him away from us.

"Let's go, man!"

"Yeah, she's probably a bitch anyway!" he calls out over his shoulder.

Pathetic. He's got no idea what could have just happened. Nor do I, but that's beside the point. All this because what, he wanted to flirt with the only girl hiker in the area?

My hand is clenched in a fist, and my body is shaking with rage. I'm ready to scream profanities at him. He could have been killed. Cade could have been in trouble. I watch them walk away, my rage hanging with me regardless of the distance they put between us. I don't understand why that had to happen.

The Leviathan licks my face. I wrap my arms around him. I don't know if hugging him is okay, frowned upon, or some sort of taboo. His head folds behind me, resting across my shoulders. The smell of warm fur and the dusty earth pulls me in. I feel at peace until I think about them coming back.

"Okay, let's go before they come back." I try to hurry him on.

Walking up the embankment they had come down, we walk a little longer. Soon, The Leviathan pushes me over to a shady spot under one of the rock formations. He noses at the backpack a few times, and I offer it out. He carries it off in his mouth.

I'm standing, observing the various layers of earth stacked in the rock formations around us. Hot angry tears roll out of my eyes, and I can't stop them.

Cade rounds the corner adjusting the hem of his T-shirt, making a beeline for me. He pulls me into his embrace, wrapping me up in his arms.

Pocatello
Preston
Malad City
Logan
Brigham City
Tremonton
Ogden
Evanston
Lyman
FLAMING GORGE NAT'L REC AREA
Bountiful
Salt Lake City
Great Salt Lake
Roy
Clearfield
Layton
Park City
Sandy
Heber City
Orem
Provo
Springville
W. Valley City
Tooele
Utah Lake
Great Salt Lake Desert
Wendover
Eureka
Nephi
UTAH
Ephraim
Gunnison
Salina
Aurora
Beaver
Cedar City
15
84
80
89
50
40

CHAPTER 20
CADE

FASTER THAN I can remind myself not to, I close the distance between us and wrap my arms around Thalia. Enveloping her tightly from behind, I bury my nose into her hair.

"You're the bravest woman I know," I whisper against the top of her head.

"Idiots like that make me wish I swore. I mean, really. Why? Why do men do that sort of thing? You could have hurt him and then gotten in trouble all because he missed the day in school where 'no' means 'no,'" Thalia says.

The anger she radiates is so forceful it ignites my own. Anger and violence won't solve this.

I draw slow deep breaths. She leans against me, wrapping her arms around mine. She pulls at them a little bit, shifting in my arms. I release her, my heart thundering in my chest. Did I push her too far?

Thalia wraps her arms around my waist. Her head lays against my chest. My hand moves up her back to her neck. I lace my fingers into her soft curls and tilt her head up toward mine.

I kiss her. Hard.

Thalia shuffles. I loosen my hold on her, a knot forming in my throat. Is she going to stop me?

Our eyes lock for a breath and then she reignites the kiss pressing her lips to mine.

The tension leaves my body as Thalia nibbles my bottom lip.

Taking it as an invitation to kiss deeper, I slip my tongue into her mouth.

Thalia melts against me. Her arms go slack, and the softest little moan escapes her throat. It's another few tender moments before I can handle breaking this connection.

When I pull away, her eyes are still closed.

Kissing the rounded tip of her petite nose, I still feel unsettled. There's a sinking in my stomach, knowing what they wanted from her. The words we heard them say. If they were shifters, they'd be dead for even talking about her like that. I wasn't there to protect her from the humans.

We were. Together. She had us both. The Leviathan reminds me of our unification.

He's been absent in my thoughts for so long that now, feeling him with me, agreeing with me and supporting me, is no less surreal today than the day before. I'm trying to adjust and remember that how it was, isn't how it was supposed to be. He's never given me any reason not to trust him. Today has further proven I need The Leviathan.

I draw a deep breath, but it's taken away seeing Thalia's blue-green eyes looking up at me with mischief in her eyes. Before I act on all the dirty thoughts The Leviathan has, I distract us both from the fact that I just kissed her for the first time.

"You were more afraid of me getting in trouble than of you getting hurt?"

"You wouldn't have let them hurt me." She shrugs and nuzzles in against me. "I had faith The Leviathan felt the same."

All I had been thinking about the entire time, as The Leviathan and I were standing between her and those two entitled idiots, was what I would do if I couldn't save her. Not because the job I've been hired to do is at risk but because . . . because Thalia Clark is mine.

Ours. The Leviathan corrects.

"You'll never be safer than you are by my side, Thalia. The Leviathan will always protect you."

I pull her down to the ground putting her firmly in my lap as I lean back against the stone wall behind us. I nuzzle myself in against her. It's more physical than we've ever been, but she isn't objecting. Not to the kiss and not to this now.

We sit cuddled, shaded from the afternoon sun for a long time. I shuffle her slightly to reach into the backpack and pull out the sandwiches I had packed earlier. *What do I say? What do I tell her?*

These feelings hit hard. I let The Leviathan take control and it cemented everything I had heard to be true. When you meet your mate, your wolf knows and will keep you with them. I just didn't . . . it's not that I missed all the signs. He was certainly vocal enough about it. There's just something, everything, about her, and I don't have a way to describe it.

Perfect. The Leviathan offers.

When Thalia wiggles and tries to move from my lap, I begrudgingly let her go. She sits, turning to face me with her knee touching my thigh.

A smile brushes across her face, and she nods. "The Leviathan is amazing."

At the mention of his name, The Leviathan preens with happiness over her approval.

"He really likes you. I've never heard so much admiration from him."

It's too early to put into words what that real feeling is; far too early for four-letter words. *Even if I'm positive that's what this is.*

"I keep getting the impression that you're a big deal," Thalia says as she rotates her butt in the dirt to look at me more. The wind picks up and blows the wayward strands from her ponytail into her face. "Some people seem afraid of you, and others are, okay, well, it's just Ansel, and I don't understand. Can you explain it?"

I take a swig of water, watching as she takes down her hair in one of those sexy hair flip scenes. I choke, trying to swallow.

After my coughing fit, I'm able to get out, "Yeah, I probably could."

"Probably could?" she repeats, eyes locked on me.

They're hard and pressing. It's a new look and a very alluring one. I half expect her to pull out cat-eye glasses and glare at me over the top rim. It would certainly play into that fantasy.

Our mate, attention to us. Sizing up? We show why we Sovereign. The Leviathan alludes to another imaginative, dirty, and uninhibited idea that has my blood rushing away from my brain. We're on the same page; that look isn't supposed to be seductive, but it sure as fuck is.

"So . . ." I pause. I don't really know where to start. "Robert Alden is my older brother. His title is Regent Alpha. Which is impressive, but I'm Sovereign Alpha, and he's ruling in my place."

"He's older, but you're king?" Thalia observes.

"From the time I was little and my wolf started coming out, everyone knew something was off. My father claimed to be The Leviathan's keeper, but my wolf puzzled people. My father groomed Robert for the throne, and it's convoluted, but he shouldn't have been next in line for the throne as he has the smallest claim." I sigh. Running my hand across her jeans is calming. And I don't think it's calming just for me. "I'm the Ardelean Sovereign Alpha. It's believed that The Leviathan and I are the bloodline from which wolf shifters were created, born, bred, cursed, whatever creation story anyone wants to prescribe through. The Leviathan says we just always existed. So, I mean . . ."

I shake my head. It's so fucked up. All of it.

"It's okay," Thalia whispers and squeezes my fingers interlaced in hers.

When she says that, I believe it. It's been, I don't even know how long since someone's told me something's going to be okay.

"The requirements to be Sovereign Alpha are messy. Ideally, it would be simple: the oldest male, born with an Ardelean gift, *and* a dominant wolf." I hold up my fingers, checking them off. "Which would be really simple because Robert is the oldest with a dominant wolf —" I laugh and lower my index and ring finger, flipping off the world. He only meets two of the requirements. Yet somehow, I'm the one who caused a significant upset in the packs' hierarchies. "Except the asshole doesn't have an Ardelean gift." I lower my hand.

"So, you were next in line regardless of if you or your father had The Leviathan?" Thalia asks, trying to make sense of it all.

With a nod, I answer, "The Leviathan aside, I would have been next in line because I have an Ardelean gift. But as it is, I was next in line regardless of whether I was their second or third child or had I been born to any other Ardelean pack. It would be my birthright simply because I have The Leviathan. Even if Robert could pull his shit together and find a gift, he would not be next." Shaking my head, I continue, "I was content with being Second. Our father choosing Robert was never problematic for me. If I could hide The Leviathan, and it would appear as though I didn't have a gift, it would rule me out of the succession altogether." I puff out my cheeks before continuing, "When the time came for me to claim my birthright, I abdicated, and now there's a lot of people, more than a lot of people, who want me to settle down with a mate and take my place back on the throne."

"That's not what you want." Thalia's voice comes out small. "It's why you understood why I don't talk to my parents about politics, it's all your life's been about too."

"It's all my life has been about," I echo, running my free hand back through my hair. "Despite what I do or don't want, The Leviathan isn't okay with not ruling. He made his displeasure clear the day I walked away from my birthright. Up until three days ago, we hadn't spoken since I abdicated the throne." I pause, looking at Thalia. "That was over a decade ago."

"Is it unusual for wolves to be separate and talk?" Thalia shuffles on the ground, pulling her hand away from mine for a moment, but I follow, my long arms not struggling to reach for her.

This is hard to talk about. How do I explain this to Thalia? I've been able to avoid talking about what I need to do for Ansel, but this could be difficult for her to hear.

I start by answering her question first. "We're supposed to work as a team with our wolves. When someone isn't mostly in alignment with their wolf, we call it a fracture. Most of the time, if you're fractured, it's life ending."

Thalia's eyes are soft, and she watches me.

I keep talking, "Ansel deals with fractured wolves; they're sent here to try to work out their shit or, in most cases, live out their days until he has to end their life. His primary goal is to keep everyone safe, but fractured wolves can be unpredictable sometimes. Ansel takes his job very seriously. He doesn't take risks but does everything he can to give people as long as possible."

I don't expect Thalia to say anything following that. I draw a deep breath. It's so hard to say these things. How do you tell someone what you feel when they have no concept of — no, maybe she will get it. My mate is smart.

That doesn't stop me from looking at our hands held together rather than meeting her eye when I say, "Recently, The Leviathan and I started speaking again and became less fractured."

Pocatello
McCammon
Preston
Malad City
Logan
Brigham City
Tremonton
Ogden
Great Salt Lake
Roy
Clearfield
Layton
Bountiful
Salt Lake City
Park City
Heber City
Sandy
Orem
Provo
Springville
W. Valley City
Tooele
Utah Lake
Great Salt Lake Desert
Wendover
Eureka
Nephi
UTAH
Ephraim
Gunnison
Salina
Aurora
Beaver
Cedar City
Evanston
Lyman
FLAMING GORGE NAT'L REC AREA
Kings Peak
15
80
84
40
89
50

CHAPTER 21

THALIA

"You're the rightful king of the wolves, despite being borderline, what? Crazy?" I ask before I can stop myself from spitting out arguably a little bit of a judgmental tone. But I'm pretty sure that's what he's saying.

Silence settles between us, and I play back my last statement. My face heats. That was rude. "Verge of what was it called? Fracturing?"

Cade gives me a firm nod, and it feels as though he's encouraging me to process this all and talk it out. It doesn't feel like judgment.

I take a deep breath and try to summarize better, with less judgment, what I understand, but it sounds outlandish. "You're asking me to believe that one, Ansel is a murderer. Two, all the people at Ansel's are craz—" I catch myself. "Fracturing, including you." I pause, remembering Cade's instructions that I stay inside while at Ansel's unless accompanied by Cade or Ansel. "Three, you don't want me to be alone outside at Ansel's because there are unpredictable people who might accidentally kill me. Or, worse, intentionally kill me? Irony here is hilarious." I flick my fingers up as I denote each item.

Instead of answering, Cade offers me a snack. I open the bag of trail mix and begin picking out the pieces I don't like, setting them aside. He watches for a moment.

The wind picks up, and my hand gets tangled in my curls as I push them out of my eyes. "Wait, Ezra is your cousin. He's also fracturing? But he also reads minds."

Drawing a deep breath, I rack my brain. Cade tilts his head, observing me and letting me verbally process this new information. He's completely relaxed while I throw around insanity and murder like it's Sunday brunch. *Seriously, always calm?*

"He can read minds, but he's fractured from his wolf, who lives in his mind? That seems like an unfair paradox." I pick up a pebble from the ground, turning the rock over in my hand.

Cade defends his cousin first. "A fracture is just one thing that can bring you here. Ezra isn't fractured. There's a balance between the animal and ourselves, and his is off." Cade picks up his hand, wobbling it side to side like one would try and balance. "He'll probably be fine."

"Okay, let's just brush past the whole part where you said Ansel is a murderer. Ezra seems nice. It's fine." I bite my lips together.

My words are sharp again and laced with sarcasm, but I'm hoping he'll start talking again. A simmer builds, and I'm feeling warmer. The cool afternoon sun isn't the cause; it's not fear, maybe anger? None of this seems logical.

"Ansel isn't a murderer. Humans view death differently than we do." Cade's hands move like a scale balancing. "It's hard when someone's broken. Some Alphas try to fix it themselves, which can be dangerous. You can be a great leader for your pack but aren't equipped to deal with a fracture. They have a choice to make, and many of them, rather than ending someone outright, risking their pack in a challenge gone wrong, call Ansel. Ansel's gift makes him the best candidate to help give them a long life before they're unsafe. Miraculously, Ansel has found that some fractures can be fixed."

He pauses, putting his hand over his mouth. Then he pulls it away, reaching over and picking up pieces of trail mix from my discard pile.

"Ansel didn't go into specifics, but he has the gift to see when and how someone is going to die. I don't quite understand how his gift works, but even with changing fate or destiny, whichever, Ansel can divine someone's death."

Chills run through my body. *Has Ansel seen my death? Do I want to know this?*

"The Leviathan and I are complicated. I don't think I could fracture from him because we are two different entities to begin with. He's not an extension of me, which is, I guess, how others describe it. We are cohabitating for lack of better terms." Cade runs his hand back through his dark hair. "My struggle with my wolf is different. I'm just different."

"Why are you telling me all of this?" I ask, the simmer of anger dissipating slowly.

This isn't something to be angry about. Cade's trusting me with something, and it's probably something wolves will never want shared with the world.

"Because there's something that's likely going to happen, and you need to know about it before it does. I don't want you blindsided." He sighs and shakes his head. "You ever start explaining something and realize it's so convoluted that you have no idea how to get it all across?"

I nod, and Cade takes that as enough to continue. "The Leviathan commands a lot of respect because of his dominance and age. He's essentially unbeatable physically and dominance-wise. There's only one wolf on the face of the earth who would ever have the chance to beat me in a fight."

"Ansel." I deduce before guessing, "Because of his wolf?"

I watch as he nods. "Ansel sees a lot of death. He kills a lot of wolves every year. Fractured wolves tend to become feral as their human half disintegrates. They're less concerned about pain and hurting other people. Alpha challenges and dominance fights are held in wolf form. It has happened that a fractured wolf has taken control of a pack by killing the Alpha in a challenge. It's uncommon but an awful thing for the pack, total decimation. Ansel's been given, by whatever deity you want to attribute it to, a wolf who is strong and as indestructible as he needs to be."

"Okay. That makes sense."

Logically, the checks and balances play out in a great design. I can see the argument for higher power involvement over natural evolution, given the complexity of one individual having these gifts.

"Wolves crave connection, and for Ansel, with his pack of misfits, attachment is still very present. Even if he tries to keep himself unattached, you spend time with someone and at the end of the day, it's not easy to kill someone you love. It's not."

Cade says these words as if they come from a place of familiarity. It's not a lecture but Cade's much more serious than usual.

"Ansel's gift means he sees it coming, but that doesn't make it easier. The fact that he pulls himself out of bed and finds a way to live life is astounding. Let alone with that goofy grin on his face."

His words are very ominous. This whole conversation brings a pain to my chest from my rapidly beating heart. He's confirmed that people come to Ansel's to die, and now what?

I swallow hard and try to speak, but it comes out with a

tremor, "Why does this sound like you're going to tell me something bad?"

"One of the wolves Ansel's had here for a long time is fracturing more. Ansel has determined there's no putting him back together. His timeline's become excruciatingly short." Cade absent-mindedly pets my leg, letting out a shaky sigh. "Ansel's struggling with it."

"Understandably so."

This sounds devastating. Ansel, from what I've met, is lighthearted. Thinking of him as killing anyone is hard, let alone someone he's attached to. I move to sit closer to Cade. He leans against me rubbing his head against the top of mine for a moment.

"I've agreed to end this wolf on his behalf," Cade says quietly.

Is it possible for a heart to stop? I'm fairly certain mine does. I try to take a deep breath. I'm frozen. My mouth runs dry. *Did Cade say he's going to kill someone?*

Cade leans forward, his blue eyes watching me for a reaction. I can't give him one. I can't move. I can't even blink.

"I'm not asking for permission. I'm telling you so that you're aware of what's going to happen." Cade's nonchalant in his information.

After a slow breath, motor function returns, and slowly I'm able to reach my hand out for Cade. I need to touch him. Cade's hand quickly meets mine. The warmth of his touch brings my heartbeat back down. The panic is cut off, and my shoulders fall from where they've crept up around my ears. He pulls me closer, wrapping his arm around my shoulders.

"I need you to stay with Ansel, first to keep him from thinking about what's happening, and second because I don't want to worry about you while I take care of it. You're human and fragile. I can't risk you being out here and getting mauled." Cade's voice is very solemn.

I can't think about it anymore. I can't think about Cade about to kill someone. Maybe, it won't happen? There's no need to talk about it just now. We sit in silence for a little bit. I watch as a large bird of some sort circles overhead. The wind blows tiny dust storms across the earth. It's really peaceful out here.

"There's one more final thing that I need to tell you," Cade says with a slow, shaky sigh for punctuation.

"Can it be any bigger than the fact that you just told me you're going to kill someone?" I ask. "Is there something worse than killing someone?"

Cade laughs. "Not worse, just different."

"Lay it on me." I nod and look up at him, ready for him to drop a bombshell.

"Wolves believe, nearly universally, that you're always going to find your mate in your lifetime. That when you meet them you know. Your wolf will recognize the soul best paired with them." His eyes don't waver from mine. He squeezes my hand gently. The sexy velvet tone comes back. Smooth, confident words come out, articulated flawlessly. "And when you find them, you're bound to them for life. Your wolf will always be loyal and protect the other."

"And mates are like spouses?" I clarify.

Cade nods and continues speaking slowly, like he's choosing his words very carefully, "I don't know how to explain this to you. But The Leviathan believes we're mates, fated to be together forever."

Fort Hall
River
Franklin
Bear Lake
W Y
Green River City
Green
Evanston
Corinne
Brigham City
Echo City
Ogden City
GREAT SALT LAKE
Salt Lake City
Bingham Canon
Alta
Stockton
Forest Cy.
UINTAH MTS.
Chapin Spr.
York
Mt. Pleasant
U T A H
Manti
Richfield
Frisco
WAHSATCH MTS.
Green River
Grand River
ELK MTS

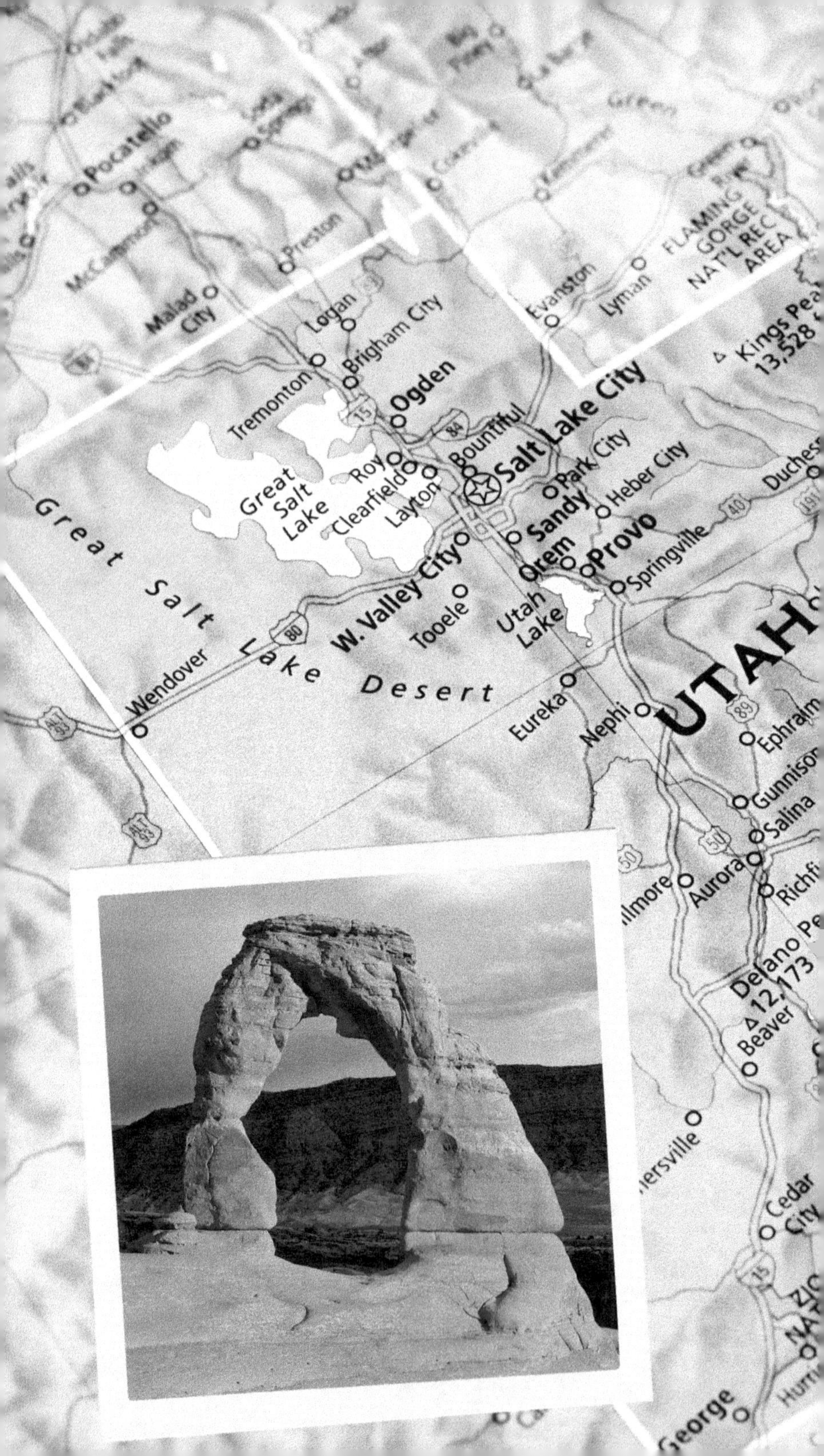

CHAPTER 22
CADE

"So, your wolf picked me." Thalia's voice catches, and I hear her heart thundering in her chest.

She stands up from the ground.

Draga mea understands. She accepts. Good mate. The Leviathan tries to give me his best 'I told you so.' But he's not seeing everything I am. Her wide eyes locking with us isn't acceptance.

"That's absurd. You can't feel that way about someone you just met. I can't," Thalia whispers. She starts pacing. "That whole idea, love at first sight, is a fairytale."

No. The Leviathan growls at her rejection.

The statement stings, but it's not totally unexpected. She handled everything else so easily. Death, destruction, and insanity are universal concepts. Love, however, isn't as universal as we'd all like to believe.

I stand up and walk to her. I pick up her hand, brushing my thumb against her skin.

"You are the first thing The Leviathan and I agree on."

"I don't know what to say."

Thalia finally gives me something to work with. I raise her hand gently to kiss her knuckles.

"It's okay. I'm not asking you to have an understanding of it all. This isn't something that has to be talked through today. But it's important for you to know that my wolf and I see you as our mate. Other wolves are going to see that too."

"Ansel said it. He called me your mate." She turns her head to look at me.

"You are. Even if you don't understand it yet," I confirm. I pull her with me as I back up to pick up the backpack, then start walking back toward the truck. "It's why no matter what happens while we're here, I want you to remember everyone here is slightly dangerous, some more than others, but they wouldn't dare harm you because tonight, they're all going to know you're mine, and they know the power of The Leviathan."

A nod, the slightest littlest bob of her head, and her shoulders slowly start to fall from their defensive position.

My heart swells. It's a start.

The Leviathan hums with pride.

From what I remember, this is what happy feels like. Even if it's temporary, I want to live in this feeling as long as I can.

"Be serious." She pushes out a frustrated sigh. Thalia pulls her hand from mine and tightens her ponytail. "Everyone seems to know something I don't. Is this what it is that I don't know?"

I offer my arm out to her wanting to pull her close, but she moves away from my hand. The truth hurts. I'm doing a shitty job explaining shifters and myself.

Puppy brain, not tell mate. Gift mate wolf. Will understand. The Leviathan gives me his one-stop shop answer to fix all problems between Thalia and me.

"Then, you kiss me and . . ." Her voice fades off, and she

looks away. Her face turns pink, and she touches her lips before saying, "No one kisses like that. I've never . . ." She looks back to me. "I've never felt attracted like this. But, your mate? That's . . ."

The way she says attracted has me biting the side of my tongue. That string of words together is a tiny reassurance of our bond forming. Her admitting attraction is a whole new form of pleasure.

The Leviathan urges me: *claim her*. It's the only thing he's thinking about. I push him back. Binding her to me isn't going to fix the issue she and I are having.

"We met you, and The Leviathan recognized you as our mate. He decided that you were worth talking to me over."

A little bit of honesty goes a long way, right?

"That sounds like a line if I've ever heard one before." Thalia's expression changes. She purses her lips and scrunches her face. Then she rips her hand from mine. "Kissing you is hot, but I don't need some cheesy movie line to have a sexual relationship with someone."

Surprised, I take a half step away from her, turning toward her, analyzing all her body language. She keeps walking, so I follow, watching her. Everything is open and accepting. Why don't her words match? I've been honest and open with her, so I'm not sure why she would think that.

Mate thinks we lie. Why lie our mate? We've spent time with her. We hunt down men give to mate? The Leviathan thinks of bloodshed as an offering of love. Then, The Leviathan settles at: *We claim her. Make her wolf. She feel it. No doubt us.*

Neither of his ideas are helpful. I should probably be disturbed at my own willingness to hunt down those idiot humans. I don't have to commit murder today.

Calling out to her, I say, "I don't believe that at all. Sex should come with a relationship."

Thalia stops dead in her tracks. I've hit a nerve, good or bad?

Stepping in front of her, I meet her eyes. "Everything you're feeling, I feel too. I'm conflicted between disbelief and attraction. I begged The Leviathan to pick anyone other than you. Every conversation he and I have is about you. It's so hard to fight him because I know he's right." I run my fingers back through my hair. *Have I said too much? Am I scaring her?* Drawing a deep breath, I lay it all out for her. "I was angry that fate would give me such an obstacle to overcome to figure out how to be with my mate. Why does everything have to be such a fight? Why couldn't love come easily? Then you smile, and my heart melts. I'll do anything as long as I'm the reason for those smiles. I'm willing to do what it takes for you."

The Leviathan paces, watching with me for her response.

She's quiet before she steps around me and starts off down the trail. Her walking away ignites the hunter within. But I must be a patient predator. Following, I let her lead the way.

A few minutes later, she turns back to me. Thalia opens her mouth to say something, closes it without a word, turns away, and keeps walking. A few feet later, Thalia turns around, motioning her hand up and down my body, then hers, not speaking.

Her face expresses disgust or anger, which one, I'm not entirely sure.

What mean? The Leviathan and I share our confusion. *Compare what? She not talk good.*

I wait, avoiding jumping to conclusions. There's a lot that could mean.

Again, Thalia walks off. It's only two steps before she spins around to face me.

"Okay, let's say I believe you, and for whatever reason, this is real. Making a ridiculous assumption that these intense feelings of . . ." Her voice trails off. She leaves that sentence hanging, biting her bottom lip before moving on, "Are real, how would this even work? We're too different. You live in Wisconsin. I live in DC. You work security. I don't even have my degree yet. You're almost thirty, and I can't legally drink. You're wolf. I'm human. You're super handsome. I'm nowhere near. I want kids someday. It's a huge want for me in a relationship. I don't even know enough about wolves to know if that's a thing. Can kids even happen?"

"You would need to become wolf for us to have children," I say softly. No sense in scaring her with the gruesome truth of what it takes to become wolf. It can't happen now. I won't let it. I switch to the defense. "I'll find a way for us to work. There's no reason I can't live part-time in DC. Peter's office is there. Long distance, when I need to see Lena and Deacon, is not impossible. School has breaks."

"You'd turn me into a wolf?" She homes in on that idea.

Of course, she'd pick something dangerous to ask about.

I push out words without thinking. "Theoretically, yes. I can't with how things are right now." I try to explain with better logic. I can't let it happen right now. It'll ruin everything if it does. "Your mother's bill makes it dangerous to be a shifter. Until things settle, it isn't responsible. It's not no. It's not right now."

The half-truth doesn't appease her. Nor should it; it's a terrible answer to her question. She's smarter than that.

When she walks away from me this time, I fixate on her hair flipping back and forth in the opposite direction from her beautiful round ass as it bounces down the trail. The fixation is so intense that I almost miss her flipping me the bird over her shoulder.

I've got to pull myself together.

With the truck in sight, I walk more slowly, letting her get there first.

Need be King. This time The Leviathan's call to power isn't angry or wrathful.

It's not one-sided or daunting. I've accepted my mate. Somehow, Thalia will be mine. I'll have to take back the throne. But, for now, I've got nine weeks to court her. To let her learn about wolves, and then when she's ready to make a decision and does choose me . . . Then I'll be ready to fight anyone I have to. I'll take back the throne, anything to keep her safe.

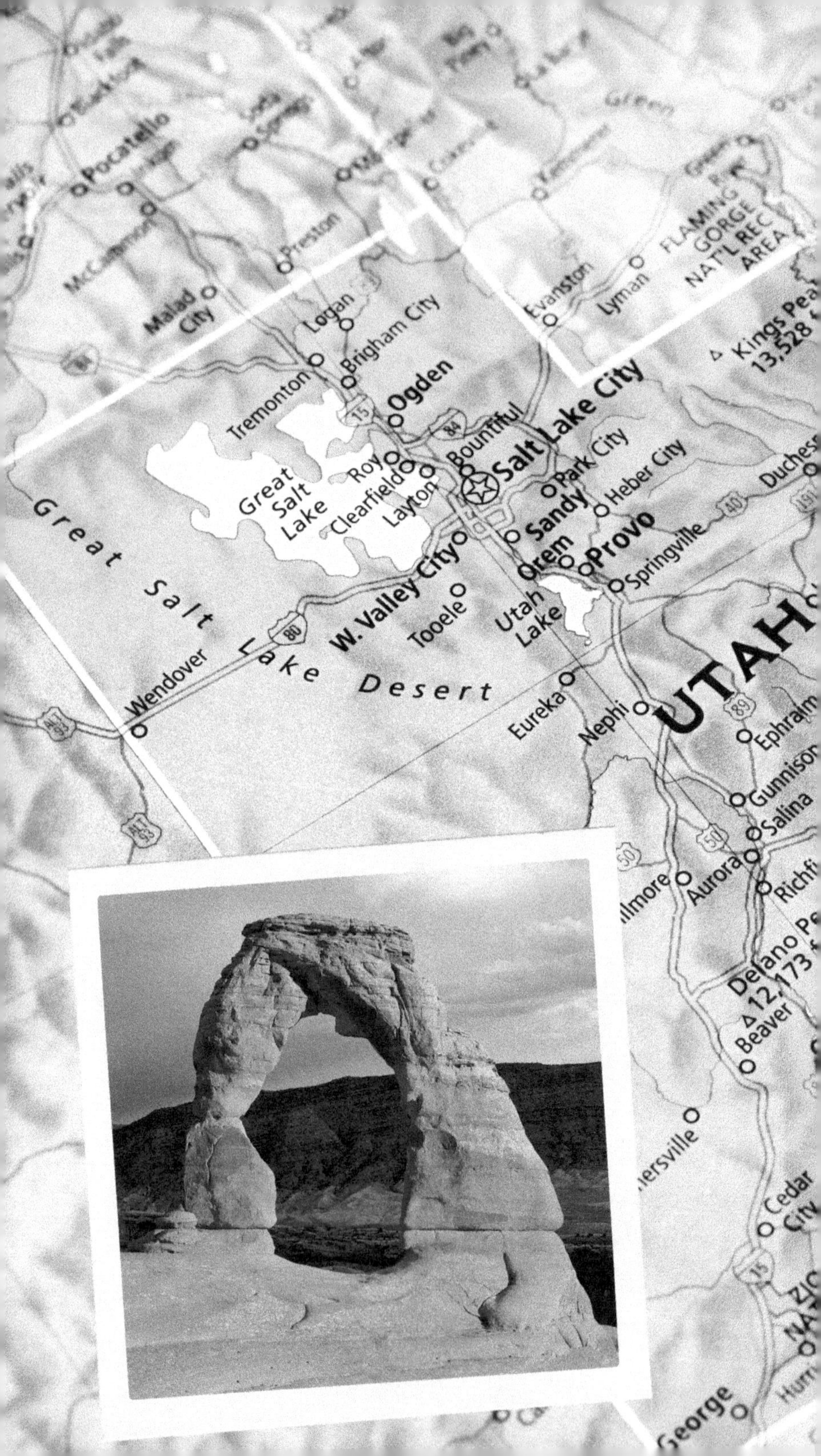

CHAPTER 23
THALIA

MICHELANGELO AND THE SISTINE CHAPEL. Cade takes me out in the middle of nowhere to tell me outlandish ideas about us being together. Just like Michelangelo agrees to paint *The Last Judgment*, if and only if it can be done on his terms. Cade's the same.

He said: *I've got feelings for you. I want to find a way to build a life.* But in typical male form won't actually commit. He won't go all the way; kids would be off the table. It's one excuse now for two excuses later.

What's worse is you can't just go around thinking about saying yes to big things like this to someone you've just met, yet here I am. I want to say yes and be open to working it out.

Another man walks into my life and sweet-talks me. You'd think I'd be immune to fancy words and devilish grins. What bodes true in my parent's circle and male-dominated scholastics is also apparently true with wolves.

But how do I go into this knowing that something I want so badly is off the table? If Cade's going to be like Michelangelo and paint a pretty picture of a bunch of dudes with their dicks out, then I guess I'll just have to be like Il Braghettone. I'll put on my big girl panties and make us decent.

No more sexy kisses in national parks.

How can I be so pathetic? He's drop-dead gorgeous, he's nice to everyone, and he seems to genuinely care about what I say. Athletic but intelligent, contributes to conversations, and can cook.

Cade is virtually perfect.

Too perfect. I was ready to jump into bed. All from what? A single kiss?

I reach the truck before him and rip open the door. Hot air burns my senses, but I don't care as I climb into the cab. Using the crank on the door, I roll down the window. The woolen seat is hot against the fabric of my clothes. It's uncomfortable, but I'm so furious not even the heat of the car is more annoying than how I feel about Cade.

How dare he!?

He's saying all these things, but in a few weeks, I'll go back to my life, and he'll go on to do whatever he does, work or time with his family. Believing anything he says will only lead to heartbreak. We're too different. We want two very different things in life. I want the house and yard, children running around, a fun education-based job. He wants . . . well, I don't know what he wants, but he's flat out said he doesn't want to turn me into a wolf which is the only way I can have kids, apparently. So, not me. He doesn't want me because he doesn't want the same life I want. I'm not settling for a pretty face.

Cade doesn't go to the driver's side like I expected. He first leans in the truck window before shaking his head and opening the door. Like I weigh nothing at all, Cade scoops me out of the cab of the truck and pins me against the side panel. Automatically, my legs wrap around him. I'm uncomfortable off the ground, but I feel safe. His blue eyes study mine like he's trying to read what I'm thinking.

I huff and avert my gaze.

"I'm mad at you," I tell him, but held up in his arms like this, it's really hard to be mad.

Gently gripping my chin with one hand, he guides my gaze back to his.

"I accept that." Cade nods. "But I want to talk about it. Can you tell me what upsets you?"

"I'm not mad you kissed me. I'm mad you're saying all these things about how you feel and that it doesn't matter because there's no way to fix it." I manage to get the words out.

My face is hot, and there's moisture in my eyes. I blink, trying to clear it.

The soft touch of Cade's thumb and forefinger wipe my tears away.

A barrage of conflicting emotions pounds in my chest. I've only known him for a few days, but life will be different when I go back home. It's going to hurt not having him in my life, but I've got to find a way to live with the pain.

"This isn't something that has to be worked out all at once," he says softly. His hand runs across my hair. "We have weeks to talk it through. Thalia, I want to make this work. I want to make us work. Ideally, I wouldn't have had to explain this to you in such a short amount of time, and I could have let you process everything more naturally. But you have an hour before people are going to notice us together, and they might treat you a bit differently than you'd be used to. You deserve to know why."

"Uhm," I start.

I should say something. I just don't know what. The dark look in his eyes brings back the kiss.

There's a hard and hot, painful throb at my core. I'm

wrapped around him like I'm climbing a tree. I'm fairly sure he felt the contraction of muscles travel down my thighs.

Cade's tongue darts out between his lips, and the look in his eyes gives away that he did in fact feel it. He leans forward and nudges my nose aside but patiently waits. He doesn't kiss me like he did before.

I can't take it, pressing forward, I kiss him. *So much for no more sexy kisses in national parks.* It's all the permission he needs. Nipping at his bottom lip, I get wrapped up in kissing him. He bites back harder on my lip, and his hand plays with the hem of my shirt. *Oh, that's hot.*

Cade doesn't take it any further. But he does press harder against me, bringing his body even closer to mine. Including a very hard cock only a few layers of fabric away. My arms, wrapped around Cade's shoulders, keep him close. I want him to stay like this. I feel so needy, and when his tongue explores my mouth, I slightly adjust against him.

Time's a social construct, and I forget it exists. When he pulls back, he kisses my nose and then from my ear down my neck and back.

His voice is a growly whisper. "If I don't stop kissing you now, I'm going to end up taking you in the back of Ansel's truck, and while The Leviathan loves being outdoors, that's not how I want to end up inside you for the first time."

Oof. That hits hard. I draw a sharp breath and bite my bottom lip. When he nibbles my ear again, there's a noise I don't want to admit to making. Ever so gently, Cade moves a half step away from the truck. Begrudgingly, I uncoil my legs and let him set me on the ground. I feel warm and run my finger across my lip.

Shaking my head, I ask, "Who'd have thought you'd have such a dirty mouth?" My cheeks flush, and my face is probably beet red. I turn from him to get back into the truck. "Should have known after seeing what you text your cousin."

"Pft, I can't wait for you to meet Dinah. You'll know that no one is safe when it comes to sexual harassment from her." Cade waits for me to be safe in the cab before closing my door.

He's really considering what it would be like for me to meet his family. I nod to myself while he walks around the back of the truck. I rub my hand down my face with the realization that I've made myself look like a huge, spoiled brat, storming off and assuming he's feeding me a line. While I'm not convinced this is a hundred percent real, I might have made a mistake by assuming the worst.

CHAPTER 24
CADE

PULLING BACK UP to Ansel's house, Thalia gets antsy seeing all the beat-up pickup trucks parked at the top of the hill. I back the truck in alongside Ansel's other truck.

After turning off the engine, I coach her. "I'm not going running with them tonight. It's okay. They're just going about their normal lives. Everyone's going to want to say hello quickly, and then they'll be on their way out. We can grab some food and watch a movie."

It seems to settle Thalia a bit more, and after locking up the garage, Thalia follows me up to the house. Walking through the front door, it's evident that Ansel's holding his pack meeting out back. Thalia goes into the bathroom while I unpack our backpack from the day.

When she's ready, I lead her out the back sliding glass door and down the stairs. She stands on my left.

Perfect Alpha Female. The Leviathan observes.

Ansel sits with his pack around the fire pit. It suits him to be a leader. In a way, I've always wished I could be more like Ansel. Leading comes naturally to him.

When we walk closer, the pack stands, and Thalia begins radiating tension. She tries to tuck herself behind me, but when I gently run my hand up and down her back for a brief moment, she relaxes.

For the benefit of his pack members, Ansel and I greet each other with official pomp and circumstance. Grabbing each other's forearms, we pull into a hug. Then breaking the embrace, his pack takes turns approaching me.

"Sovereign," Ansel's pack Second addresses me.

I nod. It's been a while since I've been out to visit Ansel, so I haven't had the opportunity to meet with his Second.

"It's good to see you, Ben."

"I wish I could say the same, but I was hoping the next time I saw you was when you were leading us again." Ben doesn't hold back his opinion but does respectfully cast his gaze aside.

He's from Robert's pack. I vaguely remember seeing him when we were growing up. I don't know why he's at Ansel's, but he's been here at least a few years.

"I understand your frustrations." I keep it respectful.

The next three pack members introduce themselves: Dale, Vito, and Sully. Then Sherman, the man from the deck, introduces himself quietly with an apology for scaring Thalia. Once they've greeted me, they step past me and give a head tip to Thalia, standing slightly behind me, almost like she's done this before. When they address her, she remembers Ansel's advice and tells them to call her Emily with small waves.

After introductions, Ansel's pack takes their seats around the fire pit. They all opt to sit on the far side of the pit, away from us, giving room to allow me the closest position to my mate.

Ansel plops down in his seat on the large wooden swing.

"Ezra says he'll be up in a bit." Ansel takes a deep breath. He chews on his top lip before saying what the somber mood is, "He's making sure Rachet settles into his cabin. It was a rough day."

Thalia sits on the swing next to him. The tension breaks. The guys all start laughing. It's a chorus of cackles. Turning her head, she's examining all of them, and not even I can help from laughing. Patting Ansel on the shoulder, I walk in front of them both to sit in a chair on her other side. Snubbed by my little human mate on her first outing with a pack. *Go figure.*

We please her. They not matter. The Leviathan huffs, defending Thalia's honor and my pride against pack traditions and customs.

"What did I do?" she whispers to me. Her face starts turning red.

Ansel pulls it together first. "Did you tell her yet?"

Thalia's head whips to look at him. "What?"

"We were exploring that," I admit lowly, bracing for some fallout from Thalia.

Ansel looks at me over Thalia's head. He gives me an obvious 'your woman, your problem' look.

Thalia turns back to look at me. There's anger and embarrassment written across her face.

"What did I do wrong?"

"Nothing," I assure her while putting my hand on her leg. "They all know that you're mine. You choosing to sit next to Ansel over me is essentially saying you're upset with me."

"I just like the swing." Thalia chews on her bottom lip, feet off the ground, swinging in a childlike fashion, before spewing out questions in rapid fire. "Why would they assume I'm mad at you? Is this a body language thing? What if I just really wanted to sit in the swing?"

"You'd touch Cade before sitting down in the swing," Ben answers for her with an explanation before I can formulate one. "It's not asking permission so much as it's informed consent. You tell Cade that you're his and that you're doing your own thing."

"Oh." Thalia's jaw drops open. If eyes could be the size of saucers, hers would be. After a few seconds, she closes her mouth. With a dedicated nod and a joking tone, she answers, "Well . . . I'm just going to play the human card."

There's laughter all around, and Thalia settles right in.

Ansel grills hamburgers and hot dogs over the fire with his massive grill grates while the pack tells stories. Sun sets around six, and the pack gets a bit antsy, ready to run. When Ansel asks if I want to run with them, it's with a heavy hint I should stay with Thalia. I feign exhaustion from the last few days on the road and lead Thalia into the house.

It's a twenty-minute game of: Thalia has never seen this classic movie before. We narrow it down to one from my memory-based synopsis. I make a note on my phone to ship him a box of new movies as part of my thank-you gift to him.

After starting the film, we sit on opposite ends of the sofa. Watching her experience the comedic happenings of the film is fascinating. Her earnest reactions while the movie dances on the screen show exactly how vibrant she is. Thalia gives emotions freely. Her legs sprawl out on the couch toward me midway through. I want to pull her into my lap, but instead, I rest my hand on her feet, petting them softly.

It's normally a dark road when wolves don't claim and keep their mates; they tend to drift slowly into insanity. They lose bits and pieces of themselves, being chipped away until there isn't anything but that one desire to possess. I can't deny she's mine. But how long do I have without claiming her? The struggle to maintain distance is already eating at me.

There are massive obstacles in my way. There're legends of claiming bites that accidentally start the process of turning their mate, but because the human half is too strong, the wolf can't take hold. The process often ends in death. It's why gifting wolves can be so gruesome. I can't claim her until I can gift her a wolf. I can't gift her a wolf until it's safe.

You bite. She will have beautiful wolf. The Leviathan pictures a beautiful dark gray and black wolf. *No problems. Puppy brain too much think.*

I shake my head; I won't risk it.

Ultimately, our situation begins and ends with her mother. Her mother's laws are terrifying. If I'm going to gift my mate a wolf, it's because it will be safe to do so. Humans and wolves will have to come to at least some sort of understanding. It could be seen as me building a pack, taking a mate. I'll have to be prepared to take back the throne to keep her safe.

Too fragile, too human, The Leviathan whispers, *fix problem. No danger has teeth. Claws defend. Make ours, stupid humans later.*

When the movie ended, I hadn't even realized it. I'd been too lost in my own thoughts of her. As if on cue, my phone starts vibrating wildly on the counter where I left it. Once I rush to it, Lena's name and number roll across my screen.

"Hey, you okay?" I answer quickly.

"Bitch is still here. We did some off-roading but finally got parked in the garage. She's nonstop with the noise. I don't know what to do." Lena huffs out a sharp exhale. "Peter's guys are staying. But it's not like Isabel is entirely intimidated by humans."

"Can you put one of the specialists on?"

Despite the anger growing inside me, I remain calm. Lena is already bristling with emotion, cutting her words short. Showing her anger, even misdirected anger, will hurt her and everyone around her.

"Hello?" the man answers. "Cade? This is Michael. Peter had our team escort your siblings home. I've been ordered to remain until it is safe."

"Yeah, what's the status?" I take a breath.

Michael is one of the best men on Peter's team. I handpicked him myself, so I trust his judgment.

"There are six unknown females. We've got visuals on them all, but they've made it evident they're not leaving without talking to you. We've yet to engage."

"Don't engage. Stay vigilant. If they breach the house, shoot to kill," I instruct. "Don't call the locals. Call me."

"Ten-four," he answers.

"When are you coming home?" Lena's voice is back. "Deacon is edgy."

"I understand. It's late now. She won't stay in the cold overnight." I remind her, "Isabel's a diva. The cold and sleeping in her car won't do. If she's still there in the morning, I'll call and see what I can do to scare her off. I can't bring work home until it's safe."

"Okay," Lena answers with a frustrated sigh. "Love you. Be safe."

"Love you too. Chin up."

It breaks my heart to hear her upset like this. I know what it means that she's backed into a corner like this. The human security detail with them should keep Isabel in line.

Looking down at my phone, I see messages and two missed calls from Lena that triggered the do-not-disturb work-around. The other notifications, all fifteen of them, are messages from Isabel, all roughly saying the same thing: Where are you? You're not with your siblings? We need to talk.

"Everything okay?" Thalia's voice picks up with suspicion.

She's come to stand next to me by the kitchen island. Her presence takes some of the edge off.

"It'll be okay. Isabel is still hanging around the house. The security team is staying with my siblings until she clears out or I get home." I give her a soft smile. "Nothing to worry about. Lena's on edge but dealing."

She nods like she understands, but it cuts to a yawn. I watch her pull her hair out of its hair tie.

I smile. "I'm going to wait up for Ansel. Why don't you go up and head to bed."

It's not a tough sell. Thalia looks exhausted, but when she walks past me to go up to bed, I snake my arm around her, pulling her close. She looks up at me through tired, hooded eyes. I kiss her sweetly.

"Sleep well, draga mea."

Thalia looks at me for further explanation. She tilts her head when she doesn't get one.

"On one condition: you tell me what *draga mea* means."

"You're only going to sleep well if I tell you what it means?" I ask, raising my eyebrow.

Thalia nods.

"It means, my darling."

Because I can't help myself, I kiss her again.

CHAPTER 25
THALIA

He calls me 'my darling.' *Swoon.* I climb up the stairs to the loft, heading to the room on the left like Cade instructed earlier today. *Wow. Was that only today?* So much happened. Was it all real?

I force myself to do my nighttime routine before I snuggle into bed. Touching my lips, I think back to that first kiss. I've never been possessed by someone like that. The feeling of his lips against mine. It was so intense. There are a lot of things that we have to talk about. Like, how exactly am I supposed to be his mate?

I wake up shivering. The blankets aren't exactly the thickest or most luxurious. It's still dark all around me. I curl myself up tighter into a ball. But my teeth are chattering; I'm so cold. *Cade's warm*, the naughty little part of my brain reminds me. He always feels so warm when he touches me. It must be a wolf thing. Maybe they run hotter?

But I can't exactly go curl up in bed with him. That's not proper. *No, no, no.* I can't possibly do that.

Squirming, I try to make some friction to warm myself up. But it's not getting better. *I don't want to forget what happened last night.* That's what Cade said when I told him we should forget about waking up cuddling. He's called me his mate. That's practically marriage to shifters. So, he wouldn't be angry about it, right?

Closing my eyes, I try to pretend I'm warm. Think warm thoughts like deserts, suns, hot saunas, Jacuzzi tubs, and hot cocoa. It's not getting any warmer. Cade made me buy more sweaters and socks, maybe because it's so cold here? Ugh. If I get out of bed and turn the light on to find more warm clothes, it'll be so hard to go back to sleep. But that's hardly an argument to go sleep with Cade. No, it's not sleeping with Cade. It's sleeping next to Cade.

He's kind of a white noise machine though. Soft breathing sounds and warmth. My whole body shakes.

Okay, on the count of three, just get out of bed and put warm clothes on. One, two, three.

There's no movement. My body does not agree with this plan.

Cade? Could I get out of bed for Cade?

One, two, three.

My feet move from under the sparse joke of blankets. Grabbing my pillow, I softly walk through my room, across the landing, and to the bedroom on the other side. The moonlight illuminates his bedroom. He's lying shirtless, in some nature of sweatpants, with the blankets pushed down around the bottom of the bed. Clearly, Cade *is* warm.

"Cade?" I say quietly.

He doesn't answer, which . . . fair, because he's sleeping. Carefully I approach and grab the blankets on my way to the head of the bed. Pulling them up with me, I sit down. Cade doesn't even stir. Gently, I curl up, facing him. Heat is radiating off him like a furnace. My frozen nose and fingers begin to thaw and feel warm almost instantly. Maybe I'll just warm up for an hour or two and sneak back to my bed. But I don't think he'll be mad.

THE BED MOVES, and the blankets shuffle. A kiss is placed at the junction of my neck and shoulder. I open my eyes quickly, only to be assaulted by the bright sunlight. Squeezing them shut, I realize I did not warm up for an hour or two and then sneak back to my own bed.

"Good morning, draga mea." Cade's voice is gravelly with sleep.

He's wrapped around me, my butt pressed against him.

Rolling slowly, I move my butt away from him, but I'm busted. Pulling my hand over my face, I squint to open my eyes.

I squeak out, "Good morning. I'm sorry."

"Why are you sorry?"

Cade's hand plays with my hair, brushing strands back. I can't imagine what state my curls are in.

"Well, I came in because I was cold, and I was just going to warm up for a little." I move my hand up to squint at him again.

Cade's hand shields me from the sun. He pushes me flat onto my back and rolls to protect me entirely from the direct light. Placing his lips on mine, Cade proves that none of his kisses are the same. With more heat than the chaste kiss good night but nowhere near the passion of the kiss at the truck or our first one, it's delicious all the same.

When he pulls back, his forehead rests against my head. "I'll always keep the bed warm for you."

"Not mad?" I ask, chewing on my bottom lip.

"Not in the slightest."

Cade's palm rests on the side of my cheek. His thumb gently untangles my lip from between my teeth.

A goofy grin tugs on my lips. "What time is it?"

"No clue. Time doesn't really exist here."

Cade moves his body more across the top of mine. None of his weight rests on me, but he's definitely more than halfway on top of me. As he reaches for his phone, the movement accentuates the delicate linework of the segmented leaves of his tattoo across his chest.

He sighs. "It's seven. Damn alarm doesn't even go off for thirty minutes. I was just too excited to find you here with me."

Shuffling off the top of me and lying down alongside me, Cade says, "Let's snooze."

The way Cade so easily pulls me to his chest and nuzzles into my hair puts me at ease. *Why was I even worried?*

It's not Cade's alarm I've become accustomed to hearing that wakes me up. It's the ringing of his cell. With more coordination than I've ever had in my entire life, Cade hops out of bed over me without hardly touching me.

"Lena? You okay," Cade asks softly.

I can't understand the sounds coming out of Cade's phone, but they're loud, and he holds it away from his face.

"I'll call her right now." Cade draws a deep breath. "I hear you, Lena. I do. If she doesn't leave, I'll hit the road today."

There's more garbled yelling.

"I don't like it either," Cade confirms. "I love you. I'll call you back."

Cade lingers, pulling a T-shirt over his head, looking like he's contemplating saying something before taking his phone call outside.

With no instructions, I head back to my room and grab my toiletries.

EVEN AFTER I shower and go downstairs, I don't find Cade in the house. Looking outside, I see Cade sitting down on the top step. He's holding his phone to his ear. Cade scrubs his hand back through his hair with the length covering his fingers, squeezing the strands tightly. I can hear the rumbles of him talking to whomever, but I can't make out the words.

Is he stressed? Am I safe? It feels like an invasion of privacy sitting here and watching him, but if he didn't want me to see him, he'd have moved away from the door, right?

I can't sit still watching him any longer. I'm antsy. There are dishes left from Ansel's breakfast this morning, I'm guessing. At least it's something to do.

I'm scrubbing the frying pan when the first phone call last night comes to mind; he told someone to shoot to kill. Why did the way he say it seem so normal? Is it because he's security or because he's a wolf?

Midway through washing the dishes, the lock on the glass door behind me clicks unlocked. I shake the water from my hands and turn to look. It's Cade. I want to ask him what's going on, but from my understanding, it's his ex, Isabel, who wants more of him than he wants to give her. I want to be involved, but am I being nosey or is it being concerned? What's the difference between those, anyhow?

I turn back and keep washing dishes. Picking up a plate, I run the dishcloth across it. Focusing on what I'm doing, I remind myself that just because he says we're mates doesn't mean this can work. Even though this hopeful, small part of me wants to work things out with him. I don't want to just be his client.

I jump, startled by Cade's hands gently wrapping around my biceps. I try to look up at him, but I feel his nose press into the top of my head. He draws slow breaths. The exhale is warm against my scalp. It's soothing. His hands release my biceps before wrapping around my middle. It feels so good to be wrapped up in him. I'm safe against his chest. Seconds pass, and then he slowly releases me, stepping away.

An ache in my chest grows. I feel the distance between us. *Why do I miss him so much?*

I glance over my shoulder to see Cade perched on a stool, focused on his hands on the countertop.

He sounds more formal again. "I've solved the issue back at the house. I'd like to take a day or two to get myself less road exhausted, and then we'll head back to my place."

I wipe my hand on the dish towel, giving myself a moment to pull it together before turning to look at him. We're apparently bouncing back and forth between attachment again.

"You fixed it?"

"Yeah. She's going to go home." He nods before pointing to the lower cabinet on my left. "You do know Ansel has a dishwasher, right?"

"What?" I try opening the cabinet; it weirdly folds down, revealing a built-in dishwasher. Sure enough, there are dirty dishes in there and everything. I puff my cheeks out in frustration with a massive sigh. "Well, shoot."

"Hungry?" He motions toward the fridge.

I nod, and Cade starts pulling ingredients out of the fridge. It's sexy watching him move expertly about the kitchen.

"How did you learn to cook?" I ask as he cracks an egg with one hand tossing the shell with ease into the trash can.

"Well, I didn't know when I . . . uh, left home. So, it was a lot of learning in the army and asking questions. You can learn how to do just about anything on the internet," Cade says nonchalantly.

"I want to know more, but I don't want to be rude by asking you so many personal questions," I admit to him.

Cade shrugs. "Why I left home?"

He looks at me before going to the sink and washing his hands.

The back door opens, and I look over to see Ansel walking in. He toes off his shoes and comes in.

"Good morning, sleepy heads." Ansel smiles. His long hair is pulled up into a messy bun at the back of his head. Shoving his hand into his pocket, he fishes out keys. Looking at Cade, he says, "Your SUV is back, detailed, and fully fueled. Guys took good care of her, as far as I can tell. They didn't see, smell, or hear anything funny. I think it's safe."

"Thank you," Cade responds.

I'm worried I've lost the opportunity to know more about Cade, but Ansel is fun to talk to.

Ansel pulls a glass and a bottle of alcohol out from the cabinet that he keeps it in. He pours himself a drink and offers one to both Cade and me. I shake my head. Cade does the same, and Ansel, not dismayed by our rejection, continues with his own glass.

Shockingly Cade continues our conversation. "You already knew that I wasn't first in line for the throne, that was Robert. And I told you that my father claimed to have The Leviathan."

"He seems like something hard to hide?" I ask. "I mean,

he's a big red wolf. If he's reincarnated, he should always look the same, right?"

"Ooo, we're talkin' about you giving up the throne. I want to hear." Ansel plops down on a stool at the end of the counter, sitting away from me.

"You don't know?" I question.

Ansel shakes his head. "I was a little busy, and by the time I heard Cade abdicated, it was almost six months after the fact. News out here travels like the old west pre-telegrams. Yeah, how did no one put together the whole red wolf thing?"

"My father was very persuasive." Cade shakes his head with a sigh. He starts chopping up some bell peppers. "He had a lot of friends and made them part of the council that helps govern the wolves in North America. In our text, The Leviathan isn't described by the color of his coat, only by his semi-mythical traits. He's supposed to be ravenous, unbeatable, a monster who brings with him destruction and realignment of power. Even if anyone suspected that his wolf wasn't The Leviathan, he was strong, and no one wants to risk angering The Leviathan," he explains.

I'm mesmerized first by the stories and second by how he makes it look so easy to cut the pepper.

"It's dangerous to challenge an alpha because losing can be a loss of your life. People try not to do that as a rule of thumb. The exception being if an alpha becomes unstable," Ansel adds to the conversation. "It's even more risky to challenge an Ardelean alpha, especially if they're the Sovereign Alpha."

Fort Hall

River

WY

River

Bear Lake

Franklin

elton Corinne Green River City

GREAT Brigham City

Ogden City Echo City Green

SALT LAKE Evanston

Bingham Cañon Salt Lake City

Stockton Alta

Forest Cy. UINTAH MTS. Ft. Uin

Chapin Spr. York Ft. Rob

Mt. Pleasant River

U T A H

evier Manti

ake Richfield Green Grand River

Frisco

llion City ELK MTS.

arowan WAHSATCH MTS. Rio San

querville

River White

CHAPTER 26
CADE

"So, you became Sovereign?" Thalia coaxes me along.

"There was a pack dinner, and my father announced that Lena would accept intention from whoever offered the best deal for her."

The Leviathan snarls within me at the memory. He seethes anger.

"Woah." Thalia looks at me, her eyes big with shock. "We talked about arranged intentions, but that seems — cold."

"There's something different about Lena, she's special, and we're very protective of her."

I don't want to give away Lena's unique situation here, not where it could come out to the world. Thalia wouldn't intentionally hurt her, but she wouldn't understand. I chop peppers as fast as I can, trying to distract from those memories.

"You're a good older brother," Thalia says.

I still, the knife mid-chop. I look at her, and she bobs once in a hard nod, confirming her statement.

"Mmmm. I wouldn't say that." I draw a deep breath. *Do I explain how I fucked over Deacon and Lena by abdicating?* Her

243

limited knowledge makes the vote of confidence less sweet, but her loyalty is so pure. "I objected. My father told me to mind my place. Instead, I issued a challenge."

Ansel's become quiet with fewer interjections.

"I had The Leviathan. It was too late for anyone to stop the coming fight. I killed my father." I wait for a negative reaction.

Instead, they're both silent. I start whisking the eggs. I can't look at either of them. Ansel would understand the necessity of the challenge, but I've looked up to him for so long as far as leadership goes I don't want to potentially see disappointment.

"You did the right thing." Ansel's voice banishes the thought.

"Well, I was Sovereign Alpha at eighteen. I'd proven that my father was lying all those years." I summarize that night. No need to get into the nitty-gritty of a challenge fight.

The eggs are whisked, and all the other ingredients chopped. I start the frying pan and continue, "Robert had been groomed to take over. I had no interest in ruling, but it was over and done. The Leviathan, of course, was glad to have his rightful place."

"Okay, but you're not Sovereign now?" Thalia tries to piece it together.

Ansel fields that question. "Cade will always be Sovereign Alpha. Only in death can the title be taken from The Leviathan."

Peppers tossed into the pan, I give insight into the why. "I abdicated to Robert because I" — *how do you explain something like this?* — "I couldn't do it. Everything I touched went wrong. Nothing I ever did was good enough for anyone. So, I stepped away and gave Robert the throne. It seemed to be what everyone wanted. But once I did that, The Leviathan quit talking to me."

"You were eighteen!" Outrage fuels Thalia's voice. "They expected you to be Sovereign when you couldn't even legally drink?"

"I don't have an answer that makes sense." I shake my head. *How do I explain the level of insanity which was my life?* I offer her a soft smile. "The Leviathan was supposed to guide me. And with my gift, I was supposed to have the ability to make wolves listen and bring about change. Once I walked away from the throne, The Leviathan left me alone and without a gift. Ultimately, wolf culture and laws don't always make sense, it's based on a lot of really old rules that don't work."

"Like why they do arranged intentions?" Thalia offers.

"Exactly like arranged intentions," I agree.

Ansel closes the door to the dishwasher at the same time the back door opens.

Ezra sulks in and, with a giant groan, protests, "Ansel, I'm about ready to kill my neighbors."

"Then you should get your shit together and go home," Ansel snaps back at him with a sassy attitude.

Ezra immediately mocks his tone. "Well, aren't you the lucky one, all high and mighty, who doesn't have to deal with a controlling brother."

"Guys." I step closer to Thalia and wrap my arm around her shoulder possessively. I press out a bit of The Leviathan's power and cut myself into their conversation. "You two okay?"

Thalia bites her lips together, trying incredibly hard not to laugh at the sass between them. She doesn't see the potential danger of the two Alpha wolves pushing each other's buttons.

I'd like to think they wouldn't erupt into a brawl in Ansel's house, but stranger things have happened.

"Yeah." Ezra sighs, deflated. "Sorry, Ansel."

"No worries. It's been tough, we're all stressed." Ansel nods as he walks over to where Ezra has sat down on a stool and brushes against him, standing there for a few seconds. He looks around his house. "You know, I never notice how boring my house is until I'm supposed to entertain guests."

"Axe time?" Ezra asks.

Ansel shrugs. "Just because you live in New England doesn't mean you're automatically going to win."

"Axe time?" Thalia whispers.

I look down to see her eyes wide and more fear than confusion painted on her face.

Kissing her forehead, I answer, "Axe throwing. We like to stay physically active. So, we play a bunch of dumb yard games because there's only so much wood you can chop, buildings to build, or miles to run."

Ansel places a six-pack into the cooler while Ezra moves to set up outside.

"Come on, it'll be fun-ish." I offer my hand to Thalia, and we slip out the sliding glass door.

Ezra pulled the wooden target out from inside the garage, set it up along the edge of Ansel's yard, and is now pulling a few chairs over to a safe zone off to the side away from where we'll throw.

"So, what's going to be the game this time?" Ansel asks.

"See . . . I figured" — Ezra gives a sly smile — "two truths and a lie."

I growl at him, but Thalia interjects, "Ooo! I love that game."

"Great, because the way we play, you're going to be the subject." Ezra laughs.

Ansel plops down in one of the chairs, shaking his head.

"Wait, why me? Don't we take turns?" Thalia questions the rules to a game that has no rules.

I run my hand back through my hair. Ezra always has to stir the pot, doesn't he?

The Leviathan is quiet, completely unfazed by the nature of what is about to happen. He's content to just spend time with our people.

I don't make a mess of it. If things get out of hand, I'll remind Ezra of his place, and it'll be fine. At least, compared to some of the other games we've played, this one is partially meant for polite company.

"See, I can tell you what both of them are thinking," Ezra says, pointing between Ansel and me. He continues, "So, it's hardly fair, and then I don't get to play." Ezra continues to explain, "Cade knows almost every sandbox I ever shit in, and Ansel doesn't know enough about anything that's happened in the last fifteen years to be interesting."

"Uh. Okay?" Thalia questions but parks her butt in a chair.

"Alright, who's throwing to go first?" Ezra cocks the axe in one hand, spinning it around. "Same rules as always: closest axe to the center gets to pick the topic. Then our lovely volunteer subject, from the peanut gallery, will give us her two truths and a lie related to said topic."

"For the record" — I flash The Leviathan at Ezra — "this is a bad idea."

Ezra laughs. "Aren't they all when they come to women?"

Ansel shakes his head and pops up out of his chair, taking the axe from Ezra. I take his seat and sit next to Thalia, resting my hand on her thigh.

"Wait, does that mean I don't get to throw the axe?" Thalia looks at me with big puppy dog eyes.

Normally immune, even The Leviathan stirs seeing that

look. *Aww, puppy.* The Leviathan whimpers urging me closer to her.

"I'll let you throw an axe. But watch them for a few tries first?" I offer.

There's no way I'll ever be able to say no to her about anything. With eyes like that, her puppy privilege is far too high. Wolves are genetically predisposed to giving in to puppy demands. Even if we don't want to, there's that push to give them everything. Good thing I never intend to tell my mate no. I'll hand her the world on a platter if that's what it takes to be with her.

The axe flies across the yard and slams into the target hard. The wood cracks on impact. Thalia jumps, looking past me down range. Ezra and Ansel walk down to look.

"Lucky first shot!" Ezra laughs. "I don't think you could have hit that more dead on the head."

"Alright, Thalia. Two truths and a lie, make them as boring as you can." Ansel laughs, clearly taking pity on me.

Put on the spot, Thalia chews on her bottom lip for a second. "Okay. I've never been to the White House. I prefer cats to dogs. I've a green thumb."

Ansel sits down next to Thalia. "Really? Cats?"

Ezra shakes his head with his hand over his chest. He staggers a step backward. "Do you wish to wound us? Cats? Really, truly, Thalia?"

"Is that the lie?" I ask, playing along with the game and giving her thigh a small squeeze.

"Pft." Ansel returns with the axe handing it to me. "You're a terrible liar."

Thalia's face flushes. "In my defense . . . that plant was dead on arrival."

The laugh comes out before I can stop it, and Thalia looks

at me with a pout. I kiss her before I get out of the chair and stand in front of the target.

Ezra pops off the top of a beer and hands one to Ansel. He offers one to Thalia just as I go to throw the axe. The distraction lands my axe in the second zone of the target outside the bullseye.

"Ohhh, we've found Cade's weakness." Ezra chuckles. "The Luna doesn't get to have fun."

"I don't drink," Thalia says to him.

"Oh, he knows." My growl isn't stifled quickly enough as I return to the seat next to Thalia.

Laughing, Ezra goes and grabs the axe. He returns and gives Thalia a wink before sending it sailing down the range. It lands perfectly in the center.

He has a devious grin when he looks first at me and then at Thalia before opening his mouth. "Alright, Ms. Clark, let's not be so politically correct. Spill something dirty."

I could just kill you now. Judah would probably only be mad at me for a little bit. I glare at Ezra.

He shrugs. Ezra can bring out the best, or worst, in people in almost any situation.

Thalia bites her lips together, but she's got that sparkle of deviousness in her eyes. I pop the top off a beer. I'm too sober for whatever she's going to say next.

"Okay, so I've started an international incident when going skinny dipping in Egypt." Thalia pauses.

I struggle but manage to get the sip down. The Leviathan is snarling. I draw a deep breath and a pull of the beer. Even the thought of someone seeing her naked sets me on edge. We're wolves, for fuck's sake. People are going to see her naked when we're together as a mated pair. But that's the problem, isn't it? We're not. *Yet.*

"My first time was in the coat closet of a meeting of the United Nations." She continues with her final one, "I was kicked out of the Vatican Museums for fooling around in the emergency exit."

Ansel's eyes meet mine. Ezra's got his head cocked. I look at Thalia. None of us are able to figure out which one is the lie. Given the limited experience I've had with her, and what Ansel observed, Thalia's a shitty liar. I adjust my jaw, confused.

"Did she just learn to lie?" Ansel asks slowly.

Thalia sits there, pleased with herself, and wiggles her butt in her seat. I down my beer because I'm not ready for this. Drinking gives me time to think. But none of the thoughts are good.

We hunt man touched mate. Then please mate best. The Leviathan nods, listing off how he wants to handle things. At least his first thought wasn't gifting her a wolf?

I should have known I couldn't trust Ezra to keep this tame.

In an attempt to determine what he can't hear using his gift, Ezra examines her. "You know, something makes me hope that it's the coat closet for Cade's sake, but I'm leaning toward skinny dipping."

"I'm going the other way. I think she's been kicked out of the Vatican but not for the emergency exit." Ansel says as he toes the dirt, taking the axe from Ezra.

"Thalia?" Ezra prompts carefully.

I'm going to fucking kill you. I think nice and loud, letting The Leviathan contemplate murder for talking about our mate that way.

She shrugs. "It wasn't at the Vatican."

Ezra walks toward the cooler, keeping his chest turned toward me, before returning and handing me another beer as a peace offering. "You can kick my ass at Solstice. This was so not what I was expecting."

The axe goes down the field again, and with deadly

accuracy, Ansel hits the center of the target, drawing my attention. I send lethal thoughts and murderous intentions to Ezra.

"Alright, a bit lighter subject?" Ansel offers. "Let's hear about your nicknames?"

Thalia shakes her head but starts slowly, "When I was in the third grade, my mom braided my hair, and the kids called me Pippy Longstocking for the entire year."

She pauses, and Ansel cuts in, adjusting his ponytail. "What's a Pippy Longstocking?"

"Beats me." I shrug at him.

We both turn to Ezra.

"Uh, I'm pretty sure that's a child left unsupervised living on an island and maybe has a monkey." Ezra squints, racking his brain.

"Pretty much," Thalia confirms.

A gust of breeze carries the scent of blood. I stand quickly, turning to face the wind. Ansel comes to my side, both of us facing the direction of the wind and protecting Thalia. One of the pack members, Zero, stumbles around the side of Ansel's house, holding his arm close to his chest. Instinctively, I step in front of where Thalia's sitting, putting myself between her and the danger. Ezra pulls out his phone and starts dialing.

"Rachet, that asshole, dislocated my shoulder," Zero shouts and it turns to a coughing fit. He tries to point, forgetting his injured arm. "He's headed south. There's nothing left."

"Take her inside," Ansel instructs me coolly.

Protect mate, end fracture. The Leviathan presses forward. He's tuned into the scent of blood and Thalia's fear in the air. The Leviathan is ready for what will come next.

I offer my hand to Thalia; she takes it, stepping out of the chair she was sitting in. I pull her close and kiss the top of her hair.

"Stay close to Ansel, I'll be back before it gets too late."

Ansel shakes his head when I try to place Thalia's hand in his.

I override him. "All the more reason to help, they need you here and steady."

I head toward the house at a jog while Ezra is on the phone next to me, talking to Ben. Ezra stops at Zero, who's leaning against the deck in rough shape. I've seen far worse and know Zero will be fine, but it doesn't change that he's in pain. With one last look over my shoulder, I see Ansel focusing on Thalia while leading her toward the house. I pull my shirt off and move out of her sight to shift.

CHAPTER 27

THALIA

ANSEL HOLDS MY HAND, tucking it under his elbow to rest on his forearm. He pats it gently.

"Come on, little human, time to go inside."

Ansel's pace is slow with small steps; we're never going to get there.

On approach, Ezra has Zero down on the ground, and Ansel whispers, "Close your eyes, you don't need to see this."

"See what?" I whisper back. *Why are we whispering?*

"Zero's a mess. You don't need to see Ezra putting him back together. We'll go in the house and play cards."

Ansel tries to stay between me and the scene, blocking it with his chest.

Despite his best efforts, I dodge around Ansel on the way up the stairs to catch a glimpse. I thought Zero had been wearing a dark shirt, but now that we're closer, I see his shirt was white. It's dark because it's soaked in blood. I close my eyes against the lightheadedness.

Ansel whispers to step at each stair before ushering me into the house. When we're inside, he closes the blinds against the afternoon sun and the scene of the yard.

Promptly heading to the kitchen, it's like this is a normal everyday occurrence for Ansel. He opens cupboards and takes out drinking glasses.

"He was covered in blood. Ansel, is he okay?" I ask, hands covering my mouth.

Ansel stops moving around in the kitchen, and his head bobs back and forth. He turns, looking at me. I could have sworn his eyes were green. But now they're so dark, they nearly look black. Then he's lost to a thousand-yard stare until his eyes turn ghostly white.

Sure, Cade's eyes have changed to beautiful gold, but this looks possessed. I step back away from him, bumping into the wall. Despite being next to the door, I feel trapped in the corner of the room. Cade's left me with Ansel and said I could trust him. But now he looks downright terrifying. *If you can't find me, Ansel is your only friend. No matter how nice someone is.*

I remind myself I've no reason not to trust Cade's statement.

With one hard blink, Ansel's eyes are back to the quirky green color I was so sure they had been.

"Yeah. Zero will be just fine." Ansel nods and then rubs his eyes a bit.

I've gotten to know Ansel in person for less than a day. This Ansel is completely different from the one I met yesterday morning. He's not smiling. He pulls out a few bottles of alcohol from the back of a cupboard. The back door opens, and I can see it's two of the guys from our gathering around the fire pit yesterday.

"Ezra's got Zero's shoulder back in place. He and Dale are taking him to his cabin to get some rest and wait for Doc. Dale said he'd button up the other cabin and give the damage a once over," the one I think is Sully reports.

Ansel just keeps nodding, pouring himself a stiff drink over ice. Is he agreeing or acknowledging? It's a few minutes of us standing in silence, waiting for something.

The other guy, who is also apparently equally uncomfortable with awkward silence, steps around Sully. He offers his hand to me.

"It's a pleasure to see you again, Emily, I'm Vito."

I shake his hand; they're rough like a laborer's hands. "It's nice to see you, Vito."

"Let's play cards, boss." Sully walks over and hugs Ansel for almost a full minute.

I divert my eyes, looking around for some indication of what I should be doing.

I catch Vito's attention. "What game?"

"Don't get too excited, Luna. We don't play poker or anything fancy. We play the old ladies' game."

Vito goes to the cabinet under the television and pulls out a bag of cards and a well-loved composition notebook.

"Hand and Foot Canasta." Sully clues me in.

Walking over, he has a half smile on his face.

Once we're all seated at the table, I notice how they've cornered me in. I'm not sure if that means anything, but I try not to seem uneasy. I try to keep myself from squirming or bouncing in my seat. I'm able to settle with tapping my toe quietly against the floor.

Ansel sits next to me, putting a glass of water in front of me. He gives me a soft smile.

"You're not cornered, you're protected. Someone would have to go over the table or through me to get to you."

"I thought Ezra was the one who reads minds?" I scratch

my head at him, hoping it means the same thing in wolf and human body language.

"You seem a bit nervous. Besides, you'll want to be partners with Sully, he's the best player here. It's more fun if you win your first time playing," Ansel says.

His smile, despite the sorrow, tries to bloom.

Vito moves about in Ansel's kitchen, putting various snacks in bowls and bringing additional drinks over for everyone. Sully goes about shuffling the cards and explaining the rules. He hands me a small piece of paper laminated with packing tape a few times over. Rules in hand and the cards apparently shuffled seventeen times, we all count cards out for hands and feet.

All the guys seem mostly normal. We're playing our hands and into our feet, and it's going really well. I keep reminding myself what Cade implied about them. I just don't notice anything that seems out of the ordinary. Aside from witnessing Ansel's gift in the kitchen, it's all so ordinary. I'm more comfortable than I've ever been in a room full of men.

We've had a late lunch and talked about starting dinner. The sun is starting to sink in the sky, and I'm getting worried about Cade. He made it sound like this wouldn't be a big deal. Was Cade sparing my feelings? No one else seems to be fazed by his absence.

We're playing the second game of Canasta when the back door opens.

Ansel leans over and looks down the hallway. He then looks at Sully. "Go get Doc."

Sully darts out the sliding glass door. Ansel pulls me out from behind the table.

"Don't look, stay behind me." Ansel keeps me close behind him.

Not having learned my lesson with Zero, I slowly look around him. Cade is clutching his side, stumbling forward through the hallway. Vito approaches cautiously, crouching down into Cade's line of sight.

"Sovereign, can you hear me?" Vito asks loudly.

I duck back behind Ansel, covering my face with my hands. The sound of Cade stumbling forward is replaced with a primal and animalistic growl. I've never heard that kind of noise. It doesn't even sound like the animals on television.

"Stay right here, don't move from this spot." Ansel is talking to me. His hands touch my shoulders.

Cade falls to the floor in slow motion. A puddle of blood quickly pools around him. My eyes are frozen open. I cover my mouth with my hands to stop the scream fighting to escape from my lungs.

Vito tries to get him up, but Cade is so much larger. Ansel walks over and helps pull Cade to his feet. The back door opens, and Ben darts in through the same hallway Cade came in.

Hurriedly Ben begins assessing while muttering under his breath. All I catch is his question. "Can we get him downstairs?"

Ansel blows a raspberry. "Let's try."

Cade growls, helping them as much as he can to get to the basement, hands holding his stomach tightly.

When they're down the stairs, I'm left alone with Ansel's instructions not to move. *Really?*

Carefully, I step around the puddle on the floor toward the top of the stairs, which Cade pointed out as off-limits before.

There's a crash of what sounds like metal on concrete. My feet move without instructions.

Bright fluorescent lights overhead don't do the sight of Ansel's basement any favors. Jail cells with thick bars and concrete are along the back wall. I follow the commotion around to behind the stairs. *Now's not the time to question the prison basement.*

Ben is filling a syringe, and Ansel is now holding Cade's stomach while Vito pulls out medical supplies. Blood is everywhere. So much blood.

My head swarms, and despite lack of movement, I'm hot all over.

"We need him awake! Don't put him under until we know it's over," Ansel instructs.

Ansel's hands and arms are coated in dark red as he presses against Cade's abdomen.

"Dead. Two miles south, follow blood," Cade answers, his voice raspy. "No sedation. Just stitches. The Leviathan," he gasps, "didn't want to be away."

Ben keeps working, filling a syringe with something. My guess is some sort of painkiller.

Time moves funny. Is it slow? Fast?

Cade's shoulders arch on the table. His body writhes.

I'm wobbly watching.

"Cade, you can't be awake for this. I'll make it fast." Ben doesn't give him an option. He jabs Cade with the needle.

I must have made a sound because Ansel's eyes are on me.

His voice is so assertive, much harsher than Cade's. "Thalia, get out of here. Close the door. Go upstairs."

My feet don't move.

"He's sedated. If she's not squeamish, there's no reason she can't stay," Ben answers with his eyes never leaving Cade's body. He goes to move Ansel's arms. "Let's check the damage."

"Thalia?" Ansel's voice calls out.

Everything looks fuzzy. I'm woozy and I wobble.
Vito stands in front of me. Where did he come from?

CHAPTER 28
CADE

THE BRIGHTNESS of the morning light is highly offensive, more so than normal. I squeeze my eyes against the light, but it doesn't block it better. How am I going to sleep until my alarm if I can't block it out? *Why didn't I close the blinds?* Every inch of me feels like pins and needles. *What did I fall asleep on?* I try to pull my eyes open. *Sleep feels too good.* This must just be first light. I left the blinds open.

I try to roll to get up. Nothing is responding. *Sleep feels good. Just a few more minutes.*

I'm cold, even lying in the brightness of the sun. My body is stiff and sore. I must have gone for a run and fallen asleep. I draw in a breath, trying to stretch. My body burns with various pain. Pins and needles are now laced with the sting of stretching raw skin. The scents of soap, metal, and stone mix with the coppery scent of fresh blood.

I'm not lying in the sunlight. It's not earth beneath my body.

Ansel's house, sitting with Thalia, the hunt, ending a life, the pain in my stomach, the sensitivity of my open wound in my hands, and the kennels all take their turn in my brain.

If I open my eyes, will I find myself in one of Ansel's kennels? Who knows how long I've been out? *Fucking Ben.* The darkness of unconsciousness grips at me.

Thalia? This time my extremities respond when I demand movement. It's slow but progress.

The Leviathan is quiet. Nonresponsive. I search for him, and he's still there, not waking.

Fucking Ben. Where is Thalia?

I sit up before opening my eyes. Pain hits me hard with a wave of nausea.

I push through it before finally opening my eyes. Surprisingly enough, I'm not in one of Ansel's kennels, and blinking through the light, I see Ansel sitting in the corner on a lawn chair, reading a book.

He looks up at me, unfazed, and then puts a piece of paper in his book, marking the page and placing it on the counter. Ansel doesn't say anything while he watches.

Blinking hard, trying to stay awake, I ask, "Thalia?"

"She's upstairs in bed," he answers softly, tilting his head to the side.

My eyes close involuntarily, and I shake my head, trying to escape the grogginess. When I move my feet, pain radiates up my torso. I force them over the side of the table, sitting up with them hanging over the edge. Forcing open my eyes, I look down. Stitches are everywhere. Deep claw marks scabbing over between stitches cover my ribs. The worst of the damage is to my stomach. Bite marks mix in with the scratches, traveling down too close to the family jewels for comfort.

Sliding off the medical table, I wobble. It takes me a minute to find my feet.

Ansel stands next to me, bracing, ready to catch me but still quiet.

"It was that close of a call; you stayed up to be down here with me?" I ask, swallowing hard, trying to force moisture into my throat.

Wolves don't want to let others die alone, not if it can be helped.

"I didn't want you to wake up in a locked kennel, alone, and wondering where your mate was. Contrary to popular belief, you're not fractured, and I don't want to treat you that way." Ansel speaks softly. "You weren't at risk of dying. I've told you, set in stone. Old age. Ben just didn't know when you'd wake up. One night of missing sleep won't kill me."

I take the first step. Hopefully, when I get moving, my body will limber up. I look for The Leviathan in the darkest parts of my mind. He's completely absent. It's back to a normal that I no longer wish to know the feeling of. After just a few short days of him actively participating in my thoughts, his absence is eerie.

I head to the stairs, unable to stay down here and away from her any longer. Ansel follows me, turning off lights and checking the doors are locked. Including the doors to the 'sleepers,' as he calls them — the cold storage for the dead bodies until Ansel gets instructions on how to care for the remains.

"Good night, Steve." Ansel's voice is tender as he says good night to the man I ended.

I'm reminded that Ansel's pack doesn't use first names but instead nicknames of various forms. Sometimes, only Ansel really knows their names. If only to use it in the purpose of death.

Halfway up the stairs, I stop, turning to watch him. On the lower landing Ansel pauses, scrubbing his hand down his face, before closing the door to the basement. He spins the vault-style lock, and my heart aches for him knowing he's grieving silently.

The darkness of night cloaks the house, assuring me I haven't been unconscious too long. On the main floor, I pause, listening. Soft breathing and a murmuring voice come from the loft, sounding like Thalia's having a dream.

"Go give yourself a sink bath. I'll get you some food. Ben said not to get the wounds wet until they start closing up, the stitches will dissolve on their own. You can use my bath so you don't wake up your mate." Ansel nudges me toward his bathroom, tossing me a pair of sweatpants.

THIRTY MINUTES LATER, I'm mostly clean-ish. Ansel sets two plates, heaping with a variety of food, in front of me at the dining table. He sits across from me, closing his eyes. My growling stomach calls for sustenance, and I oblige. I open my mouth to tell Ansel to go to bed, but he speaks first.

"You know your mate stops breathing when she's stressed?" Ansel asks quietly, one eye opening slowly to watch me.

Between bites, I nod warily. I listen more intensely to the sounds of the house. Soft breathing is still there. I'm positive it's her. The faint smell of her lingers here on the main level. It's only been a little while since she was here.

Ansel sighs but does reassure me, "She's fine, but that's a fucked up response to stress. It's fight, flight, and freeze, but I wasn't sure that was supposed to apply to breathing." Ansel shakes his head. "That's not an every human thing, right? I've never seen it before."

I swallow before taking a drink of water. Trying to explain something I don't yet know how to explain myself is hard.

"From my understanding, it's an anxiety attack, partially a response to stimuli and chemical imbalances in the brain."

"Damn." Ansel nods. "Permanent?"

I shrug. "Humans have meds for it. I guess I don't know enough about it. But it makes me wonder, if wolves had better access to medical care and their brain chemistry, what would that mean? Would we find answers to issues like tonight that could be treatable?"

"Too many wolves believe we're too invincible to be sick. I doubt a brain disease would be any different." Ansel pauses, deflating in his chair.

I can nearly see the gears in his brain turning as he thinks it through.

"Broke down and fractured is one thing. But for there to be a disease. Well, you'd have a better chance of convincing them than I ever will." Ansel rakes his fingers through his hair.

"It didn't cause any issues when you told Franco I was the one who ended his brother?" I ask. "I didn't even think if that would be an issue when I offered."

"Franco Castillo only cared that he could quit payin' me to take care of him. He couldn't find two fucks to rub together about the implications of the Sovereign doing shit he shouldn't be doin'." Ansel huffs, shaking his head. He draws a deep breath and then moves past it. "Ezra said he'll put a hole in the ground for me tomorrow."

"What do you mean? Paying you?" I put my fork down.

Ansel should be living fully off his access to the Ardelean fund. Even if he wasn't of the Ardelean bloodline, the job he does for the packs, the station of Reaper, should be an all-expense paid position. Ansel shouldn't ever have to even think about money.

Ansel waves his hand dismissively. "Robert cut me and Judah's bunch out 'bout two years ago. He told me his new plan was for each pack to pay for their wolves to be here. Partly why I grew the landscape and farmhand business."

"If he was going to cut anyone, he should have tried cutting me off." I want to growl, but The Leviathan is still slumbering. I'm enraged. "And Judah? Why didn't anyone fucking tell me?"

"From what Ezra said, it's because of how large Judah's pack is that his pack fund should be self-sufficient." Ansel runs his hand behind his neck and yawns. "It's been manageable, mostly. He sends money for Ben to be here. Musta forgot that Doc wants to be here, not *has* to be. We knew you didn't want to get involved. Until these new issues with the humans, there really hadn't been an issue."

I stab a potato on my plate, taking my eyes off Ansel, chewing my aggression through the spud.

"That sly motherfucker. Are you financially okay?"

Ansel doesn't answer and remains silent for another minute while I'm eating. But then he takes full advantage of my chewing to change subjects, hand motioning through the air like he's just brushing the previous conversation aside.

"Full disclosure: your mate passed out because apparently humans are fragile and quit breathing as a defense mechanism. Why is no one talkin' about how they've survived this long as a species? When she came to, she and I kinda had a talk through the bathroom door. Apparently, people don't just kill people and behave like it's fine. Also, veterinarians don't just stitch people up in creepy dungeon basements. Eventually, she did come out and let Ben check out her head. He said she doesn't have a concussion, but he gave her an ice pack for the swelling, said she'd be fine in a day or so. Cade, I have to be honest, I'm not sure what you're gonna do with her."

Ansel's wolf, Harbinger, glints in the low light, hauntingly looking at me through the dark. There's more Ansel wants to say, but he waits.

I take what he said and sit with it for a moment, eating slowly. It takes me a while before I can say it. They're words I never thought I'd think, let alone speak.

"I don't know what I'm going to do without her."

The realization hits hard. Without The Leviathan and his illogical arguments, I struggle to swallow. How, in the shortest time, have I become entangled in a bigger mess than I had ever fathomed?

"I was worried you were going to say that." Ansel pauses. "We need to talk about what I've seen."

Dread sinks in my stomach. I know it's about his gift. He tries to break the news of your death or a loved one's as softly as possible, but if you don't have time, you don't have time.

I nod with acknowledgment. "Did you tell her?"

He shakes his head but doesn't wait for me to ask any more questions. "It's the strangest thing, Cade. She dies twice."

"You see mixed paths all the time."

I think back to our discussions on Deacon and fractured wolves here, shaking my head, putting my silverware down. I can hardly look at the rest of the food in front of me.

Ansel's shaking his head. "Not like this. Cade, she dies twice. It's in stone but different. She's with you by your side when you go. But I don't understand how, because Harry and I are seeing that she dies . . . soonish. I would say within the next six months. Then, when she's old and gray."

I can't growl. The Leviathan isn't here; the sedation hasn't let him free of its clutches.

I shake my head. "That can't be. How can someone die twice?"

"With her, I don't see what I normally do. There're two instances, both just pieces. One young, one old. The clock strikes zero twice." Ansel shrugs at me before urging, "I don't have an answer, but you know who might?"

She can't die. She can't. Six months? I scrub my hand down my face. My stomach is in knots. *How the fuck can someone die twice? What does that even mean? An accident? A hospitalization?* I need answers. Six months isn't enough time.

My eyes snap to Ansel. "What time is it?"

Ansel looks over my shoulder to answer my question. "Uhm . . . weird question, but it's ten after two."

"Four in the morning on the East Coast." I do the math aloud. "Do you know where my phone ended up?"

Ansel points next to me. "You're not very observant."

My clothes and phone are sitting on the chair next to me.

I shake my head, picking it up. I don't bother texting. I find her contact and dial.

"Dinah," I answer him while waiting for the phone to ring.

Despite it being so early, Dinah answers the phone on the second ring. "Hey, sexy bagel. Oh, you're not going to go all formal on me now that you're top dog again, are you?"

"Top dog? No?" I shake my head. She isn't making sense. "I know you know why I'm calling. I just got trashed when ending a fracture, and I'm sorry, Dinah, but I don't have —"

"Oh, calm down," Dinah cuts me off. "I don't know why you two couldn't figure it out. You're both bright boys. To turn a wolf, you've got to take them to the edge of death; it's the only way to ask a wolf to save them."

That thought hangs there in the air.

Ansel nods. "I suppose no one has done any real studying on it, have they? Maybe we always thought it was close to death when in reality, it's new life?"

"Science wasn't super accurate back in the day. Heck, we still don't have birth control, only suppressants, and how long have they been working on that?" Dinah huffs.

I'm nearly certain I can hear her eyes rolling.

"It's not like we can exactly do experiments on it." I cover my mouth. "Do you know how she's turned?"

"Oh, come now." Dinah sasses. "Unless The Leviathan can command me to tell you that over the phone, that secret is staying with me."

I can't. She knows it. Even if I wanted to, which I've tried on more than one occasion, my gift doesn't work over the phone. I've no choice but to accept her coy games. A growl might intimidate her into more information, but I'm at her mercy, and The Leviathan is still silent.

"Cade," Dinah says softly. Her sassy attitude dissipates. "I know you pretty well. You can't . . . it's going to happen when it's going to happen. Thalia will be wolf, and she'll be fine. Don't force this."

"Thanks," I answer.

She's being cryptic, but Dinah's gift isn't black-and-white either. I take the little reassurance that Thalia will be fine and hold that hope tightly.

"Now." The softness is gone, and Dinah's sass is back. "I'm going to remind you how rude it is to call me just for a vision. You're going to apologize, and next time you think about calling me for one, you remember that I like sparkly things, fancy chocolate, concerts in NYC, and I wear a size ten running shoe," Dinah lists off coyly, pausing, as she would say, for dramatic effect. "Please be mindful that I'm not your personal fortune teller in a glass box at a carnival."

"I'm sorry, Dinah. It's my mate, and I hope you never feel the fear I just had." I also pause, for dramatic effect. "Your offerings to the goddess have been noted. Have a good night, Ms. Mona Lott."

"Yas!" Dinah laughs at the joke. "I love you. Sleep well."

"I love you too." I hang up the phone and set it on the table. I look across at Ansel. "What do I do?"

With a yawn, Ansel stands from across the table. He stretches, rolling his shoulders before tapping one finger on the table in front of me. "My one request — not that I should be making one after today — don't show your mate why she wants a wolf in bed. Either wait for tomorrow or take it outside. I want to sleep. Tomorrow, the crew's got a greenhouse build, and sorting the hierarchy dynamics after a death is difficult." Ansel's stocking feet shuffle across the floor as he calls back out behind himself, "Good night."

"There won't be any unsavory sounds from the loft tonight," I assure him. I wasn't exactly asking about right now, but we're both tired. "Sleep well, Ansel."

HAVING some reassurance from Dinah that Ansel's vision does make sense, I finish washing my plates and gently set them in the sink, keeping the noise level down for Ansel. The Leviathan begins to wake from the anesthesia. He's slow moving but immediately pushes, looking for her. *Our mate. Need her. Draga mea.*

My feet move silently across the floor and then up to the loft. I walk to the bedroom she doesn't occupy. The Leviathan demands we cross the landing to the open door of the room she's lying in. Without much convincing, I do. The door swings open, and tucked in underneath the large quilt is Thalia, curled in on herself. She's shivering.

There's no going back to the room we were supposed to occupy. *Our mate freezes. Needs more warmth. We are warm. We sleep here.*

It's a slow process, lying down with stitches and tender

skin. The healing process after a fight with a worthy opponent like that is more than a little uncomfortable. After struggling, I'm finally horizontal. It only takes a small roll, and I'm in range to pull her back toward me.

"Mmmm, Cade?" she murmurs, not quite awake.

"Shhh, draga mea, it's time to sleep."

I kiss the top of her head before my eyes close.

THE METALLIC CLANG of pans on the stovetop wakes me. The bed is too empty. I'm not surprised she isn't next to me when I open my eyes. When I go to move, the sheet moves with me. With a small tug, the stitches let go of the sheet. Upon inspection, blood droplets stain the sheets. I strip the bed before using the facilities. Then put on my clothes before heading down to the cooking commotion on the lower level.

Thalia is the source of the noise. She's magnetic, and I'm a ferrous metal. Caught in her field, I'm pulled to her. The bed sheet is abandoned in the hallway by the laundry machines. I'm stiff, and my healing skin protests, but enveloping her tightly in my arms takes priority over a little pain.

Standing behind her, I bow my head and bury my nose into her hair, drawing in her rich, heavy scent. Slow deep breaths. It's a cathartic reassurance that everything is okay. She leans back against me with my arms around her. The weight of her body pushing against my tender skin isn't unpleasant enough for me to stop her. We stay like that for a moment until I grip her hips and shift her around to face me. She looks at me expectantly. I cup her cheek while bringing my lips to hers.

I pour everything I can't say into the kiss. *Can't say just yet.* I know I wasn't near death last night, but it was a closer fight than I would have liked. The thought of something happening to me without her knowing what she means to me drives me to deepen the kiss.

She parts her lips, and I nibble on her bottom one before sweeping my tongue where my teeth just were. Then I find her tongue with mine. Thalia moves her hands into my hair, gripping the strands and pulling me even closer to her. I wrap one arm around the small of her back to eliminate any space between us at all. Cradling the back of her head with my other hand, we're held together, locked by our need for each other. The way she matches my intensity gives me hope that she's starting to feel even a fraction of what I am. I know it's all I can ask for at this point.

Love her. Want draga mea forever. The Leviathan has apparently awakened enough to start requesting hard honesty early.

CHAPTER 29
THALIA

"WHAT WERE YOU TRYING TO COOK?" Cade gives my nose a small kiss before stepping away, gesturing at the ingredients I dug out from the fridge.

"Um, okay, so." I gesture to the egg carton. "Eggs."

Cade indicates to the other fifteen or so items I'd chosen out of the fridge and the cupboards.

"Okay, and with this?"

"No idea." I shake my head. "I'm going to be honest. I don't know how to cook."

"Yeah, I figured." Cade laughs with his deep chuckle.

He puts over half the ingredients I had out back in the fridge, then switches the pan on the stove out for a different one. His hand gently wraps around my waist, pulling me to a cutting board. A knife, bell pepper, and onion sit, waiting expectantly. I watch him silently demonstrate how to hold the knife: thumb and index finger pinching the blade. He sets it down and motions for me.

Hesitantly, I repeat the motions. He pulls the pepper

toward us with his other hand, showing me how to hold my fingers curled away from the knife. It's silent communication and soft-touched corrections while he shows me how to chop the fresh ingredients. Chopping is a distraction from what I'd rather be doing with Cade. But I don't know how to ask him for it, and it hardly seems like a pressing matter.

So many times, I open my mouth to say something, but Cade's silence is a serenity I didn't know existed. Gently stirring onions in the pan, watching them turn translucent, I want to talk about what happened last night. He almost died.

Through the bathroom door last night, Ansel tried to explain it. By killing that person, Cade was protecting all of us. Some people can't be saved, and the best thing to do is honor them by not letting them hurt or kill someone accidentally. To preserve their legacy. Their loved one's memory of them doesn't need to be tainted with the last action, harmful action, they've performed. The logic of death with dignity is so educated. It's respectful.

But what gives them the right to be judge, jury, and executioner? Zero's body, covered in blood, flashes back into my mind. That certainly makes a case against the recently deceased. *I might be in the wrong trying to justify this with what I know.* I'm trying to apply my upbringing, laws, and ideals to a different culture and expecting them to fit. The life experiences of wolves are vastly different.

When the onions are done, Cade cracks eggs with one hand, dropping them into a bowl. It looks so easy. Cooking isn't so hard when he shows me how.

"Can I do one?"

"Yeah. Two hands." He demonstrates, pulling me in front of him. "Watch out for shells."

It's gooey as it slips into the bowl. He offers me the garbage can for the shell and then ushers me to the sink. We take our turns washing our hands.

Wiping his hands on the towel, he says, "I'm guessing you've quite a bit to say about last night."

CHAPTER 30
CADE

THALIA DOESN'T ANSWER.

Standing behind her while she scrambles eggs, I whisper against her head, my hands gently petting her shoulders, "Where's your head at, draga mea?"

She gives me a heavy sigh. I expected hesitancy, but Thalia's voice is steady. "I'm worried that by understanding and accepting you've killed a man, it makes me seem complacent to death. That by me accepting he had to die makes me, I don't know . . ."

"An accomplice, less human, nihilistic, or something else?" I offer, not wanting to let that hang for too long.

"Yes," Thalia confirms, evidently all the options.

Despite her answering a multiple-choice question with a nonstandard option, it's not confusing.

I try a soft smile to assure her that the change in her thought process isn't bad. "Ansel's job is to protect humans from wolves at all costs. Our laws aren't as concrete because there's no way to quantify some of the criteria we use to make

281

decisions. Steve was very sick, and Ansel gave him all the time he could. In the past, his predecessors wouldn't have taken the risk. By our laws, Ansel doesn't have to either. Understanding that sick and fractured wolves sometimes need to be killed to protect everyone doesn't change who you are. Death . . . is an unfortunate part of life. Given my and Ansel's stations within our world, we have a calling to be the end for some."

"You make it seem so easy. You killed someone yesterday."

Mate be proud. We strong and deadly. The Leviathan misinterprets what's going on.

No. I try to explain, *mate scared. She doesn't want us hurt. Doesn't like violence like wolves.*

"I did. Ending him for Ansel eased Ansel's pain. That's what mattered to me. Steve had to die yesterday, no matter which of us did it. So, I did the best I could to reduce the pain around that. I saved Ansel from having to end another friend." I kiss the base of her neck.

She nods slowly. "I'm okay, and I'm starting to think that being okay is also okay. Sometimes, growth doesn't make sense."

There's definitely tension between us. We eat in silence, but after we finish the meal, Thalia's ready to talk. She's upset, her eyes filled with emotion. Despite a substantial meal, my stomach feels hollow.

Her words are strong and almost scolding. "When you were hurt, all I wanted was for you to be okay. My heart hurt. I was afraid, and it wasn't for my survival. I felt lied to when you said no one could kill you, yet you came back looking like death."

I need her closer. Everything she's said has been fair, not accusatory. I offer my hand out to her across the table. I debate standing up, going to her, and pulling her close, but she denies the touch, not bringing hers across the table. The truth hurts. I scared my mate.

This is the second time she's been in a scary situation, but her fear isn't for her well-being, it's for mine. My chest aches with that realization.

Bite mate. Claim mate. She know wolf. The Leviathan tries to problem solve.

"I don't have a way to make this better. Last night was tough. The Leviathan and I didn't work well together." I try to explain. "But this isn't a normal thing. This isn't something I anticipate needing to do a lot of. And I assure you, if I do, my injuries should never be that severe again. The Leviathan and I are connecting better."

"Should isn't very convincing," Thalia says, but she finally takes my hand.

I squeeze her hand. "I get that. I don't know how to prove it to you right now. But, I'll figure it out."

STANDING and sitting at the dining room table wasn't terrible with my healing stitches. I'm happy to be a shifter and have significantly faster healing functionality. But sitting on the sofa next to her, watching a movie, is frustrating. Getting comfortable was hard, and she tried to baby me a few times, but I just pulled her close and let her lean on me. Reveling in her touch, I feel better just having her next to me.

A MOVIE AND A HALF LATER, Ansel comes home. He doesn't say anything, even when Thalia greets him. He pulls out a mixing bowl and an old hand beater. We pause the movie to watch over the back of the couch as he starts making cookies.

"Ansel bakes when he's angry," I whisper to Thalia.

"I can hear you," Ansel says. "Turn the movie back on, don't stop on my account."

There's a lot of tension hanging in the air. The urge to protect Thalia is too much, and I wrap my arm around her. Turning the television back on as Ansel instructed, I keep an eye on him from the corner of my eye.

Thalia's picking up on the atmosphere of the room. The scent of fear is faint but present. Petting her shoulder, I try to assure her there's nothing to worry about.

A few minutes later, Ansel tosses a sheet pan of cookies in the oven and sets his egg timer. He grabs a beer out of the fridge and sits with us. Ansel's not watching the movie. He stares at the screen, processing whatever it is that's upset him. I'll ask when the film finishes, but Ansel's insistence we finish it is an easy enough request.

Perfectly timed, Ansel's cookies are done as the credits roll.

"Do you want to talk about it?" I offer, slowly following Ansel to the kitchen.

It's then I see the problem. A rich-blue colored envelope and a letter sit on the counter. I push the letter open and start to read it to myself.

He growls. "I'd ask if you got one of these, but since you're here, I'm guessing it's at your place and wouldn't be seen yet."

The letter is written with the ridiculous frilly language that Robert likes to use. But the long and the short of it is disgusting and egotistical.

I shake the paper. "The fuck is Robert trying to prove? Did anyone else get one?"

"Just opened it. Figured I'd see if you knew anything. I think there's one for Ezra, but I don't make it a habit to open other people's mail. I dropped it off at his cabin." Ansel grumbles.

Thalia is completely silent as she sits on one of the stools at the bar. I want to include her and explain, but truthfully, I don't quite understand what this means and why Robert is trying to have Ansel, and likely Ezra, prove their claim to the Ardelean line.

CHAPTER 31
THALIA

SOMETHING IS WRONG. Last night, amid the chaos of death, Ansel wasn't his perky self, but he was more lighthearted than he is now.

Cade pulls the phone from his ear and pops it on speaker.

A woman's voice answers, "Hello?"

"Lena. You home?" Cade asks.

"Yeah, why?" His sister yawns.

"Did we get any mail from the council?"

Cade remains standing, the pages of the letter spread out before him. I watch him move his head, still examining them closer.

Lena doesn't answer right away. There's shuffling on the other end.

Her tone changes, each word coming through the line with hesitation. "Uhhh. Yeah. One for each of us. What's going on?"

"Open one, please," Cade asks.

He scrubs his hand down his face, then scratches a spot in his beard.

"It's a summons for a blood test. Cade, are they questioning the lineage?" Her voice tremors.

"Nothing to worry about. We've got gifts. This is a fishing expedition. Take some deep breaths, let's not implode. I'll fix it. It's going to be okay, Lena," Cade assures her, his voice soft. "I promise."

"Okay." Lena still sounds uncomfortable, but she seems to trust him.

Ansel takes a pan of cookies out of the oven, pulls the parchment paper off the pan, and puts the paper directly onto a cooling rack. He licks his lips, excited.

"I love you. It'll be okay. I'm calling Judah. I'll keep you posted."

Cade keeps reassuring her, nodding out of habit. It's obviously so ingrained in the body language and physical communication that he can't help it.

"Love you too," she confirms softly before hanging up.

Cade rolls his head up and looks at the ceiling. Dumbly, Ansel and I do as well.

I bring my gaze down to see Ansel making eyes at the cookies while letting out a whistle.

"You think Robert cutting us off has anything to do with this?"

"I know it. The only reason he and the council want a blood test is to try and prove we aren't entitled. Cutting you off and now trying to prove it is a huge statement." Cade shakes his head, bringing his attention back down to his phone.

He pauses, looking over at me for a moment. The anger for the letter leaves him.

Cade looks at Ansel, whose eyes are darting back and forth between us. Cade hits the call button on his phone.

It rings once, and then a man's voice answers, "Hey, how's Utah?"

"Good. You at the house?" Cade asks.

Interestingly, whoever this is didn't greet Cade.

Ansel picks up a cookie with a fork, but it's too hot and crumbles. Determined, he uses his fingers to try and pick it up, burning them and waving them in the air to cool them off. Right before going back after the cookies again.

"No, I ended up having to go into the office. Couple of kids backpacking got snowed in on the mountain without gear." He pauses. "Dinah should be home. Why?"

"I'll catch you up later." Cade hangs up the line.

"You two always that short with each other? Could have sworn you and Judah were friends," Ansel asks but doesn't get an answer.

He pops a piece of cookie in his mouth, making a face of pure bliss, eyes rolling back in his head.

I cover my mouth to stop a laugh. This seems like too serious of a time to be laughing, even if Ansel's adorable.

Ringing comes through Cade's phone on speakerphone again. I'm not even sure what questions to ask to understand what's going on. Blood tests? Like paternity? Aren't they cousins?

"Hey, spicy meatball, you free balling?" Dinah, evidently, answers the phone.

"The what?" Ansel asks, looking between us, brows furrowed. "They've the weirdest relationship."

"Weak." Cade laughs but flicks his thumb, working at the edge of the paper, almost like he's fiddling, trying to split the single page apart.

"Hey, Cade!" a man calls on the line.

"Hey, Wyatt." Cade cuts the greeting short. "Dinah, you got the mail?"

"Wyatt?" Dinah asks.

Ansel plates some cookies before sliding them across the

counter to me. I nod in appreciation, trying to stay quiet for the phone call.

"In the bin," Wyatt answers her.

Moments of silence tick by. Cade checks to see if Dinah hung up.

Another minute passes before her voice comes back. "That sleazy son of a bitch. No offense."

"None taken," Cade answers. "We all got them."

"Do we fight it?" she asks.

I can only assume she's talking about the letters.

"No," Cade answers soberly.

Looking at me first, he then makes eye contact with Ansel.

Ansel raises his eyebrows, putting his next cookie down.

We're all waiting for what's coming next. I just have no idea what it is.

Drawing in a deep breath with a sigh, Cade says, "I fight it. It's time I fix my mistake. Robert's reign is over."

The telephone line is quiet. Ansel doesn't move. It's almost a full minute before the silence breaks.

"All hail the Sovereign," Dinah says quietly.

"All hail the Sovereign," Ansel echoes.

Cade nods to Ansel. It's deep and feels ceremonial. Silence holds in the air before Cade speaks again, "Tell Judah. I'll tell Ezra. This stays within the bloodline until I get home and tell Lena and Deacon."

"I'll catch up with you once I know more." Cade's voice changes again. It's softer when he says, "Nothing's changing between us. I'm doing this our way."

"Alright. I look forward to hearing from you, Sovereign," Dinah replies before the line disconnects.

CHAPTER 32
CADE

THE LEVIATHAN HOWLS WITHIN ME. His happiness brings out my insecurities. My shortcomings and lack of preparedness are insurmountable, but I can't put this off. The media spectacle, the pack fund, Isabel's pop-ins, finding Thalia, Judah and Wyatt, and now mandatory blood tests. I don't know if I'm going to be a good leader, but I'm pretty sure I can't be much worse.

Ansel looks at me, slack-jawed. He clears his throat. "There's no going back, cousin."

I nod and turn to Thalia. Five minutes ago, the worst issue in my life was that my mate didn't believe we're mates. Now, my biggest issue is how to keep her safe and hidden away while I take back the throne. I didn't exactly think this through.

"What's going on?" Thalia looks at me, eyes wide.

How the fuck do I explain this?

Ansel answers for me, "Cade has formally declared his resolution to take back the throne. I dunno how much he's told you, I guess outside of what I told you, but he's pretty important. Him saying he wants his job back is, well, a change."

"Yeah. She has some idea." I toss the phone and letter on the counter. "Fuckity fuck fuck fuck."

We fight. Win. False king easy fight. Our mate be most protected. The Leviathan rethinks claiming and turning her. *Be safe as wolf. Draga mea. Ours. Our mate.*

I close my eyes and pinch the bridge of my nose, thinking through my next move. We can't turn her. If we've done anything right this week, it was striking a deal in exchange for keeping her safe. Turning Thalia is the exact opposite of what I've promised. Now more than ever, I have to hold up this end of the bargain.

The sound of a plate sliding across the counter has me opening my eyes. Four peanut butter cookies are on a small plate sitting in front of me. Ansel's in the middle of taking a bite of a cookie.

"What?" He stops eating it. "You're going to war; no time for snacks?"

Thalia cracks up laughing. She tries to steady herself by holding on to the counter before falling off the barstool again. Soon, Ansel is cracking up, and then I'm infected with laughter.

The sliding door opens, and Ezra waltzes in with his copy of the letter. He looks at us in the middle of a laughing fit. I see his eyes shift between us, and he reaches for the handle as he debates leaving.

Ansel pulls himself together enough to articulate, "All hail the Sovereign, want a cookie?"

"All hail the Sovereign." Ezra smiles, walking in and tossing his letter on the counter with Ansel's before hugging me.

Stealing a cookie off the plate in front of me, he looks at Ansel. "Dude, cookies?"

"I opened my letter and decided I wanted cookies, so I

made some. Then, Cade saw the letter and realized it was time to pull his head out of his ass. It wasn't like I chose the humble peanut butter cookie as the first food of the coup." Ansel turns around and digs through his alcohol cabinet before pulling out a bottle and four scotch glasses.

CHAPTER 33

THALIA

I'm not a drinker. But Ansel pours me a round, and I don't know what to do. I bring it to the living room space as we migrate away from the kitchen. Cade sits on one end of the couch while Ansel plops down in the recliner. Ezra sits on the other end of the couch, leaving me the middle. Cade gently taps the seat next to him before tossing his arm across the back of the sofa. I'm not sure about complying.

Cade tilts his head at me again before indicating I sit next to him. I'm not exactly sure where this defiance comes from, but while making eye contact with him, I fold my legs and gracefully-esque sit on the floor.

Ansel covers a laugh with a cough. I turn to watch him as he takes a drink of the amber liquid. Then out of the corner of my eye, Cade runs his hand back through his hair.

"So, is someone going to tell me more about what's happening?" I eye Ezra. Ansel seems a bit too respectful of Cade, but Ezra has a very fuck-everyone vibe about him. "I mean, I'm as excited as the next guy about a hostile takeover . . . but . . ."

"Yeah, sure." Ezra shrugs. "Cade killed his father and fucked over his mother. Think *Oedipus*, without the incest. Then cast Cade's idiot brother, Robert, as Hamlet and Cade as Claudius; except before Hamlet can actually go mad, Claudius abdicates the throne to Hamlet. Problem is, Hamlet is actually the emperor from *The Emperor's New Clothes*, and we've all known he's naked and an idiot this entire time, but he won't hear anything of it. Now, Cade, sick of seeing his brother's dick hanging out all the time, is going to play Richard Lionheart from *Robin Hood* and return as the rightful king of the wolves."

"How?" I pause, running that back in my head a few times. "How did that make complete sense and yet no sense at all?"

Cade glares at Ezra. "Really?"

"Fancy degree in folklore and mythology. It's good for a few things now and again." Ezra pulls his long legs onto the sofa, tucking them underneath himself, similar to how I'm sitting on the floor. "What's worse is that the two of you are Romeo and Juliet, if Juliet hated Romeo."

Ansel nearly spits out his drink, stifling back a laugh. "I got that one."

"No," Cade says coldly.

"Okay, fine, no Shakespeare. Pick a culture, I'll name a star-crossed lover's tale." Ezra shakes his head. "Doesn't make it less true."

"We're not in love," I retort.

"Yet." Ansel and Ezra deadpan in unison.

Yet? Why does everyone think this is . . . inevitable? Does anyone care what I think?

We're all quiet for a little while until Cade sighs. "Fuck."

"Realization just set in?" Ansel asks.

"Yeah." Cade's foot shuffles on the floor as he sinks deeper into the sofa. He sips his drink before asking, "I'm doing the right thing?"

Much to my surprise, Cade looks at me. His blue eyes are so soulful. I feel pulled in, and despite my trepidation, it's hard not to believe that we work out together.

I don't have an answer. It doesn't feel like I should. This is big for a whole group of people. A group of people that I'm not part of. I don't even know how many of them there are.

It's Ansel that answers the question. "Yeah, Cade. It's the right choice. We've all respected and stood by you because we want you to be happy. But your path has always been to lead."

Ezra confirms, "And you're not happy."

CHAPTER 34
CADE

Hearing Ezra say those four words was a resolution to a conflict I was unaware of. Dragging my eyes away from Thalia, I look at both of them.

"You're going to have to kill Robert." Ezra watches me.

The Leviathan and I know he's listening to my thoughts. The Leviathan daydreams of bloodshed. Ezra huffs before taking a drink of his whiskey.

"Terrifying how easy that plays out in your head," Ezra murmurs.

"That's always been Robert's fate. He just gets older in every vision. Robert dies as a wolf bleeding out," Ansel says brashly. "On that note." Ansel takes a bite of a cookie. "Shit's been real, it's been good. You could say it's been real good. You don't have to go home, but you can't stay here."

"New pickup tomorrow?" Ezra gets distracted.

Ansel snorts. "Yeah. I've just gotta figure out how to swing it. So, we'll be going into lockdown mode. I'd like to go through as few adjustments as possible."

"That's okay. My solution to keeping Thalia safe doesn't bring the fight to your doorstep." I nod, looking at my mate. "I've got a plan."

Ansel and Ezra both give me a puzzled look, so I elaborate. "Plan A: I challenge Robert after I get home. He's not going to want to settle this quietly. He'll want to put the challenge off until the full moon, which is almost three weeks from now. That way, he can arrange an extravagant gathering."

"You're banking on him being too wrapped up in the party to realize that Deacon isn't there." Ansel sits back in his chair, putting the footstool up.

I nod. He's catching on. Ezra smirks. "You and Lena show up, and he won't even blink because he's going to be too excited about the idea that if you die, Lena defaults back to his pack."

"He's none the wiser. Deacon stays home with Thalia." I nod, looking at Thalia. "Then, because it's the full moon, I won't be able to be challenged nor be required to present with a Second and Alpha Female until the next full moon. Which will be four weeks, and by then, I'll have just come home from taking Thalia back to DC, and Deacon and Lena can be seen as Alpha Female and Second."

Thalia takes a small nibble on her bottom lip before asking, "What if he's impatient and doesn't wait?"

"Plan B." I pause. "I issue the formal challenge, and he wants it to happen sooner. I don't have registered territory; the challenge has to happen on his property in Minnesota. He won't come to the house. I leave you with Deacon, and after it's done, I'll have until the full moon to present with an Alpha Female and a Second. I'll need to call in a favor, but I should be able to get one of the Alloways to come and house-sit."

"Alloways?" Thalia echoes.

"That'd be me," Ezra answers, raising his glass in a small toast. "Yeah. If Dinah or Judah can't make it, I'll pull it together."

"Okay." Ansel sighs. "Devil's advocate, what if Isabel shows up after she hears that you've challenged Robert?"

I draw a deep breath. "Plan C: If I can't keep Thalia out of sight, I out that I have her and see how many are stupid enough to try and come for her."

The Leviathan wags his tail at that idea. Proving his dedication to his mate stirs an animalistic part within us both. His in bloodshed and mine well, bloodshed first, mating second.

Ezra shakes his head at me. But that's what he gets for listening to things he shouldn't.

"Oh! I know this one." Ansel looks excited as he sits forward in his chair to explain. "It's like in the movie with the ring, and the woman on the horse yells at the black-cloaked dudes on dark horses to come get the little dude with the ring after she rides across the river before the river turns into horses and crushes the dudes in the capes."

Ezra looks at him and shakes his head. *The Lord of the Rings: The Fellowship of the Ring.* Arwen, on the horse with Frodo taunting the Nazgul."

"Sure, whatever movie that one was." Ansel purses his lips.

"You're not wrong, plot-wise," Thalia pipes up. "But I really don't like that plan. Can we make it like plan F?"

I look at her. Her brow is furrowed, and she's struggling like before her first panic attack. Breathing shallowly, she's staring at the floor in front of her. Her breaths become shorter and shorter as she gasps.

Ansel and Ezra look between me and her.

Ansel points. "Yeah, this and then passed out."

"Scary. Can she hear us?" Ezra asks quietly.

I move off the couch onto the floor next to her. Thalia's struggling to breathe. Her eyes are lost in a thousand-yard stare. I pick up her hand and squeeze it, trying to draw her out of her mind toward me.

"Alright, well, that's enough socializing for me," Ezra says, getting out of his chair. Before he walks out the back door, he says softly, "Cade, congratulations. Call me if you need me."

Without a word, Ansel slips out of his chair, picking up the glasses off the table and the one I've plucked out of Thalia's hands before taking them to the kitchen. I hear the back door open and close.

"Thalia," I whisper.

She's breathing short, jagged breaths. She doesn't answer me.

Moving behind her, I touch her arms softly as I wrap mine around her. I extend my thighs alongside hers until she's nestled between my legs, and I hold her tightly.

"Thalia, breathe," I command as softly as I can in her ear.

She gasps in air deep into her lungs.

The clock in the kitchen ticks out seconds toward a minute, loudly, while her body regulates.

She's still panting when she murmurs out a remorseful, "I'm sorry."

"Shhh," I whisper. "It's okay."

"What happened?" She leans aside, turning her head to look up at me before looking back at the now vacant seats of the living space. "Where did they go? And how did you get here?"

"You were having a panic attack, and we've been left unsupervised."

She lets out a heavy sigh. "Not to be self-absorbed. But, if you're going to kill your brother soon, how does that affect me?

304

Like, safety-wise?" Thalia's tone is delicately balanced between agitation and fear.

"The throne comes with a lot of different assets," I start slowly. My thumb pets the fabric of her shirt over her stomach. It's not as soft as her skin, but it's close. "Most of those assets make it easier, not harder, to keep you safe. I'll have control over the council and can override any of their decisions. Another is the direct control of the finances of my pack and majority say of other packs' contribution to the main pack's fund. Plus, I'll regain the ability to issue challenges of other Alphas. Which, on their own, don't sound overtly crucial. Together though, it means that I'll be able to destroy a pack's stability and take away an Alpha at the drop of a hat. Good leaders will want to avoid my wrath. Bad leaders will risk death, and if they do, I can help ensure a good leader sits in their place."

"That seems so harsh," Thalia whispers.

I squeeze her softly. "Someone threatening my mate is worse. If I have to prove to my people I'm willing to kill for you, then so be it. You're more important to me than any pack willing to stand between us. I'll keep you a safe distance away from the violence. You'll always have someone I can trust with you if I can't be there."

"Okay," Thalia concedes.

Her body relaxes just a bit against mine.

"It's going to be okay, Thalia. I'll never put you at risk," I whisper.

With her this close to me again, the temptation is too great. I kiss behind her ear and slowly make my way down her neck.

My lips move small distances at a time. The lower I go and the closer I get to the base of her neck, the deeper and more regularly Thalia breathes. I draw a deep breath inhaling the scent of her body. While her scent is still laced with fear, a new and much more pleasant aroma wafts into the air. Her arousal grows. I nip the base of her neck before moving to the other side. Every inhale I draw becomes more arousal and less fear. She tips her head aside, my teeth graze her skin, and my jeans are far too tight for how I'm sitting.

She whimpers ever so softly as I pull my mouth from her neck.

I whisper one of my tempting dirty thoughts, "You smell like you need to be licked until you come."

Her core clenches in my arms, but Thalia is silent. Shallow, focused breaths have replaced the inability to breathe. Her chest rises and falls over my arms wrapped around her middle.

I kiss along her hair line, nose pushing up into the bottom of her messy bun, where her natural scent mixed with soap is strong. It's a savory sweet. Her ass shuffles back closer to me. Grinding forward, I nudge her head to the other side, nibbling at her neck. Her ass rubbing against my cock is pure torture, even through our jeans.

Bite mate. Claim mate. The Leviathan urges. I ignore him. No biting, no matter how badly I want to.

She gasps when I hit a spot midway down her neck.

"I love how you respond to me. With every touch, you give me just a little more of your pleasure."

I continue nibbling and kissing down her neck.

"Ohhh." Thalia groans when I hit the base of her neck.

"I want to taste more of you." I nudge back to her ear.

She shudders in my arms.

The movement of her body against mine ignites me. I groan, feeling her ass pressed against me. The need to fuck her and claim her pounds through me with every heartbeat. It takes everything in me not to take her here on the floor.

My hand runs lower from where it's curled around her stomach. I find the hem of her shirt and press my palm against her stomach, waiting for her to object. Teasing it up her soft skin, inching closer to her bra.

A murmur of uneasiness comes with her body going rigid. I move my hand back down to where she was comfortable with it, kissing her neck again. I'm more than willing to seduce her slowly, at her pace, at least for now.

CHAPTER 35
THALIA

CADE'S HAND is so warm against my stomach, just resting there, it feels so sensual. I hesitated. I expected him to pull away, to get upset and stop entirely. He didn't. It was a retreat but not a forfeit.

Do I want this?

I think I do. His cock presses against my butt. How can I feel it through our clothes? He's got to be huge. The gentle feeling of his teeth moving on my neck is so enticing.

I know I do.

"More." My voice isn't as strong as I want, but the word comes out.

Gently Cade's hand slides slowly upward again. This time, I'm ready and need his touch.

"I wish we were back at my home. I could lay you across the bed. Worshipping your every curve is at the top of my to-do list. Followed immediately by making you moan my name and beg me to give you my cock," he whispers.

It's a promise that has my insides clenching with need. My legs and hips squeeze tight in response.

He lets out a small moan before kissing the other side of my neck. His one hand roams across my chest. The other keeps me pulled tightly against him.

I pull a deep breath at the feeling of his teeth taking more space against my neck. The small tingling nibbles from before grow into larger soft bites. I'm ragged in my exhale, leaning against him. Every brain cell is focused on how he feels: tongue, teeth, hands, and cock. It's the first time I've ever felt this in tune with a man. I can feel how wet I am. When I squirm, it's almost enough for me, a little more pressure, I could come. Each move he makes drives me closer. His hand runs under the wire of my bra.

I whine, "Please."

Cade stops moving.

Whispering in my ear, he says, "Please, what?"

"Upstairs?" The suggestion feels dirty and out of my comfort zone, but I need him.

A pleased groan escapes him. Cade stands up. The warmth of him behind me is immediately missed. I scramble forward to my knees to push myself up.

"Oh fuck." His favorite swear sounds different this time. "Add worshipping your ass to that list of things I want to do to you."

Placing his hands on my hips, he turns me toward him. Cade's pupils are so huge I can hardly see the blue of his irises. Cade presses his lips into mine, kissing me deeply, claiming. He opens my lips with his tongue and strokes inside my mouth.

A whimper escapes, and Cade breaks our kiss. His hand gently wraps around my wrist, tugging me out of the living room, around behind the couch, and over to the staircase. I ascend first. Knowing that he's watching my ass, I accentuate the swing of my hips, pushing them back and forth.

At the top of the stairs, horror hits. Cade's about to see me naked. I haven't shaved my legs in six days. I trimmed *down there* recently, but I'm not shaved. What if he doesn't like hair down there? I've soft belly rolls where he's a solid six-pack. Is it too late to back out now? I know how some guys get when you say no after saying yes, and I don't want him upset. *Cade isn't like most guys.*

"You're in charge, Thalia." Cade's voice cuts through my panic.

"I've just . . . never . . ." The embarrassment of it all rocks through me.

"Never?" Cade questions, furrowing his brow.

I expected judgment, but it doesn't feel judgy. His face holds curiosity as he leans against the door frame putting his hands in his pockets.

I bite my bottom lip and breathe deeply before letting word vomit escape my mouth. "I've had sex, but I've just never, um, had an orgasm with a partner, and I don't want you to be disappointed. Plus, I've been really busy before, you know, fleeing for my life, and I'm not exactly fresh down there, nor have I shaved my legs because we've been on the road. I'm also not, um, I look better with clothes on."

Cade lowers his head and looks at me, biting his bottom lip and shaking his head. "I'm positive you definitely look better with your clothes in a pile on the floor. I turn into a wolf, hair doesn't bother me." He pauses, locking his eyes with mine. "And I assure you, that statistic, with another partner, ends today. Those boys were more focused on their cocks than you. My focus is all you. Every moan, whimper, and plea will urge me to satisfy you."

Holy crap. His words only amp up my arousal.

He pulls his hands from his pockets and steps closer to me. I have to raise my head to look up to him. I swallow hard.

"How you squirm and writhe will be my roadmap. You'll be

screaming my name through the first orgasm. Only, and I mean only, when you beg me to stop, will I quit pulling orgasms from you," Cade whispers, his hands on my hips. They gently slide up my sides, pulling the hem of my shirt. "What do you say, draga mea? Let me worship you?"

He's always in control. Cade begging for this, for me, gives me a heady feeling of confidence.

Pocatello
Preston
Malad City
Logan
Brigham City
Tremonton
Ogden
Evanston
Lyman
FLAMING GORGE NAT'L REC AREA
Kings Peak 13,528 ft
Salt Lake City
Bountiful
Roy
Clearfield
Layton
Great Salt Lake
Park City
Heber City
Sandy
Orem
Provo
Springville
Duchesne
W. Valley City
Tooele
Utah Lake
Great Salt Lake Desert
Wendover
Eureka
Nephi
UTAH
Ephraim
Gunnison
Salina
Delta
Aurora
Richfield
Delano Peak 12,173 ft
Beaver
Cedar City

CHAPTER 36
CADE

I THINK what I see is pleasant shock.

Thalia nods, and clothes are coming off, hers and mine, as we make our way into the bedroom. Unbuttoning my jeans, I'm free from the pain of the zipper constricting my cock. It's stiff, throbbing when I imagine her pussy clenched around it. *Not here. Not now.* At home, in my bed, will be the first time I feel that pleasure. I'm lost looking at her beautiful curves. The soft pink tones of her skin. The freckles from her face dance across the top of her chest and lower.

Her eyes roam my body, and her hands move, blocking my view. I step into her space, my cock sliding up her body. I move her hands away.

"Don't hide these beautiful curves from me. I love looking at you."

She doesn't argue. I lay her back on the bed, kissing her as I cage her in with my arms. I gingerly settle between her legs, trying to be mindful of my healing wounds. Rocking against her, the temptation to sink lower and drive my cock into her is strong. The Leviathan whines, begging to take her, claim her, and turn her. Not today. Today we're going to feast and cater to her every need. This is about her comfort and her need for escape.

I slide myself down her body, kissing from her jaw, down her neck, to her shoulder, across her breastbone, and then down between her perfect tits. She squirms when I kiss her stomach. Thalia's hands move again to cover herself. I grab them and pin them to her sides, looking up at her. Catching her eyes, I place a kiss right above her belly button.

"Cade," she objects.

"No. No hiding." I hold her still, continuing to trail kisses lower. She grumbles while I pay her softest parts more attention. I need her to know how much I love them.

She does the most adorable imitation growl and squirms. I nip the soft part above her hip bones. Thalia yelps in shock, squirming against my grip on her.

I kiss lower and run my nose across her mound. Kissing just above her apex, I let my self-control go. Nosing open her folds, the scent of her arousal is overwhelming. Licking slowly, she and I moan together. Her legs squirm against me.

"Trying to stop me?" I smirk.

Thalia grumbles again, and I stand from the bed. She looks up at me with wide eyes and whines. I grab behind her knees, then pull her closer to the edge of the bed. I bring her hands under her, adjusting her hips. Leaving her hands there, I pull mine away, sliding them along her thighs. Slow and steady. I love the feeling of my fingers against her soft skin.

Dropping to my knees, I drape her legs over my shoulders, taking her in, laid bare before me.

"Fuck, Thalia."

Another whine escapes her mouth. It quickly gives way to a moan of anticipation when my fingers find her inner thighs.

With her legs over my shoulders, I taste her in long slow laps. She's so wet, and with every little noise, my cock throbs harder. The Leviathan presses me, urging me to seal our bond. *Fuck her. Mark her. Claim her.*

Long, languid strokes of my tongue against her clit. Her mewls drive me into each lap. She tastes divine. With only a few more strokes of my tongue, she's grinding into me. Her hands slide out from under her ass, reaching for me. My hands find hers where they escaped from, along her sides. She laces her delicate fingers through mine with a light squeeze. That familiar connection urges me on.

"Cade, please." Thalia begs so beautifully in objection to my silent scolding.

"Patience, draga mea. I want to hear you scream my name. One orgasm and then another, until you beg me to stop."

I exhale a cool breath against her clit.

Her whole body rocks up, trying to squirm away from the cold. I untwine my fingers from hers. She squirms but steadies when my eyes catch hers. I cock an eyebrow and give her a devious look. I laugh, wrapping my left arm over her pelvis, pulling her back to me again. Thalia settles in. I reward her patience by pulling her clit between my teeth and sucking gently. Slowly sliding my finger along the lower edge of her slit, I pay close attention. Her breath catches, but I keep moving, tentatively pressing my finger into her warmth.

I feel her moan growing in the clenching of muscles and the drawing of breath, only a second before I hear it. Her entire abdomen relaxes under my touch. Every ounce of tension floods out of her body. Casting my gaze up, I see Thalia's eyes have fallen closed rather than clenched as they were before.

With steady pressure, I slide my finger inside her pussy. Feeling the ripples, I stroke slowly. Thalia shudders, soft moans escaping with each breath.

My hips rock, cock nestled against the side of the bed while it begs to be sheathed inside her. This isn't about what I want. I need to keep my focus on her. Each noise and how she reacts deepens my desire.

The Leviathan is tuned into our mate. Analyzing every move, it thrills us. And he urges me on, *bite mate, makes ours. Claim draga mea as Luna.*

For as quiet as her body language is when speaking, Thalia expresses her sexual desire flawlessly. She arches against my arm draped across her pelvis, her heels digging into my back. When I slide in my second finger, her moans are louder, more intense, and more frequent.

My balls ache.

I break my attention from her clit for only a moment. "Fuck. You taste so good. I can taste how much you need this."

Thalia murmurs the smallest, "Mmhmm."

I find a steady rhythm feeling her body respond to me. Thalia's moans match each stroke of my tongue. I suck on her clit, holding it gently between my teeth while playing with the sensitive nub with my tongue. Increasing the pressure of my fingers inside her, I make small adjustments to how firmly I push and the length my strokes. *That's it, draga mea, show me how you like it.*

Her thighs go rigid, pussy clenching tight on my fingers. Her entire body tenses, unmoving.

She begs, "Don't stop. Please don't stop."

I repeat my motions again and again, holding that pace as she continues to spasm. I've found exactly what she needs, and I keep giving it to her. As she writhes, I only adjust to keep her held to me.

"Cade!" She screams my name, and it's never sounded so hot.

Her body panting and heaving is glorious.

It comes out as a scream four more times before she says it at a whisper, followed by the sweetest, "No more. Please, no more."

Slowly disentangling myself from between her legs, I can't keep my eyes off her. The beautiful pink tone to her skin, the messy strands of hair splayed about, and the sweat glistening on her skin are more beautiful than anything I've seen before.

My fingers are drenched in my saliva and her wetness. She's watching me as I lick them clean. Thalia's chest is still heaving as I wipe my chin against my forearm. Seeing her splayed like this, I want to close the space between us again. Thoughts of pulling her onto my cock and removing all the space between us run rampant.

Take our mate. Make ours. Give her wolf. Be one. The Leviathan coaxes.

Thalia watches me with hungry eyes. It's all so tempting, too tempting.

I stand from between her legs and climb on the bed. Once I pull her up farther away from the edge, I lie down next to her, taking away the temptation before I lose hold of my control. She turns to face me. I take the opportunity to kiss her. She squirms, murmuring in discomfort, and I move away quickly, looking for how I hurt her.

"No, come back," she beckons.

"What's wrong?" I whisper, moving closer again, pulling her arm toward me.

"I've never . . ." Her words die off.

"Never tasted yourself?" I deduce. "That shouldn't be surprising, seeing as no one's ever cared for you that way."

Thalia's eyes still won't meet mine. She doesn't say anything. I snuggle into her, kissing the top of her head and wrapping myself around her. Should I be angry or grateful that those boys before me saved these experiences for me?

Her body shudders.

I climb out of bed, and she objects. "I'll be right back."

I dart to the bathroom next door and return with a warm rag. I move her like I would a live explosive, ever so carefully, pushing her legs aside and cleaning her.

She looks away from me, embarrassed. I don't push her to try and enjoy this part. Eventually, Thalia will get used to being treated right. I finish cleaning her and wipe my face before tucking us into bed.

"I promise to be less weird in the future. It's just, new experiences," says Thalia.

The negative words out of her mouth sting me.

Others not satisfy her. Good. The Leviathan's sexism shows. He pushes the ideas of hunting down her past partners, but I force it out of my brain.

"Your experience is a nonissue," I whisper, assuring her. "You're going to quickly discover that I'm possessive and easily jealous. The Leviathan would gladly hunt down your exes simply so they couldn't think about you anymore."

Thalia yawns, looking up at me before snuggling in tighter. "How do you make red flags sound so hot?"

Her eyelids, heavy, open and close slowly.

I chuckle and kiss her forehead. "Get some rest. I'll be here when you wake up."

THE SUN'S low in the sky before I hear the door downstairs open. I've catnapped on and off while thinking about how much life is going to change. In her sleep, Thalia nearly curled entirely on my chest.

"You awake up there?" Ansel says in low tones.

"I am," I answer loud enough for his wolf to hear, trying not to startle her awake.

"I brought pie from in town. Do you two want to refuel, or should I take Ben up on his offer for dinner?"

"I'll wake her up and come down. Give you a hand in the kitchen."

I've resisted petting her for fear of waking her up. I slowly roll my hand down her back before pulling back up. Her naked body is snuggled against me tightly. I'm going to need this full-body touch again soon.

She grumbles incoherently, objecting to being woken up.

"Draga mea, it's time to get up. We'll have dinner and come back to bed."

I move her head toward me, kissing the tip of her nose.

Thalia sighs. Her whole body shivers as she does.

Lazily she moves back to the bed before whispering, "Cold."

WE'RE DRESSED and downstairs in ten minutes.

Ansel's dicing onions when we come down the stairs.

He smiles. "Good morning, sunshines."

Thalia gives him a halfhearted wave. "Hi?"

Abruptly she stops. I bump into her, my hands flying to her shoulders to steady her. She turns around to face me, eyes wide, with her hands covering her mouth.

What mean? The Leviathan puzzles in my head.

Cocking an eyebrow and my head, I try to evaluate what she's thinking, but I'm also drawing a blank. Thalia doesn't say anything but draws deep breaths. They're at least slower. I see the tension I just worked out of her starting to rise.

"What's wrong?" I stroke her hair, trying to keep her calm.

Pulling one hand from her mouth, she gestures, pointing behind her toward Ansel. I look over at him. He's fully clothed, so that's not it. He's chopping an onion with a knife, which isn't abnormal. I don't see anything strange on the counters or out of place.

When I look back at her, she's now covering her eyes with the other hand.

"I don't get it," I say quietly.

"Oh no. Did he? Was he?" Her body is rigid.

The Leviathan and I try to pool our collective knowledge, but my confused look tells her I need more information.

"Did he hear us?" she manages to whisper.

Humans odd. He hears how make mate scream. Good for him. The Leviathan and I agree that it's not a big deal. Clearly, this means something to her.

"Probably. But he was outside for a little while at least?" I move my hands from her shoulders to gently pry her hands from her face.

"Definitely heard you," Ansel confirms, also whispering.

She presses herself against my chest, and I try to stifle a laugh.

"Oh no. This is not funny. Don't laugh. He heard us . . ." she whispers, "in his house."

"Pft." Ansel raspberries his lips. "Tell her about the Solstice like six years ago."

I spin Thalia around and push her toward the kitchen. "It happened. He knows, we know, we know he knows, he knows we know he knows. It's just sex."

Her face is beet red. I'm fairly certain, if given the opportunity, she'd dart back upstairs to hide under the covers. Being the brave woman she is, Thalia sits down on the stool at the end of the bar, still covering most of her face with her hands.

"Sorry, Ansel," Thalia mumbles from behind her hands.

Ansel's eyes dart up. Raising an eyebrow, he purses his lips before answering, "Uh, apology accepted?"

CHAPTER 37
THALIA

Can I die now? Seriously. I had an awesome orgasm with Cade, the best nap ever, and then I find out that Ansel heard, at least, some of everything. I don't even know where Cade and I stand. I have so many feelings for him, but my heart says this can't just be a fling.

Both of them seem perfectly content working in the kitchen while I sit watching.

"Okay, so Solstice like six years ago," Ansel starts.

So much for sitting quietly, watching, hiding in shame.

Ansel's smiling wide, looking between me and Cade. "Alright, so Cade's just come back from who knows where. Ezra and I roll into town for an impromptu vacation, and I shit you not, it's not even noon and . . ."

A growl comes from Cade as he pours a glass of ice water, urging me to drink it.

Ansel makes a face mocking his growl, curling his lip up before finishing what he was going to say, clearly having changed the words. "He's entertaining female company on his back deck. And, uh, as Ezra would say, 'that's . . .'"

Cade growls again. It's louder and must mean something, because this time, Ansel takes a step away from him.

Ansel speaks softly, "You get the picture."

What Ansel is saying is supposed to cheer me up. Yet, sitting at the end of the counter, I see Cade standing there, and the idea of another woman touching him makes my stomach sick. I'm holding the glass in my hand but set it down after seeing my knuckles turning white from squeezing it.

Ansel steps away from me quickly. "Holy shit."

I turn around to look behind me, worried about what could possibly make him afraid. I fall from the bar stool trying to move.

Ansel catches me in his arms. "What is it with you and this stool?"

There's a rumble, and I swear the house shakes.

Ansel snaps at Cade. "Seriously? Want me to let her bust her ass? Fuck me. The two of you need to lock your shit down. Between her jealousy and your possessiveness, someone's gonna get killed."

"What did I have to do with any of this?" I push myself up and out of Ansel's arms. I was just sitting here.

"The fact that you don't know how much anger you were putting out is terrifying." Ansel walks back over to the pan. I barely catch a few of the words he mutters. "She's going to be a force."

"I warned you not to tell the story." Cade's voice is gravelly.

"What do you mean lock down our shit?" I ask, feigning ignorance.

I hope batting my eyes a bit at him warrants results.

Ansel shakes his head at me. "Are you trying to get me killed flirting like that?"

Cade is quiet. His grip on the knife is a bright white-knuckled grip, and his shoulders move with every breath. It takes him a moment, but after some silence, he sets the knife down.

"Remember when I said that I'm possessive and extremely jealous?"

"What does that have to do with this?"

Again, it feels like I'm missing a piece of this puzzle, a puzzle that I don't even have the box to tell me what it should look like.

When Cade looks at me, his eyes are the bright-flecked gold seen when I was walking with The Leviathan. "The more time we spend together without me claiming you, the more we'll struggle with other people who are potential partners to the other."

"But we can't even be sure that it's really the case. I'm not a wolf. I don't feel the same things you do," I argue.

"Do you need more proof?" Cade smirks. Clearly thinking something dirty.

Ansel laughs. "Dudes, I got to sleep tonight. Let's not start round two?"

"Sorry, Ansel." Cade quickly apologizes.

"Apology accepted."

Ansel bumps his shoulder against him. Cade nods, then bumps back against him again. *What did that mean?*

Ansel's green eyes lock on me. "I want to hear about you."

"Uh." I look to Cade, hoping for a hint of what I should do.

Something has changed. I don't want to give Ansel attention and get him hurt.

Without missing a beat, Cade starts telling Ansel about me. It's surprising hearing him repeat things I've told him. He's retained everything about my education and my goals for the future.

Ansel asks questions, often admitting that he doesn't understand my answer, and asks me to re-explain. Ansel's this anomaly with a lot of emotional intelligence, and he comes across as well educated.

"What about you, Ansel? Where did you go to school?" I ask in a break of questions about myself.

"I'm flattered you think so highly of me, but I'm not educated." Ansel doesn't meet my eyes as he plates dinner. "The station of Reaper doesn't allow for a lot of study time. I tried to get my GED a few times, but between the traveling and the lockdowns, it's just not a priority."

"If you want it, once I settle the storm, I'll handle some of your workload," Cade offers.

"Seems a bit late. I'm probably closer to forty than thirty."

"What?" I object while studying Ansel's features. He's young looking. I would definitely put him under thirty. "You're over thirty?"

He nods. "Yeah. We'll celebrate my thirty-fifth or thirty-sixth birthday with the new year."

"You don't know when your birthday is or how old you are?" As I say it, I realize how it came out.

Ansel shrugs. "I'm a bit of a mystery. The documents social services put together for me gave me a January first birthday, and the doctors assumed I was about eight or nine since I didn't know. But that's enough about me."

Cade recognizes my confusion at what Ansel's saying but, with a shake of his head, tells me to let it be before diverting the subject. "Ansel is the old man of the group, but everyone thinks Judah is the oldest because he behaves that way."

"By that logic, you're Peter Pan." Ansel laughs. "It'll be fascinating to hear the tales of you growing up now that you're a real man."

I snort, covering my mouth with my hands. Cade seems mature to me, but Ansel probably knows him better. They have history and are family. Green jealousy seeps in, and I squash it down. He has strong family ties. Those are good things.

Cade shakes his head. "Let's just hope I don't end up killing everyone like Peter."

"Wait, what?!" Ansel gawks.

The boys rib each other through dinner. It's fascinating to hear their stories. With how comfortable they are with each other, I assumed they spent a lot of time together. In reality, they only spend a couple of days a year together. It seems they have a bunch of other communication. They're very much connected, but both include me, asking my opinion and telling stories they'd think I'd like.

As we finish our dinner, Ansel stops moving. I look over at him and Ansel's eyes have turned a deep brown.

"Cade?" I whisper.

I watch Ansel's eyes go white, just like yesterday when I asked about Ezra.

Cade looks over at Ansel before he looks at me. "He'll be okay. It's his gift. Just give him a minute."

Ansel's eyes drift close. It's a moment longer before he rapidly blinks and then squeezes them shut tight.

He sighs, his shoulders heaving. "Damn."

"Are you okay?" I ask. *His gift seems painful.*

Ansel smiles. "Yeah. It's all good. No one's clock is winding down anytime soon."

"Well, that's good." I smile back.

"But I'm going to leave you to it for the night. Thalia, it's been an absolute pleasure getting to know our future Luna. Cade, I'll catch you at Solstice." Ansel pats my shoulder before clearing his plate to the counter.

Why do people keep referring to me as Luna? I need to ask Cade.

Cade walks over and meets Ansel at his bedroom door, partly blocking Ansel from walking through it. They exchange a few words in tones so soft that I can't hear. Cade's face broadcasts a lot of different things while they talk: anger, sadness, and appeasement, before a soft smile. When he nods and steps aside, Ansel pushes past him and goes into his room, closing his door.

Cade rolls his head back and looks at the ceiling before coming back to the kitchen.

Helping him take care of the plates, I ask softly, "Everything okay?"

The way Cade raises his eyebrows in shock is a new expression. His face appears contemplative while his wheels spin, probably thinking if he wants to tell me.

Cade shrugs while loading the dishwasher. "Fuck it. Yeah, I'll tell you. When shifters came out to the public, they passed emergency stipulations. They're harsh. It costs a lot of money to buy a wolf's freedom from the government. Ansel's been cut off from the pack fund. Essentially, he's not getting paid. He doesn't have the kind of money he needs available to him to pick up someone tomorrow. I'm going to take care of it because it should be taken care of to start with."

"Oh. What do you mean buy a wolf's freedom?"

Cade chews his top lip for a moment. "So, the current policy, that's been rolled out across the country, states that in order for shifters to be let out of human jails or prisons it's a minimum of fifty thousand dollars, plus any other fines and fees incurred when they bring the wolf in. There's a whole scale of unreasonable totals. Theoretically, the incarcerated wolf's home pack would be footing the bill, but Robert's pretty much uninvolved with it. So, there is no enforcement. If a pack is worried the incarcerated wolf is fracturing, they won't pay because there's no guarantee Ansel can fix their wolf."

"What happens if it doesn't get paid? They just stay in jail?" I look at Cade.

His face falls, and he looks down at the dishes. "If after seven days they're not claimed by a reputable pack, the government destroys them."

"What?" My blood runs cold.

I flash hot and cold. My body convulses in a shiver.

Cade winces. "We all do what we can to keep someone out. Death with dignity, even if Ansel ends up having to end them, it's better to go out fighting than scared and alone in someone's cage. Letting someone die alone is seen as taboo for us. We do everything to make sure someone isn't alone when they draw their last breath."

"I'm going to be sick." I rush to the main floor bathroom.

TEN MINUTES LATER, I look at myself in the mirror, eyes red and puffy, hair tied into a low ponytail. It's the best I can do to clean up.

Mom's a monster. I almost died because of what she's done, what she's doing to innocent people. It's no wonder people want me dead.

How can Cade, Ansel, and Ezra sit in the same room with me, knowing who she is? What she stands for? They've included me in their lives and told personal stories. Am I misreading all the interactions? Ansel's just being cordial, right? He's being nice because that's who he is? Ezra doesn't seem like the kind that would hold back punches, but he admitted that he's slightly terrified of Cade. Would it be enough to not be rude?

"Thalia."

I jump. Cade's standing so close he's nearly touching me. He's leaned against the door frame next to the sink, hands tucked into his pockets. My hand lands over my quickly beating heart. I look at him, drawing a deep breath.

"You're not your mother," he says softly, voice down to not disturb Ansel.

I shake my head. *He doesn't mean that.*

Cade keeps talking. It's like he can hear what I've been thinking. "We all adore you for you. None of us judge others based on what they've done or where they come from, including you. You're open, honest, and genuine. You've expressed interest in learning with an open mind. That's worth more than your lineage."

Moving without thinking, I lean against him, resting my head against the soft fabric of his T-shirt. Cade wraps his arms around me, accepting me against him. The way he holds me makes me feel like there's nothing wrong. I matter, and he believes that this situation with my mother isn't something I did. His hands rub my shoulders.

He kisses the top of my head before whispering, "I'm sorry, I didn't realize how that would affect you. I should have been more selective in my wording."

"No, you shouldn't have. This is your life. I wanted to know. How many laws like this are there? Is this part of my mom's doing?" I brace myself for horrible things. He's going to tell me it's bad.

Cade hesitates. "There are roughly a hundred emergency stipulations in place. Your mother has been involved in all of them."

"I hate her sometimes. This is one of those times." Those words come out with the acidic bitterness I'm feeling. "I don't know what to do."

"It's not something for you to fix. I'll figure it out." Cade squeezes me gently.

"Are you sure there isn't anything I can do?" I plead with him.

She's my mother, after all. There has to be some way I can intervene on the shifters' behalf.

Cade hesitates before running a hand through his hair. "As much as I love that you want to help, it's something I'll have to handle."

He leads me to the stairs and nudges me up with one hand on my low back. For a moment, I thought he would go to the second bedroom until he stalls at the top of the stairs. Looking over my shoulder at him is permission enough.

He follows me into the bedroom. Sleep takes a long time to find me but wrapped up in the blanket with Cade's warmth, it eventually does.

CHAPTER 38

THALIA

THE NEXT MORNING AFTER BREAKFAST, Cade and I head out the back door to his SUV. He's opening doors, reaching into compartments, and under seats.

As he's rifling through the car, I reflect on everything I've learned. I'm his mate, and despite not understanding all of what that entails, I'm okay for now. My mother's an awful person. The future is unknown, but Cade's plans seem to be well thought out. All I can do is live one day at a time. I think, as long as it's with Cade, that's going to be a good thing. Whatever his daily life looks like, even if it's less eventful than this road trip, spending time with him will be enough.

I take a deep breath, returning my attention to him.

He's pulling out various envelopes from all over the place. He hands them to me.

"I'm going to get us ready to go on the road. Will you please pull out all the American dollars and count them?"

The envelopes are packed with cash of various denominations in Canadian and American dollars and Mexican pesos. Not counting the Canadian and pesos, there's nearly

335

fifty thousand dollars. Why on Earth would he keep so much cash in his SUV? Leaving the envelopes on the passenger seat, I take the cash in hand to him.

"How much is there?" His attention is on wiping an oily mess off the stick thing from under the car's hood.

"Do you always keep so much money in the glove box of your SUV? That doesn't seem safe . . . It's forty-eight thousand two hundred."

"Yeah. Well, not that much. But I always keep a hundred dollars in the glove compartment for gas money or a bribe." He shrugs. "Plus, I don't tend to go a lot of places, so it doesn't get a lot of opportunities to be stolen. Would you please pull two thousand off and leave that out here, then take the rest of the cash in the house and put it on Ansel's bed?"

When I come out of the house, Cade is leaning against the passenger door, waiting for me. His smile lights up. I'm drawn to him. It's magnetizing, this warmth in my core, that pulls me toward him. I walk fast, stopping short so the door can swing open. Cade doesn't open the door. Instead, he pulls me into him, and I go willingly. Feeling his arms wrap around me, the warmth of his body feels good against my skin.

"I can't wait to get you home," Cade says softly with a devilish grin. "So many plans for you."

Heat floods between my legs. I bite my bottom lip, looking up at him. "Are they the kind of plans that don't require leaving the bedroom?"

"Oh, plenty of that. So much of that." Cade kisses me softly. Pulling away from my lips, he continues, "But it'll be nice to have some normal and get time to talk this all through, but know I mean it, Thalia. I mean all of it." His words sound like a vow. His eyes are so warm and bright against me. "You're mine. My everything."

Cade must sense my apprehension. He turns, opening the

passenger door. "I'll find a way to explain it. Somehow. There's nothing to worry about."

Cade tucks me into the SUV and hands me his phone. "Put on more of that audiobook?"

After settling into the driver's seat, Cade uses that weird wolfy, always-seems-to-know-where-he's-going GPS to navigate back out to the main highway. It takes me a minute to find where we left off. But once I get it cued up, we're immersed back in the final rise to the story's conflict.

I reach over and hit pause as we're passing the Welcome to Colorado sign.

"Okay, so for the twist, I think the big guy in the tech department is in on it?" I challenge Cade.

"You can never trust the tech guys who know how to interact with people." Cade shakes his head. With a sigh, he asks, "How did you catch that twist?"

"Oh." I shrug. "Early on, they said it was about being completely honest and vulnerable."

Cade laughs. "Damn, you're so fucking smart. I wouldn't have even thought about that. Fucking shitty of him."

His praise spreads warmth through me, and I can't help the smile on my face. I pull my hair back out of my face, trying to get cool.

I answer him, "I don't know, it just didn't seem fair for it to be her fault. She's been so supportive through the series."

The way he thinks things through, it's evident he's always in his head. I'm feeling more comfortable that whatever this challenge means with Robert, his plans to keep me safe are going to work.

"Fair enough," Cade answers, and I press play.

THE MAN at the front desk offers us a single king room. Cade smiles, not asking for something else. I want to be upset with him and reprimand him, saying I want that extra space, but I don't feel that way. I don't feel anxious or upset about it. Only five days ago — not counting the two days on a road trip across country — we were practically strangers.

Why is this so fast? Why am I not afraid?

We order pizza to the room, and he asks me to pick something to watch. I put on a history documentary about castles, testing his tolerance for my kind of entertainment. When he tells me that he's seen this one and one of the castles is way cooler in person, my heart flutters.

Cade cleans up the pizza and uses the bathroom to get ready for bed.

My heart beats a little harder. Yesterday was good. No, yesterday was incredible. Should I expect him to want me to return the favor of orgasms? While we were at Arches, he said he wanted to wait until he got home, and I think he meant for more privacy. It's not that I don't want to, but how do you handle this situation? Is there etiquette for sleeping with your security detail?

Returning to the room, Cade looks at where I'm sitting on the bed with a soft look in his eyes.

"I can smell your arousal but can also sense your uneasiness. Thalia, you're in charge of what happens between us. I have no expectations." Cade stalks closer, desire in his eyes. Walking to my side of the bed and bending to my level, he cups my head and kisses me deeply. He breaks the kiss first. "Go get changed, I want to cuddle."

My heart thunders in my chest, and I'm lightheaded from the kiss. Despite this, some of the tension melts from my shoulders. He can tell I'm nervous, so he's putting me at ease. *Dang, this man and his attentiveness.*

Nodding, I offer him a smile and let him help me off the bed. Grabbing my kit, I head to the bathroom.

"Draga mea," Cade calls.

'My darling.' *Swoon.* I turn to look at him.

"I mean it, just cuddle."

Once I return, he pulls me across the bed and into his arms. It's not awkward or forced. It's like my hesitation was enough for him. I don't have guilt about it. Especially when I hear the happy little grumble as he draws a deep breath of air and relaxes behind me. Sinking into slumber, the sound of his breathing and the warmth of his arms lull me to sleep.

WE'RE on the road bright and early, grabbing breakfast takeout from a small mom-and-pop diner. Cade punches in some directions on his phone and drives to a parking lot next to a beautiful lake. He backs into a spot, and soon, I'm holding food as he opens the hatch. Looking out over the most serene glassy water, this is, hands down, the coolest breakfast I've ever had.

Birds soar overhead. They chatter among the trees while squirrels dart in and out of the nearby shrubbery. It's not a fancy restaurant, movie, or performance, but it is one cool date. It suits Cade. He didn't ask or call it a date, but he wouldn't have found such a romantic space if this wasn't special. *Right?*

"How far is the drive home?" I ask midway through my pancakes.

"It's about twenty hours from Ansel's to home, about eleven hours left. We'll stop in Iowa this afternoon to see how we feel. Finish and get home late tonight or make the rest of the drive tomorrow. I don't want to stop in Nebraska if we don't have to. Obviously, if you have to pee, say something. I'll fuel up in a bit, and the first two hours of the state are safe, but it's that eastern side I really don't want to stop in if I don't have to." Cade takes a bite.

"Understandable. I'd rather not have to worry about you getting hurt." I give him a soft smile.

"Bears don't scare me. I refuse to let anything happen to you." Cade keeps picking at his food.

Once I've finished and I'm looking out over the lake, now seems as good a time as ever to talk about what's next. "Okay, so, I know a lot about your cousins, but I know nothing about Lena and Deacon. Which seems like an oversight since I'll be seeing them a lot?"

"Deacon sees dead people, and Lena can see your past. Literally, my life is a history exhibit. You'll fit right in." Cade chuckles and gives me a wink.

"Can you say that again? Deacon sees dead people?"

Is flabbergasted an emotion? Because I'm certain that's what this feeling is.

"Yeah." Cade shrugs, explaining in one breath. "You'll get used to it. At first, it's a little weird. Seems like he's talking to himself. Well, sometimes he does, talk to himself, that is. For the most part, he's always a little drunk or high. I'm not excusing the behavior, but if I had ghosts talking at me all the time, I might be drunk a lot too."

"He doesn't have control like Ansel and Ezra? Or you?" I wipe my hands on a napkin while Cade packages our garbage into its bag.

"None of us have complete control." Cade makes a point to catch my gaze. "Even me."

After a few minutes, Cade continues, "My siblings take a little bit to warm up to. But just give them a couple of days. They're not used to letting people in."

Oh, that's not ominous at all.

I nod. It'll be fine. Right?

CHAPTER 39
CADE

BREAKFAST IS PERFECT. Thalia looks perfect curled up in the back of my Yukon, just like she belongs there. It's second nature to simply exist with her.

Our mate perfect. Everyone love her. The Leviathan is relaxed. The constant battle between us is all but gone. It's surreal. Even his I-told-you-so attitude about her isn't annoying.

For the first time in over a decade, I'm not uneasy, even with taking back the throne and all that entails looming over my head. The Leviathan is manageable. I have a purpose that isn't based on birthright or obligation. I've found a calling, one that plays in my heart and not in my head.

When she asks about Deacon and Lena, I'm not surprised. It's always been hard for me to talk about them. I've done so much to fuck up their lives. I'll never be able to pay it back, to either of them. It's interesting how quickly she accepted that I don't have complete control over my gift. Thalia is a constant mystery of what will and won't make sense to her, and I'm loving that about her.

"When we get to your place, what's the living situation? Do you have a house? Apartment?" She's shuffling out of the back of the SUV.

"I own my home and a good-sized hunk of land. It's the house and a couple of sheds for structures. Deacon and Lena live in one half of the house, and I have the other bedroom." As I finish saying that statement, Thalia bites her lips together.

Her jaw locks tight, lips pursed.

I raise my eyebrows, waiting for something to respond to. *I've done something wrong.*

It comes slowly as I close the hatch of the SUV.

"So, what? You've got three bedrooms, and they're all occupied? Where was I supposed to sleep? I mean, this was always going to be the arrangement before we became . . . close. So was your plan to get me in your bed like some sort of Casanova all along?" She quirks a brow at me with the last question.

"I regret to inform you that bringing you to my own home was not my first or second choice of options. I can see where you'd get the assumption. My couch in the living room is huge. I have no problem sleeping on it," I answer earnestly. "We slept next to each other last night without any objection. We've been comfortable together. If that changes or we get home, and you don't want me in your bed, then you've got a massive, oversized king to yourself. I'm not here to make you do anything other than stay safe."

Our mate will share bed. Draga mea is ours. The Leviathan pushes, unconcerned with Thalia's opinion.

"What will your siblings think?" Thalia wraps her arms around herself. The spring air must be cold to her.

Gently I usher her around the Yukon and open her door.

"Sex, intimacy, and connection are very different for wolves." I remind her, making sure she's in the vehicle before closing the door. *Of course, she cares what other people think. Why didn't I consider that?* Around the front and into my side, I wait to see if she says anything before I continue, "First, it's not shameful to have a physical relationship with someone else. Second, when we find our mates, everything happens faster. Third, Deacon is going to love you, and Lena hates everyone."

"Fantastic," Thalia grumbles.

I start the vehicle and get us back on the road. "Yeah, I mean, there's still the whole part where Ezra was right. I'm hoping we don't die at the end of the story."

Or Lena doesn't kill me. I self-edit. She doesn't need to know that Lena is the potential issue. That's a different bridge to cross when I come to it.

"Morbid," Thalia answers.

DRIVING BACK across Nebraska would normally be boring. The constant looking over my shoulder for the possibility of being followed keeps me sharp. When we hit the Iowa border, and the license plates change from white to blue, my shoulders fall from around my ears, the weight of even a hypothetical altercation dissipates. The clock is late, and the sun is nearly down by the time I pull in for fuel at the pump. If I can stay awake for another six hours, we can be home and in bed tonight.

We claim our mate. The Leviathan croons, his back end squirming with excitement. *Make draga mea strong, carry our pups, rough and wild together.*

I shake my head, listening to the whirling sound of fuel. *We cannot claim our mate, and you know why. We've got so much more to get through before that's even a discussion I'll consider having.*

Thalia has drifted to sleep. It's under five hours until we get home. We would make it after Lena goes to bed, and there's really no guess as to Deacon. He's a nonissue. Then I can get up early with Lena and have a chat to get things sorted, quietly.

Tonight, I'm sleeping in my own bed, next to my mate.

Firing off a text, I let Michael know my arrival time so he and his team can make arrangements to move out. I will eventually forgive Peter for forcing my hand, but the apology won't come today. He does get a thank you text for keeping Michael, one of his top team leads, at the property as long as he did. It was a nice gesture of goodwill between us.

SHORTLY AFTER MIDNIGHT, I hit the button on the garage door and ease my black Yukon alongside Lena's bright red Equinox. My entire body shudders when my foot hits the concrete slab. It's a massive shake. Shoulders, necks, arms, and legs all spasm, releasing the tension of being away from home. I'm in the middle of a second yawn when I hear her soft voice.

"You okay?" Thalia has a soft smile on her face. She yawns too.

Nodding, I finish yawning. "It's good to be home. Shakes and yawns are stress releases."

"Okay."

Thalia's eyes drift close for a moment before her body snaps up. Struggling to stay awake, she fumbles with unbuckling her seat belt.

Continuing to unload the back seat, I hear the house door open. *Fuck.* I look over, hoping for some reprieve that it's Deacon. Through the windshield, I'm reminded my life is never easy.

Lena leans, with her arms crossed in front of her chest,

against the door frame. Her hair is pulled back tight; she's wearing her painting smock. *Stress painting, great.* And if her pinched face and squinting eyes are any indication, she recognizes Thalia.

Thalia, much to her lack of understanding, gives her a polite wave. "Hi, you must be Lena."

"You've got to be kidding me." Lena's voice is cold.

"I'm sorry?" Thalia says quietly, stepping backward.

There's not a lot I can say. Thalia is here to stay, and Lena will have to deal.

Lena walks back into the house as I round the SUV with bags in hand. With my shoulder, I motion for Thalia to follow me into the house. Inside, garage door closed and bags dropped on the floor in the laundry room, I brace for impact. *Fucking great.*

Lena is back in the dining room, which we've set up as her painting space. She's putting away her supplies. It's a violent sort of cleaning. Tension hanging in the air gives ample warning of the coming storm.

You not support her. You fail, Alpha. The Leviathan takes a jab, back to being judgmental. Hearing his frustration isn't helpful.

Thalia looks around, walking over to the island and leaning against it.

Her voice takes on the well-trained political and courteous air. "You've a lovely home."

"Expecting a bachelor pad?" I ask with a laugh, trying to diffuse the next assault from Lena before it happens.

She purses her lips, breaking the stuffy politician's kid routine. "Yeah, kinda was."

"We're wolves, not swine," Lena hisses.

Thalia turns to look at me, unsure what to say.

I growl at Lena. "I haven't even been home five minutes. We going to start shit now?"

"Bringing a client home is one thing. Bringing her," Lena snarls, eyes darting between me and Thalia before her death stare finds me, "is another issue all in itself. You're a bigger idiot than I thought you were."

Rice Lake

7

107

WISC

40

CHAPTER 40
THALIA

I'D HEARD Cade growl at Ansel's, but it was nothing compared to the ferocious sound coming from Lena now. I step behind Cade, wondering if I should make my way back into the mudroom and laundry room I had seen when we came in. Surely more distance between us would be good?

"Lena. We can talk more about this in the morning." Cade sounds firm in what he's saying and like he's gritting the words out; his fists are balled at his sides, and his back is ramrod straight.

I can't see Lena, but her voice rings through the open-concept living area. "Really? Cade, you brought home Thalia fucking Clark."

"Stop." The house shakes as that single word echoes from Cade through the space.

A door closes somewhere. I don't dare move my eyes from looking at Cade's shoulders. There's more of that terrible sound coming from Lena.

"Oh, hey. How long have you been home?" A man's voice comes from the same direction as the door noise.

My eyes dart over in that direction. I see a half-naked man standing there with his hands in the pockets of his black sweatpants.

He nods a bit before speaking. "Oh, well, okay then. I see how it's going to be. Welcome home. Oh!"

His eyes fall on me. He smiles, leaning forward a bit, squints, and then waves. "Hi. You must be the client."

I give a brief wave. The growling is still ongoing.

He walks toward us. Cade shuffles, positioning himself in a position split between the two of them. I now see the look of loathing painted in broad strokes across Lena's face.

"Bro, chill. I wanna say hi to our guest." The man sits down at the kitchen island between us. He gives me the goofiest little wave and a big smile. "Hi. I'm Deacon."

Cade directs his attention back to Lena. He steps toward Lena, and I'm torn between staying or moving.

"You're safe there," Deacon says.

I look back at him, and he nods, scrunching his face.

Can he read my mind? I'm starting to think all wolves read minds with how easily they say things I'm thinking. Though, Cade told me it was only Ezra.

I stay stone still but answer him, "I'm Emily."

He laughs. Deacon's smile is as infectious as Ansel's. "Yeah, no one will believe that."

"That's what Ansel said too." I purse my lips, fighting back the smile. I'm a terrible liar. "You can call me Emily."

Deacon nods. "There you go."

He mimics my pursed lips for a moment before looking at Cade and Lena, then back at me.

He sighs. "Standoff all because of you?"

"I think so," I whisper.

The growling echoing through the house is getting louder.

I wrap my arms around myself. *Should I move to the laundry room? It seems safer.* I take a step more behind Cade, out of her view.

"Want a snack?" Deacon asks. "I've got the munchies."

"Deacon, shut up," Cade commands.

It sounds forceful, just like the command to stop was. Deacon runs his fingers across his lips, zipping them closed.

"Lena, enough," Cade orders.

The growling comes to an end.

"I guess . . ." Cade pauses. I watch him run his hand back through his hair before looking at the ceiling. "Since you're both up. There's no time like the present."

Deacon's eyes dart back and forth between the two of us. "What?"

"The Leviathan and I will be taking back the throne," Cade says softly. "He and I are back to communicating, despite it being tense and frustrating."

Deacon's mouth is open. The look on his face closely mirrors Ansel's expression when Cade first said it. There's a moment of silence before he pulls it together.

"You, on the throne? Right." Lena sounds sarcastic. "What's next? You'll tell us she's your mate?"

I wish I could see what she's doing, but I don't want to move from the safety I've found behind Cade.

"It's true," I murmur. I don't know if it will help, but it hardly seems my input could make this much worse. "He told Ansel, Ezra, and Dinah."

"You're not right. You can't be. Your mate? There's no way. A human, this human?" Lena says with a grumble.

"The Leviathan says otherwise," Cade answers between growls.

Lena laughs, the growling beginning again. "Yeah. Sure, we all know you haven't talked to him in years."

"Things change." Cade stops growling and sighs. "The Leviathan and I are one. My gift works. You've felt it."

Lena huffs and I catch one last glimpse of her as she walks through the living space to the hallway Deacon emerged from earlier. After a moment, a door slams.

Deacon ducks in a wince. "Damn. She's pissy."

"Yeah, didn't think that any of this would go over well. I shouldn't have commanded her." Cade's shoulders drop. He hangs his head and turns to look at the two of us. "I know you've said hi, but, Deacon, do you know who she actually is?"

"Other than she's your mate, I don't know her from any other red-haired woman in the world." Deacon tries to study me. He squints, cocking his head. "Am I supposed to know her? Oh, shit. I didn't have sex with her, right? This isn't some sort of like get mad now to kill me later thing, right? I made a promise." His words come slowly at first, picking up with panic toward the end.

"Deacon. No," Cade says. He pinches the bridge of his nose, hanging his head before gesturing toward me. "This is Thalia Clark."

"Clark . . . Sounds familiar." Deacon knits his eyebrows together and cocks his head the other way before asking, "Huh, anyone ever tell you, you look like that senator lady on TV, if she was prettier?"

"Deacon," Cade prompts while I snicker. "Senator Clark."

"Oh, weird same —"

I've never seen a lightbulb moment happen in someone before, but the change in Deacon was the pull of a cord in an old dark basement.

His eyes stay on me as he turns his head to Cade before slowly drawing his eyes from me to look at Cade. "Your mate is Thalia Clark of the bloodline that is really kinda upset we exist."

"Yeah," Cade says, nodding. "My mate is Senator Clark's daughter, and I'm going to challenge Robert to become Sovereign."

"Oh, oh!" Deacon smiles. "Wait, no. This could be trouble."

"Let's go to bed." Cade sighs and looks at me.

His eyes are bloodshot. He beckons with a small wave of his hand.

Deacon sits there at the counter, fingers moving about in the air.

"Is he okay?" I whisper as I step closer to Cade.

"He's higher than a kite but mostly fine. His brain will run itself out of fumes in a little bit, then he'll grab a snack and sleep it off somewhere." Cade nudges me toward the end of the kitchen counter.

Cade's bedroom is off the kitchen, down a small hallway. When he opens the door, it's cooler inside. I shiver. Cade flips a light switch, and low lighting flips on. I take a moment to absorb the surroundings. It's a large room, but based on the size of the rest of the house, it seems to scale. It's fairly bare but has bespoke furnishings, like one-off Amish pieces.

His hands are on my shoulders, pushing me into the room farther. When I step forward, he lets me go before closing the door and latching it behind us.

There's an audible sigh from him. "Fuck, I'm exhausted."

Rice Lake 107

WISCO

CHAPTER 41
CADE

In the sanctuary of my bedroom suite, I wrap my arms around Thalia, burying my face into her hair behind her ear. I hold her firmly, trying to make her truly know she's safe.

Thalia wiggles a bit, and I let her go. She steps forward, walking away from me. There's nowhere for her to go, but I *have* to follow her. As I move, she turns around. When she looks at me, tears are running down her face.

In a small whimper, she says, "I'm sorry."

"Sorry for what? Thalia, everything is fine." I try to reassure her.

This is probably the best place for her to break down, but that's not what I want for her.

The Leviathan pushes at me, needing her. Scolding, *draga mea hurt. You hurt her.*

When I reach for her this time, she lets me capture her. Pulling her tight against my chest, she heaves with massive sobs. I hold her, unsure what released the dam she's been holding. Swaying left and right, I keep the gentle movements, trying to calm her until her sobbing stops. It hurts that she hurts, and an ache grows in my chest.

I want to ask more questions to understand why she felt she needed to apologize. However, the redness in her eyes, swollen, puffy cheeks, and red runny nose tell me to be smart. Tomorrow is a new day. I run my hand down her arm and lace my fingers between hers. Facing her, I keep watch, trying to read anything I can about what she's experiencing. Wordlessly, I lead her to the door of my bathroom, wanting to dry her eyes.

When I flick on the light, a gasp comes from Thalia, and she stops moving.

Taking a cue from her alarm, I dart my eyes, examining the space. The Leviathan and I are instantly on edge. We see nothing. I look down. Thalia's eyes are as big as saucers as she eye fucks my bathtub.

"Tub or bed?" I offer.

She nods, hand going up to her mouth, without saying anything, and starts the hot water on the tub. While she does that, I walk the back way through the bathroom, into my closet, then to the laundry room. I bypass the travel bags abandoned on the floor. Back to where we entered the house, I open the pantry and grab a variety of snacks. I pop back into the kitchen again for beverages. As expected, Deacon is gone, and the lights are off. I close the garage and arm the security system to the house. My home is now a fortress.

Returning to the bathroom, Thalia is soaking in the tub. A pile of her clothes lay on the floor, almost as if she teleported out of them. With her eyes closed, head pushed back against the end of the tub, a little moan escapes her throat that I became acquainted with a couple of days ago.

Too long. Need mate now. The Leviathan begins salivating. Fucking Pavlovian response. He's not wrong. Both of us heat with the desire.

I stand exhausted before the woman I love. I'll be damned if the first time I take her is simply blowing off steam. No matter how hard my cock is, and fuck is it hard, she deserves much better. I will give her so much better.

Sensing my eyes on her, Thalia opens hers and quickly moves to cover herself.

I smile watching her. "I've explored every inch of you and plan to do so a few dozen times over the coming weeks. Ship's sailed on being modest."

Begrudgingly she moves her hands aside.

Her voice turns soft. "You brought me snacks?"

I approach, stopping to pull out the bathtub tray from under the second sink.

After laying it across the top and depositing the late-night snacks, I whisper, "Us. And, yes."

"Oh." Thalia bites her bottom lip.

I pull my shirt off over my head and drop it onto the pile of her clothes. Her eyes rake over my body but lock on my hand as I undo my belt.

I've never found stripping sexy, but the way Thalia is looking at me, I'm beginning to find an exception. Teasing her might be fun. Belt and zipper undone, I let my jeans sag before sliding them and my boxers down my legs. Another one of those sounds I've become increasingly more aware of escapes her lips. She caught a good view of my cock twitching for her.

"Scoot forward," I urge, preparing to slide in behind her.

She does so, trying not to slosh water. "Where did you get such a big tub?"

"There's a company that makes shifter-sized things. I had them build out my bathroom." I hiss at the sensation of piping hot water. Thalia is clearly used to this temperature, as it doesn't seem to bother her. I force my body to adjust as I sink in behind her. I need the physical connection more than I'm concerned about the scalding water. Once I settle behind her, I say, "Soaking is one of my secrets. You're officially the fourth person to know I like a bath."

She tenses with me behind her. Patiently, I let her come to me. It takes a moment, but she slides back to rest against me.

Thalia's voice peaks with suspicion. "You don't tell anyone you date anything?"

"Thalia," I croon, trying a new tone hoping she understands. "I don't date. I don't have relationships. I have sex and hang out in groups at holidays. After abdicating, I wasn't ready to even consider commitment or dating. If I were ever going to consider having a long-term relationship, it would have to be with someone special. Someone I knew wasn't with me for the bloodline."

"Like Isabel?" Thalia's body tenses.

I nibble the back of her ear, then whisper my praise, "You're so possessive, draga mea. They don't matter. It's what they wanted but could never have."

Thalia relaxes.

When she rests against me, The Leviathan rests, contented by her touch.

"Please eat. We didn't stop for dinner," I coax.

She's cautious when picking through the selection. I make notes of what my mate doesn't eat. Raisins in the trail mix get set aside, and pretzels from another mix.

Her body against mine tempts me. I had barely calmed my dick down after I got in the tub, and her movements have me growing hard.

"Is that a gun in your pocket, or are you happy to see me?" she quips boldly.

I shift my hips, lifting her ass, giving her a sense of exactly how much I want her. I slip myself along her body.

"Oh, I'm more than happy to see you. But it's late, and I

have a hunch tomorrow might be a little stressful. Sleep is probably better for both of us."

In true form, The Leviathan pushes the issue. *Draga mea wants us. Wants to be bred. We will do.*

Oh. No. Do not. Go there. She is not, absolutely not, asking for that, I scold. Again he pushes the idea of puppies running in the grass, a memory from a past life. But then he imagines Thalia's stomach rounded.

"Tease," Thalia says under her breath.

"I'll drive you mad with wanting." I bend, nibbling down her neck.

I'm going to drive us both to the madhouse.

CHAPTER 42

THALIA

Banging is coming from somewhere in the house. It's the thudding of cupboard doors and clanging of frying pans. The light coming from under the doorway tells me it's daylight and a usual hour, but after being up late with Cade, I'm not sure I even want to people today. I pull the pillow over my head.

Cade left bed a while ago. He kissed my forehead and called me that pet name, draga mea, again, calling me his darling. I've never had a boyfriend give me a pet name. Not even my friends gave me nicknames. There's really no comparison either way because even when Cade says my given name, my heart flutters.

I try to drift back to sleep during a break in the kitchen clamor. I'm pulled toward thoughts of reading by a fire or scouring the archives. I'm on the edge of the stool to pull a large box out from storage. My escape to dreamland is interrupted to what's best described as someone dropping a whole stack of metal bowls down a flight of stairs.

I'm up. I'm up. I'm up.

As much as I want to march into the kitchen and give

whoever is making all the noise a piece of my mind, I don't know where Cade is. If Cade is serious about us being mates, which the jury is still out on my feelings, that means the noisy person is most likely a potentially new brother- or sister-in-law, or whatever the wolf equivalent is. Again, I'm still unsure of my feelings, but I have less than seven weeks left before Cade takes me home. Regardless of what we may or may not be, you'll make more friends with sweet than sour.

I don't know where my clothes are, but last night Cade gave me his T-shirt, and it's dress length-ish. My curves fill it out a little more than I'd normally be comfortable with, but short of finding my actual clothes, this is what I have to work with. I steel myself to be polite and deal with whoever is making the ruckus.

Entering the kitchen, I discover, as suspected, the culprit is Lena. She's pulled a blender out of a cupboard and is beginning to toss ice into it with force, it bounces around in the blender. She looks over at me and it doesn't take knowing her to see that the smile she has plastered on her face is fake. Lena wants to make my stay a living hell. She's angry and as it seems unafraid to start a squabble.

"Oh good! You're up. I was starting to believe you were dead. Which, would have been a shame." She turns back to the blender. "How are you, sleepy head?"

I smile, trying to brush off the early quips. Looking around to find a clock, I come up short.

"Yeah. Sorry. Your brother had me up late last night. We tried to keep it quiet."

"He would make that mistake, wouldn't he." Lena huffs a laugh, adding an eye roll.

"What mistake?" I poke, feigning innocence.

I know what her game is. I've dealt with mean girls like Lena. Two can play this game.

She motions to me where I stand, her fingers pulling together as she runs her hand the visual distance of my body. "Slumming it with the enemy's daughter."

It's my turn to laugh. I probe to find her weak points with Cade. "Well, seeing as The Leviathan liked me first, Cade just needed to be convinced."

Lena shakes her head. "Yeah. The Leviathan likes no one. He doesn't even like Cade."

She's salty about that. A signature eye roll barely masks her surprise at my statement. I walk around the counter to sit on one of the stools, pulling the shirt down as low as I can to protect myself from the cold chair.

I keep poking. "Oh, you didn't believe him last night? The Leviathan talks to him now."

"Yeah. Sure. He's magically going to take back the throne too." Lena pours liquid into the blender with more ice. She gives away more of what bothers her. "I'll see it when I believe it. Cade has avoided responsibility for this long; honestly, it makes sense he would want a human. There's no future with you. A genetic dead end. It is odd though. If he claims to want to take back the throne, why would he be putting his dick in the one thing that could ruin his political move."

I don't have a chance to bite back. She turns on the blender. The sound of crunching ice drowns out all possibilities of a comeback. I bide my time, lost in the reminder of the sting when Cade said, in not so many words, the same thing. We can't have children together. Not while I'm human. He said that's a conversation for the future but was it him appeasing me? My stomach flips at the thought.

Stopping the machine, Lena begins pouring out her beverage.

Before sipping on a straw, she looks over at me. "Are you even legal?"

"I guess I'm not sure what constitutes legal for wolves?" I put my finger on my cheek, tapping it and looking up at the ceiling. "Is it older or younger than for humans?"

My heart is racing. This is the most I've ever stood up for myself. Mom and Dad would have a fit if they knew I was engaging with someone. It's unbecoming of a politician and not ladylike. But they're not around, and the rules are different here.

It doesn't surprise me that Lena doesn't engage with my snark about consent.

She changes tactics. "So, Mommy and Daddy don't have enough money? You want a sugar daddy?"

"See, I don't intend to be a kept housewife." I sigh, looking at my nails. "I am, however, wondering if he's going to want to live in Georgetown or if I should start pursuing property out in Bethesda."

"Listen here, bitch," Lena snaps.

Spinning quickly, she glares at me. Her eyes are golden, similar to when I see The Leviathan in Cade.

She smirks, and I know it's because I must smell of fear. I'm afraid she can physically hurt me. I hope she wouldn't, but I'm not dumb enough to think it wouldn't happen.

"He may be fucking you. Hell, maybe The Leviathan does like you. Maybe you're even good in bed and worth his time of day. But mark my words. You'll never make Cade some domesticated city-living wolf. He values his privacy too much. No matter how good you suck dick, Cade won't give up the quiet life and sell out to the senator's idiot daughter. You're nothing more than a bed warmer. Not his first. Not his last. If you know what's good for you, then you'll spread your legs like a good little girl, take what you can get, and go back to your boring little human existence to tell all your friends that wolves do it better."

There's a pain in my chest, an awful burning that eats at my soul.

Lena's awful. She spits words like venom from a viper. They hurt. Each word pushes into my insecurities. I have to fight against the urge to curl into myself. Unfortunately for Lena, she's nothing more than a mean girl.

There's an undeniable fear of physical assault, but I can't back down now. I arm myself with everything Cade's told me, hoping he was honest. If this is going to bite back, it needs to be right. If he's said this to other women, and she knows, I won't be able to handle hearing her say it.

I look her up and down while tightening my core against the trembling. The words are hard to get out. "Think what you want, Lena. I'm not going anywhere. For seven weeks I'm going to be here. You'll have to adjust. The Leviathan and Cade agree that I'm his mate, and I'm warming up to the idea. Unless you're willing to tell me Cade's a liar, I have every reason to believe that he wants to sleep in my bed every night for the rest of our lives. We've started to talk about how to make it work long distance and how Peter has an office in DC. There's no reason we can't work."

She shakes her head, saying nothing. Lena's lack of comment is equally shocking and relieving. Now I know with certainty that he hasn't said those words to other people. If she knew he had, she would use it against me and wouldn't waste the opportunity.

I'm uncomfortable, shifting in my seat, but I need to drive my point. I swallow first. "And, for the record, he's said all this already and we haven't had sex yet."

The sound of a clearing throat breaks our death glare. My eyes dart over to see Cade leaning against the kitchen door frame, one hand hanging on to the back of his neck.

Shoot. How much did Cade hear? Will he be upset with me

for standing up for myself? Some of the confidence I felt in going head-to-head with Lena slowly dissipates, and I wrap my arms around my middle, not sure what to expect.

Lena leans back before stepping away from me. She tosses her hands up as if to prove she hasn't touched me.

Drawing her brows together, she says his name, dripping with acid as it rolls off her tongue. "Cade?"

"I am challenging Robert," he says unceremoniously. Cade takes a few steps closer to her in the kitchen. With gentle hands, he turns Lena to face him. "She's not wrong, Lena. Everything she's said is true. I wanted to chat with you this morning. It's why I texted you to meet me in the garage. I thought you'd find me when you got up."

At Cade's words, my shoulders drop in relief. *I was right.*

"Fuck you." She looks at him, then at me with her face pinched in disgust. Her eyes go back to him. Shoulders shaking out of his grasp, she raises her head. "Better find a way to stop Senator Clark, or your mating will be very short-lived. I can imagine she might even go so far as using the opportunity to press charges of endangerment against you."

"Get the fuck out of my sight, Lena, before I'm forced to put you in your place."

Any semblance of patience Cade was trying to hold on to seems to snap. I watch Cade's lip curl as he growls. The sound of his voice is that command echoing through him.

I swallow hard. It's not directed at me, but this side of Cade is different, more aggressive, than I'm used to.

Lena sets her cup down and retreats. Her whole demeanor changes. She's shrinking smaller. My heart aches. I didn't want it to be this way. Cade dropped a massive bomb of information on her. I try to put myself in her shoes and understand what this means to her. She's clearly hurting, taking the farthest distance around the island away from me toward the glass doors at the back of the house. I watch through the glass door as she descends the stairs until I can no longer see her.

Pulling my eyes back to Cade, I start trying to smooth things over. "Cade —"

"Don't." He cuts me off. "You handled her better than most people. It sounds like I'm making excuses for her when I explain what she's gone through because of my decisions. It's been hard. Had I not given up the throne, she'd be more stable. She wouldn't hurt so much. You do not have to give her another chance after that. It's a small house, and I don't want you to feel confined to my room. But I promise she'll be more respectful as she adjusts to you being here. Almost, but not quite pleasant. I'm sorry I didn't have a chance to plead your case with her. I thought she'd at least hear me out first."

"It's okay." I offer him a small smile, trying to make him see I'm sincere. I shouldn't have come with guns blazing at Lena. I could have tried to be nicer longer. I let her suck me into a dark place, and it's embarrassing. *I should have been the bigger person.* I can't look at him when I speak so I just look down at the countertop in front of me. "I can't read body language like you, but Lena's not much different from most mean girls I've met. They're going through things that I don't know about. We'll find a balance. Dad taught me a few tricks. I should have been better about not meeting her on her level."

Cade doesn't say anything, and I really wish I was better at reading him.

He starts to clean up in the wake of hurricane Lena. I drag my eyes from the counter to watch him. A few minutes later, he has most of the kitchen items put away.

"I'd appreciate knowing how much of that you meant and how much was just baiting her." His voice is low and sincere.

He's still not looking at me. I don't really want to look at him either. Shame is such a strong feeling.

What if he doesn't want those things? Just because it made Lena falter doesn't mean he feels that way.

The voice I get out is small. "I meant most of it."

It's taken a lot of debating to get to this point. The fact is, Cade's words affect me. Lena's confirmation, that Cade doesn't say these things to other girls, solidifies some of those wayward emotions. Of course, I'm still insecure about it. Of course, I want to protect my heart. His life is about to change. I may or may not be part of that change. While Lena inadvertently validated that Cade's feelings are genuine and only for me, she also slid in more things to consider. There's a mass of obstacles to overcome. Who knows if he's really willing to stick with me through the coming storm? Especially when people find out who my mom is. He'll face heat for that.

Cade is quiet and evidently doesn't have anything to say because he starts cooking. Bacon sizzles in the pan, filling the space with the smell of its salty goodness before he finds a voice.

He starts speaking slowly. "I am willing to fight to keep you. I'm going to go head-to-head with your mother on big political issues. Avoiding talking to you about them has come from a place of self-preservation and fear that I may not be prepared for your answers or political opinions, despite what you've voiced before. I also respect and understand that you've tried to stay out of your parents' politics. It's not as though I can deny this: my life is going to become political very soon. As much as The Leviathan and I want to keep you, and make you our mate, I respect your desire to stay out of it all. I'll do my best to shelter you from it."

"But?" I prompt, knowing there's one behind this.

Cade's voice is drawn out and brings a heaviness to the room. "But I'm going to need to know if I'm fighting a war on two fronts. If at every turn, I'm also going to have to defend why I can be or try to be with someone who believes the same things as her mother."

He sounds angry like it's a prediction of what he's expecting to come. Standing in front of the stove, he balls his hands into fists, clutching the spatula in his hand tightly.

Then, his voice softens, and he hangs his head. "I've tried to show you positive things about us because it seems you truly don't know a lot about wolves and shifters. We're a culture shock, and I might not be the best ambassador."

"Cade!" I cut him off. It's unusual for him to seem so emotionally charged about a subject. Unsettled by his discomfort, I try to put his mind at ease. "I don't know what her entire platform is about. But from everything I've learned, Mom is cruel. There's not a single thing I've learned or experienced that would lead me to believe anything other than shifters might not be human, but they're people. Laws and restrictions unfairly put against people aren't right. Stop worrying that I'll ever say anything against your platform. There's nothing that will make me believe otherwise."

He stops cooking breakfast and comes over to where I'm sitting. His hand cups my chin before kissing me. It's loving and tender, showing me love and devotion that I don't know how I could have earned. I know it's there. When he goes to break the kiss, I fist his shirt, keeping him close to me. I kiss him, trying to push back that same intensity.

When our lips part, Cade rests his forehead against mine.

His voice is gravelly as he says, "I wish I could accurately explain how I feel. I wish you could experience all of this, how I do."

"Why can't you tell me?" My voice comes out unexpectedly shaky.

Cade nudges his nose against mine. I push back, unsure what it means.

He's quiet before giving me one last small kiss and answering, "Because I'm letting you set the pace and what you've said tells me it's too early. You need more time."

"But you feel it." I try to understand.

His fingers slowly fall from my face before he returns to the far side of the island to cook.

"I'm willing to let my feelings belong to me, until you're ready for more," Cade says over his shoulder. "I can be patient and move at your pace."

Those words are sweet and romantic, and I'm like a heroine in a film. It's this sense of belonging and . . . Oh, no. I try not to put words in his mouth, but the tenderness he shows me, how he's gentle with me, patient, and how he says dirty things full of emotions all indicate what he's not saying. He's called me his mate, which my understanding tells me it's equivalent to marriage. *Why wouldn't it be love?*

Rice Lake 107

WISC

7

49

CHAPTER 43

CADE

IT MAKES MY SKIN CRAWL, being backhanded and self-serving, but I suggest to Thalia that we put on the audiobook while I finish cooking breakfast. I've already figured out the plot twist and confirmed it with a spoiler group on the internet, so now I need some time to process. The book keeps Thalia busy, happy, and out of her own head while it gives me time to be in mine.

The Leviathan has been brushing against my control for the better part of the morning. I wanted to go for a run and give him some time to adjust to the last day's turn of events. However, in waiting for Lena, I delayed, only to find her and Thalia in what is best described as an emotional battle for dominance. I've learned some things I didn't know I needed to hear.

This road to keeping Thalia won't be smooth. The Sovereign Alpha being mated to a human is going to be an issue, only compounded by her relation to Senator Clark. There are laws her mother could use to exploit our relationship for her own personal gain. I could be given a death sentence if I'm accused of being dangerous while she's a human. Just under seven weeks. All I need is to survive a little less than seven weeks, keeping her safe and human, then the bill is less harrowing. It'll be safer. Everything that has been brought to light is further proof that if Thalia is going to accept being my mate, our lives, okay mostly mine, would be easier if she was wolf. *Selfish again.*

We claim mate. Give her wolf. Not shameful. The Leviathan pictures Thalia smiling when we were out at Arches. Even though it's currently irresponsible to do so, it is what I want. He brings forth a memory, from his past, of puppies running about in the yard. I want that.

When it's safe, I affirm. *If Thalia agrees she wants a wolf, we will give her one.* The Leviathan still pushes, wanting time out in the world, but he's at least more content. Knowing we agree, together on something, is giving us both a boost in healing the fracture between us.

I've run and rerun the dishwasher, picked up the rest of Lena's mess, and am beginning to plate food for the two of us when Lena comes back to the house. Outside the sliding glass door, she peers in, seeing me in the kitchen. Lena quickly drops her gaze. Cautiously, she opens the back door and walks in, her long brown hair hanging loose around her face, hiding her eyes from me.

She approaches the long way, through the living room and around the couch, making her way to sit at the opposite end of the breakfast bar from Thalia. Her path intentionally was as far away from Thalia as possible out of respect. Now Lena is trying to rejoin the relationship with me, in an offering of apology.

Lena sits quietly with her head down. I grab another plate from the cupboard, making up a third. As a peace offering, I set the first plate down in front of Lena, then put the second one in front of Thalia, kissing her on the forehead. Returning to the middle of the island, on the kitchen side, I face the two of them with my own plate.

We're midway through the meal when Lena tests the waters, her voice significantly more humble. "You're serious about this?"

She refuses to look at me.

"Yeah, it's happening. Dinah, Ezra, Ansel, and Wyatt have heard. I wanted to tell you and Deacon in person, out of respect, before I go and challenge Robert."

"What brought this on?" Lena glances down the bar before staring back at her plate. "A week ago, you told Judah you didn't want this."

I click my fork hard against the plate, making a snapping sound. Thalia snaps her head up but returns her attention to her food.

Lena quickly goes back to looking at her plate again. I can forgive her for lashing out and stating the truth in the way she did, but it won't be this moment. Pack dynamics start now. It's going to be expected of us to maintain some semblance of hierarchy.

I breathe before pushing my hair out of my eyes and carefully choosing my words. "Yes, Thalia is part of the decision." I incline my head toward her. "But, overall, it's been time. The blood test and finding out that he cut off the Alloways and Ansel are the final straws. The Leviathan and I are getting settled with each other. I don't have all the answers. I do have a few plans, but . . ." I pause. *How do I ask them for this? After the years of floundering without a strong pack bond to steady them out of loyalty to me.* "I've honored my agreement with Robert. I haven't built a pack or any relationships with wolves outside of the family. But that means . . ."

"You don't have another option for the Alpha Female or Second," Lena says flatly.

I put her in her place less than an hour ago. I told her to get out of my face, and then, like the asshole I am, I ask for a favor. I ask her to be something she's not all over again, for appearance's sake.

"I accept my nomination as Second." Deacon waves from where he's been chilling on the couch.

Thalia looks around, eyes wide, before seeing his hand. She clutches her hand over her heart.

"I'll gladly nominate around you, when I have better access, but the law states that very soon, I'll need to present an Alpha Female and Second, or have to host challenge fights." I try to pull Lena into agreement, but I might have broken her faith. "I don't want to leave myself open for outside influence until I get to the bottom of whatever Robert has done."

Deacon shuffles over in his socks to sit on the stool between Lena and Thalia. He begins reaching across the counter, making a plate and a mess.

He points at Thalia's plate. "Are you done?"

"Question," Thalia pipes in while sliding her plate toward him. "Mates are like married partners? And why does it seem like Alpha Male and Alpha Female should be mates?"

Using Thalia's fork, Deacon picks up some pancake before leaning over and whispering, "Yes, and weird word choice, right? Like, did the humans get it wrong with the titles, or does it not translate? King and Queen versus Alpha Male and Female, never made sense to me either."

Thalia nods and whispers back, "Okay, so, they don't have to be mates right?"

My jaw falls open, and I look to Lena, who's watching them with intense focus. I let Deacon keep handling the questions.

Shaking his head, he grimaces and whispers, "Ew. No. It just means they're the most dominant of their gender."

"Okay, but then is the Alpha Male always in charge?" Thalia whispers back.

She's clearly fascinated, and I'm enthralled with how Deacon is chatting with her. It's not that he's not social. It's that Deacon takes a bit to warm up when he's not drunk. With how bright and clear his eyes are, Deacon's surprisingly sober.

"He's not always in control. Many successful packs run with an Alpha Female as head of pack. Human influence has made it difficult for women to be accepted as leaders," Lena answers, without a snotty tone.

I'm starting to wonder if I accidentally poisoned the food because everyone's getting along. I set my plate down.

Deacon wastes no time leaning over the counter from his stool to scoop my plate up and bring it to himself.

Thalia leans backward around Deacon to look at Lena, but Lena looks away, not meeting her gaze. Her body language confuses Thalia. With her eyebrows drawn together, she looks to me and Deacon for guidance. *How do I explain that body language without hurting Lena?*

I scrub my hand down my face. There's no way to explain it, so I just answer Thalia's other question. "So, essentially, The Alpha Male's mate, who is not the Alpha Female, is called Luna."

"Vito, Ezra, and Ansel called me that." Thalia recognizes it, her voice drawing out as her eyes focus on me.

"Awww, you are real!" Deacon bumps against Thalia lovingly. She wobbles on the stool.

Seriously, the pack house will have no stools. My woman can't be trusted with her feet off the ground.

The Leviathan growls, upset with Deacon for potentially hurting her. The sound erupts from me before I stifle it. Deacon backs away from Thalia, quickly putting the distance back between them. *No. Ours.*

"Sorry Dea. I'm working on it." I apologize as he settles back into his stool.

Thalia looks confused. I'm not even sure where to explain. *I'm the shittiest ambassador for wolves. How the fuck do I think I can do this job?*

Deacon nods. Forever the compassionate one, Deacon accepts my apology. "I get it. Unclaimed mate. Guess it doesn't matter that we're siblings, it's still competition."

The Leviathan settles, barely accepting Deacon's apology. *Lena and Deacon, out of line. Need discipline. Need pack.* He reminds me. I shut him down. He's top wolf, but if I'm going to survive being Sovereign again, it's got to be on my terms. Whatever those are.

"You'll handle the fights?" Lena's voice is stronger as she brings us back on track.

"Of course, no one will ever find out. I promise." I focus my gaze on her so she knows I'm sincere.

We will keep safe. The Leviathan agrees. He does have a heart, sometimes.

CHAPTER 44
THALIA

WE SIT around the kitchen island for a few more minutes, and Cade explains the same plans and backup plans he laid out for Ansel and Ezra. Jointly, they agree it'll play out with Robert wanting to throw a party of sorts. They're confident the contingency plans will work out precisely, if needed. I have nothing to contribute and spend the meeting observing the smallest changes in body movements. Lena leaning in and out as the conversation ebbs and flows is easiest to observe. Deacon, however, watches me intensely, and his eyes on me are unsettling.

The conversation of Cade challenging Robert begins to die, and Deacon's still examining me intently. "So, elephant in the room?"

Cade sighs. "I know. How the fuck did The Leviathan, of anyone, pick a human mate?"

"Yeah." Deacon shrugs. "Weird. But the ancestors are all sorts of proud of you and think highly of Thalia."

"Oh, joy. More old dead relatives and their judgment." Lena casts her gaze over at him.

"Shhhh." He scolds her. "I can't help you now. You've pissed them off. You know they don't like to be called old."

I am so lost, what does any of that mean? What would it matter if you make ghosts angry? I look to Cade.

"Deacon kind of explains that ancestors and spirits don't have a ton of pull over what happens in our daily life, but there's apparently some sort of interference from them we all experience from time to time," Cade explains quietly.

Does he not want the ancestors to hear?

"She's still human. Don't forget her bloodline. If Robert doesn't kill him, her mother probably will," Lena reminds us, and there's a small bite in her tone. Whatever sort of shift happened between her and Cade is clearly waning as she gets more lively. "Alright, I've got to get that painting done and some studying for school. Master's degrees don't earn themselves."

"Facts!" I chime in, hoping for some solidarity in scholastics.

There is none. Lena rolls her eyes, but I tried.

Cade smiles at me. "Alright, I've got some shit to get done. Stuff I had planned to get done because I was on vacation time. Clearly things change. I'm going to be out in the garage. You're welcome to join me. It's a little chilly today, it might snow. But we do have jackets."

"She can stay in here." Lena's tone is less snarky than it was a moment ago. "I won't kill her."

Deacon scratches his neck. "I've got to go to town today. Anyone need anything? Or want to go?"

"Hobby, craft stuff, or busy work?" Cade motions to me and then back to Deacon, implying I should give him a list.

I don't have a chance to answer. Deacon is walking away, shaking his head.

He stops. "Not you. Yeah. Anything you need, Thalia, shoot me a text."

A door closes, and I whisper to Cade, "Is he okay?"

"Not in the slightest," Lena grumbles, opening blinds at the back of the house, illuminating where her art supplies are set up.

Cade comes to me and kisses me on the forehead before instructing, "Text Deacon what you want or need. I'm just outside the garage door."

He looks over my head at Lena. "We good?"

"I promised not to kill her," Lena answers with an annoyed hum. "Get your work done."

I'VE BEEN READING for a few hours. Deacon emerged from his room and left over an hour ago. I glance over to observe Lena; she's sitting on a stool with the end of a brush in her mouth. She's been humming and muttering to herself for the last four chapters of my book. Now looking up to see the intense way she's examining her work, I realize, Lena is just an intense person in everything she does. Her eyes scrape across the painting back and forth.

She sighs. "Alright. I need help."

"Me?" I ask hesitantly, trying to pretend I wasn't watching her.

Unmoving from her place and with a toughness, she replies, "I'll go bug Cade if you'd rather."

Cautiously, I set my phone down and walk over toward her workstation. The painting on the stand is beautiful. It's an oil painting of a woodland scene with a woman wrapped in fabric, fighting the wind. I recognize it instantly.

"Oh, *Boreas*."

"Yeah, a more modern attempt with painting ourselves into the subject." She sighs. "I think I overdid making the background more realism, less impressionism."

"Do you have the reference?" I ask. "There's something missing."

Lena reaches over to the side and pulls it out, holding it between her two fingers.

Before handing it to me, she speaks slowly but not condescendingly. "He's my brother, and out of the three of them, he's made the most mistakes. I'm not trying to be mean, but you could potentially be the biggest one. I can't be the only one to see it. I can appreciate that my brother's wolf has picked you as his mate. I don't understand it, and I'm not going to pretend that it isn't dangerous for Cade to be involved with you. I'll do better to accept your place here."

I take the copy of *Boreas* and don't say anything, examining her painting and the reference photo, giving myself a moment to formulate an answer. *Did she just apologize? I mean, she didn't exactly say 'I'm sorry.'*

I see the major missing component of her painting about the same time I figure out how to answer her.

I address the easiest issue first. "It's not the structure of the realism in the back, it's that your highlight on the daffodil is too bright and not tied into the background in the lower field."

Lena looks, nodding.

Handing her back the reference, I admit, to her and myself, what I've been holding in. "I have feelings for Cade. I know you're trying to come from a loving and protective place, but I personally haven't done anything wrong. I accept you expressing your opinion, that this is a mistake, but it's not going to change how it is."

Lena shrugs. "Thanks for your eye on the painting. I saw you in a restoration class."

"Oh." I pause, confused about where we had ever crossed paths before. Then it strikes me. "Gift. Your gift lets you see people's pasts."

She nods, picking up her brush and rearranging paints. Lena bites her bottom lip and extends an olive branch. "Yeah. I'm sorry about your professor. You did the right thing in telling him no. Good morals, working for your place, and not taking the easy way through are all very important to wolves. But I know how hard it is to stand your ground when you're afraid."

My jaw drops. I've never told anyone, especially not Cade.

CHAPTER 45

CADE

WE'VE BEEN HOME for a week, and everyone has, for the most part, settled in around the house. Deacon is himself. He's been strung out less, I think out of respect for us having a guest, but for whatever reason, even when he's stoned or drunk, Thalia's befriended him. They easily spend hours together. She doesn't even question when he starts talking to the ancestors. As rough of a start as they had, Lena and Thalia have come to an understanding of sorts. Lena still pokes, trying to get a reaction from Thalia. Overall, there haven't been any major incidents.

Every day, my uneasiness grows. I know what needs to happen. I need to go see Robert. The Leviathan pushes for it. All thoughts drift back to claiming Thalia and the throne. In that order.

The longer I put off talking to Robert, the less time I give him to plan a party and the more likely he is for an instant fight. Waiting is only keeping me in a fight response. *Procrastination is self-punishment.* It's creating more problems than it's solved.

Sleeping next to Thalia is perhaps proof I'm some sort of

masochist. Every night is restful, wonderful sleep. I go to bed dreaming of all the things I want to do to her, but despite fucking my hand in the shower each night, I wake up yearning to feel her soft curves. Every morning she's glued to my side, her ass or tits pressed against me. I've tried to engage with her, but the flirting and dirty talk from Ansel's have lost their charm. She kisses back and sometimes meets my intensity, but it seems to stop there. *What did I fuck up?*

Wasting time courting. Tell draga mea we claim. Then do. The Leviathan's answer is problematic on all levels. Though, the thought of being direct has crossed my mind. *Coward. Tell draga mea want. Then claim.* The Leviathan pushes the idea of bending her over the bed. I try to block it from my brain, but for the umpteenth time, my cock presses against the fly of my jeans. Sitting out in the garage, working on the ATVs and snow machines, away from Thalia, has provided very little reprieve. Now, The Leviathan has made that impossible.

The door from the house opens. I look over from the ATV I've been working on, and Thalia steps out, closing the door quietly behind her.

She tucks one of the flyaway strands of red curly hair behind her ear. "Hey, how's it going?"

"Good, almost done. How are you?" I smile.

I don't remember ever smiling so much, but every time I see her, it happens. Even with my concern about what's going on between us, or rather, what isn't, Thalia's presence puts me at ease.

"I'm okay, just restless. Thought I'd come find you."

She wanders over, running her hand across Lena's SUV and then mine before ending at the third stall where I'm working on the four-wheeler.

"Bored?" I know the answer.

Even with the mountain of knitting supplies that Deacon

brought home, country life quickly becomes dull for someone used to living in the city.

Thalia brushes up against me before moving to sit on the shop stool. Her touch is so comforting. But I foresee the problem before her butt hits the seat. The wheeled stool is set for Deacon's height, and it spins and rolls while she tries to sit on it. I move over, depressing the lever, and it drops down slowly, putting her feet on the ground. *Seriously, no more stools.*

From my stooped position pressing down the lever, I'm looking up at Thalia's face. She bites her bottom lip, and I fight the urge to kiss her. I can smell her arousal. I have her attention.

Her bottom lip pops out when she answers my initial question. "Yeah, I'm bored. I know we're kind of in hiding, but I would take a trip to the grocery store if it meant getting out of the house."

"See." I draw it out, debating this next sentence. After that lip pop, my desire to nibble on it increases exponentially. She smiles at me, and the debate ends. I go with the forward approach. "I can most certainly think of ways to keep your mind occupied without leaving my suite. All of them require significantly less clothing."

Thalia bites her lips together and looks out the open garage door to the driveway. Her face turns red.

Moving back slightly, I voice my confusion. "Flirting, brushing up against me, you've been driving me wild. But anytime I go to initiate something with you, you clam right up. You seemed pretty on board with us before. When you fought Lena, you told me what you were saying was true. I'm concerned that I haven't been taking care of you right. What changed between us?"

Thalia releases her lips from between her teeth and looks at me. Her freckles show bright on her flushed cheeks.

She closes her eyes and releases a heavy exhale. "I can't look at you when I say this, so just deal with it." She pauses, opening one eye slightly before squeezing it shut again. In one short, forced breath, she lets out, "I'm afraid of having sex with you."

Why does our mate fear? Did we do bad? She screamed our name. The Leviathan comes forward to focus on that. One track mind. Animal.

I wait, but she doesn't say anything more. I can't sit here and let my mind, and The Leviathan, come up with the worst possible answers.

"Can I ask why?"

Her eyes are still squeezed tight and accompanied by a wrinkled nose.

Her tone doesn't convey disgust despite her face. "I've seen your, uhm. Size."

"Yeah?" I push, desperately trying not to jump to conclusions.

Her hands go to her face, and she covers her mouth. Her words are muffled, but I make them out. "I've never been with someone so, um, sizable, and the few times I've had penis in vagina sex, it really hurt. I'm positive that you'll really hurt. I'm a wuss when it comes to pain, and I'm squeamish, so if there's any, um, blood after, I'm worried I'll get woozy."

The Leviathan rolls his eyes and retreats. His faith in me for this conversation is a confidence boost on its own. Her words, well, I don't know a man who doesn't like size compliments, even if they come with awkward anatomically correct language.

Abandoning the tools, I wipe my hands on the spare rag before approaching her and gently pulling her hands off her face. I bend forward, her diminished height on the stool more difficult, but I manage. She doesn't open her eyes. I kiss her, trying to assure her that she's perfect. *Can I kiss her into seeing herself the way I see her?*

I whisper against her lips, "I promise you; those boys had no idea what they were doing. You weren't their focus. Given the opportunity, I will gladly show you that not only do I fit, but it'll be without pain or discomfort. Call me a hedonist, if necessary, but the more orgasms I give you, the more pleasure I get."

"Is that why you haven't, um . . ." Her voice dies off.

I try to put myself in her shoes. My blood runs cold. What sort of relationships has she had that this was a question for her? Humans are so fucked up. If I ask, I'll probably spend some time contemplating hunting down her ex. It doesn't stop the words from coming out.

"Are you saying you expected me to ask you to suck my cock since I ate you out?"

Thalia nods slowly, biting her lips together again. Her head falls ever so slightly.

"Thalia, this relationship is not transactional. I will never come back to you with a favor or expectation because I've done something for you. Sexually or otherwise, you're more than any exchange."

My thumbs run against the back of her hands. I crave touch and connection, but she needs this on her terms. Thalia needs to approach me.

Her eyes slowly open. Between the small bout of fear and watery quality of her eyes, it's impossible not to know how much she's hurting.

"I'm not any good at this. I don't want to disappoint you." Her voice comes out small.

"I'm not going to ask you to be good at any of this: sex, talking about sex, talking about sexual desires. I'm not asking you to have it figured out." I pull her hand up and kiss the back of it. "I'm asking that you try to talk to me knowing I'm not going to judge you. You'll never disappoint me."

The sadness in Thalia's eyes fades. She nods. "I shouldn't compare you to my past. It's not fair to you."

Her experiences and thoughts are valid. I can only do what I can to show her that it's possible for it to be different. Even if it hurts to be grouped with assholes, it's probably temporary. For now, I'll wait. She's worth it. I press one last kiss against her forehead.

"I've got an idea to get you out of the house. The Leviathan keeps pointing out how human you are. He thinks you should be able to protect yourself."

Thalia tenses in my arms. "I'm not sure I understand."

"Breathe. I'm not gifting you a wolf." I push the slightest command while trying to hide any of the dozen feelings I have.

Not turning. Coward. The Leviathan has his own commentary. *Give our mate wolf.*

"Okay." Thalia draws out the last syllable.

"Tomorrow, we'll get up early. I'll take you out and away from the house for a bit." I promise her.

She seems content with the idea. I just hope she's still on board tomorrow.

AFTER LUNCH and with the promise of a day out of the house tomorrow, Thalia snuggles herself on the couch, looking ready for a nap. Wrapped up in a little cocoon, the sleepy little face she makes is too much temptation.

I beckon for her. "Thalia, let's take a nap."

"Really?" She gleams, excited at the prospect.

Lena squints at me with judgment before shouting, "Deacon! Beer run?"

I hear Deacon's bedroom door open. "Yes! Let's go!"

He slides across the floor in his socks, arms spinning like a rockstar to keep him upright.

Lena laughs. "Alright, we'll be back later."

Lena and Deacon are out the door in less than sixty seconds.

Laughter erupts from Thalia; she tries to take deep breaths to talk, but more laughter comes out. I pick her up off the couch, pull her into my arms, and make my way to my room.

She squeaks but keeps laughing. "Did they just clear out thinking we're going to have sex?"

"Oh, yeah." I kick closed the door behind me. "I'll let you nap after you come for me."

CHAPTER 46

THALIA

I'M SET on the bed gently, as one would treat a piece of fragile porcelain from the Ming Dynasty. The Leviathan lights fire in Cade's eyes. It's powerful having both of their attentions. The look is dominating and possessive, yet I'm not captive.

I push myself up on my elbows, and butterflies swarm in my stomach. Swallowing against the nerves, I take in his posture as he focuses on me. I want him to be right about what he told me in the garage. I want it to be true that I'll feel only pleasure with him, no pain. Pulling in deep breaths, I steel myself for his next move.

Without warning, Cade descends on me. I'm very aware of the unfortunate layers of our clothes. I don't want them between us. Cade doesn't seem to mind. His forehead pushes against mine. Laying me flat, no longer supporting myself up by my elbows, back to the bed, he kisses me setting a slow pace. His body presses gently against mine but not in the heavy sense, he's leaving room between us.

It's bold, but between kisses, I let my hands explore him. I press my left hand against his chest and T-shirt, snaking the other down his abs across the smooth fabric. I find the waistband on his jeans, then the cold metal of his belt buckle. I try to pull the leather with trembling fingers, failing to release it.

Cade nips my bottom lip. "Needy, draga mea?"

"Mmhmmm." I don't have words. He kisses my ear before I can utter, "Help."

More of his weight rests against me, and I can't help but rise to meet his body.

He groans. "Fuck, give me a minute. I can't get us undressed when you're doing that."

I force myself away from him, begrudgingly retreating back to the bed. Cade, resting his weight on one forearm, easily undoes his belt. His hand then finds my waistband and works it back and forth across my low belly, slowly moving my pants down. This time, when I lift my hips, he doesn't stop me and trails kisses of encouragement down my jaw. Soon, my bare butt is against the bed, and I'm waiting for him. Gently he moves off me and then stands before shuffling his pants and boxers down to a pile on the floor. His hands skim down my thighs as my leggings fall free.

The sight of Cade pulling off his shirt is drool-worthy. Abs rippling and pecs flexing. *How did I get so lucky?* His tattoo accentuates the muscle movements in his arm and chest as I'm captivated watching. Once his clothes are off, he returns his attention to my body.

Glimpses of Cade dressing have always elicited thoughts of seeing more, but I never expected him to look this appetizing. I'm growing wetter by the second. I can't focus on anything other than watching him and how it makes me feel, the growl that feels like it vibrates the whole room, and the delicate touch of his hands running up the sensitive parts of my sides. Squirming against him, I involuntarily smile.

Can you come from foreplay?

He's watching himself touch me. The dedication to each touch lights a fire I haven't felt before. It feels like a promise of what's to come.

Cade's grip changes, pressing his fingers more firmly into the soft skin above my hips. It's the skin that pushes weirdly into my jeans. Feeling his hands firm against me, I remember there's a difference in our physiques. I try reaching for a blanket, wanting to hide it, but then he makes a soft needy sound.

"How did I get so lucky? You're fucking perfect," he whispers.

A soft groan escapes from his mouth as he pulls off my shirt. My bra is next, and he's careful with the snap and straps.

Cade swallows hard. His facial expression screams the hunger of a man starved. Which, I guess he is, with the dance we've done over the last few days, teasing us both. Seeing that fire for me banishes my insecurities. He wets his bottom lip with his tongue.

I can't answer his question. His hand gently guides me back against the bed. Instead of claiming space on top of me, Cade lies along my side. The hand pressing against my jaw drops down slowly, and hesitantly, he lets it drape on my throat. I'm squirming with excitement arching against his grip. As if understanding, he squeezes gently.

The mellow tone of his voice entices me. "You like my hand claiming your neck?"

I nod against the constriction of his fingers. He kisses me again, letting his other hand trail gracefully, circling my breast. I bring my hand over, running it up his arm. I squeeze his bicep. Smirking against my lips, he flexes. Can biceps be sexy? I think yes. Yes, most definitely sexy. He's built, but I've never really seen him use his muscles. This flex though? *Yum.*

Trying my best not to tickle him, I run my hand down his side, making sure my arm doesn't interrupt what he's doing with my breast. While he pinches hard on my sensitive, pebbled nipple, my hand finds his cock. It's erect, and my fingers wrap around it, barely touching. I return the squeeze. He smirks. His bicep might have been hard, but I'm wondering if his cock isn't harder. The warmth of his cock in my hand sends heat rushing between my thighs. I squeeze my legs together, feeling the response.

"All for you. It takes just one single dirty thought about you, and my cock is stiff. I crave you. Only say the word, and I stop. You're all I care about."

Cade's words are a vow to my ears. His hand trails, past my arm and down my soft stomach. I tense, my legs locked together. He shifts and presses his knee between us, moving to hold himself lightly above me before he slides a finger between my folds. A moan rolls out of me, and my hand squeezes the tip of his cock.

His jaw twitches as a finger gently teases my opening. It takes a second, but then his finger is grazing in and out effortlessly. I draw slow breaths watching him watch me. Cade kisses me. It's sweet but not chaste. His nose presses against mine, turning my head more toward him. I'm nearly lost in the kiss, only to be brought back as he breaks it.

My attention instantly floods to my lower lips as one of his fingers slips deeper, stroking up against the ribs of my insides. It's a surreal experience. I close my eyes to focus on what he's doing. An orgasm builds, distantly but moving closer.

I don't recognize the noises that come from me. I've never made them before, but they're about all I can come up with to encourage him to do more. I need more. Every stroke of his finger builds pressure. What I want is the pressure of his thumb against my clit. *I want more.* Cade seems to *know* what I want but coyly refuses to give it to me.

Tenderly, a second finger presses forward, entering me. It isn't painful like I anticipated. Pressure opens me, but it comes more naturally. The two fingers work in tandem. I lift my hips, wanting more touch. *Not want, it's need. I need more.* I now need his thumb. I need to come, and his thumb would give me an orgasm.

Cade's hand squeezes around my neck. I open my eyes to find The Leviathan's eyes meeting mine. I have their full attention. It's empowering. I lift my throat up into his hand, asking for more. Eager to oblige me, Cade squeezes. Despite being slightly lightheaded, I ache, wanting more. Cade nibbles my bottom lip before kissing me. His fingers thrust in and out. All the sensations: his body pressed against mine, a hand on my throat, his fingers deep inside me, his tongue playing gently with mine; I'm completely at his mercy. I love it.

I'm uneasy; now I'm more than dizzy. Nervously I'm squirming, hoping Cade knows. I squeeze the head of his cock and he moans. Cade rocks against me, pushing my hand down his shaft, lifting himself, and shuffling a bit higher.

Another squirm, and Cade's grip around my throat slackens.

In a low voice, he reassures me, "I won't hurt you."

There's a warmth and trust that comes with his vow. His hand stays above my neck, but I'm free from that pressure.

A third finger teases my entrance. Everything freezes. Every fiber of my being is on edge out of fear that it will hurt. My toes curl and my thighs clench, pushed against his knees. I try to look between us, but Cade tilts my head back up toward him.

Scolding me with one look, Cade claims my mouth again, kissing with urgency. A small part of my brain urges me to trust him. That small little part slowly begins to overtake the rest.

Cade's thumb finally presses on my clit, circling it slowly. My body tries to relax. I shudder when his third finger slides closer, waiting patiently before sliding in. There's more pressure but no pain. His fingers curl against the ridges deep inside. Again and again, he slides against them. My body rises to meet him.

"Yes, draga mea, that's it." Cade coaches between kisses.

His fingers press in and out, delving deeper, pressing up into me.

I've never been so full; I've never felt this stretched. *Sex isn't supposed to be this good, is it?*

Cade kisses my neck, nosing my ear and nibbling on it. Kisses trail lower, the same path his hands took earlier. My hand lets go of him involuntarily. The noises Cade makes as he kisses are their own brand of arousal. His teeth skate my skin and taunt of more to come. Maybe not today, but Cade clearly wants to bite.

In a small movement, he shifts and pulls his fingers out of me entirely. The warmth my core is missing from him is quickly met with his cock sliding up the inside of my leg.

I squirm as he presses against my clit. His head feels huge pressed at the apex of my folds. I whimper in a worry. Biting my bottom lip, I look at Cade.

"Trust me, Thalia, you're ready," Cade vows.

The hand playing with my tit traces lazily down my center to my clit. His fingers slide against it, and I throb in response. His eyes lock on mine, just watching. It's calculated.

He whispers, "One word. At any moment, tell me to stop, and I will."

Nodding, I wait for pain, breathing shallowly.

Cade kisses my lips before watching his cock sink into me, replacing the hollowness I felt from the retreat of his fingers. Full, so incredibly full and warm, but no pain.

Cade presses forward, whispering, "Fuck, Thalia."

I draw a quick deep breath from the new sensation. He freezes. I'm not even sure he's breathing. I nod, lifting my hips, grinding, looking for more of him.

Calculating and watching, Cade yields, giving me more. His slow pace, set for my care, drives me nuts. I push myself up toward him, trying to get more, trying to get him closer to me. Snaking my hands around his shoulders, I try to pull myself to him more. It's more intense than a need.

Is there something stronger than need?

Cade slips deeper into me. Deep. I'm breathing, I think. His pelvis grinds against mine. Are the noises I hear from him or me? My fingers dig into his back, pulling myself closer to him. I don't want any space between us.

"You want me, draga mea?" Cade noses my ear, pushing my head aside, kissing down my neck.

I try to use words, but all thoughts are just needy noises wrapped up in the obsession of feeling his touches.

Cade grinds hard, fucking me. His head pushes against my deepest point. It's intense but not tender or painful. Cade's teeth graze against my neck, and he pulls them away slowly.

"Fuck," Cade whispers. "You take it so good, draga mea."

Cade's slow, grinding movements morph into pleasure-filled thrusts. While the dexterity of his fingers rippled each pleasure spot, there's nothing that's ever come close to rivaling the feeling of him fucking me. I'm panting.

"Cade, please." I'm begging, and I'm not even sure what for.

I need more. I need him deeper. Closer. I need. The whisper of an orgasm echoes in my core. It's there, but I can't seem to grasp it.

Frustration hits, and my eyes lock on his. "Please."

His weight shifts. Carefully running his hand between us, his thumb finds my clit. Then he's pressing and circling.

My orgasm slams into me.

"Cade! Cade."

Toes curling, I'm falling over the edge of pleasure. Body tensing. Breathing short. I can't focus on any one thing further than how good everything feels.

Cade's hips meet mine with a yearning intensity. He fucks me through my orgasm, thumb working my clit.

"That's it, Thalia, come hard for me."

And I do.

Then for a second orgasm? Then a third? I can't count. Numbers don't exist. Is it just one orgasm if you never stop and adjust or change positions?

I beg, "Don't stop."

He doesn't. Everything I ask for, he gives me, repeating each motion perfectly over and over again. It's exactly what I need. My throat feels sore from screaming his name. My body feels one with his.

"Thalia. Fuck."

Cade's body curls into mine as he comes. I clench around his cock. Pulling, keeping him in.

A feral snarl echoes from his chest. He turns his head away from me, biting into his arm. Cade drives a few final, quick thrusts into me before his body sags as he works to steady himself. Slowly, his cock slides out, and he lifts his weight away from me.

I shiver at the absence of his body heat. But Cade drags me closer to him and then envelops us in a blanket. He kisses the back of my neck, and I'm lost in the fog of my brain.

Cade must have moved from the bed because, after a few moments, the feeling of a warm, wet rag glides along my skin. He gently moves my legs, keeping the blanket on me. My head is woozy, and my eyes are heavy. Closing them briefly, I only become more alert to the sensation of Cade cleaning me. More time passes, and the bed sags, his warmth is back.

I peel my eyes open to see him examining me. Steel-blue eyes study my face.

Kissing my forehead, he tells me, "Sleep, draga mea, I'm here."

Content, exhaustion grips me, pulling me to sleep.

WHEN I START TO WAKE, it's to the sounds from the main living space again. A quieter set of noises, but they're there. Cade's next to me, so it must be Deacon and Lena back from their beer run.

Cade shuffles in bed, a soft sleepy smile on his face. From my position, flat on my belly, I watch him in the low light of the bedroom.

"Mmmmm, that was some nap." Feeling the warmth of his body against mine, I move closer, whispering, "I had no idea sex could be like that."

Cade wraps his arms around me and effortlessly pulls me closer. His strength amazes me. Trailing one hand down my back, he kisses me tentatively.

His voice is a bit gravelly from sleep. "I'll do better next time."

"I don't think you understand, I'm saying that was amazing." I nuzzle against him. *How can he be so cozy?* "I loved it."

"Oh, I know." He nibbles my ear before whispering, "I'm still learning what you like. It'll keep getting better."

I involuntarily smile.

Chills hit me, and words come out of my sleepy mind

before I can fully process them. "Can I ever really have this life? Is this something we'll be able to do?"

Cade squeezes me tighter. The more he hugs me, the more uneasy I am about his answer.

Releasing me from the hug, Cade moves us so our eyes meet. "I'll find a way. If this is what you truly want, after you're not required to be here with me for your own safety, I'll find a way to make it work."

"I want to be wolf." The words come out.

Apparently, orgasms destroy my already limited brain-to-mouth filter.

The look of shock on Cade's face surprises me. We talked about this at Arches. Granted, I didn't say I wanted to be wolf then, but I did say I wanted kids. So why does he seem surprised at my admission?

It doesn't take too long for Cade to formulate a reply. "Not right now. But, yes, if you still feel that way after getting to taste your old life again, I'll explain more about the process. You can make an informed decision."

It wasn't exactly a yes, but it wasn't a no. Either way, it's sobering. He talks about my requirement to be here, my safety. It almost sounds like Cade expects that I'll never want to come back. Some sort of vacation symptom? You escape reality so far that you never want to go home? Why does life here, with all of them, seem so possible?

I snuggle myself closer, breaking our eye contact. His hand pets my hair, and I feel connectedness. *Is this love?*

Neither of us have said it. How can I love someone I've known for two weeks? How can I be so ready to spend the rest of my life with someone? Why can't I answer those questions? Am I naive?

We manage to pull ourselves out of the cocoon of blankets and get dressed.

Leaving the sanctuary of Cade's bedroom, I expected critical looks.

But Lena and Deacon are sitting at the counter and barely glance up when we walk in. Plates piled with food and two different bottles of beer sit in front of them.

"Come sit down, little red. Let him get you food." Deacon pats the stool next to him.

Cade's hand on my low back encourages me.

Deacon smiles at me. "He likes to care for his people. It's an alpha thing. Literally can't help himself. So, get used to it. Judah and Ansel are the same way."

"Oh, so are all alphas' love language acts of service?" I ask, mostly to myself.

"Pft. That's not his love language." Lena laughs. "I made the boys take the tests when I took psych freshman year. We were figuring out if it applied to wolves, given our sociological differences. Touch and quality time are so necessary for us, so it seemed that those would be the default."

"Were they?" I lean forward, past Deacon, to look at her.

The science is fascinating; I start thinking through what I observed about the wolves I've met so far.

"We all scored pretty steady across the board in those categories, but there were a bunch of differences in our higher categories," Lena answers.

"Huh, that's cool."

The scientist part of my brain wants to ask more questions and comb through the data, but it would be weird to ask. People don't like invasive questions about how their brains work. *Don't be weird.*

Deacon nudges me gently before whispering, "He's big on physical touch and quality time."

Cade shakes his head. "Between the two of you, it's

impossible to say if I'm going to be able to convince my mate to work with me or if you'll scare her off."

"Aww." Lena nudges Deacon, who bumps into me again. "Look, he's all embarrassed."

Cade's chewing on his bottom lip, and he is, in fact, blushing. I prop my head up on the counter with my hands, watching as he makes our plates of food. He sets my food in front of me along with utensils and a drink. Leaning against the counter, he stands with his plate.

"Dude, we need more chairs." Deacon realizes.

"We're not going to live here a lot longer," Lena says softly.

"Oh," Deacon says quietly, "It's weird talking about going home. Can we just move the pack here?"

Silence seems to be an answer. I eat small bites, feeling incredibly awkward about this conversation. Not even Lena, who seems like she has something to say for everything, speaks. I wish I had more of an understanding of what it means for Cade to be taking over the pack again. No one's really saying what a challenge entails.

Cade sets his plate down, looking between the three of us. He draws a deep breath. "We can't move the pack here. They'll need the stability of places they know, usual commutes, and their family homes. I don't know about the main pack's dynamic. For all we know, I'll be breaking up a healthy pack dynamic by killing Robert. I can only imagine what that's going to do to Courtney. I've put this off too long. Tomorrow, Thalia and I are going to the range. I'm going to give her tools to defend herself. Then, I'll challenge Robert. We'll see where the rest of the month takes us."

After finishing the few bites left on my plate, I expect to be whisked away to Cade's bedroom. Instead, the four of us move to Cade's massive couch. He sits stretched out, long legs running down the sitting space of the couch. He pulls me close, pulling me into his lap. I'm lounging mostly on him. When Lena and Deacon settle in on the couch, we're all connected through touch. Lena's feet extend from her side of the sectional to meet with Cade's. And on the far end, Lena and Deacon snuggle up, sharing a pillow. As we get settled together, it's strangely familiar and fitting.

"You weren't kidding about the big couch. There's plenty of room. I don't have to sit on you." I wiggle.

Cade nips my ear. "Are you comfortable?"

I assess and rotate my hips a bit, moving them to lie more naturally along his body. "Yes."

"Good. Then you lie here." He wraps his hand around my waist, and there's no further argument.

Physical touch, his love language.

Midway through the movie, Lena makes snacks, bringing back a bunch of different things for everyone. Cade carefully moves me but keeps me touching him. We go from one movie right into the next. I find myself carefully petting his arms, tracing imaginary patterns, and tracking along the veins in his arms. For a while, I don't know where I begin and he ends. It's a whole new experience, vastly different from our unity in sex. I've never felt so connected to someone on any level.

CHAPTER 47
CADE

"Have you ever fired a gun before?" I ask Thalia as she opens the back of the Yukon, looking around the gun range.

"No." She stretches, and her voice is puzzled. "You brought me to watch you shoot, right?"

"No," I draw out slowly. "I mean, you'll watch a few times but welcome to firearm safety."

I pull out the targets I brought with us and walk her down range to a few of the target stands. She helps me put up the farthest targets first, traditional bullseyes, and we work our way back.

When we get to the closest target, I offer her some options. "Would you like to shoot me? Lena? Deacon? Your parents? Or this hideous alien thing I found on the internet today?"

Thalia looks at me like I offered to shoot her parents. "You're kidding."

"Okay, so ugly alien it is." I tuck the rest of the choices back under my arm.

"No. Yes." She corrects herself. "You brought pictures, of your family and mine, to shoot with a gun?"

411

"Well, it would be weird if I actually brought them instead of just their pictures," I answer, pinning up the alien. "It's good stress relief. Take a few good shots at who's making you mad, and suddenly, you're less mad and clearer about things."

"Put Mom up there," Thalia says softly.

Following her instruction, I pin Senator Clark up next to the funny-looking alien with too many eyes and not enough heads.

Thalia's nerves are evident. I walk her through basic gun safety multiple times. The first time she holds the small pistol I brought for her, she's nearly vibrating. But I intend to have her able to hit the bullseye on the closest target with it. It takes some prompting and walking her through the steps. She repeats it back to me, checking each step and completing the movements, working the slide, eject, and safety on the gun. It's impressive watching her brain work. Each process becomes natural, and soon, she's nodding to herself as she confidently handles the metal.

I pull the loaded clip out of my back pocket. When she hands the gun to me this time, I swap them out.

"You're working a live weapon," I warn her. "This will kill."

She freezes but goes back through the drill again. Flawlessly.

Then she looks at me. "I can do this part all day, but something tells me you didn't bring me here to make sure I could load and unload it."

"No, I brought you here so I know I can give you a gun and a few loaded clips and trust you to take a few wolves out in the event we're attacked." I pause. *Do I tell her?*

Our mate fierce. The Leviathan scoffs at my underestimation of Thalia's ability to handle the scary thoughts. He underestimates the implications of what I've already told her.

412

Thalia's eyes are wide, and she blinks dumbly at me. "It's that possible?"

"The Leviathan worries that you're not wolf." I hesitate but nod. "I won't give you a wolf right now, so this is your next best defense. If a wolf attacks you, you've got very little time to fire. Each shot you take must be lethal."

She swallows hard, looking at the gun in her hand. I can tell the metal feels heavier to her now that she's not blind to its purpose. This isn't a general how-to; it's the possibility of life and death.

Thalia looks at me. "Show me how to shoot it."

"I'll make sure you're competent to do this, and then I'll pull out the big guns. We'll have some fun, okay?" I try to ease her mind a bit. This was supposed to be work and pleasure. Telling her the purpose sucked the fun out for her. I pop a smirk, walking her to the bench. "Besides, how many of your co-workers can say they've fired assault rifles for fun?"

"Bookworms don't fire guns," she sasses back.

"Mine does." I smile and kiss her softly, putting a pair of earmuffs over her head.

I admit to being nervous. Thalia's arms shake as I help her move them into position, and the smell of fear is in the air. If this weren't necessary, I wouldn't do it to her.

When I nod and encourage her, Thalia sends the first bullet down range. I expect her to put the gun down and step away. Most civilians do. No, my mate is special. Thalia sends two more shots down the range.

Squinting a bit for focus, I see she's hitting the target.

Ten rounds go quickly. And when she's sent the last one down range, she goes through the process of confirming she's empty, locking the safety, and setting it down on the bench.

Fuck, this is sexy.

Thalia looks at me. Her eyes are bright behind the safety glasses, and she pulls the ear muffs off. When I pull my muffs off and the plugs out of my ears, she speaks.

Her voice is nervous, but it's pure excitement. "I think I can do better. But I'm pretty sure I did okay."

"This isn't a test. There are no grades." I holster the gun. "Let's go see what you did."

"I know it's not a test. It's like the quiz before the midterm. Really important to get the answers right so you know what to study." She follows me to the target block.

There are holes in her mother's face as well as several in the faces of the ugly alien. A couple of shots are nowhere near things you'd shoot at. It's not a cluster you'd see from a marksman, but it's also weirdly specific for it to be rogue shots.

I knit my brows together and casually ask her, "Where were you aiming?"

"This one and this one are misses." Thalia points to the obvious outliers. "I was trying to hit the alien between the eyes so those aren't the best. Kind of high. But the ones on Mom are low."

Thalia's shots on her mother's face are around her mouth and cheeks. Nearly silencing her, which could be Thalia's subconscious, given the scary accuracy of her first shots with a firearm.

Mate perfect. You doubt? You puppy brain. The Leviathan quirks.

"Is it that bad?" she whispers.

"Thalia, you're within inches of your target points. For someone's first time shooting, this is the best I've ever seen."

I look at her, wrapping my arm across her shoulder as I pull her close. I keep looking at the near-perfect shots.

"So, can I shoot the big one now?" Thalia looks up at me. "I have a good teacher, and I'm a quick learner."

My heart melts in my chest. Safety glasses never looked so sexy.

I stoop slightly to kiss her, claiming her mouth. She moans, and I'm rock-hard. Why is a woman with a weapon a turn-on?

She breaks the kiss. "Are you kissing me to distract me from getting to shoot the big gun?"

I laugh. "No, but make that little noise again, and I'll bend you over the bumper of my Yukon and show you a distraction."

"Or show me your big gun?" Thalia waggles her eyebrow at me with her innuendo.

I pull her close, putting her hand against my hard cock in my jeans. "This one?"

She bites her bottom lip with a gasp. "Mmhmm."

Thalia darts away from me back toward the SUV.

Silly mate no outrun us. The Leviathan and I join chase.

It's only a few yards back to the SUV, but I catch her easily, throwing her over my shoulder in a fireman's carry. I turn my head toward her hip and take a teasing bite of her ass through her jeans. My jeans are too tight as I plot what I'm about to do to her.

I set her down, turning her away from me. Wrapping my hand around her to the button on her jeans, I pop it open. She doesn't object when I slide my hands around the top of her waistband. I sink to my knees, pulling her jeans down her legs.

Thalia lets out a timid shriek before whispering, "Cade, what if someone sees?"

I assure her, "It's my private range."

She squirms as my fingers pull on the cotton of her underwear. The stench of fear doesn't accompany her uneasiness.

I kiss the bottom of her low back. As I kiss my way down, Thalia squirms when the cotton slides down her legs. I stand behind her again. Nibbling on her ear, I loosen my belt. Once

I'm free of the button and fly on my jeans, I free my cock one-handed. I use the other to run up the back of her shirt and unclip her bra.

Seemingly shocked, she looks over her shoulder, mouth agape.

I run my thumb along her bottom lip. "That face makes me want to watch you gag on my cock."

Her eyes dilate, and she presses back against me, her ass brushing, settling against my cock. I'm throbbing. My moan fills the air as she wiggles that perfect ass against me. She feigns innocence, looking surprised when I respond to her effect on me. I see the coy smile and gleam in her eye.

If she knew how little control I had over myself, would she test it as much? Her humanity sits on a precarious wall built of a single promise. With every booty wiggle, that wall threatens to topple.

Ending my torment, I push her forward, as threatened, bending her over the bumper. Her perfect, soft ass is presented to me, and I run my hands across it, giving it a small but firm tap.

Thalia wiggles more. Putting my hand across the low part of her spine, I give her another small swat.

A murmur comes from her.

"Do you like that, draga mea?"

She murmurs again, but this time, it's clearly one of approval.

I swat her ass again. Giving her four more before I can't not feel her wetness anymore. The hand from her low back migrates lower. My fingers slide down, sinking into her folds. She's dripping wet. Thalia's warm core greets my fingers.

Her body tightens when I press one deep inside her.

"Breathe. I promised you it would fit, and it did. Let me make you feel good." I encourage her.

Thalia spreads her legs, rotating her ass into the air more. Seeing it so high, I smack it a bit hard. Her pussy clenches tight on my finger as she squeaks with shock.

I see the full presentation of her pussy. The beautiful sheen of her wetness draws me forward.

I'm down on my knees without further thought. Nose buried into her, lapping her folds. I move my finger, gliding it now against her clit. Loud moans pour out of her. Needy little mate tells me how good I make her feel.

Pulling my hand off her ass, I fist my cock, moaning while tasting her. I push a second finger into her, stretching.

"No." Thalia objects.

I freeze. My heart pounds in my chest as I withdraw the second finger. She didn't smell of fear. I start pulling out the first finger. *How do I make her okay? What did I . . .*

"Fuck me," she mewls, ending that thought. "No more fingers, I want you."

Her command banishes my fear. I easily obey. The Leviathan doesn't even flinch at her commanding us. I stand and slide myself along her soft skin. She's soaking wet. *How sore will this make her?* She's squeamish. This might be too quick.

"Now," she draws out in a whine, her ass pushing back into me.

Her pleas for more are too much to resist. I comply. Slowly sinking into her, I let out a long moan. I press myself against her, letting her adjust to my cock filling her depth. Her walls clench on me. Slowly, I grind back and forth, encouraging them to loosen. I offer low moans and kiss the back of her neck. My hand slides along her side, up under her shirt. Tenderly, I lift her tits upward, allowing access under her loosened bra. I caress the underside of her breast before massaging it in my hand.

A whimper of pleasure escapes her. I rock my hips, keeping a steady rhythm, pressing into her. Abandoning her tit, I slide down her stomach and across her pelvis. My thumb and index finger find her clit. She screams out when I do. Excitement but not the sound of her orgasm, yet.

She presses her hips to my quick, firm touches. Working the grinding to my advantage, I rock into her. Thalia's pussy clenches down. I hear and feel her getting closer. Every thrust is met with a satisfied mewl. I stroke her clit, remembering how her response sounded before. It takes only a few more moments, and I find the perfect pace for both of us, her body working toward orgasm, each breathy noise an instruction for more.

When Thalia screams through her orgasm, I lose my composure, fucking her harder. One hand pulling her hips toward me, the other supporting us against the SUV. The urge to bite her is strong.

I turn my head and bite into my shoulder again. My vision flutters black and white. Shaking my head, I try to sort it, coming back to normal slowly. Thalia clenches herself around me; I'm nearly completely emptied by her actions, cum pouring from me to her.

Collapsing over the top of her, I growl lightly against her ear, "Something tells me that last squeeze was intentional."

"Mmhmm." Thalia giggles coyly. "You're not the only one who can learn what we like together."

I separate from her and wipe her clean with the spare towels in the back of my SUV.

Nearly twenty minutes later, we're put back together. I sit in the back of the vehicle, pulling her into my lap. She curls up against me.

"So, we can still shoot the big gun, right?" she whispers.

I nod against her head. "Yes, I'll still let you shoot the big gun. Let's go get your targets, we can frame them later."

Thalia is, quite honestly, perfect in every way.

CHAPTER 48
THALIA

I'M NOT RECOGNIZING the person I'm becoming with Cade. That isn't a bad thing though. I'd have never considered having sex outside. Screaming an orgasm into the wild? Unheard of. Enjoying shooting an assault rifle? Irresponsible. Sitting in silence with a massive wolf's head resting in my lap? Beyond my wildest dream.

After shooting, Cade asked if I wanted to go for a walk. The Leviathan's eyes had overtaken his silvered blue. While I could have used a nap, it seemed too important to snooze through. The Leviathan let me set the pace, so I chose to mosey along, looking at the barren woods. What does Wisconsin look like in later spring and summer? It's not that it's ugly now; I've never really had the chance to be in someplace so removed from crowded streets and towering buildings. What do green forests look like when in full color?

As we sit next to a small lake on a log, the sun starts to dip down in the sky. The Leviathan nudges my stomach before standing up. He shakes his whole body like a dog after a bath and stretches out like a cat waiting for me. I smile and step into his space. I barely have to crouch to wrap my arms around his neck, soaking in his warmth and the smell of his fur. He leads me back down the path, walking beside me again.

We're walking for a few minutes before he stops. Poking his nose into my side when I look at him, he looks off slightly into the woods.

I focus on the brown, looking for whatever he's trying to show me. A small movement in the twigs and then nature's camouflage isn't good enough to hide it. A deer is walking through the woods. If it's aware of us, the deer is clearly not concerned with our presence.

The Leviathan steps forward, waiting for me. Following his lead, we walk extra slowly. I keep my eyes on the deer, watching it pick through the underbrush, looking for food. As we get closer, the beautiful doe's eyes lock on us. It freezes for the briefest seconds, then springs off. The white tail flashes as it darts away.

This deer is living its life as a normal and everyday thing. But to me, it's magic, a whole other world I'm being drawn into with every step. Natural splendor around me brings comforting emotions I don't expect.

You would need to become wolf. Cade made it sound possible, though I'm certain the word he used was theoretically. In a life of science, 'theoretically' holds a lot of variables. Would his people not accept me if I weren't wolf? The family of his I've met thus far have seemed mostly accepting of me. And, even then, Lena's clearly coming from a place of love and worry for Cade.

I look down at The Leviathan now that we've reached the SUV. He trots off around the side of the vehicle. I'm alone for a few minutes, and then there's the sound of popping joints. Then Cade is pulling his shirt over his head, rounding the other end of the SUV.

"What happened in that head of yours?" He pulls me into his arms.

"Nothing." I lie.

"Mmmhmm."

Cade's tone tells me that my lying has not improved. Stupid shifter trick.

CHAPTER 49

CADE

I'M STARTING to believe that Thalia dislikes The Leviathan. Every time they spend time together, she gets quiet. While two instances aren't quite a pattern, it's enough to make me question if I'm misreading us.

The ride back home is quiet but free of tension.

When we pull into the driveway, Lena's SUV and Deacon's bike are missing. We have the house to ourselves. As if on cue, Thalia's stomach lets out a giant growl when we walk into the kitchen. Her hands fly to cover it.

We provide for her. Make her favorite food. The Leviathan demands, as if I'm supposed to know what that is and magically have the ingredients. We've had deep conversations, but I haven't picked up on the surface-level things yet.

"Hungry, draga mea?" I ask.

She turns to look at me before nodding. "Yeah." She sounds sad. "I can help?"

I nod. "What's your favorite food?"

"Okay, don't laugh." She stops pulling her hair into a ponytail to point her finger at me.

With a shrug, I wait for whatever words could possibly come from her next.

"I love grilled cheese and refuse to be told it's not real food."

There's no holding it back. I laugh, and I laugh hard.

With her hands on her hips, she glares at me.

I try to get it under control. "It's not the fact that it's your favorite food. It's that you're talking to someone who has grown up literally across from the dairy state, and you think I'm going to judge you for a love of cheese and bread."

Thalia's little face pouts before pursing her lips in false anger. She storms off around the kitchen island and sits on the stool.

"For laughing, I am not helping."

Hand over my chest, I pretend to be wounded. "Oh, no. Whatever will I do? A grown man left to make a grilled cheese all on my own."

My antics are not appreciated if the little scowl she gives me is any indicator. *Has she just been masking her feelings? Are these her real feelings? Maybe it's both The Leviathan and me?*

I assemble sandwiches for the griddle with various kinds of cheese and lunch meat. The logical part of my brain tells me not to ask questions I don't want the answers to. However, I can't get her reaction to The Leviathan out of my thoughts.

If she not like one, it you. She like me. The Leviathan insists. *I perfect. You no.*

"Can I ask you something?" I start tentatively.

Thalia's eyes go wide, clearly aware of my unsettledness. "Um. Sure?"

"Does it bother you when I shift?"

I'm not sure I'm picking the right word for that sentence. Points for trying to communicate that question, right?

You puppy brain. The Leviathan retreats, leaving me alone with one final insult.

"What?" Thalia furrows her brow, her jaw drops, and she shakes her head. "Why would you ask that?"

I keep layering cheese and deli meat into the sandwich and bite my tongue before trying to articulate. "After both walks with The Leviathan, you're distant. I don't want to be making you uncomfortable. I don't have to shift around you."

"No." Thalia shakes her head.

My expression of confusion must drive her to continue talking.

"I adore spending time with The Leviathan. If anything, I wish we had more in common."

I listen carefully, setting the first sandwich into the pan.

Thalia continues, "Okay, you know the other day, when we were talking, you said you wanted me to set the pace? That you think I need more time?"

You could hear a pin drop while I wait for her to say more. That conversation has run through my head multiple times a day. She doesn't speak.

I break the silence, answering her, "Yes. I remember."

Even after answering her, Thalia is silent. It's agonizing. My heart is pounding and feels like it's in my throat. She's just watching me make dinner. I'm fairly certain she's moved on from the conversation. Her head is off thinking of other things.

"It's difficult because you've been so good to me, and I'm not used to being treated this way, but I'm not even sure what's real. You keep saying that I've got to go home and that things are going to change. And I really want to be able to justify this. There's no prudent way for me to go about getting you to understand that I think this is just for the . . ." Thalia starts rambling.

It sounds a lot like the 'it's not you it's me' speech that I've heard Lena give boys from time to time.

She grumbles, "I'm messing this all up."

I brace for impact.

"I love you."

The spatula hits the floor. For a moment, I'm weightless. Everything. Everything falls away. *She loves me.*

How did I get around the counter? How did I pull her into my arms? How did I end up kissing her like a man running out of minutes to live?

Not a fucking clue. Thalia is now sitting on the counter, legs curled along my sides, keeping me close. With her hand in my hair, she claims me back.

The tide had been out. I had been stranded out to sea, and now, hearing that, I've been brought to shore.

The smoke alarm going off crashes me back to reality.

"Fuck!"

I quickly disengage, moving around the counter. The grilled cheese has gone from grilled to charred. Tossing them onto a plate, I rush them out the back door to the deck. When I come back inside, Thalia is trying to fan the beeping smoke alarm.

I turn it off at the control box in the pantry.

Thalia's jaw drops. "You just turned it off?"

"Yeah, reset, it's part of the —" I stop talking, looking at her.

The house doesn't matter.

Her lips are red from kissing, her hair mussed from being entangled with my hands.

"I love you too."

Thalia beams at me. "Yeah? You love me so much you tried to burn the house down with me in it?"

I can't be this far away from her right now. I close the

distance between us. She laughs and wraps her arms around my neck when I pick her up. I say it again, "I love you."

She's looking me square in the eye and shakes her head ever so slightly full of sass. "I was hoping you'd say that because I could feel it. But I needed to hear it too."

CHAPTER 50
THALIA

H E L O V E S M E. His words sink deep into my bones, and insecurities begin to fade. Warmth soaks my soul. Is it perfect? Do these four words solve our issues? No. There's still hope that love will be enough and we can work it out.

I have believed grilled cheese was my favorite food for my entire life. Sitting in Cade's kitchen, I find out I've never really had grilled cheese. There are no words to accurately explain my love of the sandwich that this man has made me. A traditionalist would not approve of calling this a grilled cheese. But there is, in fact, bread and cheese, so in my book, it counts.

Cade expertly layered three different kinds of cheese and deli meat, and used the most amazing bread and butter. I'm in heaven. Sitting here eating my sandwich, I've never had such an experience. Maybe it's the fact that I said 'I love you' and he said it back. But this sandwich could easily be my last meal, and I'd be a happy woman.

WE'RE FINISHING LOADING the dishwasher, okay, I'm loading the dishwasher, and Cade is telling me I'm doing it wrong, when the door to the garage opens.

"Someone remind me it's illegal to kill stupid people." Lena's voice rings out.

The door thuds, and then I hear her head thump against it.

"It's illegal to kill stupid people, most of the time," I answer, trying to help.

Cade turns to look at me, pointing a stern finger. "No. Do not encourage her homicidal tendencies."

Lena looks at me, walking into the kitchen. "Maybe you having..."

She freezes, standing perfectly still. Her eyes glass over. I assume it's because she's having a vision similar to Ansel's. Cade turning back to the dishwasher, confirms he is not worried.

"So, how does she drive if that can happen at any time?" I meant to think that in my head, but the words came out of my mouth.

Cade looks at me, grabs a spoon off the silverware rack in the dishwasher, and tosses it at her in a gentle lob. Despite the glossed-over look in her eyes and having stopped mid-conversation, Lena snatches the spoon out of the air without a problem.

With a smile, Cade says, "She can't hear us, but it's like her brain continues to keep her safe. It's the same for Ansel and Dinah."

"Well, that's cool." I nod.

Cade rearranges the dishwasher and runs it.

"A mate isn't such a bad thing." Lena finishes her sentence, continuing to walk.

It's evident that to her, this is just a usual thing.

Cade ignores her statement about me. "What do we want

to do tonight? It's potentially my last night of freedom. I'm headed to see Robert tomorrow."

The way Cade says 'last night of freedom' makes my heart hurt for him. He truly seems to feel trapped by the upcoming responsibilities. Guilt creeps into me about how he spent today teaching me to shoot. Surely there's something he'd rather have done instead. Then again, I'm positive he had a good time . . . at the SUV.

More insecurity hits. I haven't even taken the time to know what he likes or doesn't. Everything I know about Cade relates to how he reacts and responds to helping others. We've talked a bit about his music tastes: eclectic. His movie tastes: adventure and mystery. His book preferences: involved without being complicated and preferably plot driven. But I don't know his favorites of anything. I don't know.

What does Cade do for fun?

Air is hard. I can't get it in. I'm trying to breathe. It's getting hard.

"Cade?" I hear Deacon's voice. I'm finding it more usual that he seems to materialize out of nowhere. His voice is concerned. "Is she okay?"

I'm looking for Deacon. I find him with his head cocked, watching as he steps closer to me. It hurts me knowing Deacon is scared. I swallow back everything I've just thought about and try to assure him.

It comes out in a gasp. "I'm fine."

Cade places his hand on my shoulder, running it across my back. There's that commanding tone, spoken softly. "Breathe, Thalia."

My lungs seize, and I cough, trying to draw a deep breath. After a coughing fit, Cade hands me my water glass.

"Let's finish dinner and go watch a movie."

CADE CARRIED me to bed after a double feature on the couch. Wrapped in his arms, I drifted to sleep, with the last words I heard being, "I love you," spoken in his groggy, sleepy voice. But this morning has come too early.

Begrudgingly I've helped him get dressed into a three-piece suit. Despite how sexy and confident he looks, my heart aches at seeing him look back at the three of us with a sobering look before walking out the door.

Deacon runs his hand across the back of my shoulder. "Don't worry. He's not going alone. The last keeper of The Leviathan is with him."

CHAPTER 51
CADE

I PULL up to the guard shack at the beginning of the Regent pack property. As I roll down the window, the guard walks over. He doesn't look at me. Not from respect but out of carelessness.

Flat and unwelcoming, he demands, "Name and nature of business."

"Cade Alexander Alden. Self-explanatory," I quip with a smile. *It was funny.*

The guard doesn't recognize me or my humor. His demeanor is impersonal. I've met palace guards and secret service agents with more personality.

He looks at me, furrowing his brow. "ID, please."

Granted, the family resemblance isn't strong between Robert and me. Surely his distrust and lack of recognition are because he's younger.

I let him do his job, pulling my wallet out of my pocket, sliding out the ID, and handing it over between two fingers. He goes into the guard shack with my ID, then picks up a landline phone. Sitting there watching him on the phone, the minutes tick by.

My cell phone rings: *Robert Alden.*

I hit the answer button. "Hello."

"Are you at my house?" Robert asks snidely.

"Yes. I am," I answer in the same tone.

'My house.' I shake my head, letting it go. Judah and I don't use formal greetings because we value the other's time. This isn't about respect. Our fight for dominance has always been there.

The Leviathan's hackles rise, as do the hairs on the back of my neck.

"Thank you." Robert hangs up the phone.

Manners were a nice touch.

A few minutes more, and the guard walks back with my ID.

"Follow the driveway to the left, park along the garage stalls to the left, and leave your keys in the vehicle," he commands.

We kill later. The Leviathan makes note of his face, observing him.

We are not walking around killing pack members you don't like. One thing is for sure though. We won't be leaving the keys in the vehicle.

Pulling through, I watch the gate close through my rearview mirror as I drive to the main house. The trees and bushes along the sides are well maintained. I round the bend where the driveway opens to the house. It's as it always was. White, opulent, and completely out of place among the conifers. The mansion is stately beyond reason. I park where instructed but lock the vehicle, pocketing my keys.

At the front door, I knock and wait patiently.

Courtney opens the door, her smile quickly fading when she sees me.

Apprehension coats her voice. "Cade, please come in."

I cross the threshold, and she quietly closes the door behind me.

She looks at me with a soft smile. "I suppose you're here to see your brother."

"I am," I answer softly, trying not to give her any reason to be upset by my presence.

My failure to prearrange a visit falls well outside the norms, and Courtney is already piecing together the nature of my visit.

"It's —" Courtney starts, her blonde hair glistening in the foyer light. She stops herself, unwilling to lie for the sake of being polite. "Robert's in the office. I'll take you."

I'm not in need of an escort. However, it is her home. She's a good host. I've never had anything against Courtney. She's from the pack and was a few years older than me, but I've never really known her.

Along the way, I dissect the house, trying to find indicators of something that would explain the changes with Robert. I don't expect a sign or anything labeled as 'fucked up shit,' but a look around doesn't hurt. In ten years, the house has only changed in decor. It's now clean, minimalist. Empty. There are no family or pack photos; there's no indicator that anyone lives here. Is it a decorating choice?

Down the hallway, toward the back of the house, we stop outside the double doors of the Alpha's office. Courtney knocks on my behalf before walking away without another word.

Unsurprisingly, Robert keeps me waiting. I'm ready to open the door and barge in unanswered when he finally calls, "Come in."

Despite our phone conversation less than fifteen minutes prior, Robert looks surprised to see me. We're not alone in his office. It never occurred to me that he could be having meetings. Two members of the high council are sitting in chairs around Robert's desk. Winston Hemsworth, the Third or Fourth, and Beatrice Moore turn their heads to look at me.

"Cade!" Winston, a friend of my father, beckons with a halfhearted smile. "It's good to see you."

He lies.

Beatrice genuinely looks pleased with my arrival. "Robert didn't tell us you'd be coming by for this meeting."

"It's good to see you both, Beatrice and Winston. Unfortunately, I hadn't made Robert aware of my visit today. This is as big of a shock to him as it is to you." I smile.

Now I'm grateful Lena insisted I wear a vest and tie today. As was the case with Thalia's parents, I need all the bonus points I can get.

My eyes finally land on Robert. His smile barely hides the grimace.

"Yes, little brother, what is it that brings you by today."

I look at the council members one last time before trying to plead with Robert. "Perhaps we should have a conversation in private first, it won't take but a few moments."

"Nonsense." He gestures to the council members looking appalled at the idea and shakes his head. "Whatever you have to discuss can surely be said in front of my advisers."

"Regent. I believe it's best we speak in private." I try to be firm without commanding.

I'd rather not alarm the council members, but I can command him to do this in private.

"Come, Cade," Beatrice says softly. "Robert says it's fine."

"Cade, I'm sorry, but we're really quite busy. If you had called, we'd have had time to chitchat and catch up." Robert tries to dismiss me like a petulant child.

The Leviathan growls. I let it out. We're no longer willing to be spoken down to. The three of them sit at attention. I allow the growl to fade slowly.

"This is your notice, Robert. At the next full moon, I'll be reclaiming the throne."

"Is that a challenge?" Beatrice asks.

Robert's jaw hangs open. "Cade, you can't be serious. It's been a decade. You can't truly come back now and think I'll hand the people back over to you. Not in the midst of shifters being outed to the public. The politics of all this are far too sensi —"

I snarl.

Smartly, Robert stops speaking. I always let him bring out the worst in me. Best intentions fall by the wayside.

My fuse is short, and there's bite in my words. "Robert, your incompetency in dealing with the humans is part of my grounds for taking back the throne. You can either step down gracefully with your life and I'll keep you on as a personal adviser, or we'll call a challenge and The Leviathan will end you."

"You weren't fit to rule then. You're not fit to rule now." Robert accuses. "Leave now. The three of us will pretend this conversation never happened. Your behavior is exactly why we've decided that the Ardelean wolves must submit to lineage tests."

"Your blood test is you trying to justify taking the pack fund from the Alloway and Abbot packs." I don't split hairs. "You're angry I'm back because you know I'm going to find out that you've done something big, and you don't want it coming to light."

Winston, afraid to meet my gaze but not respectful enough of my power, chastises me. "You haven't done anything to better yourself forward for this position. Robert's been doing the best he can, given the constant issues with the humans. We're near a critical point in the negotiations. Two weeks from now will be a terrible time to change political hands. The humans don't operate on a lunar schedule. They won't understand a new person coming to the table. If you're upset about the blood tests, we will call it forgotten. I'll call your cousins personally and apologize."

"Don't patronize me, Winston. Why is it the only Ardelean wolf without a gift needs to challenge the lineage of those with them?" Pausing for a moment, I let The Leviathan's eyes forward. Winston shifts in his seat while I continue, "I've had a decade to learn and grow. Simply because it hasn't been on your radar doesn't mean it hasn't happened." I turn my attention back to Robert. "I have a list of grievances, Robert. They begin with the pack funds and end with Senator Clark. I'm giving you the option to step down and keep your life. Come the full moon, I will reclaim my title as Sovereign. You know how to contact me if you'd care to arrange a peaceful handoff or want to have the fight sooner. If I don't hear from you, I'll show up here the night before the full moon."

Robert still hasn't bothered standing up from his desk. I turn to leave.

"Don't come into my home and threaten me, Cade. I know where you live as well. It wouldn't be difficult to visit your little hovel unannounced either." Robert threatens.

I turn back to look at him, raising an eyebrow. It's bold of him to make a blatant threat. At least he finally had the decency to stand to speak to me.

"You're more than welcome to show up at my home unattended. I came alone and asked to speak to you in private. I've offered for you to keep your life. I'm not required by our laws to do any of those things. Remember that."

There's no need to say goodbye. I close the door behind me.

Less than a minute later, I've reached the foyer and am almost to the door when Courtney's voice comes from above. "You've challenged him?"

I turn to face her on the walkway of the upper floor. I remember all those years ago what the view looks like. How I stood there before descending and claiming my title.

"I've offered him the opportunity to step down. I'll be coming the night before the full moon. Talk some sense into him, Courtney. I've given him all I can."

"I understand," she states. It's unemotional and peculiar as she ends our conversation. "Drive safely."

Out at my SUV, I walk all the way around before unlocking the door at a distance, as a precaution. The instructions from the gate may have been nothing more than a formality, but there's no reason not to take a lap around. There's no scent that anyone's been close to my SUV.

Back down the drive, I don't have to wait long before being let out of the gate. Robert's threat lingers in my head. Would he show up with a hunting party? The question isn't if he's stupid enough for it. I know Robert has made impulsive decisions before.

I'm miles down the road before I click the call button in my car. It only rings once.

"Cade?" Thalia's voice floods the vehicle.

"I'm okay. I'm headed home. I'll be back in about three hours." I sink into my seat.

Knowing she'll be in my arms soon helps banish the tension of the meeting.

I hear her let out a loud exhale. "I'm really glad you're okay. I miss you," she says earnestly.

"I miss you too," I answer, and an unfamiliar lump grows in my throat. I cough to clear it. "I'm going to let you go. I've got to call Judah."

"Okay. I'll see you when you get home. I love you." She says it so effortlessly.

My heart swells, and The Leviathan preens. "I love you too."

Surprisingly, The Leviathan hasn't chimed in, despite actively listening. Even more unnerving is that he doesn't offer up crude scenes of fucking Thalia or replays of her beneath us. My space, in my mind, is my own. There's balance. *Is this how it's supposed to be?*

You earn right to choose. He answers. Instead of Thalia, he pushes back fantasies of violently dethroning Robert.

Despite how monumental his actual acceptance of me is, there's no time to enjoy it.

I hit the call button on the screen again. The phone rings several times. I'm anticipating it going to voicemail when it picks up.

"You on the road again?" Judah answers casually.

"Yeah. Had to see a man about finding a moving company." I can't help but smile at my own dumb joke.

"Damn." Judah fumbles around with something. "How'd that go over?"

"Well, about as good as one might expect. Movers are expensive, you don't seem to know what to do with such a big house, you didn't like the neighborhood the last time, and get off my lawn before I light yours on fire."

"No shit, the little punk threatened you?" I hear Judah's work Jeep start up.

"Mmhmm." I confirm. "Told me off for showing up unannounced. Didn't help that Winston Hemsworth the Fourth —"

"Third." Judah corrects. He would know that, golden boy Alpha.

"Third, and Beatrice Moore, were in his office when I arrived." Traffic slows as I enter the first sleepy town on my drive home. "I tried to talk to him in private, but he wanted to treat me like a petulant child. So, I had to inform him of his last day in office with them in the room. Winston tried to convince me I wasn't suited. Then offered to waive the blood tests if I backed down."

"Not worth it. We'll take the tests and prove lineage. Then there really won't be any reason for any of us to be challenged." Judah sounds hopeful. "Wait, I'm assuming you didn't take the deal."

"I didn't. I'm serious. I'll reclaim my title as Sovereign with the moon." I assure him.

Judah speaks again, "I believe you. You're going to do great. I'm headed into a pack meeting. We'll catch up after you know more."

CHAPTER 52
THALIA

CADE COMES HOME, and he's starting to strip before the door closes. He's moving like he can't get out of his dress clothes fast enough. By the time he hits the kitchen, his fly is undone, and he's no longer wearing his shirt, tie, and vest. He doesn't stop walking until he's nearly on top of me. One arm wraps tight around my shoulder, the hand snaking into my hair at the base of my skull, while the other runs down my spine and slides into the back of my yoga pants. Even his legs seem to spider monkey around me as his instep touches my pinky toes.

"Ahem." I hear Lena clear her throat.

We've been friendly-ish. By no means are we even slightly friends, but there's a respect between us. This pushes my button. I tense.

"Shhh, Thalia, not worth it," Cade whispers.

I'm more aware of his warm skin pressed against my face as I feel the vibrations from speaking in his chest and hear his heart beating. I nuzzle him a little bit and settle.

He's right. Fighting with Lena over a hug is a dumb hill to die on, in the history of dumb hills to die on.

Once I've settled, Cade pulls away. "I'll be right back, let me get out of the monkey suit."

Cade's back a moment later in black sweatpants and a gray T-shirt. Am I a pervert for wishing they were swapped? Did I just fall for the gray sweatpants lust? Probably yes to both. Do I care? Mmmm, probably not.

The laid back, nearly cocky smile Cade gives me when he sees me checking him out is only slightly embarrassing. I look away, watching him from my peripheral as he pulls Lena in for a quick hug and then Deacon.

"And how was brother dearest?" Lena asks as 'dearest' drops off her tongue with her special brand of poisonous tone.

Cade huffs. "Pretentious, condescending, and most certainly up to something."

Deacon snarks, dripping sarcasm, "Nothing changes with him, I take it he was thrilled with the idea of moving his ass out of your chair."

"Yeah." Cade runs his hand back through his hair. The locks he had mostly tamed earlier shuffle out into the more rugged places they naturally hang. "I need a fucking haircut."

I must let out the sad noise I thought I had made in my head.

Cade looks at me before saying, "Or not."

A smile escapes.

Lena gives an exasperated sigh. "Alright, what's the game plan? What did Robert say?"

"It was mostly him trying to talk me out of it. I told him when I'd be back. Honestly, I expected more fireworks. Though, with Winston and Beatrice there, who knows?"

"Awww, how is good old Winny, that bastard?" Deacon goes to the freezer, pulling out a bottle of vodka. "Anyone else too sober for this?"

No one answers. He mumbles something I can't

448

understand while curling his lip in a mocking expression.

"Robert made the threat that he'd show up here unannounced. I don't know how serious it was." Cade shakes his head. "There's something off about the whole blood test issue. It doesn't seem like it was Robert's idea."

Lena growls.

"I know. Which is why we're not going to do them until it's mandatory." Cade nods. "If it truly comes from the council, they may have wanted to do all of us to take suspicion off questioning him. Once he's gone, maybe they won't care."

Cade pulls Lena in for a hug. "I'm doing what I can."

She grumbles again and shakes her head against his chest.

"Want to go for a run?" Cade offers her.

A knife of jealousy sinks into my chest.

"I call dibs on staying with Thalia." Deacon beams when I look at him.

"You okay with that, draga mea?" Cade asks with a soft smile.

It's clearly something he's torn about.

I nod. He's home and he's safe. A run with Lena can't be dangerous.

Cade and Lena go around the side of the house. A few minutes later, I watch the red fur of The Leviathan bound off, followed slowly by a soft-gray colored wolf.

They barely disappear into the tree line when I turn to Deacon. He pulls his head back, eyes wide, in response to my glare.

"I want dirt on Cade." I look him square in the eye.

Deacon casts a Cheshire grin, rubbing his hands together. "What do you want to know?"

"What am I getting into?" I ask as Deacon starts rifling through cabinets.

"Ahhhhh," Deacon croons before clarifying. "Am I talking

you into or out of taking Cade as your mate?"

Deacon picks up the mass of snack foods he's located in the cupboards and heads to the main area with the sofa, tilting his head. I take his cue and follow. He sets the assortment down between us and starts snacking, waiting for me to answer him.

"If Cade wasn't your brother, would you tell me to date him?" I ask back.

"Oh, absolutely. He's loyal as fuck. From my understanding, ladies have never left . . . uhm, unsatisfied. He cooks, cleans, and has manners. He's a wolf, so he has a temper, but when he acts on it, he's still in control. As far as wolves go, Cade's about as good as they come."

Deacon rambles and forgets what he's saying all at once. But he does sell Cade well.

There's another question I have to ask.

"But he is your brother, so, would you still tell me to date him?" I ask.

Deacon points his finger at me while the other hand digs through a bag of candy. When he pulls his eyes off the sweets to look at me, there's a smile.

He nods in confirmation, but his voice is sad. "Yeah, I would. You look happy together. He is all those things, but you're going to need to remember that he's an Ardelean with a gift. Granted, as far as they come, his is far less crippling than the rest of ours."

I'm trying to think of my next question, silently munching on a salty snack.

Deacon volunteers information. It's more of a rant. I can hear Deacon's uncharacteristic tone of being bothered.

"You should know, Cade gets a reputation for being selfish for walking away from the throne. It's easier to paint him that way. Many of our father's mistakes and shortcomings have been blamed on him. Many think of Robert as the noble ruler.

Nothing Cade did was going to be good enough. He let their words . . . he let other people tell him who he was."

Deacon is quiet, eating his chips, clearly done ranting.

I process a moment before picking up a cookie out of the package. "What do you think, about him abdicating?"

"When Cade should have been picking out which university to go to and worrying about his intended's first heat, he was ruling our people." Deacon pauses. He takes a bite of a cookie before he speaks, this time seeming a little less sharp. "Hard to paint him as selfish for walking away from that sort of pressure. It's hard to be mad at someone who's dead, so you pick the person who isn't in your face every day."

Deacon is looking over my shoulder. I turn to look, and nothing is there.

When I look back, Deacon looks at me. "You're not haunted. It's one of the usuals."

I look back again, but still see nothing.

Deacon chuckles. "Unless you've developed a new gift yourself, you can't see dead people."

"Oh, sorry." I suck in my top lip.

"Why?" Deacon squints at me. He draws out his words. "Did you kill them?"

I squint back at him, repeating his tone. "If they're ghosts you normally see, how would it make sense if I killed them?"

"You make an excellent point, my friend." Deacon pops out of our squinting match. He shakes his finger knowingly with a smile. "Should I be asking you what your intention with my brother is?"

"My intention?" I put my hand over my heart in mock offense. His face is painted more seriously than I expected. I change to match his earnestness. "I love Cade. A whole lot even, but I don't know the dumb stuff about him. I want to get to know him better. But it doesn't feel like there's time."

CHAPTER 53

CADE

DEACON IS A GOOD BROTHER. It's no surprise he's my favorite. Competition isn't exactly stiff, but he's legitimately a good person once you get past the recreational drug use, drinking himself into a stupor, and having literal conversations with ghosts. As the days have dragged on, waiting for my challenge of Robert, he's been mostly sober and around. I've seen more of him in the past two and a half weeks than in the last six months.

Some things don't change, his lack of work ethic being one of them. When he finds me, the work for the day is done. I'm splitting the last of the logs for the wood burner, which heats the house.

Deacon saunters out, crossing the yard. He plops himself down on the splitting log and looks at me. "Your mate wants to get to know you better."

Direct and to the point, I keep stacking. "Fair. How do you know that?"

"You should take her on a date. She told me when you and Lena were out running," he says.

It's not a suggestion despite the word 'should' being in there.

"What do you propose we do?"

It appears he has all the answers today. I wait for a viable suggestion.

"Drive her into the Twin Cities, and take her to see the stupid cherry on the spoon at The Walker." Deacon is nodding, pleased with his suggestion.

I scratch my head. "That's not exactly low profile. There are plenty of wolves who work in the city."

"Touché." He frowns, defeated. "It's got to be something she's going to enjoy but you also have knowledge about. She thought shooting was fun, but obviously, that seemed like business. Though, based on the blushing, it sounds like you flexed some exhibition muscles. I give you seven out of ten for that."

He raises his hand for a high five. I shake my head. Not having any of my shit, Deacon high-fives himself.

I wait for him to come up with another viable option that isn't waltzing Thalia Clark around in the middle of Ardelean pack territory.

I've finished stacking wood, and he gasps. "Okay, what about a cave tour? I know you've spent sixty-nine years in the car, but they're outdoorsy-ish." He pauses. "Are caves outdoors or indoors?" Scratching his head, he says, "I'm not sure it matters, they're nature-y. They've got cool history, and she can get cave kisses and Cade kisses."

I cock my head. Honestly, I wasn't expecting an idea that made sense or that I could actually see us doing. I don't know if a cave is an outdoor or indoor activity. I wonder if Thalia knows.

Pleased with himself, Deacon walks away. Over his

shoulder, he calls, "You can thank me by picking up more beer on the way home!"

I scrub my hand down my face. It's true, I will pick up his favorite beer from the brewery on my way home.

BACK IN THE HOUSE, Thalia is in the middle of counting her stitches on her project. Her tongue sticks out of her mouth, and her hands move the little threads back and forth. I wait a few minutes, leaning against the wall, watching her. When she figures out whatever it is she's counting, there's a movement of thread, and she puts her needle into its designated spot in her project.

"What's up?" She draws out the question, eyeing me.

It's not fair that my mate is so sexy all the time. Apparently, I can't keep her locked in the bedroom for days on end. I let go of the lip I've been biting.

She licks hers.

If mate wolf. She have heat. Heat means bed for days. Puppy brain, not give wolf, coward. The Leviathan corrects me.

Pushing him out of my mind, I answer, "Come with me to shower?"

Thalia bites her bottom lip.

Since our bath when we first got here, we haven't spent any time getting clean together. Which is a shame, I love the way she looks naked.

Thalia stands quickly, walking to get in front of me before sauntering. Her hips sway back and forth purposefully.

Licking my bottom lip, I follow dutifully.

I strip off her clothes first.

She giggles. "I thought we were getting clean."

"I can multitask." I push her into the bathroom, pulling off my clothes along the way.

CHAPTER 54

THALIA

CLEARLY IMPATIENT, Cade turns the water on as hot as it goes. Stripping me, he plants kisses on every section of skin he exposes. With my leggings around my feet, he kisses each leg as he steadies me, pulling them off.

I watch him, unsure what to do with my hands, but not wanting him to stop.

He pulls me toward the shower, stepping in first. Forgetting about the hot water, he hisses, writhing out of the way as it hits him. Adjusting it colder, he tests it this time. His other hand is still attached to me.

With the glass door closed behind us, we're in a rainforest worth of humidity. I can only imagine how poofy my hair is getting.

The look on Cade's face, the intensity in his gaze as he rakes me in, and the look of possession in his eyes all remind me he's not the least bit concerned with my hair.

The water pours over us from the rainfall shower head as he pulls me closer to him. Cade kneels on the tile floor. With his head between my tits, he looks up at me while grabbing hold of the soap and a rag.

"Oh, so you were serious about getting clean." I tease. "Here I thought I was getting more orgasms."

I try to step away from him, but Cade wraps his arms around me. Finding a nipple with his mouth, he bites down gently.

I bite my tongue, squirming.

"Multitask." Cade chastises before traipsing kisses back across my chest to the other side.

I squirm as he nibbles. Closing my eyes, I tilt my head up to the water, letting it fall over the top of us.

Cade kisses lower. Slowly. The soapy rag slides against my skin, along my sides and under my breasts. It's such an intimate feeling.

I keep my eyes closed, soaking in the feelings of his care. Cade's free hand wanders, slowly and gently, up the side of my leg. Rag abandoned, both of Cade's hands run across my body.

One hand finds it's way between my legs; without hesitation, his fingers slide into my warmth, teasing me.

I try to tell him how good it feels, but no words come out.

Cade's hungry for me. He doesn't slow down, pushing two fingers into me at once. I'm tight. I wasn't expecting his rough touch, but it's a new kind of wild euphoria.

My hand finds and fists his hair. I take a deep breath, moving closer and tilting my head toward the ceiling. Water flows over my face. I hold my breath, focusing solely on feeling his fingers work me. Pressing my inner sensitive spot with long strokes of his fingers, he provides a firm, but in-tune, grinding against my clit with his thumb. Staying there, under the flow of warm water until my lungs scream to breathe, expedites my pleasure.

I bend forward, clearing the water from my face. My lungs

gasp for air, and my stomach clenches, nearly causing me to come undone. All I feel is lust. I need more.

Cade must hear how close I am because he makes a needy noise before coaxing, "That's it, draga mea. Come for me."

His words are all I need.

I wobble, my orgasm taking me, but Cade wraps his free arm around me, holding me close. His soaking wet brown hair is pushed against my stomach. Steady in his hands, I'm a panting mess, feeling so much pleasure.

He's not done. Cade's fingers slowly retreat, but his touch doesn't break. I'm lust drunk. My mind is hazy as I watch the water roll down his body. He trails kisses up my body on his way to standing. He nibbles my ear, causing a shiver.

"Dry off and get warm. After I get clean, I want you to make me dirty again," he murmurs.

I turn to look at him. His blue eyes are heavy with desire.

I face him and counter, "After *I* get *you* clean, I can definitely do that."

Cade's shock doesn't go unnoticed. I'm feeling brave. Embracing what I feel between us, I start to explore.

For the first time, I really drink him in. Slowly, cautiously, my core warms, thinking about what I want. It's exciting and has me salivating.

I want to try giving head. Will he know I've never done this before? Probably. Is it going to stop me from learning? No. *Like all subjects and skills, this can be mastered.*

His cock is hard, reaching for me, but I'm not ready to move that fast. Instead, I grab the rag and start with his shoulder, covered in tattoos. Building courage as I work my way down, I trace the delicate line work and shapes that accentuate the curvature of his muscles.

At this distance, I notice the smallest details. Leafy patterns cover the top of his shoulder. Two wolves are running up the central part of his bicep. I keep exploring downward, finding a blank space on the inside of his forearm. I trace it again.

"What's this space empty for?" I look up to see his confident panty-melting smirk.

He darts his tongue over his lips before answering, "Your name."

My jaw falls open. We've said I love you. We've talked about the future. Nothing permanent has been discussed. Cade saying that feels so massive.

Cade moves in slow motion. He pulls the washcloth from me, cleaning himself between peppering kisses on my skin.

This is what stunned feels like.

I know I should speak, ask questions, do something. I just can't move past his words and my reaction.

My brain whirls as he walks me out of the shower, carefully dries my skin, and begins dressing me. I'm obsessed with watching and feeling how he cares for me. When I try to help, he bats my hands away with soft kisses and small growls. He's so attentive. *Why won't he let me care for him?* He runs his hands around my calves and up my legs to my stomach, then squeezes the little rolls, making the happiest little grumble. He bites his lip.

He slowly clasps the bra behind my back and then, from behind, allows me to help get my arms into the sleeves of my T-shirt. He kisses the nape of my neck, and I shiver.

"I love you," he whispers.

I nod in response but can't leave it unsaid. "I love you too."

Cade moves away from me to get dressed. *Now's my chance.*

My heart rate accelerates. I want to try and make him feel as good as he makes me feel.

Cade tries to walk away, but I wrap my hand around his forearm. With the lightest touch, Cade allows me to direct him. I pull him around and then back him into the bed. His eyes hold a million questions and a slight glimpse of mischief as he lets me push him to sit down.

Our height difference gives me perfect access when he's seated on the bed. Standing between his legs, I can kiss him without reaching or moving to my tippy-toes. His breathing seems shorter as I kiss him. I rest my hands on his strong shoulders, and Cade rests a tentative hand on the side of my hip, but he doesn't stop me.

My knees press against his, and Cade widens his legs, allowing me to shuffle closer. As athletically inept as I can be, I try to mind my knees in relation to his growing erection. Once I'm close enough, I drag my nose across his cheek like he does to me. I nip his ear, repeating all the motions I've felt him do to me. The smallest gasp leaves his mouth. I'm starting to lose my nerve. New things are always scary, but this is . . . I want this. Fear isn't always bad.

As I kiss down his neck and collarbone, Cade squirms, almost rising off the bed until I catch his gaze and he settles in. His pupils are massive — his blue eyes turned nearly black.

Cade's cock is hard and presses against me. I look down only for a moment on my descent to the floor. My knees come in contact with the carpet, and I'm pretty sure my heart is rattling my rib cage.

His voice comes out as a small whine. "Draga mea." He draws deep, heavy breaths between words. "You don't have to do this. It's not reciprocal."

With my tongue out, I press it flat along the bottom of his shaft, licking up to the head.

Cade groans. He lifts his hand slightly before I watch him hesitate and put it down. He fists the sheets, gripping the bed.

I don't know what I'm doing, and I hope it doesn't show. His reaction tells me that, at the very least, I'm doing this right.

With a light grip, I wrap my hand around his shaft. My hand trembles. I feel so many different things.

"Fuck." Cade pants watching me, his body tensing.

Licking him again, I guide the head into my mouth. It feels significantly larger than I anticipated. I press my tongue against the underside, working the shaft with my hand slowly. I try to focus on Cade's reactions to learn what he likes and what sets him off. I'm overwhelmed with the foreign — but not unwelcome — sensation of his cock moving toward the back of my mouth.

With his size in my mouth, it feels so awkward. I feel lost. I'm drooling down his shaft. It's uncomfortable and messy. My toes squirm.

Cade's hand finds mine wrapped around his cock.

Defeated, I pull him out of my mouth. *I've failed. I know it. He hates this.*

Hunger still burns in his eyes as he looks down at me. I feel like he's ready to consume me.

"Let me help you? Or, let me fuck you?"

I hesitate. Cade's lips pull into a soft encouraging smile as his other hand wraps into my damp curls. He works his shaft with his hand wrapped around mine. I try to memorize what he's doing. I notice the change in pressure as he guides my hand along the silky-smooth skin. Watching is intoxicating. My pussy clenches, empty, wanting more, but the desire to have him in my mouth is stronger. I look up, ready to beg to learn more.

"Open," he instructs. "If you're uncomfortable or want to stop, just tap my leg. But if you're not tapping my leg, I want your other hand working that sweet little clit."

Cade's dirty talk sends a hard throbbing between my legs. I'm ready to try with his urging.

I open my mouth for him. He raises his eyebrows and shifts

his gaze to my hand resting on his leg. *Message received.* Begrudgingly, I slide my hand into my leggings. *I can't focus on what I'm doing if I'm playing with myself.* I barely touch my clit, and it throbs with need. I moan and fight the urge to close my eyes at the feel of my hand between my legs.

I let Cade guide my head. Slowly his cock works deeper into my mouth, but he's gentle. I'm trying to focus on what he's having me do. Drool continues to escape from my mouth. It runs down my chin as I adjust to the feel and size of him. Pressing my tongue against him, I try to swallow saliva, but it's far too much.

So many sensations.

With his cock in my mouth, I almost forget about the fingers playing with my clit. *Multitask.* That's what he said earlier. I can multitask . . . I think.

Cade groans, panting.

Something warm and salty coats my tongue. My first taste of his cum. It's different than I expected. Not bad, just different.

Cade coaches me. "Relax your jaw. I want to feel your throat. Breathe now."

His words are so hot. *Breathe?* I draw a breath and find out why. It's momentarily impossible. My airway is cut off by his cock. Cade is quick to let me move my head back. Even as gentle as he is, my gag reflex kicks in. I gag around him but don't pull away. My body fights back, but I want, no, I *need* more.

"Fuck, you take me so good, draga mea."

Cade's praise is all the encouragement I need to do that again. He guides my head back down his shaft, and I let him. Slowly pushing himself deeper into my mouth.

My head bobs quickly, in time with the hand working my clit. The feeling of warm wetness on my breasts startles me.

I've apparently drooled through my T-shirt. I'm doing an excellent job at getting us dirty again.

Cade quickly removes the hand in my hair. But I don't stop. It wasn't bad.

I moan and watch as Cade's fingers intertwine in the bedding. I'm not taking him as deep as he pushed me; it's hard to make myself go that deep. The pain of the heave from deep in my stomach is a small deterrent. Only small amounts of bile rise.

I pull myself away from watching him and back to the task at hand, repeating the motions he showed me.

"Fuck, Thalia. If you don't stop, I'm going to come right down your throat."

He arches his back, and his leg tightens next to me. His words confirm that I'm at least a decent student.

His hand falls away that had been guiding mine along his shaft next. I'm in complete control. The feeling of him at my mercy is powerful. *I'm pleasing him.*

Cade's body is seizing. His breathing is short and quick. I look up at him, seeing The Leviathan there. *Is he holding back?* Cade groans, his body rigid under my touch.

I press harder with my tongue against the bottom of his shaft. It's throbbing in my hand. I moan again; the vibrations must feel good to him. I increase the tempo on my clit. The sounds and sensations of panting around his thrusts, bobbing my head, and my moans have me on the edge of an orgasm.

A massive feral sound echoes through me as Cade comes. The sound accompanies a feeling of warmth as his cum fills my mouth.

I lap, trying to swallow it back. It mixes with my saliva and runs out of my mouth, coating my already soaked chest.

The pulsing of his cock in my mouth is so seductive. I bring my focus to my fingers still working my clit. I pull Cade's cock from between my lips, moaning hard.

Moving my hand from his cock to the bed next to him, I have to steady myself. I'm lightheaded from the lack of air, but choosing his dick over the air I breathe gives me an awesome rush.

I keep moving my fingers, chasing my orgasm, wishing it was his hand on me instead of mine.

He tilts my head to meet his eyes as he leans forward on the bed. Cade's eyelids look heavy, but the look only adds to the sex appeal.

"Come for me, Thalia."

At those words, a gentle command, I unravel.

He pulls my hair firmly; it's only the slightest amount of pain. But that pain is washed away with an intense kiss. Cade's tongue claims my mouth.

It's too much. I'm screaming into his kiss. He doesn't break it, taking my scream and the air as it leaves my lungs. My body shudders with the release. I'm still lightheaded, so I close my eyes. It feels like the world wobbles. When I open my eyes, I realize the world did wobble. Cade had lifted me off the floor. His arms wrap around me as I straddle his lap.

"You're fucking perfect, you know that, right?" he whispers in my ear. He lies back, pulling me down to the bed with him. "You're more than I would have ever thought I could be worthy of."

His praise is everything. It doesn't matter that I'm covered in the mess from going down on him. All I want is for him to tell me how good I did.

He cuddles with me, petting my hair. His forehead is pushed against mine. My insides are tingly and warm with a connectedness, love, that I feel toward him.

My grumble when he leaves the bed doesn't go unheard.

Cade assures me of his intent to return. "Let me clean you."

Cade pulls off my soaked T-shirt before retreating to the bathroom and returning with a warm damp rag. Wiping my face down slowly, he cleans everything from my chin to my bra and back again.

CHAPTER 55

THALIA

I'D SEEN the pole shed a few times while walking around the yard and when we'd gone to the gun range, but it didn't seem important. Cade and I walk down the driveway, and he unlocks the side door. *It makes sense, this is where Deacon keeps his motorcycle.* There are four additional cars and three motorcycles.

Cade pulls a set of keys out of what looks like an electrical panel before unlocking the rolling garage door.

Eight fluffy wolf feet are prancing around, noses sniffing the door as it slides up. The fluffy gray one looks like the glimpse I caught of Lena, and there's another white and cream wolf with darker bands, which I assume is Deacon.

"Hey, guys." Cade shakes his head. "Really?"

Deacon spins in a circle, all four paws coming off the ground.

"Deacon wants to know if he can say hi." Cade seemingly translates.

I look at the fluffy wolf and open my arms. "Whatcha waiting for? I'm going on a date. Places to be."

Slowly, with his head down, Deacon approaches. I let him smell my feet as he works his way up. Then he pushes into me expectantly. He's smaller than Cade so I stoop down a bit to wrap my arms around him. He sighs a big huff before squirming. Then as fast as he was spinning, he darts off, barking and nipping at Lena as they run.

"Ready to go?" Cade smiles while walking over to a dark-blue classic Mustang and unlocks the passenger door first.

"Uh, sure. We're not taking the Yukon?" I walk over to the vehicle sporting a wide-banded stripe, flocked by two thinner ones up the sides.

Cade shrugs. "We can, but I figured a change might be good."

"You know, had I not recently become well acquainted with your size, I'd think driving a muscle car was you trying to compensate. You don't seem like the muscle car type." I walk between him and the door motioning to his pants and car as applicable.

"Do you aim to wound me?" Cade laughs at my joke, shaking his head. "What is the muscle car type?"

"More . . . pretentious." I try to explain. I motion to his clothes. "Not so approachable looking with jeans and a thermal Henley. I mean, you hardly look preppy."

Cade nods. "I'll make a note to drive the muscle cars only in my dress suits starting after today."

DESPITE HAVING A MUSCLE CAR, Cade drives just as respectfully as he did in the Yukon. He's not trying to speed or weave in and out of traffic.

He feels too far away, despite being physically closer in the Mustang than we were in the Yukon; we're not touching and should be. I slide my hand into his lap, and Cade pulls a hand off the steering wheel to hold it.

"What's your dream car?" Cade asks slowly. "What do you drive now?"

"I don't have a car currently. I don't drive a lot, truthfully. There's not been a need. I have a license, but it's not my favorite activity, and, living in the city, there's always transport," I answer. He asked a second question, but between the muscle car we're in and the massive SUV Cade drives daily, I'm not sure I want to answer it. "I haven't really given my dream car any thought."

Cade rolls his eyes. "You're still a terrible liar. I'm not going to judge you. What's the dream?"

"Okay, but the last time I told you not to laugh, you did." I remind him of his betrayal relating to the grilled cheese.

"I promise. Think of it like *The Great Gatsby*, the cars matter — an allegory." Cade waves his hand.

I furrow my brows and tilt my head to look at him. He doesn't have a college degree but makes complex literary references.

I'm quiet too long so he prompts, "You okay over there?"

"Yeah, sorry. I just, you surprise me sometimes. You'd think I'd know better by now, but you constantly make references to literature. It's weird that you don't have a big fancy degree." I swallow while cringing at myself. It feels like that might have been a bit insulting, so I change the subject, answering his original question. "For the longest time, I really wanted Herbie."

Cade squeezes my hand, drawing his lips tight. I can just *tell* he's stifling a laugh.

Glaring at him, I voice my frustrations. "See, I knew you'd laugh."

"I didn't laugh," Cade defends. "I think it's adorable, and I just fell in love with you a little bit more. You'd look adorable in a vintage beetle."

Trying to divert the subject of my dream car — an impractical tin can — I turn the conversation back toward him. "Tell me something about you I don't know. Something from when you were little?"

"I've never had a dream job," he says slowly. "I know it's a thing for humans. Fuck, even other wolves wanted to be doctors, veterinarians, astronauts, or whatever. I think I even heard of a human kid who wanted to be a garbage man. I always knew there was no point in dreaming of something else. It's always been expected of me to be pack Second, take a mate, and settle into my place at the left hand of the Alpha."

Rice Lake 107

WISC

7

40

CHAPTER 56

CADE

Thalia's thumb rubs against the denim of my jeans. Mindlessly stroking the fabric, she seems to have more to say. I wait patiently for more questions, just enjoying the ride with her.

"I know nothing about you," Thalia says quietly. "I feel so much for you. We've said I love you. We've talked briefly about plans for the future . . ."

She stalls out, checking my reaction.

I help her. "You feel like you don't know basic information that you learn during dating?"

"Exactly." She nods. "Is this how it is for wolves? I really like how things are progressing, but I don't even know your birthday."

"October second," I answer the easy part of the question. "As for how it is, kind of? When we find our mates, like me finding you, it's pretty instantaneous. The draw to be with them. You've got the rest of your lives to figure out the simplicity in life."

With nearly an hour's drive to the cave, I let her ask me questions about everything and anything. My favorite color: blue. My favorite non-wolf animal: bats. What got me into classic cars: a bet with Ezra. Thalia didn't like my answer about what I had for a dream job or what I did for fun as a child. I can't blame her. From what I know, humans are encouraged to dream about careers and fancy ideas of what they want to do. Humans aren't typically groomed for certain jobs. They sure as fuck don't spend their entire day working toward goals to be the pack Second. I don't even want to tell her what that entails.

We're pulling up to the cave when she goes bashful again. Her back and forth between comfortable and uncomfortable is still concerning. I wait for her question, trying to reserve my fear that Thalia could go into withdrawal mode entirely. I've turned off the car before she asks the question.

"You said draga mea means my darling, but why?" She bites her lips together, pulling her hair over her shoulder.

I smile. "It's Romanian."

"You speak Romanian?" Thalia's eyes go wide.

I shake my head. "The Leviathan; his first non-ancient and verbal language. It's what he started calling you when he wanted you. I guess I should have checked with you on a pet name."

"I love it." Thalia doesn't hesitate. "I love you both."

Love is a warm feeling that saturates even the darkest parts of you. Right now, there isn't a depth where darkness can hide from the warmth of Thalia's love. I lean across the car, my hand finding her cheek, and pull her to me for a kiss. The Leviathan pushes forward, and I let my eyes go gold.

"We love you."

I DIDN'T THINK AHEAD to book a private tour. Hindsight is 20/20. We head down the stairs for a small safety presentation about not touching things, watching our heads, and, if we, for whatever reason, need to leave, don't wander off.

Thalia nearly dances with excitement as the tour guide starts explaining the tour. Despite the height difference between her and the children on the tour, there's no variance in the excitement level.

Once we reach the first level, she drags me around a rock pillar, said to be good luck. When the tour guide asks open-ended questions, Thalia leans down and whispers the answers into various children's ears.

Mate smart. Loves pups. The Leviathan doesn't hesitate to point out.

As we descend lower into the cave, there are ceilings at various heights. Thalia walks effortlessly underneath them; very rarely does she duck. I, on the other hand, find myself crouching under nearly everything. The benefit, it puts me at the right level to plant kisses across the nape of her neck.

She snickers.

We enter a chamber that's supposedly haunted, and she steps back against my chest. The tour guide says she's going to turn off the light to give us a feel of total darkness. Thalia grabs hold of one of my hands. I snake my arm around her waist. The lights go out, and we're plunged into total darkness. It's true, there's absolutely no light. Even with The Leviathan, I can't see anything.

I am unashamed to admit that I take advantage of the opportunity, running my hand down along the front of her body. She lets out a small gasp before I run it back up. The tour guide counts down to turning on their flashlight, and I pull my hand back to a publicly acceptable place.

When the light comes up, Thalia's poker face is on. I scent her arousal, but without that, I'd assume she's just fine.

We see cave bacon and some straws and hear a comical story someone made up about some of the cave features, linking them all together in a compelling way. When we're plunged into darkness in the second room, I mind my manners, letting her and the children talk about the rocks that glow in the dark and under blacklights.

BACK ON THE surface of the world, Thalia is beaming. "That was so much fun!"

Her smile is infectious. She waves goodbye to the children, and we walk around some of the trails. As we're exploring, we see their mini-golf course.

"Ohhh! This looks so cute." Thalia walks over to a giant dinosaur egg that's bigger than she is. "We should come back and play sometime."

"We'll have to bring Lena." I nod. "She loves mini-golf. But if you mention it before she tells you, she'll deny it. It's kinda her sign she likes you."

Thalia shakes her head, recognizing the ridiculous nature of Lena's inconsistencies. I shrug, leading Thalia back to the car.

When she rests her head against my arm, I wince slightly. Her head hits where I sunk my teeth in to stop myself from biting her.

Claim mate. Can bite her not us. The Leviathan reminds me that my pain is my own fault.

"You okay?" Thalia asks, looking up at me.

Squeezing her hip, I say, "All good."

"Oh!" Thalia moves off my shoulder. "Your arm, where you've been biting."

"It's okay." I kiss her forehead. "Nothing I can't manage."

"Why are you doing it?" she asks, looking at the spot about where the bite mark is.

"Biting humans is dangerous. There's a small chance that if I bite you and claim you, like I would another wolf during sex" — I swallow hard, trying to finish this sentence — "it could gift you a wolf and bond us before you're really ready."

Claim mate. The Leviathan reminds me how badly we want her.

Thalia's features scrunch into her thinking face, her eyes drawn together and lips pursed. I don't know what she's going to say next, but I've laid it out there and answered her question. It's all I can do, right?

Claim draga mea. You know fix. The Leviathan huffs.

WE'VE TALKED about the cave and stopped by a local restaurant that serves root beer in glasses straight out of a freezer when Thalia finally asks the question I've been waiting for.

"Why won't you turn me?"

She's not looking at me from the passenger seat. Instead, she stares out the windshield.

Anticipating this question for the better part of an hour doesn't make her question any easier to answer.

"It's not safe to do so. It's currently legal, but I'm worried it'll become illegal for us to even exist. I don't know what our future holds, and I don't want to possibly put you at risk like that. Not until I'm sure you're safe and that you're sure you want this."

Rice Lake 107

WISCO

7

CHAPTER 57

THALIA

We're home before sunset and are playing battleship, which I thought was a weird game for them to own, but it's kinda fun.

Lena comes through the door after school.

After pleasantries, which are cordial as usual she asks, "Hey, did you get the mail?"

"No, there wasn't any," Cade answers, closing his half of the game. "You expecting something?"

"No, there just wasn't any. Seems weird." Lena shrugs, dismissing it altogether while tugging her hair out of the bun she had it wrapped in.

"Fridge." Deacon's voice comes from somewhere in the house.

I wasn't aware he was home.

"Deacon." Lena groans.

She separates three midnight-blue colored envelopes from the stack she pulled off the fridge bin.

"If you don't talk about it, it doesn't exist. It's reverse manifestation," Deacon answers from the abyss he's hiding in.

I get off the stool with a hop, walk over to the couch, and peer over the back. He's not there, but he sounds too close to be in his bedroom. *Where the heck is he?*

"Cade Alexander," Cade adopts a snooty tone as he reads his letter, "Your formal challenge of the Ardelean Pack Alpha, Alpha Regent Robert Douglas Alden, has been accepted. You shall arrive no later than seven thirty in the evening on the eve of the full moon. Please bring with you the genetic proof of your lineage and claim to the throne as well as the parties you will be presenting as Alpha Female and Second for the Ardelean pack. If you fail to appear with the aforementioned, your challenge will be considered null and dismissed. Signed, Robert Douglas Alden, Alpha Regent."

"Alexander?" I ask. *Interesting middle name choice.*

"Mom claimed it was important for everyone to have a traditional name available, in case we wanted to be doctors or some shit," Deacon says.

I finally find him, lying on the floor of the foyer.

"But your name is Deacon." I try to logic through how that would be considered traditional. "And you're Lena."

Cade points his thumb over his shoulder toward Deacon. "James Deacon." And then points to Lena. "Kathleen Meredith."

"No wonder you go by Lena." I try to make a joke.

Lena, opening her letter, adds, "Yeah, I'm not very merry." She starts reading, "Kathleen Meredith. Both of which are spelled wrong." She shakes her head with a huff. "You are formally invited to the pack dinner and wolf run of the Pink Moon. Dinner will begin precisely at five thirty. Cocktails and socialization will be hosted on the pack lawn beginning at four in the late afternoon. Dress code is formal evening wear as we will be hosting a formal challenge of the Alpha Regent." She quits reading out loud. Her voice spikes as she calls out, "Dea, come open your letter."

"No, the world is spinning," he answers. "You do it."

Cade rolls his eyes but proceeds to open Deacon's letter. His eyes dart back and forth.

"That son of a bitch."

"What?" Deacon asks.

"Please be ready to meet with possible matches to fulfill your duty to the Ardelean pack. An intention will be arranged for you following the Alpha challenge." Cade rolls his eyes. "He's truly clueless."

"What does that mean?" I ask.

Intention was like engagement, so an arranged marriage seems like what they're talking about. *Can they really force them into this?*

"It means" — Deacon's voice is closer so I turn to see if he's moved, and I jump. He's standing next to me — "that Robert thinks he's going to kill Cade and then force Lena and me to be mated into far away packs so we can't or won't challenge him to avenge Cade."

"I need an Alloway." Cade scratches his head. Cade turns to look at me. "Was it plan C where we get Ezra to come hang out with you?"

Silence between the four of us is awkward. The clock on the wall chimes that it's now 9:00 p.m. I'm exhausted and want to curl up with Cade in bed, but now isn't the time.

A loud alarm blares in frequent beeps from the pantry where Cade's control box is for everything.

"Did the driveway sensors go off?" Cade asks between beeps.

Deacon shakes his head.

Wolves howling outside send shivers down my arms.

Lena goes to the pantry and over to where Cade went to

turn off the smoke detector. The alarm stops beeping, and the windows of the house all turn opaque. She's pushing buttons.

"Two at the front door, I don't recognize them. None have gotten close enough that they could have seen in the back windows. House is secured."

Cade moves quickly, grabbing my wrist and heading through his bedroom, bathroom, and finally into his closet. He pulls out guns from the safe. He loads the handgun I shot just days earlier. When he hands it to me, Cade gives me an expectant nod. I do the same drill I did earlier today, working the action and demonstrating it's loaded. He hands me two full clips.

"If it's not Deacon, Lena, or myself, shoot. Shoot to kill. Don't worry about anything else." His words come quickly; they're controlled and informative, just like when we first met. There's precision in everything he does as he leads me through his closet into the laundry room, locking the door behind us. "The laundry room is the most defendable position in the house because you can see both doors from the corner. I'm putting out a distress signal to Corinth Security. Peter and the team will monitor the house remotely, and if needed, the local police will show up. They will announce themselves as police, and it will be many hours from now. Don't shoot the police. Stick with the alias Millie and Adam have given you."

Cade's words make it sound like he's anticipating not coming back. *He has to come back.*

"Wait, you're coming back, right?"

Pulling me into his arms, he whispers into my ear, "The Leviathan and I will do everything we can to come back to you. I don't know what's going on. You need to know what to do if I'm no longer here to protect you."

I nod. "Emily Elizabeth Miller."

"I love you," Cade tells me before letting me go. He walks

over to the door to the pantry and gives me the last instruction, "Lock this behind me."

"I love you too," I answer.

This better not be the last time I get to say that to him. I lock the door and back myself into the corner sitting on the floor next to the vacuum and the steam mop.

CHAPTER 58

CADE

Deacon is looking around the living room. To the average observer, it would appear he's seeing things that aren't there. His head darts back and forth like he's trying to keep up with a conversation. Knowing that he's listening to ghosts makes it more explainable but not less eccentric looking.

I walk through a spot in the house. A shiver rolls through me. *Fucking spirits.*

"What have we got?" I ask.

Lena's eyes are glued to the screen, watching the security system flip through the cameras. "So far, it's just the two of them. The driveway sensor was set off a few times now. One SUV and one car pulled up; they had 'sota plates."

"Bold of him. Turn on the lights. Make it daytime. Thalia has been told to shoot to kill anyone who isn't the three of us. She's locked in the laundry room."

I watch the feed with Lena for a few moments before tapping the screen, sending the distress signal to Peter. He or my team will take over monitoring the situation and call the authorities if needed.

The SUV pulls up the driveway. Isabel's SUV, to be specific, comes to a stop in the driveway.

Lena snorts, correcting me. "Bold of her."

A knock comes on the door.

As I leave my place in the pantry, I make eye contact with Deacon, who shakes his head. "It's not a trap. According to the ancestors, it's the same old song and dance. Isabel wants an Ardelean."

We kill false mate? Bitch not worthy of bloodline. The Leviathan's bloodlust starts very quickly. He's salivating at the idea. Probably not a good thing that I'm equally tempted. We'll see how much she pisses me off.

Another knock on the door. Persistent fuckers. Through the peephole on the door, I see Isabel standing there, poised to speak. My hackles are raised. I run my hands through my hair before glancing behind me. Lena stays back in the pantry, out of the line of sight. Deacon, on the other hand, sits on the back of the couch, where he has a great view of the door and any drama that may unfold. Unfortunately for his view, I'm not letting her in the house.

I open to find Isabel's fist ready to knock again.

"Oh." Her blonde hair hangs neatly. "I see you're home this time."

"Seems as much, yes."

I step forward and turn the lock on the knob as I cross the threshold. She's forced to back up, but only far enough to let me out. The deadbolt clicks behind me.

She tries to drape herself against me by placing her forearm against my shoulder and wrapping her hand around my head. I brush her off with my hand and growl.

She croons, "I've missed you. You sounded angry on the phone."

"Stop." I let the Alpha command out, harnessing my gift and The Leviathan's power.

Those in the woods still too. The animals of the night pause their noises. I show her my disgust as I push her away from me.

Unable to continue her attempted flirting, Isabel stands there. Her jutting bottom lip and sad puppy dog eyes are pathetic.

I point her down off the porch and command again, "Move."

Isabel huffs, having no choice in her compliance. She flicks her head defiantly away from me. Her bratty behavior may have had some allure when we were younger, but I was wrong about what I wanted. I was wrong about what she was offering. Isabel paints a pretty picture of the inside of the birdcage to make you feel like it's exactly what you want. Once she's lured you inside, you find yourself ensnared.

"Cade, we need to talk," Isabel says the four words no man ever wants to hear from a woman.

I keep indicating with my arm, forcing her back away from where I've positioned myself at the bottom of my stoop. We're illuminated by the floodlights strung up in trees and the porch lights behind me.

"I've nothing to say to you, Isabel." I let those words come out with the ice-cold tone I feel for her in my heart. "We've been over for years. I'm sick of having this conversation with you at all hours of the day. Go home."

"You've taken a Luna. I'm here to challenge her," Isabel says, like she's learned a well-kept secret that she can use against me.

She runs her hand into her blonde hair, tucking it behind her ear.

Her continual flirting causes The Leviathan to growl at her hubris.

There's only one way she would have heard something like that.

I roll my eyes and shake my head, glancing around the clearing at the front of my house. Her friends, her own little she-wolf army, stay by the vehicles and tucked into the tree line. They all have enough sense to be fearful.

With a sigh, I bluff. "I don't know what you're talking about."

"I've been told that you're claiming a mate. I've come to challenge her." Isabel rephrases with confidence.

She adjusts her posture, standing taller with a cocky smile. Isabel's wolf is a fierce fighter. There's reason for her to be confident that she could win a challenge.

My intention for this exchange was not to be rude, just forceful and direct. Yet, a crack of laughter escapes before I can rein it back in for composure.

Isabel glares, unamused. "Is tradition funny to you, Cade?"

"No, Isabel. It's not. That adds another element of irony. I'm not a Pack Alpha." I remind her with a coy smile. "The Sovereign cannot form a pack after he abdicates the throne. Deacon, Lena, and I live here free of pack status. Law states it takes five wolves to be a pack, there aren't enough of us here. You can't challenge someone for a position that doesn't exist. Furthermore, there's no one for you to challenge."

"That's not what I've heard."

Isabel cocks her head, raises an eyebrow, then crosses her arms below her chest. She's purposely pushing her tits up, trying to seduce me. I think.

The Leviathan, taking the same cues from her as I did, wrinkles his nose and bares his teeth. *Make her stop. She wolf disgraceful.*

"I don't know what you've heard, who you heard it from, or how you heard it."

I raise my head and relax my posture a bit. Tucking one

hand into my pocket, I lean into the bluff that I've got nothing to hide.

"You've been seen with a woman, and you've apparently made it clear she's your Luna." Isabel takes a moment, her resolve faltering. When I don't engage with her hearsay, she continues, "You've issued Robert a formal challenge. You're going to use The Leviathan and take back the throne. Then you're going to take whomever this bitch is as your mate. I am challenging that."

No. She no talk draga mea. The Leviathan snarls and snaps.

I hold him back. *She's bluffing. She's trying to get a reaction.* She's heard a rumor and is fishing for information.

I shrug, extending my arms, demonstrating I have nothing to hide. "Your information is wrong. Yes, I've challenged Robert, and I intend to take back the throne. The Leviathan and I are both ready to accept our position. Eventually, I'll take a mate. Until then, your challenge is invalid."

"Don't insult my intelligence, Cade."

Isabel takes a tentative step toward me, testing my resolve.

Lulling her into a false sense of security, I let her move back toward me. It's a slow saunter, her hips swinging wide, trying to get my attention.

False mate sick. The Leviathan observes the way she acts and how her wolf isn't steady inside her. *Not worthy. Filth.*

Apparently, The Leviathan didn't get the memo of trying to be cordial.

Isabel is within touching distance. I glare, flashing her The Leviathan's eyes and flaring my nostrils. Smartly, she stands still.

In a low tone, she whispers, "I know you're with a human. Don't disgrace our people taking a human mate. You can't even properly claim her. She's unfit to rule."

Whatever reaction Isabel wanted from me doesn't come.

Her eyes go wide when I don't react. Self-doubt flashes across her face. She second-guesses all her information.

I shrug and let the power of The Leviathan forward. Stepping into her personal space, I wrap my hand around her neck before I snarl.

Quickly, Isabel whimpers, looking away in submission. She struggles to escape. My hand is tight around her throat.

I smile, pulling her close to me, and whisper in her ear, "When and if I take a mate, it will be none of your damn business. When and if I take a mate and you come to challenge that mate, you better have your affairs in order. I will fight all challenges against her. Most importantly, it will be my personal pleasure to put you in the ground."

Fighting harder to escape, Isabel puts her hands on my arm. I hold her neck for a few more seconds, letting the panic of cutting the blood supply to her brain set in, before I let her go. She swallows hard, walking backward from me. I look around at her pack of she wolves.

Now that she's stepped away, I make sure to say it loud enough for them all to hear. "If you want to talk about me, talk about the facts. I've put my father in the ground and buried my mother as a result. After I reclaim the throne, anyone, and I mean anyone, who comes to challenge myself, whomever I select as my Alpha Female, whomever I select as my Second, and whomever I eventually choose to take as my Luna, should come ready for death. I will take the challenge personally. The Leviathan will not be appeased by submission. Death will follow in his wake."

Isabel's friends back away from her. Many begin climbing into the vehicles or retreating through my woods. Isabel smartly keeps her head down, not looking at me as she backs herself to her SUV. The stench of her fear causes my nose to wrinkle in disgust.

When she hits the comfort of her SUV, she says quietly over the open door, "I'm going to find out who she is, Cade. You won't take a human mate, not if I can do something about it."

I stand with my arms crossed over my chest, watching each and every one of them leave my line of sight.

Oh, Isabel. I can't wait to see how you fail after I strip your father of his position in the Alpha council.

After a few more minutes, I hear the front doorknob and deadbolt unlock. I turn, knowing that's the sign the unwanted visitors have left the perimeter of our security system.

Deacon leans against the door frame. "I'm not going to get to fight my own battles?"

"Really?" I yawn, giving a shake to let off the tension.

I quickly move to the door and push past Deacon. Lena is coaxing Thalia out of the laundry room.

I pull them both into a hug, holding them tightly. The countdown to ending Robert is on. Until I take back the throne, life is in limbo, and I'm sick of waiting to control my future.

CHAPTER 59
THALIA

CADE LETS Lena and I go, kissing the top of my head. Then pinching the bridge of his nose, he turns to his siblings.

"I shouldn't have to ask this, but I'm going to anyway. Have either of you talked about Thalia to anyone?"

Deacon shakes his head. "Haven't seen a living wolf in months."

"I may dislike her, but I'm not stupid," Lena answers.

Cade sighs and runs his hand back through his hair before walking over and pulling his phone off the charger. He presses some buttons and then holds it up to his ear.

"Ansel, you need to lock your shit down. Isabel LeFleur knows that I was seen with a woman, human woman, and that it was assumed she was my mate."

Cade growls, and there's a darkness I haven't ever seen or heard. It's scary. Even with how angry he was with Lena when I first got here, this is more intense. The hair on the back of my neck raises.

"The only one I know who has ties there is Ben. So, you tell me who the fuck talked to Isabel."

My stomach drops. Ben was so nice; Cade doesn't think he would have talked to Isabel? That doesn't make sense.

"Dale and Ripley. Names and packs," Cade demands.

He snaps his fingers at Lena, who brings him a pad of paper and a pen before retreating to her bedroom. Cade writes down the information that Ansel is providing him.

He snarls, "Ansel, you need to deal with this. It's treason, and I won't tolerate it."

Deacon comes over and wraps his arms around me. I only realize my body is shaking once I'm wrapped in his arms.

He whispers, "It's okay, little red. He's only a little mad at Ansel. Ansel will be fine."

That doesn't make me feel a whole lot better. Treason doesn't seem like a word that should just be thrown around. And just because Ansel is fine doesn't sound like someone else will be.

"You'll know which one it was before the morning." Cade pulls the phone away from his face and looks like he's going to hang up before his shoulders drop, and he puts it back to his ear. "I'm sorry. I know you didn't do this. But Thalia is fucking mine. I hope you never have to know what this rage feels like. And that bitch just fucking threatened my mate."

How safe am I?

Deacon pulls back his arms before offering me his hand. He leads me over to the big sofa. A blanket hits me from the side, and I hear Lena giggle. She's returned with her hair wrapped into a braid and in pajamas. I spread the warm fabric out around me.

Cade starts placing another call. "Adam, I need you to run some numbers and connections for me. I know it'll be a lot of work, so any overtime you need is approved. Any resource at all is at your disposal."

Settling into the couch, I watch Deacon toss a frozen pizza in the oven and Lena disappear into the pantry. By the time Cade finishes making phone calls, an impromptu movie night is happening.

CHAPTER 60
THALIA

WHEN CADE EXPLAINED what happened with Isabel, I knew I wasn't getting the whole story. I've wanted to press him for more information. Continually, I feel like I'm being left out of important conversations. I'm not sure if it's because I'm my mother's daughter or because I'm human. *I guess it's probably a bit of both.* Asking Cade directly about what's going on only results in half answers and explanations. Sometimes he struggles to find human parallels between protocol and rules, but other times, it feels like deflection.

Since the Isabel incident a week ago, Cade has made it a point to be intimate every night. It's been fantastic. I didn't know you could actually have sex like this every night. Tonight, it's going to be different. *Can you have withdrawals from orgasms?*

Tonight, he'll come home and won't be in any shape to do much more than eat and sleep. He's assured me at least a dozen times, today alone, that this will be a cakewalk for him. I want to believe him, but I don't.

Seeing Cade being put back together by Ben was traumatic.

I've tried not to think about where he's going and what I've been told will happen. I get woozy and it's difficult to breathe. If that was a spur-of-the-moment fight, what sort of damage would an intentional fight cause?

This is something he has to do. People are counting on him to do what they consider right.

I couldn't beg Cade to stay, even though I wanted to. I watch Cade get dressed into another expensive black three-piece suit. He looks so polished and put together. The silver tie brings out the haunting silver-blue of his eyes. Despite my small objection, he did get a haircut. It's shorter than when I first met him, but not awful.

When we emerge from Cade's bedroom, Lena is fiddling with her purse. I gawk at her little black dress that's daringly short. Deacon is stashing little individually wrapped candies into his all-black suit. He looks like a high-end version of Johnny Cash. If it weren't for them looking so ritzy, I'd say they were headed to a funeral.

One of their brothers is going to die tonight. Black is appropriate.

A few minutes before needing to leave, Cade anxiously looks at the clock on his phone, and the driveway sensor goes off.

The timing of Ezra's arrival is very wizardly. Ezra pulls up to the house and walks to the door but doesn't bother knocking. After letting himself in, he greets Cade with a low nod and a handshake. It's very formal. He nods lower to me with a cheeky smile, pretending to tip an imaginary hat. Then he turns and wraps Lena in a hug. He's still holding her while bumping fists with Deacon. Given that his gift is based on touch, and he's very selective about touching people, it seems odd that he'd be willing to give both physical displays of affection. I know why he won't touch me, his deal with Cade, but I still feel left out.

Knowing that he was willing to drive halfway across the country to stay with me and keep me safe is something I can't explain. Mom and Dad throw money at problems to make them go away. Wolves, it seems, show up.

"Thank you for coming." Cade gives him a soft smile.

Ezra shrugs. "It's not every day that my second favorite cousin takes my first favorite cousins to the fanciest full moon party to finally murder my, and everyone else's, least favorite cousin."

"Are you allowed to pick favorite cousins?" I ask before my brain can stop my mouth. "And is Deacon the favorite or is Lena?"

"I'm the favorite," Lena says with a smile.

She's still nestled under Ezra's arm.

Deacon pulls out a single-bite candy bar from his pocket and unwraps it. "It's true. She is."

Ezra shrugs. "It's not that I dislike Deacon, but he's the only one who scares me. No offense, Cade."

"None taken." Cade adjusts his tie.

We stand in silence, stuck in some strange limbo.

Cade looks at me. He gives me a soft smile that doesn't reach his eyes, but his words are so warm. "I love you. I'm coming home tonight. It'll be late. I'd tell you not to wait up, but I know you will anyway."

Ezra stands with his hands in his pockets. "Or if you fall asleep and he calls, I'll wake you up. It's going to be okay."

Cade looks back and forth between us. "Ezra, I'm formally waiving our agreement. If she consents, I'll hold my end of our deal."

"Wait, what?" I ask, trying to remember this agreement with Ezra.

Was it something I was aware of? Did he say?

"He's saying I can, if you're willing, use my gift on you, and he still won't ever use his gift on me." Ezra smiles at me, sliding his hand almost out of his pocket before pushing it back down. "Not something we've to think about right now."

CHAPTER 61
CADE

AT THE GATE, the same guard as last time flags me through without second guessing. I'm directed to park in front of the main garage. Apparently, they saved us a place. I'm not sure it's out of hospitality, but it's convenient. Waitstaff opens the door for us. Lena stays between Deacon and me; she looks calm and collected, but I know better. As we make our way through the front door and out to the back, the people we pass go from talking to silence or hushed whispered tones.

"Cade's back. It's true. He is planning to challenge."

"Does he have a chance of winning?"

"Are we sure he's even going to be a good leader?"

"If Cade takes the throne, who will save us?"

"He can't be worse than Robert."

The whispers follow us onto the back patio.

I find Courtney's blonde locks before I realize she's standing tucked against Robert's side. She looks uncomfortable, as if standing next to him is the last thing she wants to do. His black suit and the royal Ardelean blue sash and tie coordinate with her dress. They're flanked by some council members whose names I don't recall.

"Ah, Cade, I wasn't sure you'd be joining us." Robert looks at his watch.

We're fifteen minutes early, but clearly, that doesn't stop him from trying to create an appearance of undermining me.

His insolence has The Leviathan on edge. We snub him, addressing Courtney first. "Courtney, you look lovely as always."

She smiles softly but says nothing.

"I wish I could say it's good to see you, Robert, but we both know how this ends." Finally, I say what The Leviathan and I are both feeling.

"Come now, brother, is that any way to start the evening? It's a beautiful moon tonight, and we've an excellent dinner prepared."

Robert parts from the council members and hastily strides toward me. I straighten my spine. He tilts his chin up slightly to look me square in the eye.

He enunciates clearly, "You think you know how this ends. You've always been overconfident in your abilities, little brother. Your wolf won't save you. I know you're confident, and you have The Leviathan, but my wolf is a true monster."

The Leviathan scoffs, rolling his eyes. While The Leviathan is highly interested in the fight to come, we're both unamused by Robert's taunts. Anyone wanting to compare dick sizes isn't worth engaging with in a pissing contest. My silence is enough of a response to his childish remarks.

"You've come for your last meal? We didn't assume you'd come to dinner, so we put your invitation for later in the evening." Robert extends his arms, motioning to the council like they had anything to do with the invitation.

It will be his *last.* The Leviathan grumbles. We become more aware of the small crowd of curious pack members gathering around us.

"Kathy and Jimmy, it's good to see you." Robert looks first to Lena and then to Deacon.

Deacon ignores him.

Lena, per usual, cannot keep her sass contained. "What's with the pomp and circumstance? Are you really going to make us sit down, break bread, and pretend to be a nice happy family one last time? Can't you just let Cade kill you so we can go home?"

Her statement sends murmurs running wild through the ever-growing crowd. Hesitantly, I pull my eyes from Robert to glance at them. Pack Alphas from across the states are present. Isabel stands next to her father. Her bright green dress stands out among the suits and other dresses. I'm certain if it weren't for the fact that I'm about to commit Robert to the ground, her dress would be the talk of the evening as she intended it to be. She gives me a coy smile and a wave. *Disgusting.*

"Come now, Kathy." Robert calls her by the wrong name again. He's baiting her, using it on purpose. "Surely it doesn't have to be all business."

The Leviathan pushes hard with a monstrous growl. I let it rumble through me.

Robert pauses, his attention sliding back to me. "Then again, did you bring the results of your blood test and the comparison report from Romania as required?"

"Yes, signed and sealed." I reach into my breast pocket and pull out the envelope. I see Beatrice, the only person I trust on the council, among the crowd. "Mrs. Moore, would you do the honors?"

Despite knowing, despite having a gift, and despite proving it to myself again and again, my heart flutters as she opens the first envelope.

What if I'm not of the Ardelean bloodline?

The Leviathan shakes his head. *Puppy brain. We are the Ardelean bloodline.*

With a trained nail, Beatrice slices open the envelope.

She skims before reading aloud, "Dear Mr. Cade Alexander Alden, you are a direct match for Revecca Ardelean, The Pricolici. You are undeniably of the Ardelean bloodline. Given the nature of the match, you should expect a visit from The Pricolici in the near future."

"Well, now that's an interesting turn of events," Deacon says coolly. He steps up from beside Lena to look squarely at Robert. "You still want to fight this out, or are you going to step down?"

The peanut gallery of the pack and esteemed guests goes silent. Courtney approaches him, and when she presses her hand on his shoulder, asking him for attention, he raises his hand to her.

There is no letting him step down. Time slows down as I watch her cower. Too many memories of our father rush back.

We move as one. The Leviathan nearly takes my skin before we've reached him. Robert has very little time to react. Blood is pouring out of him before he's even into wolf form. Our teeth sink straight into his shoulder, the bone hard against our teeth.

Pulling with everything he has, Robert tries to kick at our soft stomach, barely tearing his shoulder free.

We're back on him in the blink of an eye. His fangs find our shoulder, but it's no match for the grip of our teeth sinking into his neck. The fluff of his silver-gray fur fills our mouth, followed by the taste of blood.

With a flail, Robert pulls hard enough to unlatch us from his neck. We keep hold of part of him as a partial prize. We drop the flesh from our mouth.

Robert attempts to intimidate The Leviathan, circling before he charges.

Lowering our body to the ground, we take Robert's charge into our shoulder at an angle. We push him over our head before turning and slamming our front feet into his chest. This time when our jaws lock on Robert's throat, he has nowhere to go. He makes a pathetic last-ditch effort, using his back claws to try to rip open my ribs.

The Leviathan laughs wickedly in our head. *Sad too easy.*

Despite his feet pushing against my chest, Robert's time on this earth is over.

We pull hard on Robert's throat. With a thrash, his neck is shattered and between our teeth. His body lies limp, blood pouring out onto the pristine lawn.

We walk away from Robert's lifeless body. I stand as wolf, making eye contact with other various members of the pack. No one looks back in challenge. Eyes divert from me with every glance.

I harness back The Leviathan's anger inside, forcing us back into human form.

"Are there any challengers?" I say no louder than I have to.

The wolves surrounding the lawn can hear me.

It's a long and eerily silent sixty seconds. The wind chills my body, but I force myself to stand tall. There's a small chance someone is dumb enough to challenge me.

"I, Cade Alexander Alden, take my place as Sovereign Alpha of the Ardelean Pack. I present before you tonight with my Alpha Female, Kathleen Meredith Alden, and my pack Second, James Deacon Alden."

With the formalities over, I leave my shredded suit where it fell and begin walking, naked, back to the house. Lena's heels click on the pavement behind me, and with how people move farther away from my right side than left, I know Deacon is there, scaring them off.

They all stand. Anyone sitting rises to their feet as we pass. It's the highest respect. Choruses of acknowledgments, both joyous and remorseful, are spoken as I pass by. I make it to the entryway of the house that adjoins the formal sitting room. A housekeeper greets me with slippers and a robe, offering them to me. I put them on.

With a large smile, she quietly and directly says, "All hail the Sovereign."

When I nod in acknowledgment, she motions for me to follow her. She leads our trio down the hallway to a guest room.

Once we enter and she closes the door behind us, she starts, "I'm Lauren. I had hopes that, well, I had to guess your size. But there are clean towels and clothes. I'll have a few plates sent over and have the main courses served to the guests who choose to stay. I'll keep them and the council contained. I've loyal staff, and they'll work on pulling documents and the things Robert stashed. We were all rooting for you."

I nod along as she talks. I'm trying to digest what she's saying, but my brain hasn't fully adjusted from the desire for bloodshed. I hope Lena's focusing so she can keep it in order.

Lauren gives a little bow and goes to leave.

I clear my throat. "Lauren?"

She turns back, eyes wide.

I offer her the best I can do at a smile. "Thank you."

It shocks her. Knowing she should say something she squeaks out a "you're welcome" and flees down the hall.

Deacon flops down on the bed. "Alright. You get cleaned up so we can get out of here, Imma grab a nap, and Lena should call Thalia."

Lena opens her clutch and hands me my phone. Bringing it

with me into the adjoining bathroom, I open the messaging app. There're a few messages from Ezra and one from Thalia, but I don't open them. If I read them now, I don't know if I'll be able to stay and finish this. I put my phone down and close my eyes, trying to find more strength.

Life has come full circle to me standing in the shower letting the water rinse familial blood from my body. Robert managed a few good kicks and bites. They're virtually nothing compared to helping Ansel with the fractured. When I step out of the shower, there's only one scrape on my ribs that still hasn't stopped bleeding.

With a towel around my waist, I open the door to Lena and Deacon sharing food from different plates. Deacon sees me and comes over to take a look.

"Uff dah." Deacon shakes his head. "I don't know that butterflies are going to hold this together."

It's twenty minutes of them applying some pressure and wrapping my ribs and the wound before I'm able to get dressed.

Deacon had grabbed the bag of emergency clothes out of the car. While I appreciate Lauren's gesture of dress clothes, my reign starts now. I'm not going to spend my life in suits and ties. I'll put them on for the media and circus but not among family and pack. Life is going to be approachable, no more pomp and circumstance.

I manage to get a pullover sweater on. While it's a bit warm for my liking, it was the only top we brought that doesn't show much of the bulk of the bandages holding the tender skin of my ribs together.

Walking down the hall, I adjust my posture and stride to

hold more control. Is it probable that someone will challenge me tonight? No. But the chances are never zero. Appearing perfectly fine is the first step to preventing more bloodshed.

We follow the sounds of people talking to the formal ballroom. It's a massive space and is generally set for tables for this occasion. When we get to the doors, I remain just out of view and turn back to look at Deacon and Lena.

I open my mouth. "I —"

"Don't say it." Deacon stops me. "You're not getting rid of us. We're not making you go through this alone. It was always supposed to be us together. She and I've talked about it a few times, but it's always been the three of us."

Lena nods in confirmation before picking a stray hair from my sweater. "We'll figure it out."

Their approval is all I need to make the last few steps into the room. It takes a few minutes before the sound in the room dies out; council members begin standing up at their tables. Alphas, Males and Females, from other packs stand next. I walk to the center of the room before approaching the table that would have been set for Robert and Courtney. Rather than taking a seat, I turn to address the room.

"I am aware that this transition will be difficult. I appreciate your patience with me while I sort through Robert's estate. To Robert's advisers, the pack council, and other Alphas who are here this evening: please email your availability for meetings. I want to meet with everyone to determine the momentum of the packs. Lena and Deacon have stepped into the roles of my Alpha Female and Second. Anyone who wishes to challenge them will be challenging me directly. I will fight every single one of their fights for them." I wait to let those instructions and the information sink in. "As far as other advisers and appointed council members, nothing is decided or set in stone. The team I assemble to help me will be those who are best fit for the job. Tradition and nepotism do not apply."

A few seconds of hushed whispers pass before a shout comes from the back. "And what about the humans?"

"With your . . ." I pause and change tactics. I let my eyes roam across the hall. *Ask for help, show openness to assistance from others*, I remind myself. "If Robert has a team or an individual coordinating his correspondence with the media, please reach out to me immediately. If you know who that person or team lead is and they're not in attendance, I'd appreciate their information provided most urgently."

There's silence. I don't have any further instructions, but what feels right comes to mind. *Show compassion and admit to being willing to learn.* "It's going to take me time to get up to speed. I failed you all before. I'm determined to do and be better. Your patience is appreciated. There will be changes, and I am aware many of you won't like them. I'll know more in the coming weeks."

More whispering happens, and I give them a minute. After a few minutes, I have everyone's attention again.

"Thank you all for being here. Please, enjoy your dinner, and for those who have been instructed to reach out to me, do so."

My phone buzzes in my pocket before I even leave the ballroom.

Unknown Number: Hello, this is Henri Greene. I'm your publicist, as when you took back the throne, the primary publicist walked out. I know everything about what was going on with the media and am available anytime to bring you up to speed. I would like to schedule a meeting for you and the press within the week.

CHAPTER 62

THALIA

IT'S BEEN HOURS. Cade hasn't called. Lena and Deacon haven't either. I've tried pacing around the house and needlepoint. I've tried watching a movie and taking a bath. I open and close the refrigerator for the fifteenth time.

"Thalia, Luna. I love you. But you've got to stop." Ezra sighs. "Your mate is fine, and you're driving me nuts."

"How do you know that?" I accuse.

My tone is sharp even though he's trying to help. It's just not as helpful as he wants it to be.

"I've seen Ansel's vision, Dinah has predicted this from an early age, The Leviathan is fucking terrifying" — Ezra pauses and shakes his head — "and because you're only worried not devastated." Ezra lists them off with his fingers. He only has four, so he comes up with one more. "Because I know Cade doesn't walk half-cocked into anything. If he wasn't sure how tonight would go down, he wouldn't have gone with Lena and Deacon. He would have taken me."

"I thought he had to take an Alpha Female and Second." I draw my eyebrows in, questioning him.

Ezra sighs. "Neither Robert nor the council truly have any authority over Cade. They can make requests, but Cade's wolf and his gift, mean no one tells Cade what to do. Plus, according to Dinah, when they open his blood test results, it's going to be life altering."

"What does that mean?" I snap.

He's trying to help, but I'm scared, and the only thing I want right now is Cade.

With a shrug, Ezra walks closer to me. I can see he wants to comfort me but is trying to respect my privacy.

He smiles softly. "Dinah is cryptic on a good day. She doesn't like to speak in absolutes when she talks about what she's seen in the future. Your guess is as good as mine."

"I thought you could read minds." I pull my eyes together, trying to convey that's a question.

Ezra shrugs again, which seems to be his default answer. "It's not that simple. Growing up with a mind reader, my sister and parents learned to block me out."

"You have a brother too, though, right? Judah?" Focusing on him is easier than dealing with thinking about Cade.

"He's my twin and we've got the whole weird freaky finish each other's sentences without me even being in his head. There's no point." Ezra laughs. He walks into the kitchen. "Let's start cooking up a feast for Cade. He'll need to eat after his fight."

CHAPTER 63

CADE

We've tossed Robert's office, the Alpha's suite, and made a sweep of anywhere we've scented him in the house. I've pulled documents out of closets, Courtney's old purses, under beds, bathroom cabinets, and the wine cellar. We've found seven external hard drives and three laptops. It took a few times, but I cracked the wall safe and emptied it. There were a few hundred thousand dollars in cash mixed with various documents. With Lena and Deacon working with me we're an efficient team. Lauren has somehow managed to keep the guests contained mostly to the public areas. I'm not certain we've found all the items that Robert has hidden. It's a start.

There's only one thing left to do. I find Courtney in the vacant patio, sitting at the base of the stairs. She's feet from where I ended Robert's life. Robert's body has been moved to the family tomb to wait for internment. Blood-soaked earth leaves a red hue, reflecting in the moonlight. If Courtney hears me approach, she says nothing.

I sit next to her quietly. Trying hard to put myself in her shoes, I feel so much sorrow.

With a low voice, I speak, "I'm sorry that it had to end this way."

She shakes her head. "I'm not."

It's alarming to hear, but I don't want to pry. It's a delicate situation.

"We've gone through the house. I believe I've found all the paperwork that I need to try and make the transition. Obviously, there's no way to say for sure, but now that I've severed your mating bond, how you or your wolf will handle the change —"

"Fate didn't give me to Robert. He claimed me, and it's been a long time," Courtney interrupts. "I'm embarrassed to face the pack. I'm not sad he's gone. I'll be fine."

It seems I can add Robert's mate to the list of people I've wronged.

I draw a breath. "I'll have to move into the main house. The Alpha suite is yours, and I will never —"

"I don't want to stay," Courtney interrupts again. She pauses before her voice turns pleading. "Don't make me stay."

"Wherever you want to go, I'll sign off on the paperwork," I answer. I drop my voice. "I want you safe and happy."

"You have my cell?" Courtney asks. She turns practical quickly. "I'll coordinate moving out."

I nod. She clearly isn't grieving. I guess grief isn't universal. What I think she's feeling isn't relevant. I can only respect her wishes.

"Thank you," Courtney whispers. She still hasn't turned her head or moved to look at me. "For killing him. For freeing me."

"You're welcome. I'm sorry it took me so long," I answer.

She says nothing more, and it seems I've been dismissed.

Slowly, in case she has more to say, I stand to leave.

THE VEHICLE STOPS MOVING, and I hear the garage door.

We left the Regent pack property three hours after we had arrived and managed to bring home six large boxes of rummaged findings.

I tried to climb into the driver's seat, but Lena insisted on driving. The pain in my ribs and the shoulder above them throbbed, and exhaustion and hunger were settling in, so I didn't give her any argument. Healing is hard fucking work.

I fell asleep as soon as we crossed the front gates. I don't remember anything else on the ride home.

Now I'm halfway sitting up, and the back door opens. Thalia is there. Tears are streaming down her face. She's wiping them away on the oversized sleeves of my sweatshirt between sobs. My pain is irrelevant to whatever caused this intense reaction from her. I move quickly from the SUV to her.

Our mate cries. Why cry? Who has damaged? The Leviathan grows suspicious of Ezra. Ready to do battle again.

I deflate, abandoning the tension The Leviathan reignited.

Oh. I fucked up.

I wrap her in my arms, enveloping her, and apologize. "Shh, draga mea. I'm okay. There was never any danger. I should have called you."

"You could have died. I could have lost you. I don't ever want to go through this again. Please," she forces out between sobs and hiccups into my chest.

Unfortunately, those aren't things I can promise her. There's so much uncertainty in the days to come. I pull her close to my chest, holding her tightly.

I should have called her. *I failed her.* It never crossed my mind that she would see a possibility in which I wasn't coming home. After all the reassurance, she wasn't sure because how could she be? She had no idea.

Swaying back and forth, I rock her until the tears stop.

EZRA HAS food nearly done cooking by the time Thalia and I re-emerge from my bedroom. It took a lot of coaxing for her to understand I truly was okay. Being stiff and sore is normal. The blood didn't help the case. She looked like she was ready to pass out when I removed the bandages.

"So, what's on the docket tomorrow?" Ezra asks, taking a pan from the oven while I plop down on the stool in the kitchen.

Scrubbing my hand down my face, I scratch my beard. "I'm assuming some of the council will show up here, wanting to start talking over things. I'll have to text my team with Peter Corinth. I'll see about using them to rummage through all the shit we've collected and try to figure out what Robert was doing. Hopefully, Adam and his tech friends can figure it out quickly. The pack publicist reached out already. She wants me to do some media stuff in the coming week. I just hope that someone, somewhere, will be on my side."

"You're not alone." Lena hands me her phone.

The social media site she's showing me is blown up with activity; my name is in bold letters. Various levels of excitement flag the posts and comments.

Thalia reads over my shoulder. "Wow, word travels fast."

I can't help but agree. "Fuck. Well, that's . . ."

I hand Lena's phone back to her.

She muses with a laugh, "At least it doesn't seem like anyone had a chance to take a photo of you post fight. No dick wagging in the wind."

Thalia's eyelids are heavy, and she doesn't say anything about the comment of me being naked in front of others. She's crashing from the adrenaline.

"Want me to put you to bed?" I lean against her, trying to comfort her.

"Only if you're coming too." She yawns.

Ezra sets down a basket of blueberry muffins, a plate with a variety of fried chicken, and another plate with pan-seared steak.

He smiles at her. "No can do. He's going to need all the energy he can get."

"Don't remind me." I pull Thalia into my lap.

While I'm occupied adjusting Thalia, Lena reaches over and pulls a muffin out of the basket. The Leviathan growls but gives her all the privilege that's due to her status.

"Elephant in the room," Deacon says, looking at us.

I shake my head. "What?"

"How" — Deacon's face scrunches with confusion — "do you plan to keep her hidden if we've got wolves coming to the house nonstop?"

"Ezra?" I look to the king of keeping secrets.

"Flood the house with your scent, all three of you, and in all areas of the house. In the event anyone asks, you've got a human housekeeper. Then, keep her in your clothes, in your room, and have one of you with her whenever possible. Put a speaker near your suite's door playing talk radio or television or some shit, and just keep it playing all day. There's no reason anyone should question you beyond that." Ezra smiles.

"Do I want to know how many times you did that trick to your parents?" Lena asks, setting down the muffin.

"Oh no, that's a Judah trick."

Even my jaw drops hearing that. *The golden boy isn't always so golden.*

CHAPTER 64
THALIA

CADE'S SPOT in the bed is empty and cold. When I roll over, I notice a few small spots of blood. With a grimace, I begin stripping the sheets.

I've tossed them in the washing machine and started a load when Cade finds me in the laundry room. I smile at him, but he has a dark look in his eye.

He spins me around and pushes the front of my body against the machine as it starts the first cycle, vibrating against my chest as he holds me there. His body covers mine as he bends me over the top.

He kisses the back of my neck before pausing briefly. "Good morning."

My response comes out as a mix between a moan, a giggle, and a greeting all at once. "Good morning."

"We don't have long," he whispers. "Let's go back to bed. I want breakfast." With a moan, he adds, "Please say yes."

"Please, hmmm?" I ask, pretending to hem and haw over the answer.

He holds my hips with a bruising grip, and I grind back

against his hardness pressing into my low back. I clutch the washing machine in front of me, encouraging him. I bite back a moan as he brings one hand around, finding my clit through my pajama bottoms.

"Mmhmm." He confirms. "Please."

Cade alternates between kissing and nipping at my neck as I continue teasing his cock with my hips. He moves the hand that found my clit to my waistband, sliding it between the fabric and my skin, down the front of my pajama bottoms.

My heart beats hard in my chest.

I gasp as he finds his way into my panties and gives me gentle pets. "Yes. Oh. Mmmm, yes. Yes!"

The security panel chirps from the pantry.

"Fuck." Cade growls. He freezes, murmuring, "Please be Ezra and Deacon."

Cade's hand retreats as a second and third chirp ring out. I push back, and he frees me from the washer. He whines — a sound I didn't expect to hear — and when I turn, he's almost pouting.

I kiss him softly and then give him a soft smile. "So, company today?"

"And I've got to keep you out of the limelight," Cade grumbles as he rests his forehead against the top of my head. "I'll message Deacon to bring you food from town. I'll keep meetings as short as possible. But just over three weeks and your mom's bill goes to vote, and then it'll be safe for you to be seen. Then we'll have to talk about what we look like publicly. Though, all I want to discuss is how many nights a week I get to spend *not* sleeping in your bed."

Cade pulls down some sheets out of a cabinet for me. Then pulls his T-shirt off and gives it to me. I don't have a lot of time to object because he walks into his closet and upon returning, he's pulling on a polo. A knock comes on the door.

I nod in understanding. I know he cares about my safety above all else. I know this is temporary. It just feels so strange not being his first priority.

DEACON SNEAKS in through the back door to Cade's bedroom. He turns the television up a bit louder than I had it when he walks in. Sitting down on the bed with two bags full of food, Deacon gives me an ear-to-ear grin before I have time to adjust to someone in my space.

The change in atmosphere makes me grumpy.

Sitting next to me, Deacon pulls his head back in a sharp movement, drawing his eyebrows together, lips wrinkled into an unusual shape.

He speaks quietly, "You okay?"

"Yeah. Sorry. Cade told me you were coming, but I didn't know when." I try to explain what I'm feeling. "It's like when you've been alone for a while, and then someone comes into your space, but you're just not ready for it, and then they're everywhere, all over you. Not that you're doing anything wrong. I like hanging out with you. It's just . . ."

My voice falls off and Deacon does the opposite of what I expected.

He pulls me close to him, wrapping his arms around me. "It's just that you miss your mate and don't feel like you matter. I'm not the Alden you want to be spending time with, and it's frustrating to feel like you're just in waiting."

I snuggle in. The truth is, he does feel really good and comforting. Despite the strange smell of cigarettes and who knows what else, Deacon is comforting. He lets me go after a few moments, and I feel better.

"How did you do that?" I ask.

Deacon shrugs. "We have a lot more in common than it seems."

I bite my bottom lip, trying to process everything he just said.

He starts opening boxes. There's so much food that I have no idea where to even start. Handing me a fork, Deacon picks up some pancakes with strawberries and holds them out between us.

Twenty minutes into a home renovation show, Deacon's picked through various boxes of food, rotating sweet and salty. My belly is full, and I'm content, which he intuitively just seems to know.

Leaning against him, I ask quietly, "You have anxiety, don't you?"

Deacon draws a deep breath. "It's not simple like it is for humans."

I nod, willing to let it fall away. We sit in silence, watching TV for a while longer.

I use the bathroom and come back to the sound of the front door slamming. Deacon jumps and scrambles off the bed, getting between me and the door.

"Fuck!" Cade shouts, causing Deacon to relax.

"Well, that meeting went well," I say, highlighting my obvious lack of knowledge about what happened.

The door to the bedroom opens, but Cade doesn't come in. Deacon nods for me to follow him out. When we ask Cade if he wants to talk about it, he shakes his head, locking down his emotions.

I've no more than given Cade a hug when his cell phone starts to ring. It's frustrating, but I understand. I do. Logically, Cade's just taken over a country. He's a king, and if I'm going to be in his life beyond the next three weeks, I need to adjust to the fact that his world can't revolve around me all the time.

The last month has been a luxury of Cade's full attention. Is the new normal something I can handle?

I sit on the couch, pick up my knitting, and weave stitches of a red cowl scarf. There's a lot to think about.

Cade's voice is soft. "Thalia, draga mea."

Groggy, I sit up to see him leaning against the door frame.

"I'm done for the day. Sent out a pack newsletter, and thanks to Lena, everyone knows I'm not taking any more calls or texts tonight."

Cade walks lazily across the living room to sit on the couch next to me.

I yawn and wipe the sleep out of my eyes. His hands caress my face, the setting sun giving the room an orange glow.

"You've got nap marks, let's get out for a walk for a bit."

"Oh, I see how it goes. I need to take The Leviathan for a walk? My turn to walk the wolf. You did it yesterday." I joke, standing up and moving straight into his arms.

Cade's chest vibrates with his laugh. "Dog walker joke?"

"I'll do better next time. Snacks and walk?" I use my cutest voice, reserved for an adorable puppy.

Cade shakes his head and kisses me. It's sweet and tender.

CHAPTER 65
THALIA

TODAY IS MORE of the same. Cade and I manage breakfast and the morning together on the back deck. While I'm casting off yesterday's scarf, Cade is skimming through various documents. While it's not talking, at least we're in the same space in our comfortable silence.

Lena called out the door that the driveway alarm was going off, and I find myself in his bedroom. Deacon is nowhere to be found. So today, Lena and I watch trashy celebrity reality television. This is the longest we've been in the same room together, unsupervised.

I want to ask her questions. I've learned a lot of information about wolves from Cade, but there are some things no man will be able to explain. Well, not that he wouldn't try, but men generally don't have a full understanding of women's issues.

I swallow, building courage. It's been a long day of constantly psyching myself up to ask.

"Why don't you just ask the question before worrying that I won't answer?" Lena side-eyes me with a smile.

It's almost friendly.

"That obvious?" I scrunch my nose up.

Lena nods, turning the volume on the television a little louder. She shuffles in the bed to face me.

"Okay, what is heat?" I quietly and quickly blurt out the words I'd been trying to reorganize to make them sound more polished. They're not. "I assume it's like with animals? Oh, that sounds bad. I'm sorry."

"Shh. It's fine." Lena shakes her head. "Where you see comparing us to wolves as a bad thing or disrespectful, to us, it's what we are. Duality is the nature of our lives. And, yes. It's very much like what happens with natural wolves. Obviously, I can't say for sure what it's like for animals, but it's very uncomfortable. Your body is demanding to be bred. You're bombarded with hot flashes and incoherent thoughts. There are days of not wanting to get out of bed, and the only thing you can think of is what your wolf is dying for . . . to be fucked, repeatedly."

Her matter-of-fact sardonic tone gives me all I need to know — heat is awful.

"But you didn't ask that out of pure curiosity about our physical health." Lena is uncharacteristically softer with her next statement. "Cade told you he wouldn't give you a wolf, which would be the only way you'd ever have a chance of pups, kids," she corrects herself, "with him."

"How did you know?" I ask softly, squirming in my seat.

The reminder of the divide between my world and Cade's is brought back to my mind, front and center. Despite his proclamation and conviction that we're mates, I can't help but feel that he's hesitant about us because he doesn't want to make me wolf.

"Gifted," Lena admits.

Her hand rests on my knee.

"Oh." I wonder how much she's seen about me.

"If Cade won't give you a wolf when things calm down for him" — Lena makes eye contact with me, reassuring me — "I will find a way to get you a wolf."

"You wouldn't do it yourself?" My mouth speaks before my brain can tell it not to.

Lena bites her lips together. She runs her hands through her hair like Cade does, the auburn brown locks fluffing out over her shoulders.

"I can't, but I would if I could."

"Sorry. I'll eventually learn not to ask personal questions. I just feel so left out of everything. It's like I'm just the token human." I voice my frustration.

Lena picks up my hand, holding it for a moment. I look, and her eyes are glossed over. Can she look at people's pasts on command? I don't dare pull my hand away; what if it's like waking someone during a nightmare? Well, that's probably an old wives' tale, but you never know. Shifters weren't supposed to be real, so who knows what else is possible.

When she closes her eyes and wrinkles her nose a moment later, she says, "First, no one sees you as the token human or the tagalong. Second, I can promise The Leviathan will give you a wolf. Cade's um . . ."

Her hesitation alarms me. *Breathe, she hasn't said anything bad, yet.*

I ask quickly, "Cade's what?"

"Okay, listen, we're not girlfriends. We aren't even really friends. You're my Luna and my brother's mate. It's not friendship we're growing, it's acceptance of each other's place in his life." Lena clarifies. It feels a bit rude, but she's trying.

Nodding along, I hope she finishes the sentence she left hanging.

"Cade's barely missing biting you. Him not wanting to give

you a wolf isn't disinterest or rejection. There's something more to it that we don't know. Whether it's work related, or he doesn't think you're ready, or he's afraid of something, I don't know. Your guess is as good as mine, but the fact that he's fighting the urge to claim you in bed, tells me he wants you on a level that I can't explain."

"Oh."

Mortified, what's stronger than mortified? Whatever it is, that's what I feel right now. Lena can see anything in people's past, and she just saw us . . . intimately.

"Calm down. I live with Deacon. That man has had more sexual conquests than he has days working some sort of legal job. I've seen way more intense things. I'm just glad the living archive of your life listened to me for this request." Lena shrugs. "Any other female wolf questions?"

I shake my head. *None that I can ask right now.*

CHAPTER 66
CADE

USHERING THE PUBLICIST, Henri Greene, and the council member out the door, I'm so ready to be done for the day. I'm grateful for Henri's organization — stacks of papers with summaries typed on them and her newest implementation in my life: lists of shit for me to do — but it all boils down to burying me under a shit ton of stuff.

I'm resting with my head against the front door, taking my first deep breath of the day, and I hear the door to my bedroom open. With it, I can hear my shower running. I get the idea to join Thalia, but as soon as the thought enters my mind, my hopes are crushed.

Lena and her shit-starting voice drown out the sound of my shower. "So, what's the deal with everything going on?"

Her open-ended question invites me to jump to the conclusion of what she's asking about.

"Care to be a little more specific?" I ask, turning around.

I run my hand across the back of my neck, trying to stretch out from being crouched down over screens and documents all

539

day. I'm not dumb enough to fall for her tricks. At least, I hope not.

Lena waves her hand about the house. "This, us helping you. You've named me your Alpha Female and Deacon as your Second, but it seems the positions have been reduced to babysitting the human."

"You're finishing school. That's always been the deal. I want you to embrace something that's just for you. You deserve this. I'm giving you a chance to be as normal as possible." I try offering her my logic as I step back toward the kitchen. "Finals are coming up and it's the end of the year. You don't need this mess."

"And me?" Deacon leans against the door frame on the other side of the house, by their rooms.

When I look at him, he has his arms crossed over his chest and his feet crossed at the ankles, completely dependent on the wall for support.

"You're supposed to be getting sober." I remind him, pointing at him. *Et tu Brute? What the hell is going on?* "That was our deal. If you truly wanted to help, you had to be sober. Or you would accept the position of Second until I could find someone I trust to take over your place."

Deacon pushes off the wall and shrugs. He crosses the living room space.

"I'll work on it," he says nonchalantly.

"That it, this settles it?" I offer my arms out, waiting for more shots to come.

They say nothing, and I begin moving back into the kitchen, away from the front door, as my stomach growls. I hope Lena's curiosity is satisfied.

I've been Sovereign for two days, and I'm already under a microscope. Henri, both the biggest pain in the ass and closest ally I have when it comes to the council, is placing insurmountable pressure on me to fly out and meet with Thalia's mother in a few days. I'm running out of excuses as to why it's not as urgent as coordinating with other shifters. I expected the scrutiny and pressure from the pack but not the two people closest to me. They're part of the reason I did this, to begin with.

Lest you hope in one hand, shit in the other, and see which one fills up first.

Lena's not done with me, much like the publicist coming back with more questions. Lena walks over to me.

"So, tell me why you're not gifting your mate a wolf and claiming her?" she asks while opening the refrigerator.

She tilts her head back, indicating that she's expectantly awaiting my answer.

"You think now, arguably the most volatile time for shifters to be alive, is a good time to be gifting another being a wolf?" In a matter-of-fact way, I try to diffuse. "It doesn't seem like a good time to put my mate's life in danger."

"Now's as good a time as any. It's currently not illegal to make other wolves," Lena presses, uncharacteristically interested in my relationship with Thalia. "Unlike in the coming weeks when your mate's mother ruins all of our lives."

Ah, there it is.

Not speak to Alpha this way. The Leviathan pushes forward a growl, but I hold him back.

"How does she feel about that?" Deacon presses, drawing closer.

Am I really outnumbered right now?

"We've only had a couple of discussions on the matter. It's not the time." I grit my teeth and try to make it clear with my tone that I'm done discussing it.

Lena shakes her head, her eyes hard like she's trying to

pierce my skin. She sets the plate of steaks down on the counter.

"You're just going to let your pet human's mother destroy us all, taking all of us down with you because you don't want to do the job."

"How the fuck did you even jump to that conclusion?" I raise my voice.

The Leviathan and I vibrate with rage at the accusation.

"I heard you," Deacon says coolly. "You keep pushing off meeting with Senator Clark. You keep saying you want to meet with other shifters first. If it's not because you're giving up on the legislation, what is it?"

I turn to face them both. "Seriously. You don't trust me?"

"We trusted you not to sleep with the enemy, but the only thing you've managed not to do is turn her. Which, arguably, would be the smartest move." Lena gasps, jumping to conclusions, the right conclusion. "That was the threat, wasn't it? Someone, somewhere, is threatening to bite Thalia and push Senator Clark's hand . . . that's why you have Thalia, isn't it? You're the only idiot big enough to try and keep her safe."

Slamming my fists down on the countertop, I hear something crack. "Back the fuck down, Lena. Or so fucking help me."

"So, what? Clearly you and little red are in a bit different position than before. You playing double agent now or . . .?" Deacon's voice peaks.

"No!" I'm seething, cutting them both off. The idea of commanding them into silence, in order to not have to discuss this, crosses my mind, but I need this settled. "You want to know why I don't give a flying fuck about what Senator Clark is doing? Senator Clark and I have a deal. I bring Thalia back human, and she will cut out whole sections and pages from that bill. Full sections on sterilization and limitations on family sizes are going to be completely removed. The death penalties for misdemeanor offenses, reduction on the statutory for what is or is not considered endangerment, and the revocation of due process are all updated. So, forgive me while I focus on something other than what Senator Clark is doing in Congress because I've got that fucking covered. Staying out of that media circus gives it time to cool off."

"How do you know she'll keep that end of the deal?" Lena spits, and I see the gears in her brain working.

"I told her that if the bill goes to law before I bring Thalia back and passes without the changes we negotiated, then Thalia doesn't come back home human." I snarl.

The fuck did I do to deserve this scrutiny from them? Not bite my mate? Is this really over the fact that I'm making responsible choices for what feels like the first time in my life?

"You're so sure that she'll come through?" Deacon asks with a growl of his own.

Lena covers her mouth, eyes going wide.

I turn to look at what she's seeing. My heart drops through my stomach.

"Fuck you!" Thalia screams.

Her eyes are wild, and wet hair falls out of her messy bun. She's standing at end of the hallway leading to our bedroom.

I stand between my siblings and her, unsure who she's yelling at. After a day with Lena, there's a tiny hope that it's not me.

"Fuck you, Cade!" she screeches with a dedicated point at me.

Well, that clears that up.

"You fucking used me?"

She swears again, and it's unsettling. I've never heard her swear, and now it's three times in ten seconds.

Our mate not take this tone with us. Disrespect. She's not wolf not know rules. The Leviathan shakes his head. He examines her closely, coming to the same conclusion I am: this is a fucking disaster.

I take my eyes off her to motion to Lena and Deacon to leave. There's no need for them to be involved with this. Thalia is glaring at me when I turn my full attention back to her.

I walk across the kitchen and step into her personal space. I hope the proximity brings her rage down some.

Her hand goes up, pushing against my chest, blocking me from her, and pushing me back out of her space.

"No!" she commands.

Anger paints every feature, from her flushed skin to the scowl on her lips. Her entire body is rigid. I stop pushing in and let her take the lead.

Our mate no talk to us this way. The Leviathan isn't helping.

"Draga mea, please talk to me," I ask, keeping my voice down, trying to invite a more calm state.

It's a hostage negotiation tactic, but I'm willing to try anything to get her to hear me.

She shakes her head. Lip curled up, sneering as she spits, "Don't you 'my darling' me. You're a fucking asshole, Cade. You. Used. ME."

"I didn't use you." I hold still while she pushes a single finger against my sternum. I'm forcing words out past the lump in my throat. "I've never used you, and I never will."

"First, you used me to cut a deal with my mom, then you used me for sex, and now you're using me to be this perfect mate that everyone will love." She punctuates each point with her finger, moving it up against my chest, landing right above my heart. "I'm just a political move for you. Someone you can manipulate to do your bidding."

Is that what she really believes?

I shake my head, wrapping my hand around her wrist. "Thalia, none of that is true."

"Are you going to deny it, Cade? How am I supposed to know you're telling the truth? How do I know you're not just using your gift to make me believe you!"

She tries to pull her hand from mine, but I'm still a wolf and she's still a human.

Holding her hand against my chest, I shake my head and try to lay it all on the table. "The deal I cut with your mother had nothing to do with you. I hadn't even truly met you. I was an opportunist. I had something your mother wanted, and she has something I need. No leader in the world wouldn't have tried to cut a deal. The deal was made before I ever could have known you were my mate. This was never a hostage situation. I'm not keeping you from your family in exchange for them doing what I want."

"You just said the only way you're giving me a wolf is if my mother doesn't come through," she snaps back.

"That's not what I meant," I defend. "Gifting you a wolf is complicated, and I can't reduce it down to a single choice and one conversation."

"And your gift?" Thalia spits. "Have you ever used it on me?"

I can't tell her what she wants to hear. I won't lie to her. I hang my head, hoping this doesn't explode.

"I've used my gift on you. But only to pull you out of your panic attacks."

"I want to go home." Thalia cuts me off.

She pulls on her wrist, bringing her other hand to push against mine. I let her go this time.

I snap my gaze up to meet hers.

"You can't go home, Thalia." I plead my case to her logical side. "Regardless of what's going on between us, it's still not safe for you in DC. I can't guarantee your safety away from my side. Taking our feelings out of this, your safety comes first and foremost."

Tears well in her eyes, and it guts me.

"You used me for your own gains. Why did I ever believe that you understood why I have tried to stay out of politics? You were just doing the same thing my mother has always done. But what's worse, you didn't even bother telling me. I'm nothing but an object to any of you."

"Thalia, I love you." I wrap my hand around the back of her head, drawing her eyes to meet mine. "I love you. My deal with your mother happened in a split-second decision. What I feel for you now came after. Everything about us together has grown since I've gotten to know you. Our relationship has nothing to do with her or the bill."

Thalia squeezes her eyes shut and lowers her head. "I don't believe you."

She pulls farther away from me, and I let her go, balling my fists at my sides.

"All those lines you've fed me. I almost believed them." She shakes her head, wrapping her arms around her middle.

Walking away from me, she turns back to look at me, and her tears fall from the corners of her eyes. "The fuck did you have to fuck me for? You literally had women camping out on your front lawn. Was it necessary to use me like some whore?"

My mouth opens, but nothing comes out. The Leviathan is speechless. We're both stunned by that accusation. Her words tear like sharp claws in battle. I would take wounds from fighting a fractured wolf or an Alpha challenge over this any day.

Keeping my eyes on her, I pull out a stool from the counter and sit down facing her.

How the fuck did we get here? How did I love you turn into a means to an end?

Running my hand back through my hair, I look at her. "Thalia, I don't understand how we went from talking about a deal I cut with your mother to you and me together. What am I missing?"

"If you can't see it, then I can't tell you. You need to take me home, Cade," she demands again.

Our mate goes nowhere. She learn what means to be ours. The Leviathan seems so sure of her place with us. Despite not understanding how she drew this conclusion, he thinks the best course of action is to confine her here. I try to trust his instinct with more tact.

"I can't just take you home, Thalia. It's not that simple," I inform her. "You've got to talk to me. I can't fix this if you don't talk to me."

"I want to go home," she repeats. "We're done talking."

"You're not going anywhere until we talk this out." I try a firmer approach. "Where did you get this idea that I'm using you for sex?"

"Don't deny it, Cade. I'm just the key to my mother's campaign. You keep me happy and send me back with a glowing review of shifters to my parents, and it's another feather in your cap against the onslaught of what this bill could mean." She crosses her arms in front of her chest. "You seduced me into thinking I mattered beyond the bill to keep me on your side."

"Are you serious?" I run my hand behind my neck, pulling on my shoulder.

"Don't patronize me. Make arrangements. I'm not staying here. Your services are no longer required," she demands before marching off to our bedroom.

Heavy footfalls echo anger through the house. I let her walk away to give her time to cool off.

One thing is for certain, I'm not letting her leave without a direct order from Peter. I fucking love her, and I'm not going to lose her. Not without a fight.

I hear her rutting around in my room and assume she's packing. Between the sounds of banging drawers, there are hundreds of different sentences cursing my name.

The Leviathan whines. *Make her see.*

CHAPTER 67
THALIA

HE LIED TO ME.

He used me.

I've never felt so betrayed in my life. It's a sinking feeling that falls through me over and over again. It pulls me lower and lower with each passing thought.

I can't stop crying. After packing the little bit of clothing and knitting supplies I've accumulated, I'm curled up in a ball on the floor between the dresser and the wall, facing the corner. I tried to be on the bed, but all I could think of was the amazing sex. The sex that now seems dirty.

He lied to me.

He used me.

Chills run through my body, and I shiver uncontrollably.

Did he ever love me? Did he ever truly want to get to know me? He's such a con artist, driving me places, taking me on dates, sharing interests. It's textbook manipulation. One foot in the door, gaining my trust little by little.

After hearing about the true nature of our relationship, everything makes sense. Cade never really wanted a life with me. He told Lena and Deacon the only way he'd give me a wolf was if Mom went back on her deal. Which he probably knew wouldn't happen, so it was an easy empty promise. There was never a chance he'd give me a wolf. I let him feed me that line, that we could talk about it later. *How could I be so naive?* He kept me happy and content. Once again, I'm just a bargaining chip. Or is this blackmail? What's the difference, anyhow?

What's worse: Ansel, Ezra, Deacon, and now even Lena all covered for him. They've all painted him as a good person. That he's tried. Did he really? No. He fucking lied to me. He hasn't tried. He gave up on a job before, so why wouldn't he give up on me? Quitters are as bad as cheaters. Ready to throw in the towel if it doesn't suit their needs. What kind of future would I ever have with that?

What else has he lied about? Lena lied too. I can't even trust that I'm not pregnant. We haven't used protection. I have been mostly consistent with my birth control, but it's not guaranteed.

Sick to my stomach, I scramble, barely making it across the bedroom into the bathroom to pray to the porcelain god for relief.

"Shh."

Cade's here. He pulls my hair back. Hand rubbing my back.

"Get away from me."

I move away from him in the small space enclosing the toilet. I'm trapped in here as he stands blocking the door.

"Thalia, talk to me." Cade offers me his hand to help me up.

"What didn't you lie about?" I'm bitter.

I won't believe anything he says, but I want to see what else I need to worry about.

Cade shakes his head dismissively. It feels so fake.

"I haven't lied to you. None of what I've told you has been a lie."

"That's just it, isn't it?" I try pushing myself off the floor. My socks slip on the tile.

His arms around me steady me. "What's just it?"

"You just didn't tell me." I pull away from him, recoiling at his touch. "Just like you didn't tell me about using your gift on me."

Letting me go, he backs up. I'm no longer trapped in the bathroom. I move past him back into the bedroom. If I go back to my spot on the floor, there's no escape. He'll have me cornered again.

I move quickly to the living room, pulling my phone out of my pocket. Cade said it would call his boss, which is my only option. It's clear he has no intention of taking me home.

I open the screen and scroll to *Peter Corinth*.

The phone only rings once. "Thalia, are you okay?"

"I'm firing Cade. I want to come home. Call my parents and let them know," I say firmly.

There's still emotion in my speech, and I breathe, trying to force myself calm. Tears are hot as they run down my cheeks. My nose runs, and I wipe it on my sleeve.

I hear the back door to the house open. Lena peeks her head into the kitchen. She sees me on the phone. Deacon stands behind her watching.

I turn away from them. Not like they won't hear me, but I can't look at them.

"Thalia, is Cade there?" Peter asks.

"Yes. He's here. I've made him aware that his services are no longer needed. I no longer feel safe in his care."

My voice is more level this time, but my stomach clenches in a knot. His betrayal stings again. I fight back another heave.

"Can you put him on, please?" Peter is kind, his voice soft.

Having moved across the house effortlessly, Cade is next to

me, offering out his hand. I hand him the phone, careful to avoid any contact.

Cade listens to Peter for a bit before saying, "I don't fully understand what's happened. She's perfectly safe here. Regardless of my position change, there's no risk to her in the slightest. If anything, she's significantly safer here now."

Unfortunately, I don't have their hearing. I can't hear Peter's half of the call. My shoulders shake as I fight against the uncontrollable sobs of grief for all the happiness I thought I had found.

Peter is speaking again, and Cade scrubs his hand down his face. There's silence a moment later; I don't hear the muffled sound of Peter's voice. Peter must have said something to agree with me coming home.

Cade shakes his head as he responds, "I understand, we'll make the flight. Thank you."

Handing the phone back to me, Cade walks away.

THE LAST DAY WAS AWFUL. Peter tried to get us on a flight sooner, but this early morning commuter was the best he could do. Even private planes weren't running, apparently. It's not Peter's fault I broke the cardinal rule and got involved with the hired help.

There's been no break from Cade. He canceled all his meetings yesterday. He was uncharacteristically short in tone, telling them all to go away, and by 10:00 a.m., his phone had quit ringing. Anywhere I went around the house, inside or out, Cade was always just a few feet behind me. He would just sit close to me. I'm certain I caught him following along with what I was knitting, counting stitches off on his fingers. He tried on multiple occasions to talk to me. But mostly, he respected that I didn't want to talk.

What's worse is that part of me wants to. This tiny little part wants to forgive him, no matter how many times I remind myself I'm angry, that I'm hurting, and that he lied to and used me. It wants me to hear him out. It wants to talk and see if he has something to say that isn't going to feel like a knife stabbed through canvas.

I love him.

But holding on to my anger is easier than facing the heartbreak I'm sure I'd feel if I talked to him. Self-preservation at its finest.

Cade guides me through the airport with precision. The security gates and check-in pass in a flash. As he leads me to the front of the gate, I see we're the first people here for the flight. Looking out the large glass windows brings me no joy. I choose a seat facing away, looking at the empty terminal. Empty, like how I feel inside.

The large sigh that comes from Cade as he sits down rattles through me. He slumps back in his chair, legs kicked out in front of him. It's probably him stretching out before being crammed on a plane. He told me that flying is hard for him.

I want to lean over and put my head on his chest. I want to snuggle against his shoulder and for him to tell me that we're both going to be okay.

No. No, I don't.

Cade clenches his fist and lets it go, his long fingers stretching out.

When Cade speaks, velvet tones brush against my skin, causing me to shiver. "I've given you time. I'll admit I haven't given you space, but well, it's not in my nature. I really want to talk about this."

I shake my head. I can't. There's nothing to say to him.

Dropping his hand, he sets it gently on my thigh. I bat it away.

No, you don't get to touch me and make it better.

"I wish you'd just talk to me." Cade pushes again.

I look at him. His eyes are dark. He looks sleep deprived.

I shake my head. "I've nothing more to say."

He hangs his head, breaking my gaze. We sit in silence for a long time.

Cade starts talking. "I've trained and worked hard to have a firm grasp on my temper and how I react to others. When people yell or shout, I listen and wait my turn to talk."

I stand up. I can't sit next to him. I can't hear his side of things. If I do, I'll change my mind. I'll forgive him. I'll . . . I'll want to go back home.

Home.

At that realization, my insides seize, and I have to hold back the sob trying to crawl out of my chest.

Cade doesn't follow me when I stand up, walk over an aisle of chairs, and sit back down.

As people start to fill the gate for boarding, Cade comes and stands by me. We wait for the final boarding class. He looks at the gate attendant and then at me.

I'm standing there, dwarfed by his side.

"Last chance, draga mea. We don't have to go. But the minute we get on this plane, there's no going back. I can't undo this."

His hand raises to brush a strand of hair out of my face. I wince and turn from him to board the plane. He follows quietly.

CHAPTER 68
THALIA

"Senator Clark, it's a pleasure to meet you again." Cade offers her a warm smile, but it doesn't reach his eyes.

"Cade." My mother pauses. "I guess I'm uncertain what to call you now formally. Mr. Alden? Sovereign?"

"Cade is fine," he assures her and offers her a seat at the table.

We're back to where it all started. I'm seated between my parents across from Cade.

Peter breaks the awkward silence. "This meeting is, in my professional opinion, premature. However, we've been informed that Ms. Clark is no longer comfortable using our protection services and is asking to be returned to you in order to use a different security service."

"With it being so close to the passing of the bill, and now with Cade leading his people, my need for protection seems unnecessary." I try to defend my decision.

They've all hidden from me the fact that I'm a pawn. No need for them to think this is a temper tantrum. It isn't. Cade used me, physically and emotionally. I just want to go home.

"Cade, what is your opinion?" Dad questions.

"I think this is a terrible idea," Cade responds.

"Pumpkin, I think you should listen to Cade. I'm sure there's been a lot of commotion with him being in the public eye, but you're still safer with him." Dad pats my hand like it hasn't been four days since Cade became Sovereign Alpha.

I'm so over everyone thinking they know what's best for *me*.

My mother is uncharacteristically silent. I look to her for help. If she hates shifters, maybe I can sway her to my side.

"Mom?"

"If you want to come home, I will absolutely support it. We can increase security at the house. There've been no issues there. You can stay with us until we get you a new apartment." She smiles, stroking my hair and shoulder in an uncharacteristic loving gesture. "Besides, now that Cade is in the public eye, we don't want you to be seen standing at his side."

Cade draws a short breath, and I catch him fight a wince. I draw my eyes from him and put on my best puppy dog eyes to look at Dad.

"Can we have pancakes for dinner? I missed you."

Hitting him with the pancakes will get him on my side. Is it emotionally manipulative to do this? Probably. Do I care? No. Anything I need to do in order to get away from Cade. Anything at all.

"Of course, pumpkin. If you're sure this is what you want." He holds my hand. Then, turning to Peter, he says, "Can we employ your team for additional security at the house?"

Peter answers quickly without having to think. "The only team I have available is Cade's. As it appears you are firing Cade, I don't have any additional assistance available to you at this time."

"We'll call the other companies. Surely, they'll make space to accommodate us." My mother waves her hand dismissively.

After weeks of watching how wolves interpret body language, I can see where Cade sees her as angry and not fearful.

Am I making the right decision? It's only a few more weeks. I can surely just hole up in the bedroom at his place. It's not like we even have to see each other. He slept on his couch last night.

It's too late. Mom and Dad think it'll be safe. I trust them more than I trust Cade. He admitted he couldn't be objective when we were talking about wolves. It's time I do research myself. There is a possibility Mom is on the right side.

"Thank you for upholding your end of the arrangement. I've brought you the most updated copy of the bill. I'm sure you've already been briefed on it based on the media coverage." My mother slides a thick stack of documents across the conference table.

"The pleasure was mine." Cade shakes his head slightly. His hand hovers over the document before finally sliding the stack closer to himself. "I look forward to seeing you at the interview later."

He stands and turns to leave, giving a small nod, dismissing himself. His lips are drawn tight. I've never seen this look on his face.

"Ambassador and Senator Clark, Ms. Clark, it's been a pleasure. Peter, I'll debrief with you later."

CHAPTER 69

CADE

THE LEVIATHAN IS SILENT. We're both in mourning. Walking the hallways back to my office, every fiber of my being screams to go back to her. I can't. She's made her decision despite my best efforts. I couldn't get her to open up to me. Having to walk away from Thalia hurts more than walking away from my people when I abdicated. The sense of failure I felt back then is nothing compared to this. *I failed my mate.*

Millie calls my name as I walk past her. I shake my head, opening the door to my office. Closing it behind me, I toss the updated bill unceremoniously onto the desk. The bill is thick, despite the fact that entire sections should have been cut. It lands with a solid *thump*. I strip out of my flannel. Not the most professional, but what the fuck do I care?

My door opens. I look to see Millie leaning against the door.

"Closed door still means not interested in a conversation, right?" I growl.

Millie shrugs. "You aren't okay."

"Not okay is just going to be my new normal. Right now, I have to do what I can while I still can. Get Adam briefed on security for the meeting today. I'll need you with Lena at all times." I move on as fast as I can from talking about Thalia.

My impromptu trip to DC for no apparent reason was unexplainable to the council and the pack publicist. No one outside the Ardelean bloodline knew that Thalia was at the house, so it was only fair when questions started cropping up. So, I asked Henri to arrange a formal interview and public forum between myself and Senator Clark. Lena booked herself a last-minute plane ticket, citing the fact that I should appear more supported than Robert was. While her argument is valid, her flying in this afternoon before the meeting is less than ideal. Hopefully she isn't crabby or anxious from being with all the people on the plane.

Millie continues to stand there. If she doesn't want to give me space, then so be it. I strip off my jeans and begin putting on my dress pants. It's not like she hasn't seen me in my boxers a hundred times before. Buttoning my shirt, I look at her. She's glaring at me.

Tired of this already, I huff. "What?"

"I've never seen you so defeated. In all the years we've worked together, I've never seen you completely devoid of anything." She shakes her head. "You won a huge victory today for your people. Adam told me all about the deal after he reviewed the security footage. But at what cost was this victory? You're not selfish by any means, but I've never seen you so willing to roll over and take it up the ass from someone else. Why aren't you fighting for her? It doesn't take a rocket scientist doing brain surgery to figure out you're in love with Thalia Clark."

"Yeah." I hang my head. She's known me for years. Even if I could hide my torment better, she would see through me. "I've run from my responsibility to my people for too long. I've chased my own happiness and my own life, hurting thousands of people in that process. That pile of papers is the start of what needs to be done. No matter how I feel about Thalia, I've got to let her go. She'll marry someone who can make her happy."

"Hardly fair to the woman you settle with." Millie points out.

My brain cycles back to the woman I'll probably settle with. On paper, Isabel and I make the most sense. She won't mind settling for only owning my last name and not my heart.

The Leviathan leaves my consciousness. He's barely a blip in my thoughts. I've disgraced him once again.

Pulling my suit jacket on, it's time to defend my mating circumstance. "Marrying the Sovereign comes with a lot of compromises. Not having my heart will just have to be one of them. Women marry for wealth and fame all the time. What does love have to do with it?"

"Woah. Dude." Adam walks up to the hallway. "What did you do with Cade? 'Cause the Cade I know wouldn't ever speak of women that way."

"Yeah. That Cade died about thirty-six hours ago." I pause, picking up the papers off the desk. I'm sick to my stomach looking at them. "Good news, you don't have to work for him."

Duffel and stack of papers in hand, I usher them out the door, closing it behind me. I walk to the front desk, not bothering to swing by Peter's office. At the front desk, Alice is typing on her mechanical keyboard. The loud clack of keys should have blocked out the sound of us coming up the hallway, but before we get there, I hear her voice.

"You better be wearing a tie." She's sharp.

I step in front of the desk, showing her that I am, in fact, wearing a tie. She looks at me and rummages through a drawer pulling out a lint roller.

She walks around and starts rolling my suit. "Wouldn't kill you to not be covered in dog hair."

It's too much. The pressure and her statement get to me, and I start laughing. I can barely breathe between laughing. The three of them stand there, looking at me before Millie catches on and she starts laughing.

"Oh!" Alice catches on, and she's laughing too.

Adam still hasn't caught on. His eyes dart around, looking at us for an explanation.

"It's not dog hair." I take a deep breath. "I don't own a dog."

Adam rolls his eyes. "Good grief."

Alice is satisfied that I've been deshedded and looks at me. "Your brother used to wear a fancy sash with his suit."

Footsteps come down the hallway toward us. Alice looks at me. "You should go to Peter's office."

I shake my head, knowing that in thirty seconds, I'll be seeing Thalia Ann Clark, most likely, for the last time. The masochistic bit of my heart begs for the last look of the love I've lost.

CHAPTER 70
THALIA

I HOLD my head up high, trying to channel my mother's persona. I'll just be the perfect little chess piece they've all made me out to be. Walking tall, I try not to look at him as we walk past and enter the elevator. It's futile.

My eyes lock with his. I don't know that I've ever seen Cade sad. But it's a look I won't ever forget. I watch him close his eyes and turn away before the elevator's doors close. Hopefully, that'll be the last time I see him. It'll be easier to rebuild my heart when he's not there every day to pull it apart.

"What happened?" My mother's interrogation starts the moment we've left the inside of the Corinth Security building.

"Nothing. I just don't think that, given Cade's new position, it's safe for me with him," I answer.

Where are these tears coming from? I blink them away.

My mother, ever the politico, continues, "It certainly doesn't bode well. Though, I suspect my reaching an agreement with him is going to boost my approval rating. It seems the public approves of Mr. Alden significantly more than his brother. He didn't have you with him when he murdered him?"

Our conversation continues as we move into the town car. Dad sits up front, and the two of us tuck into the car's backseat.

"Did he?" My mother presses.

I shake my head. "No, Mom. It's fine. I wasn't there."

"Left you unsupervised?" She looks more excited than appalled.

"No, I wasn't unsupervised. He had someone highly qualified to protect me."

I cover for Cade. Why? What does it matter? Mom can rake him across the coals for all I care. Right?

She makes a noise of displeasure but doesn't ask any further questions.

My phone vibrates in my purse. I pull it out to see a message from an unknown number:

> Unknown Number: Doesn't sit well with me you not having Cade's number.

A contact card opens with Cade's, Lena's, and Deacon's phone numbers and email addresses. There's no indication of who sent it to me. I debate deleting it. My finger hovers over the button. But I can't do it. I move on from the numbers.

Logging into social media, I check all the things Millie and Adam kept updated for me. Their trip to the Maldives has photos of beautiful beaches and various books and shops. There's fancy coffee and food. It all looks exactly like things I would do. My usual contacts all seem pretty content with me having taken some me-time away. There aren't any questions that my captions are different or that I've been distant. *I haven't missed this, and I haven't been missed.* It's flavorless looking at these posts. Maybe once I figure out how much of my life has been messed up, I'll just go to the Maldives and see if I can experience it myself.

Social media has piqued my curiosity; I type Cade's name into the internet search bar. There are nearly a hundred new news posts, some less than four hours old. The only photos they've seemed to find of him are candid photos from what I'm guessing are holiday events at the Alloways with Judah, Dinah, and Ezra.

An article from only five minutes ago catches my attention. Cade Alden Invited to Meeting with Congressional Party.

"Are you okay coming with us to the meeting, pumpkin, or should your mother go alone?" Dad asks, almost like he knew I was looking at the headline.

Do I want to go? I look at the pictures and the articles. "Yeah. I'll come with."

CHAPTER 71

CADE

I'VE CHANGED CLOTHES, ridden in a different vehicle, and am at a new location. Yet, the smell of Thalia still hangs with me.

The Leviathan doesn't seem to believe it's abnormal. It's the only comfort he and I have found together. Sitting in one of the historical rooms of the Congress building, I'm surrounded by the smell of the old wood walls, oil paintings, large tapestry drapes, and carpet. It should be enough to keep me busy smelling other scents. But The Leviathan and I still smell her.

Henri made sure I was briefed on the questions, cameras, and protocols by the news team. It's surreal to be on this side of the chaos. I'd much rather prefer standing in a suit with an earpiece off to the side like Michael and the rest of my security team.

I'm seated on a small stage, elevated, uncomfortably so, above rows of chairs. Millie sits next to Lena, chatting with her in the front row on my side of the table. They've always gotten along well, and I'm grateful Peter has agreed to let me hire my own team.

I pinch the bridge of my nose, trying to relieve some tension. Then go back to the questions they're going to ask in the main forum that Henri provided me with. One of her various lists is canned responses to common questions. All I have to do is memorize them and then make them sound natural. The second half, where I'll be taking questions from the public, will require me to think on my feet. In an additional list, Henri gave me general talking points. I play them back from when Lena read them to me on the car ride here. I didn't have time to review the last of the important lists of today: the rebuttals Senator Clark might give. She doesn't scare me. I need the court of public opinion on my side.

The scent of Thalia grows stronger. I look up from the document to see Senator Clark, her staff, and her newly hired security team filing through the doors, barely twenty minutes from when we're supposed to begin. *I wonder how she was able to find a new security company so quickly.* I'm sure Senator Clark smells like Thalia because they've spent time together. I stand, out of respect, when Senator Clark approaches the table we'll share. As I scan the group of people entering, I find the real source of the smell. Thalia is here.

"Cade, it's been a long time." Senator Clark uncharacteristically cracks a joke.

I give her the best smile I can muster. Under normal circumstances, if my heart hadn't just been shattered, it would be funny.

"Yes, yes, it has."

"I assume you've found everything in order." She pulls out her chair to sit.

Resuming my position in the chair two down from her, I nod. "Yes, if this is truly the document you plan to sign into law, there are no objections from myself or my people."

"Excellent. You'll find I'm a woman of my word." Senator Clark waves to Thalia, who politely waves back.

She's changed her clothes; her beautiful wild red hair has been wrangled into a more polished look. It doesn't suit her, but somehow, it's still beautiful. Stunning but different. I see the security detail they've hired. The air smells of wolves and large cat shifters. The hairs on the back of my neck rise as I glance at Lena, and she smells it too. Stiffening her back, she looks past Millie toward their side of the room.

My phone vibrates in my pocket. I look at Lena, who has hers in her hand. I pull it out for one last check before putting it on silent.

> Lena: I don't like the wolves. I'm fairly certain they're LeFleur. I don't remember her brothers' names.

I nod, muting my phone.

The host or interviewer or whatever he would like to be called, arrives at the table. We do some last-minute checks, and soon, the room is filled with people. It's loud, and there's movement all around me.

The Leviathan fights for us to move to talk to Thalia. *By our mate. Other males touch her. Unacceptable.*

So, he's apparently only willing to communicate when he can see her. *Fan-fucking-tastic.*

Introductions are made, and I'm already counting down the minutes until I can escape. My head is on a swivel, constantly checking on Lena and then on Thalia and her security.

The preplanned questions fly by. I don't know how my answers are going over with the public. I should care more, but I just can't find it in me with her so close. My attention is split, and I try to focus on the questions being asked, but I'm still constantly aware of Thalia.

When we open the forum for questions, my attention is split three ways: the person asking questions, Thalia, and now Henri.

"What is it that shifters want? Why, in your opinion, have shifters come out now?" A woman stands at the podium with her hand resting on the lowest part of her stomach.

Dinah informed me once that it's the sign of a woman who recently found out they're pregnant or lost a child. I wonder how true that is right now. *Why am I even thinking about this right now, any distraction is a good one maybe?*

"I don't think anyone woke up and said, 'let's just out everyone to the humans.' I'm not sure what happened on the day when we were brought into the public eye. I wasn't there. For centuries we've lived alongside humans undetected, just skirting society or interacting on the smallest scale possible. Now, we're moving to a time where everything is so connected that there's no way to effectively be apart. What do we want? A future. We want the right to exist, have families, live our lives in the same way we always have, in peace."

"Yes, but what about what the people want?" Senator Clark chimes in. "The people want safety."

"Who doesn't?" I'm about to say something and it's either going to go over really well or it won't. It's Henri's problem. "We all want safety. I would find it hard to believe that any person, shifter, human, or otherwise, doesn't want to feel safe. Safe to live, work, raise a family, or take a walk through the national parks. Safety, for humans, hasn't changed. You're no more at risk than the day before our people were found out. You're only now aware that people, shifters, near you don't feel safe."

"Hardly," Senator Clark argues. "You can't tell me that your animal doesn't make you safer."

I know what I want to say. I look at Lena, who casually looks away, examining a painting on the wall.

Looking down the table at Senator Clark, I smile. "The negotiations that our people have come together for on your bill, while significantly easier for us to live with, make us very much less safe. Large swaths of legislation leave us very much exposed for our lives to be ended at no fault of our own. We've done everything we can since our people have lived side by side with humans to keep you safe. That includes policing our own and keeping it out of the public eye. We're not asking to be held to a different standard. We only ask that we're given the ability to maintain our status quo in policing our own and when we violate human laws, we're given the same due process."

The senator sits back in her chair. The room is a shuffle of people conversing, and I'm unsure if I've made a massive mistake. When I glance to Lena and Henri for an indicator of what's going on, they're smiling widely, and it seems to have gone over well.

AFTER TEN MINUTES of wrapping up, people start filing out of the room. When I hop off the platform my legs are wobbly from sitting so long. The Leviathan and I still can't pull our focus from Thalia. One of her new security specialists flashes his wolf to me. His face is so familiar, but I can't place it.

The Leviathan snarls urging me to put him in his place. Luckily for the young security specialist, The Leviathan understands my plea to not shift with humans so close.

"Earth to Cade." Lena's voice breaks my concentration.

I focus back on the group.

Henri has a massive smile plastered on her face. "You did phenomenally. Senator Clark barely had anything to say to your responses. A little off script a few times, but you did flawlessly."

"Thank you." I look at Michael, finally getting to do something normal — security-related protocol. "When can we depart?"

"Transport is ready," Michael responds.

CHAPTER 72

CADE

Days pass, and they're all the same. Henri has arranged dozens of meetings at my request. She's becoming more than just a publicist. Her organization system is constantly adapting to help work with how my brain processes things. Apparently, there's a whole psychology to how people manage and organize tasks. It goes over my head most of the time. But I follow her lists of shit to do and things to talk about. It's helpful having the box to check off.

We don't fly back from DC to Wisconsin. Instead, we drive, zigzagging to meet various packs and see other shifter territories. Everyone I meet says I'm different from Robert. That they appreciate my approach. I'm not sure what that approach is, because I'm just trying to get through one day at a time at this point. I spend most of my time trying to not let everyone know I'm dying inside. The council has applauded me wildly in phone calls and emails. After a week of meetings in various cities across the country, Lena and I finally make it home. Well, the Wisconsin house.

As we pull up to the house, Deacon's music accosts my ears.

I can hear his music over the engine of the SUV, the air conditioning, and through the windows of my car. I park my SUV outside since moving boxes are packed and stacked neatly in my garage stall. The windows and doors to the house are wide open.

"What are the chances he's been kidnapped?" Lena deadpans.

I blow my lips in a raspberry. "Probably not high enough."

With rock, paper, scissors, I lose and have to brave the sound system and tinnitus that comes with it.

I find Deacon scrubbing the floor with a brush. He doesn't look up when I come in. After walking to the house's sound control panel, I turn the music down to a tolerable decibel. My ears ring with an echo to the small exposure I had walking into the house. I can't even imagine what his ears are doing.

"Hey!" Deacon looks at me. "I was listening to that."

"So was the rest of the county." I can barely hear myself.

"Alright. You don't need to yell. Sorry." Deacon raises his hands for a brief second before going back to scrubbing the floor.

It's muted, and I read his lips and body language to get better answers.

"Seriously, Deacon, what are you doing?" Lena asks, kicking off her shoes at the door.

"There's a bunch of people headed here today, wait, tomorrow, wait. What day is it?" Deacon asks.

"Monday," Lena and I answer together.

"Tomorrow." Deacon confirms. "There's a bunch of people headed here tomorrow to start moving our shit. I thought you set it up."

I shake my head. "Because, apparently, I don't get to decide when we move."

. . .

CURRENT TO-DO LIST:

- Move to Minnesota.
- File paperwork for Courtney.
- WTF did Robert do with all the money?
- Give Henri a raise.

I'M IN SURVIVAL MODE. Lists of shit to do.

CHAPTER 73
THALIA

I'VE BEEN STARING at the numbers on the screen for seven days. I have a new apartment and don't go anywhere without my new security detail. Which means I'm going nowhere that isn't mandatory because the two of them are awkward. They aren't inconspicuous like Cade was, and they're opinionated about what I'm doing. It's like Mom hired her own personal spies to keep me in line with her agenda.

The only plus is that I've been reinstated at the Smithsonian. Also, I've been granted extensions on final papers for this semester. But none of it brings me joy. I was one of the first to find out about this fall's art installations: art made by modern shifter artists and some never-before-displayed art from their private collections.

I can't focus on any of it. I smiled at the news and shared enthusiasm with my peers, but there's no real joy. It's just a reminder of how different my life has become without them. I feel like the frame that once housed *The Storm on the Sea of Galilee* — my insides cut out, left threadbare and without purpose, waiting for the canvas to be returned.

All I can think about are their phone numbers stored in a simple text message.

What was my life like before my time with the wolves? After everything that's happened, I'm not me anymore. I see everything differently. The body language of other humans gives me a perspective on the intention behind conversations. A few times now, I've thought I recognized other people as shifters. Not that I would ask them.

I need to move on, to let it go. But there's no closure. Without answers as to why he used me, I'm stuck wondering about my place in all this. I need answers to the questions floating around in my head. Need it enough to use the numbers.

One thing is certain, I'm not texting Cade's number. It'll be emotional manipulation. He could even try to use his gift. *Does it work long distance or through text messages? I guess I have no idea.* Lena and I weren't close, and I know for a fact that she's loyal to Cade. She would just as quickly block my number on his phone before texting me back. Deacon seems more grounded. He seemed hurt by Cade too. If I'm going to trust anyone to give me the truth, it'll most likely be Deacon. I don't know what I can believe or what answers he can give me. Maybe it'll do more harm than good. Maybe he'll just push an agenda for Cade too.

I'm not getting answers from stalking them on social media. Their publicist does a great job highlighting all their excursions and interactions. Candid photographs mixed with posed portraits and roundtable meetings. I'd be lying if I said I haven't watched every news clip, looked at every photo, and thought of him every hour of every day.

Cade doesn't look well. He looks more tired than the first day I met him when he had driven through the night. He looks worse now than the day after he ended the fractured at Ansel's.

Well, minus the blood. He's worn out, and his movements seem regimented as if on autopilot.

Answers don't come from staring at their phone numbers on my screen all day either. I text the number listed for Deacon.

> Me: Hey, is this Deacon?

There's no answer, I don't even know if this is the real number. How will I even be sure I'm talking to Deacon? My phone lights up with a new notice.

> Deacon: Hey little red, I was wondering how long it would take before you texted one of us. Did Adam not give you Cade's number?

My breath catches in my throat reading his nickname for me, and tears sting the backs of my eyelids. *No, I won't feel sad.* I take a deep breath before texting him back.

> Me: How do I know this is really Deacon?

I wait a few more moments, how on earth am I going to know for sure it's Deacon? My phone lights up again. A picture of Deacon holding the scarf I made and accidentally left behind graces my screen.

> Deacon: This was for me right? Cade doesn't look good in red.

> Me: Yes, if you want it, keep it. I don't want Cade to know we're talking.

> Deacon: 10-4, TL doesn't have to know. You safe?

I read his message again, ten-four means acknowledged, but TL? What could that ... *oh, The Leviathan.*

> Me: Yeah, perfectly safe. I have to know Deacon.

> Deacon: Know what?

> Me: Was everything he told me a lie?

Deacon doesn't answer for a little bit. Maybe I misread him.

I put my phone on my bed and begin pacing my room. This was a mistake; I can't possibly remember everything Cade said. I can't expect Deacon to know what Cade lied about. Who knows how sober he was? I'm just opening a can of worms ...

My phone lights up, and I rush over to it.

> Deacon: It was shitty that Cade didn't tell you about his deal with your mom. But he wasn't lying to you about any of it. Lena says that TL is burning him up inside over losing you. They got home earlier today, he's not awesome.

> Me: What does that even mean? Burning him up?

I watch, waiting for a response. It doesn't come.

I order dinner in, and the driver comes and goes without a response.

Deacon is funny when intoxicated but very inconsistent. Why would he magically be sober and reliable just because I want information?

Morning rolls around, and I wake up to a message from him.

> Deacon: IDK how much you want to know.
> Cade didn't lie about how he feels & sees you.
> I just know what he's like with you not being
> here & it's not good.

> Me: Why didn't he tell me? Why did he keep
> me in the dark?

Deacon's answer doesn't come through, and I didn't expect it to. Hardly fair that I ask him questions that Cade should be answering.

Work and school are more of the same. The subjects that used to enrich my life are still muted. It feels ridiculous, but I text Deacon anyway.

> Me: What do you mean about me not being
> there?

I'm growing illogically mad at him. It's stupid, I know. Deacon isn't Cade's keeper. It's not his responsibility to take care of me. I'm literally nothing to him. He doesn't owe me anything.

I'm probably just adjusting to life coming home. I was away for a long time, and there are a lot of changes in my life. It'll pass. I can't hang on to the what ifs of a disaster of a relationship. Throwing myself into my work and focusing on what's happening seems the most logical option. Change my perspective, right? After all, I've only been apart from Cade for eight days. This is just post-vacation blues. It must be.

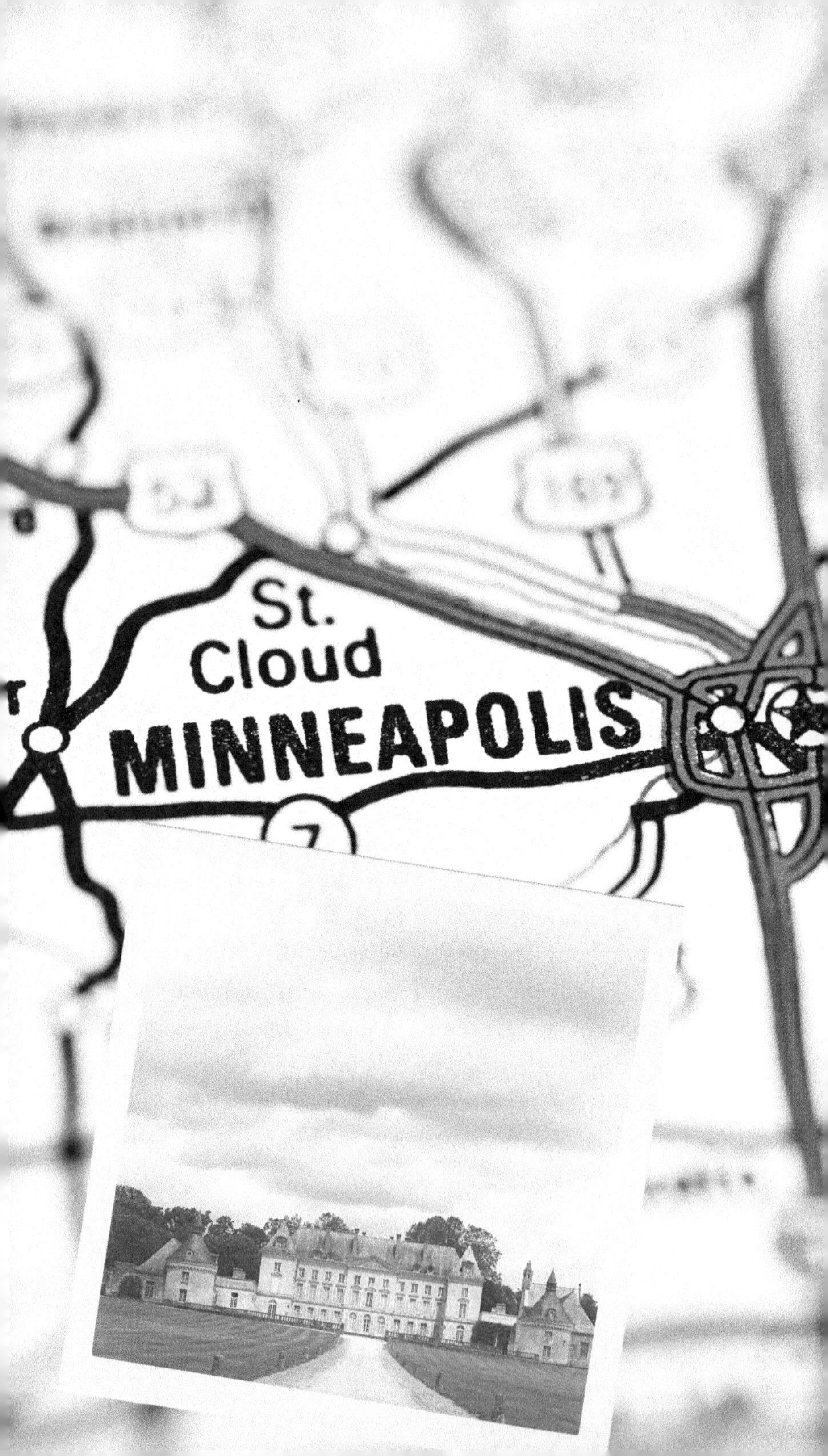
St.
Cloud
MINNEAPOLIS

CHAPTER 74
CADE

IT'S BEEN fifteen days since I last shared a bed with Thalia. It feels like time's moving at an odd rate. It's neither quick nor slow. Some days and moments drag on, and others, I'm frozen as the world swings around me. Climbing into bed every night, I try really hard not to think of how empty it is. But my pillow still smells like her. We've moved houses, and I've changed bed linens, but her scent still clings to the fluff inside. It's sweet torture.

Lauren and her staff take excellent care of us. It's hard with the three of us trying to settle in.

There's a pile of memories that we haven't quite been able to address. Lena doesn't want to talk about it. Deacon's using every substance under the sun even more now than he ever did in the Wisconsin house. He made a promise to Lena a long time ago, and I'm not even sure a promise is enough to keep him alive.

The Leviathan stews in anger. From within my mind, he sulks between thrashes of anger, grinding against me as he desires bloodshed from any and everyone around us. The apathetic silence from before we met Thalia is gone. Now, being without her has triggered silent rage. There is no reprieve from him. Even my dreams are coated with dripping loathing.

THE ALARM GOES OFF, and I can't pull myself out of bed. I silence it, lying there, trying to grab any sleep that isn't restless.

There's a knock on the door before Lena calls, "Hey, it's almost eight. You're not up. Deacon says the old dead people think they'll be arriving around eleven. I got a text from the publicist saying you didn't answer her texts this morning. You okay?"

I'm anything but okay. Unfortunately, it's not an option for me to not be okay. At least for now, while I'm still sane enough to function and do my job, I have to do that.

It's hard, but I pull myself away from her scent and into the bathroom. Trimming my beard shorter than I normally would, I try to remember that I'm no longer wearing it a certain way because it makes her happy. I'll schedule another haircut again this week. Maybe.

TODAY MUST-DO:
- Fire Robert's CPA.
- Hire a new CPA (maybe do this first).
- Find out what Robert did with the money.
- Schedule meetings with West Coast shifters.
- Give Lauren a raise.
- Schedule haircut.

. . .

My to-do list for today is blessedly short. But the things I can't write on there are the things I don't want or need people to know I'm doing. This list is benign enough. But when you start writing things like 'find a replacement Alpha' and 'hold on to your sanity a little while longer,' that could be red flags to those around you.

CHAPTER 75

THALIA

My ADVISER CALLED me first thing this morning, telling me they needed me to come in as soon as possible. I rushed to the office, worried that I'd done something wrong. That I'd messed up.

The bus doesn't drive fast enough. What if I lose my place at the Smithsonian? What am I going to do? Even after I graduate, losing a job at the most prestigious institution? No one will hire me after that. It's a good thing I haven't had breakfast. My stomach is in knots. I've been distracted lately, but my feedback has been good. They would warn me before firing me, right? I would get warnings? Oh, unless it's a huge mistake. Did I ruin something? Did someone break in? It has to be all my fault.

Breathing is hard. I can't come up with air. Until his voice is in my head. *Breathe in. One, two, three, four. Hold. One, two, three, four.* I follow along with the words taking breaths and cycling through. My breaths come easier. It does nothing for my stomach because it's not my voice in my head doing the counting. It's his.

THIS MEETING IS A WHIRLWIND. My brain has crashed at least three times.

I've been hand selected to personally assist them in curating and authenticating pieces for this fall's collection. The shifter art exhibit.

I asked for time to think about it. I don't know what came over me. They looked so confused but are giving me two days to decide.

Sitting here, staring at the informational email they've given me, I almost feel like I shouldn't take this. It's an honor to be selected, as an intern, for this kind of project. It doesn't sit right with me.

I've picked up my phone a hundred times to call Mom and Dad. They'll be, well, they'll fake being happy for me.

Lena's paintings would be stunning on display. My mind drifts back to her take on *Boreas* and some of the other original works she's done.

A lump forms in my throat and hot tears fill my eyes. I blink them away and close my laptop.

Picking up my phone, I'm sure I'm going to call Mom and Dad this time. There's a notification. It's been six and a half days, but Deacon's name pops up on the screen.

> Deacon: Sorry. Cade's in a rough place. I really wish you'd message him. I've tried talking to him about coming to DC to see you. He won't budge. He went as far to say if he goes to DC TL won't let him come home without you.

It's my turn to make Deacon wait. I'm so angry with more half answers coming from the wolves. The nerve asking me to message Cade.

Deacon: I miss hanging out with you little red. It's hard not having your smiling face around here. I'm sorry if you ever thought I didn't like you.

Me: I liked you too, Deacon, but I feel lied to.

Deacon: No one has wanted to lie to you. I didn't know about the deal Cade made. I also know Cade doesn't use his gift for his own benefit. He's not the self-righteous type.

Deacon: He loves you. It's fracturing him.

Me: What?

My stomach drops with Deacon's last message. But, of course, there isn't another answer. Even after I call my parents, per their request, in which they tell me nothing eventful and make boring small talk for half an hour, Deacon doesn't message me back.

I'm in bed, but it's impossible for me to fall asleep. What happens if Cade fractures? The fractured wolves are Ansel's problem. But then I think about the wolf at Ansel's that Cade killed. Will that happen to Cade? Will Ansel be forced to kill him? He has to fix them or kill them. Ansel is the only one who can kill Cade.

I can't think about this. Whatever is happening to Cade has nothing to do with me. It can't. When Cade ended the fractured at Ansel's, he said him and The Leviathan didn't work well together. Clearly, that hasn't changed.

CHAPTER 76
CADE

I DON'T SLEEP MUCH ANYMORE. An hour here and there at most, and when I do, I'm haunted by the memories of what I've done wrong. Giving in to her demands and taking Thalia back to her parents was the worst thing I could have done. What hurts more is that I walked away with a bad gut feeling. I left my mate behind, and knowing she's vulnerable is the worst plague of all.

These nightmares are fictitious, building inside from my worst fears: her being taken, them hurting her, her death. They wake me from the little sleep I find.

My dreams don't only happen when sleeping. They strike me throughout the day. Any moment alone or break in the conversation, my mind wanders with no sense of urgency back to what I've done wrong: I made a deal with her mother. My not telling Thalia broke us. It seemed so insignificant at the time. Why didn't I just tell her? How many times did The Leviathan call me a coward for not claiming Thalia? Maybe I wasn't a coward for not claiming her, but he wasn't off the mark completely. I was a coward for not telling her the truth when she told me in earnest she wanted to be wolf. None of it matters anymore. I made my bed, and now I get to lie in it — alone.

CHAPTER 77

THALIA

ALMOST TWO DAYS pass before the notification sound I set for Deacon plays.

> Deacon: IDFK Ansel has been calling Cade daily. Last I heard Ansel was cautioning him to slow down. That he's burning out.

Ansel said that Cade always dies in old age. That it was locked in stone? But what if it isn't? I take deep breaths. It's not my job to worry about Cade. I push down the fear that has worked its way into my bones and ball up on the couch. He isn't mine. I'll have to distance myself from him. Deacon too.

Putting my phone away does me no good because the television begins playing a clip of a meeting Cade had today with the Governor of Minnesota and the congressional committee they formed for shifters.

The media calls his look 'Cade Casual.' Normally, he wears a combination of chinos with polos and dress shirts. Today's look was dark-blue chinos and a short-sleeve, collared shirt. His tattoos down his left arm are on full display.

I see all I need to know about Cade's mental state. He's moved on.

The spot on his arm, where his tattoo was unfinished, which he told me was reserved for my name, has been filled in. His armband ends midway down his forearm.

I pick up my phone and text Deacon. Rephrasing it a few times and backspacing from the shaking of my fingers pushing the wrong buttons, I finally send a message.

> Me: If your brother truly missed me, then he wouldn't have already moved on to someone else. His tattoo is completed. We talked, and it was where he reserved space for my name.

Almost immediately, my phone begins to ring. Deacon's name pops up with the accept button right there, waiting for me to click it.

"Hello?" I answer. My voice squeaks.

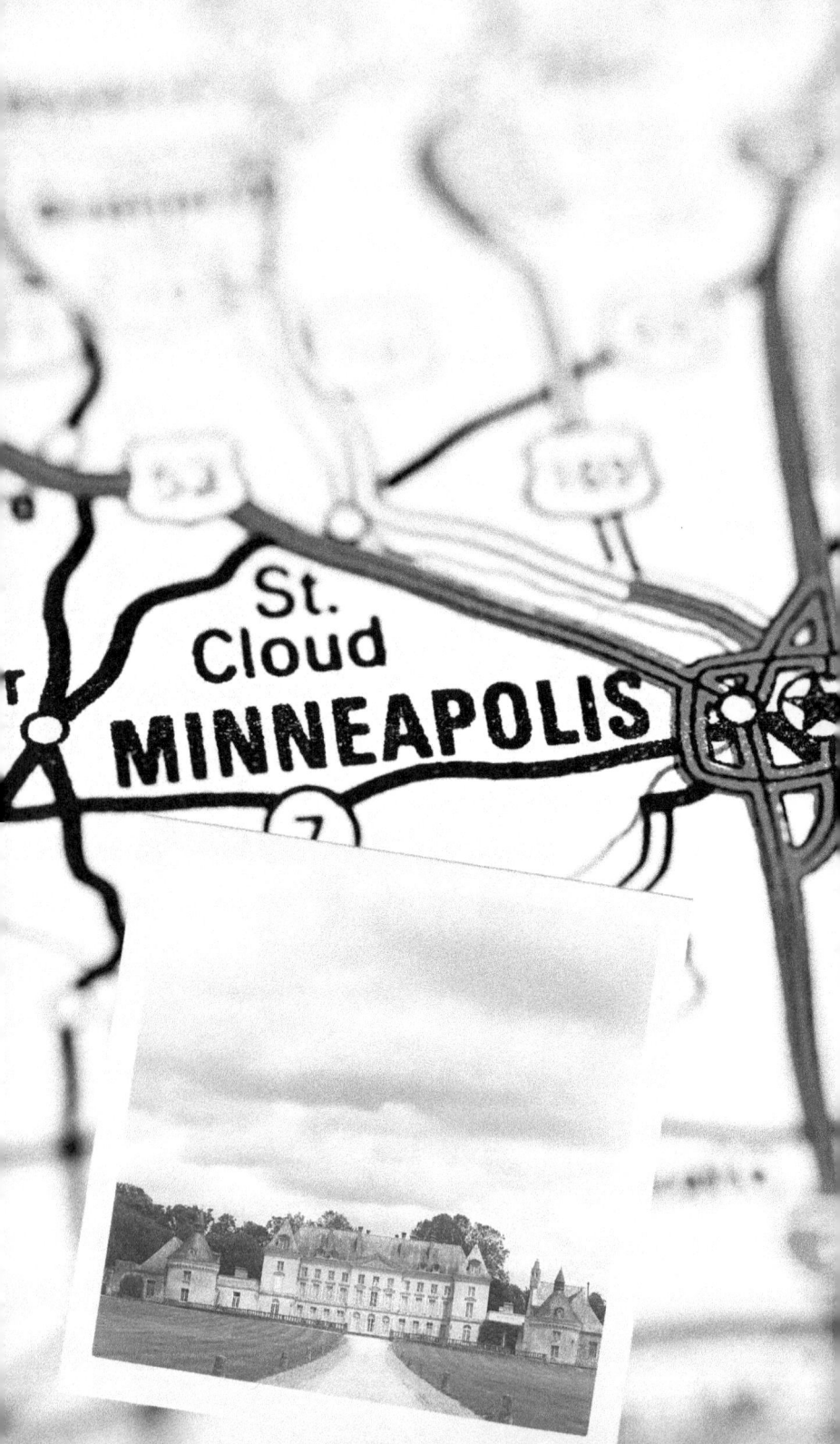

CHAPTER 78
CADE

It's late, and I'm exhausted, but I'm writing tomorrow's to-do list. It's easier to wake up to a list of tasks than clueless or without objectives.

Shit to get done:
- Quit putting off firing the high council.
- Reinstate Judah's access to the pack fund.
- Reinstate Ansel's access to the pack fund.
- Begin building the small council.
- Get Lena started with plans for Summer Solstice.
- Fi

Per usual, I stop myself from writing: find replacement Alpha, call Ansel about ending me, and intimidate Adam until he gives me Thalia's phone number. The list of what I wouldn't do to talk to her again, even if it's just to say one last goodbye, is very short.

The door to my office slams open, rattling as it bounces off the bookcase behind it. Deacon rushes through in its wake.

He's yelling at his phone, "Don't hang up. Seriously, no, please don't hang up, just wait."

I step around the desk, the panicked look in his eye putting me on edge. *What's the issue?* I try to figure out what's going on between his frantic movements and pleading.

Deacon slams into me, hard. He pushes me down to the ground and sits on my chest, wrestling with me as I try to push him off.

"Deacon. What the fuck? Get off me!"

He pushes my arm out to the side.

"Hold still, shut up." Deacon snarls like he's not the one causing the issue.

"Is that your foot in my hand? Disgusting."

I struggle to get away. What the fuck is he doing?

I hear the shutter sound effect from his cell phone.

"Sent! Little red?" Deacon yells at the phone.

Little red. He's talking to Thalia.

I stop fighting. I don't care what he's doing to me. I listen for her voice.

"Little red?" Deacon asks his phone again. His voice drops. He's pleading. "I sent you a picture. Look. Please don't hang up."

There's no answer. My voice must have scared her off. Deacon watches seconds tick by. The phone line disconnects.

CHAPTER 79
CADE

Thalia hung up on Deacon. He told me she thought I had moved on.

The council members all eyed my arm today but said nothing. The two-day-old ink has yet to blend in with the tattoos I had done over the last six years. I think the glare I gave them made it known I wasn't talking about it.

Robert listened to no one about anything, and now everyone has a petty squabble of some nature to attend to. The information I've given the council today about embezzlement doesn't surprise them, which is why, against my better judgment, I haven't let them go yet. I'm positive they're hiding something more. I'm keeping my enemies close for now; none of them know what's really going on in my office. I give them half-truths and let them learn things at the same time as the general public.

I got the money back that was embezzled and am working to reallocate the funds. This has been enough to lull them into a false sense of security that I'm off their trail.

Peter let me hire a team permanently from Corinth

Security, and they're working around the clock. Not only are they the chosen security detail for my family, but they're also following paper trails behind the scenes to uncover what's going on. There are too many inconsistencies.

This particular meeting has devolved into a pissing contest. Each of the council members from the non-Ardelean packs across the country, all seven of them, are trying to plead a case as to why they're special. They try to one-up each other with fucked up reasons as to why their contributions are low or why they need leniency.

I can't keep the complaints straight; I can't keep names straight. Focus on any level for longer than two minutes at a time would be fantastic.

It doesn't sit well that Thalia hung up on Deacon last night. He said she normally texts him back. Well, after I commanded him and gave him no choice but to tell me.

My cell phone rings on my desk, loudly, interrupting the conference call. At this point, I would take a call from a telemarketer to get out of this meeting. Peter's name flashes across the screen with the strobe light going off on the back of my phone in emergency mode.

"Cade, this is incredibly —" Winston begins.

He gestures to my phone. With some self-preservation, he falls silent under my glare.

"You'll excuse me." I pick up my phone and stride out of my office.

Protocol would have it that I ask them to leave, but my gut instinct tells me that waiting isn't an option. I'm down the hallway before I answer my phone.

"Cade?" Peter's voice comes across the line, waiting for me.

"Yeah, Peter, what's wrong?"

I'm waiting for a shoe to drop. *Adam? Millie? Are they okay?*

"Are you sitting down?" Peter asks.

"No." The knots in my stomach churn once more.

"Thalia Clark has been abducted. GDK Security reported a disturbance in her apartment. When they responded, she wasn't there. Her parents received a ransom note this morning."

"Cade!" Lena's voice echoes through the house. "Cade!"

She keeps shouting, running closer.

I meet her halfway down the hallway. She has a large box in her arms. The scent of blood hits me. *No, please don't let this be* . . . Dread pushes my shoulders to my ears.

As soon as she hands it to me, I set it on the floor and rip it open. Vacant dead eyes, glossed over in death, greet me. I move the head aside, examining the mangled carcass. My nose crinkles at the sight.

I speak to Peter, phone pressed between my ear and shoulder. "I got one too. Mine came with a coyote missing its heart."

"The trickster?" Lena whispers.

"They mate for life." I nod and look at her. "Tell the council our meeting is rescheduled. Get them out of the house."

"Cade, you there?" Peter asks.

"I'm here." My voice comes out in a growl.

The Leviathan howls inside me. His bitter loathing toward me, laced with slow-burning anger, is lit ablaze.

I don't blame him. I hate myself too. This wouldn't have happened if I had pushed harder for her to stay.

I stalk through the house to the back staircase and up to the room I've claimed as my own.

"Book a flight. I'm coming to DC. What do you know?"

"GDK lost track of her twelve hours ago. They notified the authorities ten hours ago. The press knows something is wrong, but they don't know what. The Feds are doing the usual transportation checkpoints, et cetera," Peter lists off.

"Useless, two hours after she's been missing. They're out of the city. And, by now, there've been too many people in the apartment for me to get a good scent. Get the details on the GDK agents who were at the press conference the day I brought her back. Tell Adam I want to know everything about them, including where they took their last shit. She had an ex — one of her professors. I need his info too," I demand quickly. There's no time for niceties.

"Cade, The Clarks have specifically asked that you be brought in for questioning. They think you may have her. They want you in police custody." Peter stresses the severity. "I'm fairly certain the police are on board at this point."

I laugh. As it comes out, I feel like a hyena cackling. "I have so many things to say to that. But I'll start with: if I had Thalia, I wouldn't have snuck her out of her apartment in the dead of night."

"Adam's getting the information sent to your phone. Do you still want a flight to DC?" Peter keeps on track with the conversation.

"I'm packing," is all I answer.

Years of experience take over. I'm not even thinking, just packing.

"Millie just updated me. She says the Feds have footage of a man carrying Thalia into the back of a black cargo van. They can't get the plates." Peter keeps relaying information as it comes in.

I put in my earpiece and pull the phone away from my face to see what the beeping on my phone is. Adam's already starting to send info on the wolves.

Alice's voice on Peter's end of the phone is too garbled for me to make out clearly, but I'm busy reading. If she says something that I need to know, Peter will relay it again.

I mute my phone and yell, "Deacon!"

Every second that ticks by is agonizing. I need more information.

The Leviathan has no logical thoughts. He's still refusing verbal communication. The only thing The Leviathan feels is hatred. It grows, and I harness it as fuel for the hunt. Exhaustion is staved off only by the torment of knowing someone has our mate.

"Lena told me. You want me to come with and see if I can talk to anyone the cops can't see?" Deacon asks.

"I know it's a longshot, and I know it's —"

Deacon shakes his head at me, cutting off my sentence. My heart sinks. *I've hurt him too much to ask for this.* I don't ask Deacon to use his gift regularly because of how much chaos it causes him to open the paper-thin door that he tries to barricade closed to the spirit world. *I don't deserve his help.*

"Bags packed." He assures me. "I'll wait for you at the car. Lena is clearing out the council. I called Judah and Ansel."

I'm floored. If I had longer to let Deacon's kindness soak in, I would.

"Cade!" Peter's voice comes from my cell.

I unmute the call. "Yeah. Go again."

"You coming alone?" Peter asks.

"No, book Deacon with me." I pause and confirm. "You're sending my detail here for Lena."

"Copy. You're on the next flight. Leaves in two hours. Our boots are on the next flight to the pack house." Peter confirms.

The phone disconnects.

A sharp pain rips through my abdomen. Every muscle in my chest seems to go tight. Clenching my hand and bringing it to my chest, I pull my hand away, expecting blood from being shot. My whole left arm is tingling with pain. There's no blood. Deacon is next to me, supporting my weight.

"Cade?" he asks. He's nervous, anxious. "Cade, can you hear me?"

I nod, unable to answer. I wince again from the pain. The tension I'd been carrying in my shoulders floods up into my jaw. I try to breathe through it, but my heartbeats are too big. My lungs can't draw air.

The Leviathan fights, thrashing inside me. If there were any sort of mercy from him, he would force the shift and take away the pain. But he doesn't. Blood rushes through my ears, pounding in my head. If this is what fracturing all at once feels like, it's a mercy that Ansel ends them quickly.

CHAPTER 80
CADE

PASSENGERS ON FLIGHT 1178 to Washington, DC, should count themselves incredibly lucky that Deacon sat in the seat between me and the aisle. I might have ripped off every single person's head. From the man who fell asleep and snored the entire way through a two-and-a-half-hour flight, to the toddler screaming "stop the fire truck," and the teenager who constantly spoke at a louder-than-normal speaking volume about how he's not afraid of shifters, I was at my wit's end.

Their noise and annoyance don't dissuade The Leviathan. Nothing around us fazes his pacing in my brain. The fury I keep contained is ready to be unleashed on the first person we find associated with Thalia's kidnapping.

My thoughts are dark, vicious, and consist of murder. When I find her, there will be no mercy. Shifter or human, they will be decimated. The Leviathan has no objection.

WE'VE FOUND our way to Thalia's apartment. Deacon only needs a few moments, and he's used his gift. In a stairwell, he talks with a recently departed building resident. It yields information I'd already assumed. Growls and glowing yellow eyes accompanied the men who wore body- and face-concealing clothing. There's no way for me to scent any shifter that may have been in the building before us. It's too contaminated. I feel lost on our way outside. It was a long shot.

Deacon stops dead on the sidewalk. I turn back to encourage him to come with me.

"North Carolina. Whiskey. Romeo. Echo. Seven. Seven. Four. Nine," Deacon says. He repeats, "North Carolina. Whiskey. Romeo. Echo. Seven. Seven. Four. Nine."

Plate number. My phone is unlocked and dialing. It doesn't feel quick enough. I snap my fingers, urging it to go quicker as I call the tech desk lines.

"Hello."

The voice that answers our technical services line isn't Adam's. I can't expect him to always live at the office. *Damn it.*

"Marjorie, it's Cade. I need you to run a North Carolina license plate: whiskey romeo echo seven seven four nine. Cargo van fitting the description from the Clark abduction." I pause for a moment. "Please."

I hear the keyboard clacking. Marjorie speaks. "I'm so sorry, Cade. Millie made it seem like you and Thalia had gotten close, this must be incredibly hard."

Note to self: Millie needs an ass chewing on keeping my shit private. I wait quietly, not saying anything. It's only a few more minutes before she comes up with some base information and a promise to keep looking. I type the address into my phone. It's a long shot to go where the van is registered to. I'm willing to follow any and every lead.

In the SUV, Deacon looks at me. "Wait, just to be sure, you didn't see the cop with the old-style police hat on, did you?"

"No, I didn't," I answer, focusing on the next destination.

"Oh, cool, well, he saw a redheaded woman tossed in the van, and poor bastard has been trying to radio it in this whole time. I hope someone helps him stop." Deacon shrugs off his statement.

Normally, I'd remind him that he's the only one who can see him, but I'm afraid that today of all days, Deacon would want to go back and talk sense into him, let him know we're on it. But I'm not wasting time to appease a ghost.

CHAPTER 81

THALIA

My head hurts, and everything is dark. My body weighs too much. Everything hurts. My stomach hurts the most.

I peel my eyes open. Something is blocking out the light, only allowing a dull glow. I'm not at home.

I try to breathe, but air isn't coming in. Focus. Where am I? *Oh no, where am I?* I swallow hard. *Where am I?*

He warned me it wasn't safe. Cade said the risk hadn't been resolved. I wasn't safe. I didn't believe him. *Why didn't I believe him?*

Banging on the door, I scream at the top of my lungs. It hurts; the sound hurts my ears. No one's coming. I try screaming again, yelling for help at the top of my lungs. I walk over to the window and try to yell out, hoping someone on the street might hear me. My fists, fingers, and arms hurt from banging on the door, ripping at the fabric stapled over the window, and trying to escape.

CHAPTER 82

CADE

"CADE, a hungry wolf is a dangerous wolf. You haven't slept, and you haven't eaten," Deacon urges.

He brought out a plastic sack of food from the gas station. We're filling up one of Peter's SUVs at the pump.

"I'm not hungry, and I need to be dangerous."

I don't know where we're going. According to the GPS, we're headed into the mountains. I don't know what we're walking into. The more desperate The Leviathan is, the better. It doesn't feel like we're going in the wrong direction. Feelings don't equate to facts, but until Adam is awake and can get me better info than Marjorie, this is what we're dealing with. This is the path we're taking.

Deacon puts a sandwich in my hand. "Listen, I get wanting to be able to rip anyone to shreds. I love her too. But if you eat me, I can't help you."

To appease him, I take a bite of the sandwich. Much like the food of the last couple of weeks, it's tasteless. I force down the sandwich, and Deacon hands me a pop. I try to hand it back to him. The Leviathan doesn't do well on caffeine.

Deacon shakes his head. "We're not driving through the mountains without you awake. You haven't slept. I'm the suicidal one, not you."

I crack open the lid. The carbonation in the soda burns, but outside the physical element, it's sweet and sugary but not appealing. I force it down. I can't save her if I'm not alive to do so. Deacon has a point.

My fear that the address would lead us to a dead end has come full circle. The address we pull up to is in a residential neighborhood. Deacon and I sit, looking at the house. It's the size of a postage stamp with a well-groomed lawn and tiny front porch swing. There's no van in sight.

I look at the clock; it's been over twenty-four hours since Thalia was abducted. The sun is peeking up over the trees to the east.

"So, we going to go out and talk to the locals?" Deacon points down the block. There's no one there.

I look at him, knitting my eyebrows together, and he gives a realizing nod that they're not living people.

Before opening his door, he looks back at me. "Why don't you take a ten-minute nap? I'll figure out what I can."

Deacon's not wrong. I can't keep running on fumes. The caffeine is burning off. The jitters died over an hour ago, and my eyes are heavy.

I struggle and fail to stay awake. Deacon's request for a catnap kicks in.

The door to the SUV opens, and I spring awake. Deacon ducks in fear of my snarl.

The sun, higher in the sky, indicates I've lost more than ten minutes of time. Deacon holds two travel mugs of hot beverages in his hand.

I rub my eyes, trying to distribute moisture. I'm guessing they're dry from sleeping upright.

"Where the fuck did you go? How long was I asleep?" The words are all punctuated by growls.

How did a ten-minute chat with ghosts turn into a coffee run?

"Wave to Miss Gertie, she wants us to bring her mugs back, and I promised we would. So, we'll have to not die." Deacon climbs in. He sniffs the cups, then hands one to me. "Yours is hot cocoa. Mine is coffee, and it's Irish."

As instructed, I wave to the little old woman standing on the front porch of the little postage-stamp house we're parked in front of. She waves back to me before hobbling into the house.

Once she's safely inside, I turn my attention back to him. "Deacon, where the fuck are we going?"

"Oh, right. Back out and take a left." Deacon points, then hands me a donut that he's fished out of the bag from our earlier gas station stop.

I take it and don't ask questions. Deacon seems confident with what we're doing and where we're going.

After he's had a donut and pointed us left and right a bunch of different times, he says, "Miss Gertie's grandson was bitten and turned before shifters were outed to the public. She's known about us for a while. He's a wolf who got caught up with a bunch of mountain lions in the area. She loves him a lot, but he didn't adjust well. Anyway, he's been trying to get close to the new local pack."

"There's not a pack in North Carolina," I answer. "The closest pack is Georgia."

"Oh, see, I asked Gertie about them. They're from

Minnesota, moved down here for warmer weather about the time Senator Clark started putting in new laws."

I listen to Deacon, trying not to rush him.

"They've been building themselves a home just off the Appalachian trail, where apparently he was bitten." Deacon indicates the next turn. "Also, Miss Gertie says she saw you on the news, and she thinks you're very handsome. If she was a few years younger and you weren't clearly head over heels in love with Thalia, she'd make you her fourth husband."

There's a whole lot to unpack there, but all I'm focused on is following signs through the curvy roads toward the Appalachians.

APPALACHIAN
Clarksburg
Elkins
Mount Sterling
Paintsville
Pikeville
Hazard
Norton
CUMBERLAND GAP NAT'L HIST. PARK
Abingdon
Bristol
MT. ROG
NAT'L REC
Harlan
Corbin
Middlesboro
Kingsport
Elizabethton
Boone
Johnson City
Mt. Mitchell 6,684 ft
Greeneville
La Follette
Morristown
Norris Lake
Knoxville
Asheville
Waynesville
Hendersonville
Brevard
Maryville
Oak Ridge
SOUTH FORK
NAT'L RIVER
REC. AREA
GREAT SMOKY MTS. NAT'L PARK
Greenvill
Bluefield
Hinton
Marion
Wythe
Radf

CHAPTER 83
CADE

THE CLOSER WE get to the mountains, the more on edge I am. The Leviathan is pure rage.

We hit the end of Deacon's directions, and he looks around. "There's no one here."

"Appears not."

My lips pull up into a snarl. I'm squeezing the steering wheel so hard it creaks. I don't have time for dead ends. There's a building development, just as Miss Gertie said there would be. But there aren't any workers, no cars, no visual indicators that someone has been here recently.

We've come too far to not get out of the car. I leave the SUV door open, stepping out into the humid air. Birds chirp in the air, and woodland creatures run underneath.

The Leviathan presses to take our skin. This is the first time he's shown interest in being out since the last time we saw Thalia. I trust him. Stripping my shirt off over my head, I kick off my sneakers.

"Okay. We're shifting." Deacon gets out of the car slowly.

"Stay with the SUV," I command.

633

Deacon says nothing; it's not like he has a choice but to stay here. The command and my gift from The Leviathan still work. *Interesting.*

Deacon shakes his head. "Fine, but take your phone with you. That way, I can track you if you get into shit."

The Leviathan and I struggle. It's a hard shift. We're fighting each other about the process, but we adjust.

Deacon ripped apart one of the T-shirts in my bag and tied it into a collar-like sling. The Leviathan hates the feeling of it around his neck, but he carries it without arguing.

APPALACHIAN
Clarksburg
Elkins
Mount Sterling
Paintsville
Pikeville
Bluefield
Bluefield
Hinton
Wytheville
Marion
Hazard
Norton
Abingdon
Bristol
MT. ROG
NAT'L REC
CUMBERLAND GAP NAT'L HIST. PARK
Harlan
Corbin
Middlesboro
Kingsport
Elizabethton
Boone
Johnson City
Mt. Mitchell 6,684 ft
Greeneville
Morristown
La Follette
Norris Lake
Asheville
Knoxville
Maryville
Oak Ridge
SOUTH FORK NAT'L RIVER AND REC. AREA
GREAT SMOKY MTS. NAT'L PARK
Waynesville
Hendersonville
Brevard
Greenville

CHAPTER 84
THALIA

My throat hurts. The sun is sinking. No one's come to save me. Why kidnap me if they have no intention of keeping me alive? Tears roll down my face, and I wipe them away. I'm lying as far as I can from the door. *Is this where my life is going to come to an end?*

Ever so softly, the sound of a door unlocking catches my attention. The door creaks, swinging open slowly. No one's there. Doors don't just open themselves. That door was locked. I'm sure of it.

Inhaling sharply, I freeze on the spot, straining my ears to pick up any other noises. I wait for something, anything to happen.

Nothing.

It's not too dark to see but dark enough to be extra cautious. Slowly I stand up, skirting the wall, trying to look in the hallway outside the bedroom door. My heart thunders in my chest. I draw short quick breaths trying to stay calm and make level decisions. I don't see anyone. I don't see how this door would have opened. Am I imagining this?

Run.

Hallway, stairs going down. I follow them, looking for a door. I find a front door. It's locked. I try to unlock it, but the door doesn't move. I run to the kitchen and try that door. It's locked too. Rummaging through the cabinets, I look for anything I can use as a weapon. Of course, a gun would be nice because, you know, that's what my security detail taught me to use. I find a knife. It's a crummy little steak knife. But better than what I started with?

I feel my heartbeat in every part of my body. I need to find a way out. *It's a trap!*

CHAPTER 85
CADE

THE LEVIATHAN ALLOWS me to shift back to human form. Night has fallen. Standing in the trees, The Leviathan tunes in to the sounds of maniacal, evil laughter. A chorus of seven cackles, by the sounds of it, a hunting party.

I pull my phone out and crouch low, blocking the light. I text Deacon.

> Me: Figure out how to get as close to me as you can.

I don't wait for a response and put it back in the makeshift bag around my torso. The Leviathan helps me stalk quietly through the woods. Bare feet nimbly pick across brush and leaf litter. The scent of green wood smoking before trying to burn covers the air as I pull closer. It hangs low among the trees, skewing the scents through the area. I pick up a few independent scents from the group laughing ahead, but it's not enough. A waft of air smells like Thalia, but I'm not positive.

I skirt around the fire, back across the wind line. No sense in letting them smell me either. If they lit the green wood to create smoke and distort scents, I'll use it to my advantage.

I stalk within a hundred feet of their bonfire, unseen. I settle in, listening.

"So, will she take an animal or just die?" one asks, gesturing toward the house.

The Leviathan calls for blood. She's here. We both know it. I hold him back. We can't see her; we can't find her if they're all dead.

"Isabel said it doesn't matter if she does or doesn't," the second says, taking a swig from his beer.

A third stands up.

I crouch lower, nearly lying prone, but he walks the other way off to a cooler.

As he walks back from the cooler, he says, "Yeah, but wouldn't it be just perfect if she became a cat? What's he called? Cale? Cade? The Lochness? Not only is his mate the daughter of the senator he hates, but then she'd be a cat. Wolves get touchy about mating outside the species, right?"

A man comes from the house. "She not lookin' too good. Sure there ain't nothin' we can do for her?"

"Nope. Either an animal will save her, or she dies. Nothing to do but wait," another one chimes in.

"Her screams though. They were sure pretty." This voice comes from a man who leans back in his chair. I recognize his voice. The wolf from the gatehouse. "Too bad we can't have more fun with her. Tight piece like that. I don't understand Isabel. She wants this bitch out of the way, so what better way than to ruin her for any other man."

My blood runs cold. I'm burning with anger. My eyes glance across each of them, formulating the best plan to take them out. Control is necessary.

We will slaughter. All. Eight is not too many. The Leviathan is so sure of himself. *Let out. Will destroy.*

"Don't be sick. Chasing her and turning her is one thing. Forcing yourself on her is another," the second one says.

Maybe he lives. We need one to confirm the story.

"Possibly killing her is fine, but having sex with her isn't?" the wolf from the gatehouse says. He stands up from his chair, stepping toward the house. "Besides, what Isabel doesn't know won't hurt her."

The Leviathan can't be contained. Four feet hit the ground, and the smell of blood overpowers the scent of burning wood.

CHAPTER 86

CADE

WHEN FILLED with rage and left to act without my restraint, The Leviathan can kill six shifters without any issues. He left two of them alive. Well, alive-ish. We'll see how long they survive. And if Thalia's dead, they will be too.

They've left her on the floor on a pile of blankets that reek of mildew. The relief at seeing the rise and fall of her chest quickly turns back to rage when I see the blood and cuts covering her body. I approach quickly but cautiously. If she does shift for the first time, I don't want to risk hurting her by subduing her in a small space.

Our mate no animal. Must give her wolf. The Leviathan is so sure of himself.

I shake my head. *She's perfect human. This wasn't her choice. This wasn't how this should have been.*

She is death. The Leviathan confirms again. *Give ours wolf, give draga mea life.*

Thalia draws a ragged breath. I hear the gurgle of blood in her lungs. Her face is shades of black and blue. Her eyes can't open, and the little movement from her body drawing breath is gone. Her heartbeat is faint, too faint, as it slows.

I'm not even sure she can hear me. "Draga mea, I'm so sorry."

The Leviathan doesn't waste time shifting into wolf form. He's as gentle as he can be with this final assault on her body.

Thalia's scream when The Leviathan bites her feels like an indication the wolf is going to take. Her painful yelp nearly shatters our eardrums.

The Leviathan allows me our body back. It feels like I'm waiting for a miracle. Then, it happens.

I can sense her wolf.

I pick her up and carefully carry Thalia around the carnage of the backyard to the plush overgrown side yard covered in clovers.

I listen for the two The Leviathan left breathing. They're still alive, for now. A wolf and mountain lion, their bodies, healing slowly, are nothing to worry about.

Our mate's wolf beautiful. Gray-black fur. Dark as night. The Leviathan pictures this beautiful animal. He pictures running with her and claiming her. *Did not need violence. Claimed ours. One bite for King of Wolves. Anyone Wolf. Like The Pricolici give wolf in one bite. Claim our mate. Turn her in one bite. Turn everyone, one bite. Kept diverting bite. You coward.* The Leviathan berates me, giving me this information now. Repeating it.

There's nothing for me to say. I did divert the bite. Part of me, deep inside, knew what would happen if I did. I've never heard of someone who wasn't on death's doorstep being turned, but why risk it? I knew all this time she would end up wolf, and rather than being at home, in the comfort of family, I let this happen instead. She's transitioning in a bed of clover after being chased and tortured. This could have been in our bed on clean sheets.

Watching Thalia breathe is the only thing I can do. There's no way I'm leaving her side. Each breath grows just a little bit stronger. I don't know how long we sit and wait.

Soon. The wolf grows strong. The Leviathan shuffles his paws in anticipation.

Her body snaps as the wolf takes over. It's a nasty transition. Slow and painful, it takes her body time to go through the motions. I've seen hundreds of transitions but nothing so torturous.

When it passes, I'm eye to eye with a very angry black and gray wolf. I move to my feet, crouching and holding myself as close to the ground as I can. Ready to shift if needed.

She's fucking gorgeous.

I told you our mate beautiful. The Leviathan reminds me. The condescension isn't missed.

Thalia draws in long deep breaths. As she makes her way to her feet, her movements are uneasy and uncoordinated. Her body's weak. Malnourished and coming back from the brink of death, I'm surprised she has any energy at all. What's worse is that combination with wolves is potentially deadly. I don't have an offering of food to sate her wolf.

She's watching me. I see her wolf analyze and recognize. It's a very Thalia expression.

Headlights come up the driveway as we stand there. She tries to flee. Her feet tangle, and she falls onto her chest with a loud thump.

"Shhh, draga mea. It's Deacon." I kneel next to her. "We'll get you cleaned up, fed, and home."

She whines, and my heart breaks.

I wrap my arms into her fur, holding her closely. "I'm so sorry. I'm sorry."

CHAPTER 87

THALIA

I CAN'T FOCUS. The entire world is loud. There are sounds of voices and yelling. Vehicle doors opening, slamming closed, and driving on different surfaces. It all sounds like it's happening right in my ear. A helicopter flies low overhead and I wince because it sounds like it's right on top of me.

The lights from the ambulance and police cars are overwhelming. The flashing emergency lights are the most disorienting. The ambulance I'm sitting behind has a harsh light; there's flood lamps put up nearby. Headlights of cars, SUVs, and a firetruck flash and flicker everywhere.

The EMT asks a lot of questions. She pokes and prods. My body is tender all over, but I'm not in excruciating pain. Nothing like the pain before. It feels like a lost memory. Did it even happen? It must have. I'm hot and dirty. There's bruising and scabs. But I'm not bleeding? Is any of it my blood?

"You're sure you don't want to see a doctor?" she confirms again.

It's like she's urging me to go to the hospital but can't advise me to. This time she's making sure I'm looking at her. I heard her the first two times. I hear everything. I'm guessing this is what wolf healing looks like.

"I feel fine. It looks a lot worse than it is. I just want to go home." I nod, assuring her.

I'd read that shifters hear, see, and smell better. It made sense when I apply it to everything that I'd learned when I was with them. Is that what this is? I'm a shifter.

Is this my new normal?

Drawing a massive breath, I push those thoughts away. I don't want to think about that right now. I can't think about that right now. I just want to have a massive plate of food, climb under the blankets, and sleep until I'm no longer numb inside.

Cade stands at a distance, maybe a hundred feet away, constantly watching me, sometimes directly and others just out of the corner of his eye. Police officers and federal agents approach him. No one even tries to call him away.

They keep talking about the men and the bodies from the back yard. I heard one of them scream while they loaded him into an ambulance. His screams matched his laugh. That's how I know that those men, those bodies, are better off dead.

Am I in trouble? I draw a deep breath. The scent of blood in the air hits my nose. *It was self-defense. Whatever I did, if I killed them, they took me first.* The law would be on my side. I'm pretty sure. Worse comes to worse, Mom will handle it. She won't let this *incident* tarnish her career.

Unless, it was Cade? He came for me. It's possible . . . it is possible that he'd kill for me. Would he be in trouble? I swallow hard. How can I protect him if he's in trouble? No, I don't have to protect him.

He didn't have to come for me either . . .

Cade's wearing his signature Henley and jeans. It's like the first day we were together all over again. Everything has changed, yet nothing has changed at all. Cade's taking me away from a dangerous situation. But this time, when someone came into my apartment in the night, they took me and not just pictures.

A federal agent walks over to Cade. With his back to me, he begins talking to Cade. Unable to read his lips, I can't determine what he's saying. I focus, trying to hear Cade's response.

"The two gentlemen still alive confirmed your story. We've found Isabel LeFleur and she's in custody. What would you like for us to do with her?" I hear the man talking despite the distance and that his back is to me.

This is handy.

Cade's voice is crystal clear. "It's a pack matter. Have transport arranged back to Minnesota. I'll deal with it myself. Have the Clarks been notified?"

"They know you've found her alive and that we have people in custody. There's a large push for details, but given the complexity of the situation, it seemed best to have further contact go through you," he says, nodding to Cade.

"Am I good to take her?" Cade asks without physically indicating to me at all.

The agent does look at me. It's uncomfortable having his eyes on me. I look away, still listening.

"You'll make her available for questioning?"

"Yes. She just needs a few days to adjust," Cade says.

Movement catches my attention, and the agent walks away from Cade quickly.

Cade starts walking toward me. I hear growling and look around. He's twenty feet from me when he stops moving.

"That's coming from you," Cade says quietly. Putting his hand over his sternum, he shows me what to do. "Feel the sound in your chest."

I mimic him and feel it. I try to stop it. I don't know how. Why? How?

Breathing becomes hard. I force air into my lungs, but the growling only sounds scarier.

"Thalia, settle." His voice is firm and commanding.

The rumbling inside ceases. It's like I had no choice in it. He said it, so I did. *Like the panic attacks before.* My body feels relaxed, and while I'm aware of everything going on around me, it's like nothing can bother me.

He moves slowly, letting me watch him.

When Cade gets close to the gurney I'm on, he whispers, "Let's get you out of here. Then we can talk."

Cade fidgets. It almost seems like he's trying not to touch me.

Why would he want to touch me? We're nothing to each other. He lied to me. He doesn't want to touch me because he doesn't want me now that I'm not human. I'm not important to his cause. He lied. He's never loved me.

"Thank you for the clothes."

That's probably the dumbest thing to say in this situation, but it's what comes out. I'm drowning in one of his Henleys and a pair of sweatpants.

There's a small smile on Cade's face. He shuffles. "You don't have shoes. I'll carry you to the SUV."

There's a small part of me that wants him to carry me. I want the closeness. Even if the feeling of his body against mine is a lie. I won't give in to it. Cade's the enemy, but he's my ticket out of here that doesn't involve hospitals.

I stay strong and shake my head. "I think I can walk."

I try to hop off the gurney onto the ground, but somehow, the ground got much closer to my face than I remembered.

Cade's arms wrap around me. His voice is low. "Yeah,

something tells me you don't have any fuel in the tank to walk that far."

Effortlessly, Cade pulls me up and into his arms. I'm draped across him bridal style, warm and protected. I'm wrapped up, held against his neck.

Each breath I draw pulls in more of his scent. The woodsy and warm scent I attributed to him before has changed. It's richer and more complex. *Are there words for all these smells?*

I want to object and try walking again because I don't want to need him the way I do.

He's lied to me. He's lied to me. He's lied to me.

I keep that thought, fueling rage to burn against the softness and care he's giving me. Even though he feels like home.

A black SUV is parked just down the road, on the very edge of the police line. Deacon gets out of the passenger seat when we approach, opening the door for us.

"Hey, little red." Deacon smiles.

I smile back. Then remind myself that he lied to me too. He told me that Cade was honest and trustworthy. It's partly his fault I hurt like this.

I force myself not to smile. Cade tucks me into the back seat. Before he closes the door, he looks at me like he wants to say something, but no words come. Deacon takes the driver's seat.

"Ancestors say the police have the media held off down the main road. I looked at the map, and we can take Miss Gertie's mugs back to her on the way back to DC." Deacon points to spots on the GPS in the car.

"We can't go back to DC. I don't have what we need there," Cade says softly.

"New wolves generally take two or three days before they shift a second time, you're not thinking of getting her back home first?" Deacon pulls his hand to his mouth as Cade nods through his question. Deacon's eyes are so wide that I can see the bright whites. "Cade that's two days. With a new wolf. In an SUV. Across the country."

"I want to go home," I say. "I want to go to *my* home. Not Wisconsin."

"There's no going home." Cade's voice is cold. "You don't have any control over your wolf. I can't take you to DC until you can shift at will."

"Then call my mom. She'll find a property in upstate Pennsylvania. I'm not going back to Wisconsin." Anger rolls through me.

Deacon shuffles in his seat, almost as if he's trying to get away from me.

"Your mother has no jurisdiction over you right now, Thalia. Given our last conversation, I understand you're not thrilled with me. I'm the Sovereign. Until you have control, you're with me," Cade says, his voice remaining calm. It feels emotionless.

CHAPTER 88

CADE

I'VE HEARD the human phrase about their higher powers not giving you more than you can handle. I'm beyond a doubt certain, if that is a universal saying, it does not apply to wolves or, at the very least, not to me. Because from where I'm sitting, my life just became more than I can and will be able to handle. I'm Sovereign, rejected by my mate, and just gifted said rejected mate an Alpha wolf who quakes enough force to scare Deacon. I'm not even sure I scare Deacon.

Thalia sits fuming in the back passenger seat of the SUV. Arms crossed over her chest, glaring out the window, she's blissfully unaware of the Alpha wolf she harnesses. I rack my brain, trying to remember what I've learned about bitten wolves.

Anger, violence, volatile. The descriptors don't bode well for this trip home.

The Leviathan is constantly focused on Thalia. *Mate mad. Wolf feral. Will calm. Needs time.*

How much time? I ask, but The Leviathan doesn't feel like answering more questions.

Lore says it's days between shifts, but I think I remember hearing it could be weeks before she's fully settled. Until then, we'll see uncharacteristic anger, the likelihood of wanting to fight everyone, and explosive mood swings. *Fucking great.*

"So, let me guess, you'd rather we didn't drive by Miss Gertie's and get her the mugs back today," Deacon says sadly.

"She's a timebomb, Deacon. I have to get her someplace she can detonate. We will personally drive down, thank Miss Gertie, and bring her mugs back. Just not today." I nod.

I owe that woman a lot more than two travel mugs. If it weren't for her being willing to talk to Deacon, Thalia wouldn't be alive.

Gifted strong wolf. Great mate. The Leviathan paces, *why she not like you. I not know.*

I know, and I don't know that I can fix this. Once the bill had passed, I had hoped I could spend some time in DC, trying to get her to see me. I just had to survive long enough to see if she would give me a chance.

"This is ridiculous. Take me home," Thalia argues again in the back seat. "I'm not a bomb. I can hear you. I'm fine. I need a nap. That's it."

"She knows, right?" Deacon asks quietly.

"Knows what?" Thalia snaps at him.

"Little red, you're a wolf," Deacon tells her softly lowering his head in a cower.

He's pressed as far against the driver's side door as possible while still being in the vehicle.

Thalia growls. It's vicious as she spits, "Yeah. I figured that out. But I feel fine. I don't understand why everyone's making a big deal out of it."

"Deacon, drive," I use the Alpha command. "Thalia, quiet."

Thalia tries to object, but it comes out as a grumble as my Alpha command stifles her ability to talk back. Her wolf is unsettled, working to try and carve out space inside. Thalia might feel physically okay despite her injuries, but that's shifter healing. Her behavior, though . . . is that because she hasn't developed a full consciousness of her wolf? I refuse to believe it's Thalia. There's no way the woman I love is truly this way. *I fucking hope not.* Regardless, if I've got to command her wolf into submission like this for the next day to get her home, where it's safe, so be it.

AND, so it fucking was.

I've never considered the Regent pack property home, but today, driving through the main gate, I've never been so relieved to be home. Trading off driving with Deacon through the night, I've had to command Thalia to behave nonstop, and Deacon's been jumping out of his seat nearly every time she growls. I want to take my mate to bed and sleep for two days, but she's not my mate right now. Her wolf isn't settled, she's pissed off at the world, and I'm sure my to-do list has exponentially grown while I wasn't here. There's no rest for the wicked.

"Never pictured you as a gated community kind of guy, Cade," Thalia quips as the wrought iron slides closed behind us.

I slam on the breaks. Gripping the steering wheel, I grit my teeth. I'll take this attitude from Lena. Not from her. I don't have to hold it together on the road anymore. She wants to behave this way, then I'll show her the consequences of it. Mate or not, she needs to learn the hierarchy and how shit works.

The Leviathan agrees, growling.

Deacon, choked awake by his seat belt, looks around.

"What's wrong?"

"Get out!" The command is part growl and part yell.

Between her witty remarks and The Leviathan's constant desire to claim her, I'm at my wit's end.

Deacon gets out of the car and leaves the door open, his eyes wide, body half crouched, ready to move, eyes darting around, determining whether we're looking at the car to blow up or each other.

Thalia gets out of the car and stands with her arms crossed, looking back at the gate, which is the opposite direction of me.

"Deacon, drive up to the house, please, and tell Lauren I need the guest suite next to mine made up."

I glare at Thalia, hoping she feels the heat of my eyes.

"Oh, Lauren, she the new mate?" Thalia doesn't even bother looking at me when she throws that punch.

Outside of Deacon's wolf form, he normally doesn't run, but he sprints to close the car doors before hopping in the driver's side, the SUV peeling off up the driveway.

The wind blows her scent to me. We're both filthy and disgusting. Dirty, bloody, and smelly from the days without a bath. I start walking away from her, shaking my head.

The mountain of fast food we got on the ride home wasn't the most nutritious fuel for her body, but it's enough to walk the half mile home. Of course, she's free to walk herself wherever she wants around the property. The gate house won't let her out without approving it through me, and the sentries have confirmed that the six-foot-high fence is intact and clear all the way around the property. So, unless she can figure out how to shift and jump it, there aren't a whole lot of options for her.

Her footfalls sound behind me, and I slow down, letting her catch up. She's content to walk behind me.

I try diplomacy. "Lauren is the chief of staff for the pack

house. You'll be nice to her. She's a wonderful woman."

"Never saw you as the kind of person who would let someone clean for him. Figured you were a hard worker." Thalia keeps jabbing.

Years of dealing with Lena have toughened me. I'm not going to get into her petty attacks.

"But that was all a show, wasn't it? We were playing house, it wasn't maintainable because that's not who you are."

Thalia wins. The pettiness is enough.

I turn to face her, The Leviathan with me, our eyes bright gold.

I push back. "And this? Is it really you? Because the Thalia I got to know, the one I grew to love, she didn't behave this way. Bitchiness isn't a trait of wolves. It's a character flaw."

Thalia doesn't say anything.

I shake my head. "The woman I fell in love with was the least judgmental woman in the world. She sat at a table and played cards with Ansel and his pack of partly fractured. She spent hours on my sofa talking to my brother like he was her best friend. Even when he was stoned out of his mind or talking to dead people. And when she went and held her own against the biggest bitch I know, she used facts and tangible ideas over petty jabs at character."

"That woman is dead when it comes to you," Thalia snaps. Her eyes gleam gold.

It's too soon for her wolf to come out again. I shake my head.

Our mate strong. Will push for our dominance. Then we claim her. The Leviathan sees right past the part of our relationship that's broken.

I don't know how to fix it.

Tears well in Thalia's eyes when I say nothing.

She sneers, "You've no idea. That's the worst of it. It's like you've no concept that you've hurt me."

"You won't talk to me. How am I supposed to know?" I step toward her and plead.

She shakes her head and looks away. "You fucking used me. You broke my heart. Now my life will never be the same. It's all because of you."

"You're right."

She looks at me with her jaw dropping.

I finish my thought. "There's nothing for me to say. If that's how you want to see me, if that's all the further you want to look into what's happened, then there's nothing to say."

"When can I leave? Or am I hostage here too?" Thalia diverts again.

"You can leave after your next couple shifts. You're not stable until then," I answer, then walk away.

Hostage. She was never a hostage with me before. Comparing me to them is a low blow. It doesn't stop her words from cutting my flesh like the fangs she'll learn to use soon.

"I've plenty of control. I haven't turned into a wolf and bitten your head off. That's got to be proof enough." She argues with me.

"It's because you can't. According to The Leviathan, you can't shift again for another day or two, something to do with you two making peace about sharing the same space." I try to explain what The Leviathan tells me in actual words rather than his broken sense of right and wrong.

"That's bullshit!" Thalia shouts.

I keep walking. "Suit yourself. If you can figure out how to shift back and forth on your own, I'll personally book you a one-way ticket home."

Our mate not settled. No shift. The Leviathan pushes me to go back to her. He doesn't understand why I'm grieving her. *Go back. See our mate. Hold her.*

CHAPTER 89

THALIA

CADE WALKS AWAY, leaving me alone on the driveway with no shoes, dressed in his oversized clothes. At least he's rich enough for a paved driveway.

I'm stewing my way up to the house before I reach a split in the driveway — a jarring turn to the right or more to the left and up a hill. *Great, which way to the stupid house?*

A strong pull inside me says left and up the hill. I'm tired and hungry and follow my gut feeling. Would it kill people to have signs in this sort of situation?

I come up to the most ostentatious house I've ever seen in the States. It's massive and looks nothing like what I would picture Cade having been raised in. In the driveway, men are detailing the black SUV we drove here. I can't believe I didn't realize Cade was used to coming from this kind of money. He seemed so different. The suit in the beginning said it all. Peter Corinth doesn't have to pay well. His security specialist comes from money. Cade truly is king of the wolves.

I stand at the front door, debating opening it or ringing the bell. Maybe if I stand here long enough, it'll open by itself.

The door does open, but not on its own. Lena's sporting a snotty smirk, and she leans against the door frame, arms across her chest, blocking my entry.

"Aww, Miss Clark. You look like death and smell like piss."

"Lena," I answer coldly.

I hate that she's been right about all of this. I should have listened to her when she told me I was just the girl warming her brother's bed. I would have the same attitude problem as the one honest person in this house.

"Oh, do come in." She moves, making way for me.

I walk into the house. It's in a state of organized disrepair. Renovations? Work seems to be happening in all the rooms as she leads me up a staircase.

She opens a door and ushers me in. I expect her to close me in here and leave me alone, but instead, she shows herself in, closes the door, and looks me up and down.

"You're going to look so hot as a wolf." Lena smiles.

It's uncharacteristic. I stare at her, hoping she understands that her joy is confusing. If she notices my confusion, she ignores it. *What the hell is with the 180 on the attitude?*

"Come on, let's get you cleaned up. I'm not living in the same house with you like this." She shows me into a bathroom and starts turning on fixtures. "I'll call in a few favors and get someone out here who can cut curly hair tomorrow. We'll get you put back together and so hot, you won't notice the length loss."

"Lena, I'm perfectly capable of cleaning myself up," I try to explain to her.

"Mmhmm." She nods, turning on the hot water in a massive steam shower.

Before leaving, she looks at me with golden eyes. "Listen, I know you're mad at him. I know you don't understand that he doesn't get what he did was wrong. Getting your shifts under control, running back home, and being your mother's perfect, freshly minted wolf daughter isn't the life you want. Forgive him and get over it."

"Oh, so what, you and I are friends now?" I snap.

Shouldn't I want friends? Even if she's a bitch?

"Uff." Lena laughs, putting her hand over her heart, mocking me. "Deacon wasn't kidding about being afraid. You're going to be one hell of a queen bitch."

"What?" I ask, furrowing my brow at her.

"Get in the shower. I'll bring you some clean clothes."

As Lena leaves, I want to tell her there's no way I'll fit her stuff. She isn't stick skinny, but the curves she sports are significantly tighter and more intentional than mine. But I don't argue. When they don't fit, we'll find a second plan.

I don't know how long I scrub, trying to get clean. Dried blood covers my body. I've barely managed to get blood off half my body. The water runs murky brown across the white tile floor. Tears are streaming, and I can't stop them. I don't know what I'm doing. Why is getting clean so hard? This is pathetic. I only want one person to help me deal with all this, but he broke my heart. And that betrayal still cuts deep.

Lena is back, knocking on the bathroom door. "Thalia, do you want some help?"

"Any tricks for getting blood out of your hair?" I call back, angry tears running down my face.

"Several. Do you want me to come in?" she asks softly.

I'm trying to come up with an answer. I'm not a prude, but Cade's sister shouldn't see me naked. Lena doesn't come in, apparently understanding my dilemma. I keep trying to scrub my arms clean.

Tears are in my eyes. My stomach is growling. Everything seems so hard.

The door opens.

"I'm fine, Lena. I'm sorry."

It's not Lena. Cade's smell wafts in through the steam from the shower. His presence in the bathroom seems so large. I swallow hard. The sound of jeans and his shirt hitting the floor reaches my ears. I turn and face the wall, wiping tears from my eyes. It feels pointless trying to hide crying.

"Shhh, draga mea." Cade rubs my shoulders.

The gentleness of his touch breaks the dam, and I heave with sobs. He doesn't falter. He just stands there, comforting me and letting me cry. My shoulders shake less under the calm of his touch. Cade offers no words of comfort, but his hands carefully work on cleaning me from the top down.

His fingers on my scalp pull gently through my wet curls. Through bleary eyes in my peripheral, I see him shake wet strands off his fingers, leaving a sizable discard pile of loose hairs. I catch a glimpse of myself in the mirror, and between my reflection and the growing pile, I understand Lena's comment about a hairdresser. I remember the ripping and pulling and snarling so close to my head. It explains the jagged pieces and shorter areas. It's hideous.

I stand, arms wrapped around myself as he works, neither of us saying anything. The water circling the drain begins to run clearer, not the russet-red color of blood.

Cade grabs a washcloth. Holding my hair, he cares for me, washing the blood from the back of my neck down. Somehow, it's effortless for him. I'm not in any pain until he hits a spot on my right shoulder.

I wince, stepping away from him. That whole shoulder is tender and angry feeling.

"I'm sorry," Cade apologizes softly. He works the skin more gently. "The Leviathan says once you and your wolf become more connected, the bite that gave you your wolf will become less painful."

"You saved me?" I ask.

Cade doesn't say anything, but a look over my shoulder is all I need to see.

"And you wish you hadn't." I accuse.

"No," Cade says quickly. "I don't wish that at all. I wish you'd hear me out, but at least, for now, you're clean."

Cade leaves me alone in the large shower. He dries himself off and dresses while I turn off the water.

I can't talk with you if you won't stay in the same room with me.

When I come out of the bathroom wrapped in a towel, Lena is sitting on the bed with a pile of clothing. Graciously, I take them into the bathroom and put them on. Weirdly, the clothes she brought me are big, which feels strange considering Lena's smaller than me. Maybe they're not hers. They smell like her. Maybe she was just carrying them. She's a few inches taller than me, but her curves look more muscular than my soft ones always have.

She looks at me with laser focus as I emerge from the bathroom.

"Oft dah, your wolf is burning you up." Lena looks at me with what looks like concern. "For science, I wish we had a pre-bite set of measurements."

"What?"

Lena isn't making sense. First, something strange about Deacon being afraid of me, and now this.

"You didn't notice how much we all ate when you stayed with us?" Lena asks.

I shrug. "I don't know. I assumed it was a Midwest thing."

"Oh, for fuck's sake." Lena puts her hands on her hips and glances at the ceiling. With her sigh, her shoulders, stomach, and everything slumps. Another short breath and she says, "You're a wolf now. You're an Alpha Female. And, honestly, I'm jealous as fuck, because, of course, you have an Alpha wolf.

That's The Leviathan for you. Wolves need to eat, a lot. We don't have three meals a day just because food tastes good, which is a good enough reason all on its own. New wolves burn fuel while settling. Even if your clothes hadn't been destroyed, I'm fairly certain they'd be too big. You're wasting away. Come on, move your butt. I'm hungry."

Following Lena, I ask, "Deacon's afraid of me?"

"Deacon isn't afraid of a lot of things, but yes, you're now on that short list of shit that scares him." Lena holds open the door.

"Because I'm a wolf?" I ask, trying to catch up.

I don't understand any more than when I was human. *Are there wolf classes I can take?*

"No, because you're as unhinged as I am but have dominance like The Leviathan," Lena explains.

"I'm not unhinged." I object. *Rude.*

"Oh, okay." Lena laughs. "That's not the story Deacon tells."

I want to ask her what she means by that, but we're walking downstairs and there are people around.

I freeze at the last step. A crew of men laugh as they work on some area of the living space off to the left. My heart thunders in my chest. I swallow hard, my skin breaking out in a sweat. Their laughter puts me on edge. My feet are stuck. I can't force myself forward.

Lena stops, looking back at me. Her expression softens. Briefly, I see perhaps the first bit of nurturing and softheartedness. Mask firmly back in place, she turns and looks at the men in the living room.

"Gentlemen," Lena barks. It's a sharp, angry sound. She cuts into them with a glare. "Some respect for the Luna."

The men go silent, taking steps away from the staircase and

lowering their gazes to the floor. No one looks at me but Lena. She waits for me offering her hand.

Softness seeps through her words. "It's okay. They wouldn't dare hurt you."

With Lena's coaching, I walk past them.

"Thank you, gentlemen," Lena calls with a complete change of tone, waving over our shoulders. She wraps her arm around me. "I'm really sorry you've felt unsafe. You don't have to worry, the work crew is pack. No one here will hurt you."

I'm in the twilight zone. I'm sure of it.

Lena leads me into the kitchen. We're rooting through one of several fridges. It feels so weird to be in a residence with a kitchen this big and industrial. I'm looking around and wobble.

"Thalia, why don't you sit down? I can kinda, not really, cook. Let's catch up." Lena smiles at me again.

Is she just being nice to me because Cade fucked up? Is this her job in the pack? Why does she suddenly care about me? If she didn't care, would she be doing any of this? There're so many questions. Weird doesn't even begin to explain this.

CHAPTER 90

CADE

Do I regret saving her?

She asked me that. Does she really not know how much I love her? Am I wrong, and this is how love is supposed to be?

Who am I kidding? I would never regret saving her.

I'm dressed again and back in my office. I have over a hundred emails from the last two days. Opening and combing through the excruciatingly dry contents sounds less painful than the phone call I have to make.

I dial the number slowly, double-checking each number before I hit the call button. The phone rings twice.

"Hello?" Senator Clark answers.

"Hello, Senator. It's Cade Alden," I start.

"It's true then?" she asks. "My daughter is with you?"

"Yes. I was able to save Thalia's life. She's healing well. Given her state, I've brought her to my home to recover."

I try to highlight the fact that Thalia is alive.

The line is quiet for a moment, and I hear sobbing sounds. I don't know what to say. There's no formal protocol for this situation. So, I do what I know how to do, wait.

673

"Cade?" Ambassador Clark's voice gets louder. "This is Darren. You're confirming that Thalia is alive, and she is now a wolf."

"Correct. I rescued Thalia from where she was mauled and bitten by various shifters. She's had her first shift as a wolf. If it weren't for the wolf accepting her, she would be dead." I pause, pinching the bridge of my nose before offering, "She's currently having a meal. But I'd be glad to have her call you in about an hour."

"Is she safe?" Senator Clark asks.

"Very safe. I can't extend an invitation for you to visit just yet. She needs to have some time as a wolf. But, with how strong —" I catch myself before calling her mine. "With how strong and determined she is, I believe Thalia will adjust within a few days."

Senator Clark cries again. Did I make the right choice in saving their daughter? I don't regret saving her, but am I the only one?

"Please keep us posted. If she wants to speak with us, please have her call us," Darren says. "Thank you, Cade."

"You're welcome. I will do so."

The phone disconnects on their end.

Our mate is perfect. They will love her wolf. The Leviathan shows his lack of understanding of the situation.

CHAPTER 91

THALIA

I'M NOT ALONE. I'm never alone. There's this whole other entity in my brain lurking in the depths of my mind. It should be alarming, shouldn't it? It should feel more intimidating than this, shouldn't it? Cade explained The Leviathan like a snarky, ever-present pain in the ass. The Leviathan can be alert and focused on different things than Cade.

She's, well, not. I know she's there. It's like thinking you've seen something out of the corner of your eye, but when you turn your head, nothing's there. Not alone is the only way I can explain it. Even then, it doesn't do the feeling justice.

Dusk is falling, and from the balcony of the suite that's been made up for me, I watch Cade shift. Seeing him shift for the first time makes my skin crawl, but he's there, going through contortions that look painful, only to give way to The Leviathan stretching. Despite Cade never complaining about the pain of a shift, my body aches thinking about what that must feel like. The Leviathan takes a few steps before looking over his shoulder. I assume The Leviathan can see me standing in the window watching him.

An eerie howl comes from him. It's a long, drawn-out note. A chorus of others pick up in the forest surrounding the property.

I'm drawn with wanderlust, wanting to go off to explore the forest. But the woods don't seem quite safe for a human at night. Then again, I'm no longer human. *Why does that feel like a good thing?*

I FIND my way downstairs the next morning, shortly after nine. Lauren, Cade's housekeeper — and apparently a saint — is in the kitchen, standing while working at a laptop, holding a toddler on her hip.

"Good morning!" she chirps. "Are you feeling okay?"

I nod. "Is there coffee?"

Without hesitation, Lauren moves across the kitchen, stopping at the fridge to grab some milk before opening a cupboard where an espresso machine hides. She pushes a button, and a grinding noise fills the room, followed by the heavenly scent of coffee. Then she pours milk into a metal pitcher and lifts it to the machine.

"Oh, that's too much trouble. Just a regular black coffee is fine. Like one of those pods?" I try to stop her.

"Nonsense. This is better, and I don't mind. Cade and Deacon don't like coffee. It's an excuse to make myself one as well." She smiles over her shoulder at me.

"Should I at least hold him for you?" I offer my arms out to take the child.

Lauren looks at me hesitantly. "Yeah, that'll be good."

"What's his name?" I bounce him, and his little face lights up, giving me warm fuzzies.

"Horace." Lauren shakes her head in disapproval. "Evidently, it was a family name."

"Oh! He's not yours."

Apparently, my ability to discern what to say aloud versus in my head is lacking, even with my new wolf.

Lauren laughs, looking at me. "No, I'm not mated. I've been working too much for any of that funny business. He's my sister's. Kept wandering off while she was trying to get the garden put in. So, I said he could come and run about the house."

"Cade makes you work so much that you don't have any time to date?"

I'm angry for her. I ball my fist and fight the urge to track down that jerk and give him a piece of my mind before getting her answer.

"Well, seeing as how Cade's had his job for less than a month, I'm not hanging the blame on him. He's sending me home left and right." Her voice changes, mocking his deep tone. "It can wait until tomorrow. No one cares if it's dusty. You have staff to do these things. Tell me how many more people you need, and I'll hire them."

She's smiling while making the espresso. The way she's smiling turns a pit in my stomach.

Her hands stop working, and she holds her arms out to take Horace from me. "Alright, that's enough of that."

I hear a rumble, and it feels nearby.

Horace's face scrunches up as he starts to cry. She bounces him a bit.

"It's okay. She just thinks that Aunty Lauren is moving in on her mate. She doesn't know that Aunty Lauren was younger than him growing up. Yeah, and we've seen him all scrawny and scraggly. We don't like knowing what our dates looked like before they got hot, do we?"

"He's not my mate. I'm sorry. I didn't realize I was growling." I step back, my eyes welling with tears. Putting my hand on my chest, where Cade demonstrated the first time it happened, I try to get it under control. *Why am I so bad at this?* "Is it always this hard?"

Lauren smiles, setting Horace on the floor where he clings to her legs.

She shrugs. "I've always been a wolf. I can imagine, like most things, the transition is the hardest part. Take the house, for example. Despite Cade being a complete 180 from Robert, we're all adjusting to different standards, schedules, and requests. They're all easier changes. But there are new feelings. I had to explain to my staff that the house isn't going to get smaller and that less daily busy work doesn't mean less staff, it means getting to do things we didn't have time to do before." Lauren moves about the kitchen, Horace following her everywhere. "I guess what I'm saying is that it's scary and new. You don't know how things are going to go, so of course, it's going to be hard. But, if the wolf didn't think you were strong enough for it, she wouldn't have chosen you."

She hands me a hot latte. "Cade told me your drink order. I don't quite have everything we need for the fancy stuff, but this should be good. I'll be sure to order what you like in the future."

"Oh, that won't be necessary." I smile. "This is perfect, thank you."

Lena slides into the kitchen, socks skidding across the floor. "Coffee?"

"I swear you can hear this machine from anywhere on the property." Lauren laughs as she starts making Lena a cup.

A few minutes later, Lena and I head out to the patio.

We barely get seated at a stone-top table when she starts. "Listen, you're getting really bitchy."

"Oh, like you're one to talk," I quip back.

Again, why can't I stop my mouth? Can I pretend it's caffeine deficiency?

"It's time you woman up and admit that this is the new normal." Lena continues around my smart mouth, "I'm the bitchy one around here. There's only room for one. Seat is full. You'll have to find a way to get back to being the nice one. Accept your wolf and your mate. Fucking deal with it."

I don't feel like myself; I don't know how to be that person anymore. I'm not sure she still exists. My body is tense, and no amount of stretching or breathing brings it back to feeling anything close to normal.

"I'll do what I can," comes out of my mouth, but it's still sharp and pointed.

It's not how I mean it. Lena is trying to be nice, in her own way. I can tell. *I'm the broken one.*

We are not broken. This is just new. The soft voice in my brain speaks. It's startling but feels like someone kind, compassionate even.

"Alright, I've got to go paint. Evidently, the Smithsonian is doing a shifter exhibit, and someone spilled the beans that I paint." Lena picks up her cup of coffee and gives me a pointed look, lifting her brow. "You were cc'd on the email. I'd say thank you, but I'm scared shitless of people seeing my work. So, until I have a handle on that. Cheers."

CHAPTER 92

CADE

I'VE BEEN UP since dawn and am finishing breakfast in my office when my phone rings. The gatehouse icon pops up on my screen.

I answer it quickly. "This is Cade."

"Cade, the transport with Isabel LeFleur has arrived," the guardsman informs me.

I check the clock. The transport must have made good time and driven through the night to get her here this early. It's not even nine.

The Leviathan rumbles, excited. *Kill her. Avenge mate. Rip false mate limb from limb.*

"Have transport meet me at the mausoleum," I answer, closing my laptop.

I don't bother stifling the growl. By the end of the day, everyone will know The Leviathan reigns in blood.

"Ten-four." I hear the gate opening before the phone disconnects.

There's no sense in holding a public trial. She's guilty in the human court of law and within our own. Simply for conspiring

683

to kill a human, the sentence is death. Thalia isn't ready for this kind of closure. She's not accustomed to the blood lust of revenge. Closure for humans doesn't come from watching someone draw their last breath, mostly.

My mate is kind and smart. She will learn to be a wolf and she will learn to be a strong Luna for her people. I never want her to learn of this darkness. Keeping her away from this execution, this part of shifter life, will ensure her innocence remains intact.

"Can I witness?" Deacon asks from where he's leaning on the doorframe.

His wolf's dark eyes hold mine.

I nod. Opening the drawer of my desk, I pull out my handgun. While running the holster into my belt, I follow as Deacon leads the way out of my office.

"Do you want me to notify her parents?" Deacon asks when I catch up to him in the hallway.

I shake my head. "They know it's today. Transport will have to drive right past their house. If they show up or not is on them."

Deacon and I walk in silence down to the cemetery. Traditionally, trials, subsequent executions, and challenges are held out on the lawn of the house. But in keeping Thalia out of this darkness, I'll kill her where she'll be buried. Walking past the drive that leads toward the rest of the packs' houses, there's no movement. It appears Isabel's parents won't be joining us.

Once we arrive, the transport team opens the SUV and pulls Isabel LeFleur from the back. Her hands locked in handcuffs behind her don't humble her. Her head held high in defiance, she tries to shake her shoulders and escape the grip of the transport guard.

"Piece of work," Deacon greets her with a wry smile as one of the guards hands me the keys to her cuffs.

"Really, Cade?" Isabel looks around the pack's cemetery. "I don't even warrant a fair trial? You're going to kill me for this?"

"Trials are for humans. Wolves have laws and ultimatums. You've broken all our laws. I have nothing left but death for you." I pause, taking a moment to look at her. *Is this really all because of me?* I was going to tell the transport team they didn't need to be here, but it wouldn't hurt for them to bear witness to her confession. "What happened to you, Isabel? You've always been driven, but I never thought you'd have this darkness in you."

"I'm not the one who betrayed us," Isabel spits.

Her eyes lock on me with a glare, and her wolf's bright yellow eyes push forward.

Why did I expect her to be remorseful? There's no redemption for her. There's no point in looking. Any fleeting sympathetic emotions I have toward her fade.

Kill false mate. End this. The Leviathan presses me. When I let his eyes shine past my own, Isabel smartly recoils.

"How did you get the info on her? Your brothers?"

I don't know that she's going to give me answers. But thinking back to the press conference, they make the most sense. Although, until recently, they hadn't been in the security game.

She rolls her eyes, shifting her body.

The cuffs jingle and Isabel snorts. "Hardly. Once Senator Clark discovered they were shifters, she had them removed from the security detail. Seems she was only interested in allowing one shifter to protect her precious daughter."

Deacon growls, reminding me of his supportive presence behind me and to my left.

He speaks, "No, you're smarter than that, aren't you? You

went to DC when no one was watching you. Slipped away like the weasel you are."

Isabel takes a step back, and Deacon moves forward to stand shoulder to shoulder with me.

He snarls, "Answer me, Isabel. Who did you find willing to give you Thalia?"

"Having your psycho do your work for you, Cade?" Isabel taunts, unaware of the blood boiling hot with rage underneath my skin.

I clench my fist, holding it tight.

Break bones with teeth. Cut flesh. Bleed. The Leviathan's bloodlust reaches new heights. The thought of shaking her body until it's lifeless and nothing more than a blood stain is appealing to both of us.

We have to wait. Many more will have to die, based on what she says. I try to steady him, explaining the situation. I need more information first.

Deacon is the calm one right now. He might be loud, but between the two of us, he's holding the most control. I'm seconds from snapping. I haven't been this angry in a long time. She always had a way of bringing out the worst in me. But now, she's on the receiving end of The Leviathan's rage.

"Typical." Isabel rolls her eyes. "Speechless and unable to complete the work."

When I step forward, Deacon's hand latches onto my forearm. His fingers press against Thalia's name, permanently etched on my skin.

"Who, Isabel? Who was stupid enough to think that taking a senator's daughter would solve everyone's problem?" Deacon probes. Then he barks out a dark laugh before saying, "Because we all know you aren't smart enough to think it up on your own."

The insult sets Isabel off. Deacon knew it would.

"You've no idea how many people wanted her turned. But I was the only one who managed to do it. Of course, it helps that there was a wolf at her school program already obsessed with her. He was so ready to turn his little protégé into the perfect mate. But I told him to wait." Boldly Isabel steps forward. "It was going perfectly until she suddenly went on sabbatical."

She's nearly chest to chest with me. I grind my teeth to stop myself from opening my jaws and ripping her throat out in my human form. My toes tear into the soles of my shoes as I grasp onto razor-thin control to keep from shifting. The Leviathan pushes hard, trying to escape from within me. Deacon's hand on my arm is the only restraint I have left.

"Doctor Dorset has sticky fingers so it was no problem for him to get her keys. Thalia isn't very observant. The only problem was he kept visiting her. I couldn't keep him away." Isabel shrugs.

Releasing my arm, Deacon snarls next to me, "You really thought that murder would solve this?"

"No." Isabel turns to him. "I proved it." She smiles, looking Deacon up and down, biting her bottom lip. "The minute Thalia Clark was bitten and made wolf," Isabel says while turning to me and sidestepping toward Deacon, "by my pack," she continues as she inches closer to Deacon, "Senator Clark's proposed laws magically became favorable for shifters."

"I hate to break it to you, Isabel. But there are two things very wrong with what you just said, so let's get the facts straight." I step closer, circling her. I lower my voice as I walk behind her. "I'm the one who turned Thalia. And the laws that were all dropped? Were already being dropped because of what I negotiated with Senator Clark. It had nothing to do with the fact that your joke of an independent pack took my mate, nearly killed her, and caused me a fucking nightmare."

Isabel turns to look at me, eyes wide. "No."

The Leviathan pushes forward. I snarl, "What's it like dying, knowing you're doing so for nothing?"

Deacon's hands wrap around her biceps before spinning her to face him. She snarls, but Deacon only has to laugh and flash Isabel the demonic eyes of his wolf before she stops.

Unlocking the handcuffs, I walk them to the transport and hand them to the driver through the window. The SUV pulls back out, heading the way they came in. As I turn back around, Deacon's already let her go. It doesn't matter, her final breaths on this earth are few.

I draw the gun from my holster, and Isabel's eyes go wide.

She shakes her head. "That's not how this works."

"I'm Sovereign. I'm The Leviathan," I deadpan.

I click the safety off, keeping my eyes on her. Setting my jaw, more excited than I should be, I watch her whole demeanor change.

"No, I deserve an honorable death." Isabel's voice shakes. Finally, she becomes aware of the severity of the situation. The fear coming from her hangs thick in the morning air. She begs, "I should get to plead my case. I shouldn't have to die alone."

The cackle from Deacon is bone-chilling, and even the hair on the back of my neck stands on end. Isabel steps away from him, walking toward the rest of the cemetery and the thousands of acres of forest.

"You're not alone, Isabel," he mockingly tells her, stepping closer into her space.

I chamber a bullet.

"This isn't right." Isabel fights.

At that, I pause and cock my head at her. "What's not right is that you had my mate ripped from her apartment, chased through the woods like an animal, and left to die in some rotten house smelling like her own piss." I'm yelling. I've kept my cool this long, but I can't contain it any longer. I shake my head. "I'll give you this one last pathetic piece of decency, not that you would have ever done it for Thalia. Run. If I don't shoot you, then Deacon can tear you limb from limb."

Isabel panics, her eyes wide as she starts to run. Deacon doesn't even bother.

The muzzle flashes, the recoil kicks, the smell of gunpowder permeates the air, and there's ringing in my ears. Three repetitions.

Isabel's body hits the ground, barely twenty yards from me.

Take a few good shots at who's making you mad, and suddenly, you're less mad and clearer about things.

I close my desk drawer with the three brass casings and my handgun. I scrub my hands down my face. Knowing Thalia is safe, putting together the final pieces of the puzzle of how she was in danger, and tying up the final ends help with the uneasy feeling I've been having. Helps, but I've effectively avoided Thalia for the last twenty-four hours since I washed her in the shower. Removing blood from your hair the first few times can be tricky. Rightfully so, Lena called me an asshole for even thinking Thalia should be left to do it by herself.

I can't avoid her forever, though. Her shift is getting close. We all feel it. Thalia's been grumpy and, as Lena called it, 'hangry.' I haven't been much better. Being surrounded by her scent and having her right next door to me is testing the limits of my control. During the night, I've walked to her door at least a dozen times, always forcing myself back to bed. Only after standing there for minutes, fighting the urge to open it.

Aside from this morning, Deacon has made himself incredibly scarce. Despite Thalia presenting as an Alpha wolf,

Lena has done what Lena always does, stand her ground and pretend she's not cowering inside.

The Leviathan is full of excitement. He doesn't understand that Thalia doesn't want us, and her wolf might not either.

I find Thalia out on the patio; Lena glances at me before excusing herself from the table and taking her mug with her. I catch her eye and motion for her to sit back down. No way in hell I'm talking to Thalia for the first time alone. The midmorning sun beats down, creating warmth in the fool's summer day.

Casually, I sit down next to her in one of the cushioned chairs.

Thalia puts her coffee cup on the table before turning to me. If looks could kill, I wouldn't be dead, but I sure as hell would want to be.

"Can I get the being-a-wolf lesson over with so I can go home?" Thalia's voice is sharp and full of uneasy energy.

No wonder Lena's struggling to be around her. From the flurry of texts I've received, it seems like they only had a good time when the hair stylist came to the house, working out what to do with Thalia's butchered hair.

I nod, giving her a soft smile. "Yeah, we can try shifting. You've been restless. It's a little early, but it's probably time. The Leviathan says it's better to try and do it and call your wolf out rather than waiting until she pushes out on her own. Apparently, it makes it more pleasant."

"It'd probably be easier on you if we go and shift together first," Lena offers Thalia with an I-know-something-you-don't-know tone clearly directed at me.

It's not an awful idea, and it's fairly well thought out, but she's my responsibility.

Thalia looks at Lena, eyebrows up, surprised by her kindness. "Why would you say that?"

"Um, my wolf is less, big and less . . . intimidating than Cade's."

Lena skillfully leaves out the real reason, knowing Thalia won't know the difference.

"Yeah, that works for me." Thalia turns to me, questioning the rules. "I only need to shift, it doesn't matter who with?"

"No way. I bit you, so you're mine." I tease while getting closer to her, biting my bottom lip.

It's forward of me, but she's still my mate. I still want her with every breath.

"Eww." Lena pinches the bridge of her nose.

"No, the saying is, 'I licked it, so it's mine.'" Thalia shakes her head, equally disappointed in my antics.

Apparently, I'm not as funny as I think I am.

"I can certainly spend a few hours licking you to prove how much you're mine."

The Leviathan brushes against the surface, but I hold him back. A replay of fucking her in the back of the Yukon flashes in my brain. I get closer to her to try to nibble her ear.

Thalia, who must have equally erotic memories, blushes before lifting her hand to try and smack me.

I grab hold of her wrist. "Feisty."

Lena groans before sliding her chair back, grabbing her coffee mug, and walking off. "Okay, you two crazy kids, have fun."

Thalia's eyes turn back to me, her pupils blown wide. Then her eyes fleck to gold. Her wolf is right there.

I pull the inside of her wrist to my mouth and kiss it before releasing her. Shrugging my shoulders, I nod my head toward the woods suggestively, giving her one last lip bite before standing up and heading that way.

"Let's take a walk. You probably don't want to strip down and be naked in front of the entire staff."

We leave the patio and head across the lawn. Neither of us speaks until we reach the first running trail of the woods.

Thalia tries to bring up how fleetingly temporary her stay will be. "I called my parents. Mom's upset that it's jeopardizing her career, but Dad confirmed they still love me and want me to go home."

"They're more than welcome to come and pick you up and take you home if that's what you all wish to do."

The words come out of my mouth, but they're not the ones I want to say. Hopefully, after this shift, they're not the ones I'll have to use anymore. *No, I love you. You can't leave again*, is on the tip of my tongue. I'm hoping her wolf will help. If her wolf gets a taste of freedom, and she recognizes me as her mate, then staying will be the easy choice.

We reach the first open space among massive, intentionally planted pines. It's a casual undressing point with benches and a lawn box to keep clothes dry if it rains or dew sets in.

I pull off my shirt and motion for her to do the same.

The Leviathan is ready; my skin tingles with his want to take our form. He presses himself against me, but I hold him back. He argues. *No, we shift our mate will follow.*

She has no idea how to shift. You want to just guess her wolf does? Or do you want to be back and forth in forms all day? I argue with him. The Leviathan grumbles in response.

"So," Thalia says expectantly.

The wolf has left her eyes, and she's holding her arms out like she's waiting for me to hand her a basket of answers. She raises an eyebrow.

"I've never had to explain it before. For me, when I'm working with The Leviathan at least, once we agree to change forms, he helps push me into it. My skin tingles, and I just let go. I let myself fall into my wolf." I pause, realizing how unhelpful that must sound. "It's like that first stretch after a nap or a yawn that moves your whole body."

"Next are you going to tell me to think wolf?" Thalia asks.

I shrug. "If that's what helps."

"Okay." Thalia purses her lips together, shaking her head. She changes the subject. "Are we ever going to talk about us?"

Blindsided, I pause. "The last time we tried to talk about it, I didn't get too many words into that conversation."

"But . . ." She hesitates. "You want to."

Thalia's body shivers. The conifers casting shade overhead cool the forest floor. It's colder in the shade than in the warmth of the patio, but I suspect the energy of a nearing shift rolling off her is the true culprit. It won't be long.

I puff my cheeks and blow out air, giving myself a moment to formulate words. "Yeah, I wish we could talk about why you don't trust me. I feel like, after the time we've spent together, I deserve at least the benefit of the doubt."

Thalia's eyes flood gold again, but this time, they don't fade back to green. I unbutton my jeans. Her body shudders again.

I urge her, "Thalia, draga mea, take off your clothes."

She manages to get her shirt and pants off, but her bra is shredded. The beautiful black and gray wolf pulls out of her body. The Leviathan barely waits for me to get my pants down, and we're in wolf form together.

CHAPTER 93

THALIA

I'VE NEVER FELT MORE alive. The world is more colorful. The ground, the forest, the cerulean blue of the sky are all more vibrant and alive. All the stress and pressure from earlier has fallen away. It feels like I can think and adjust. Is it just post-workout clarity? Is that a thing? I've never been one for running. Runners high? Is that what it's called?

"I feel her." The words come out as I think them. "I feel . . ."

The problem is there aren't words for these feelings.

The Leviathan fades as Cade shifts back. I watch Cade roll his shoulders.

"Full? Not alone?"

"I didn't know that I was empty until her." I try to explain. "Which is ridiculous because I was a full person before."

Cade smiles, picking up his clothes. "You weren't empty before. You're not more full now. You're different, and different isn't bad."

I've been caught watching him. Cade pulls on his pants, tempting me with a sly grin.

"Let's go get cleaned up. I want to check you for ticks."

Moment ruined. Involuntarily, my body recoils from the ground. I look down, expecting to find one crawling on me. Cade chuckles until I glare at him. He puts his hand up in mock surrender, pulling himself together. I'm going to be a shitty wolf if this is how I react to one run.

"You'll get used to it." Cade steps closer to me.

I can feel the warmth of his body. I bite my bottom lip, thinking of the last time he made me feel this warm.

"Get dressed, I don't want people seeing you naked just yet." Cade motions to my clothes.

"Ever. I don't want people seeing me naked, ever."

I breathe deeply, thinking about how awful that would be. I'm not even thrilled about Cade seeing me naked. We're not sleeping together. He shouldn't get to see the cow for the milk. Okay, I don't know if that analogy applies. But he shouldn't see me.

Cade doesn't say anything. I'm more aware of how close he is.

He's ours, a voice inside my head whispers. I'm pulled to him, not by his arms, but by something inside me. I bring my hand to his chest above his heart.

"I love you," Cade says quietly.

"And I love you. That's not the problem." I want to be wrapped in his arms. But the physical closeness might complicate things. "But I think I've been a real bitch to you the last couple days, and I'm sorry."

Cade's quiet. He kisses the top of my head before wrapping his arms around me. My body relaxes, tension escaping. Complications are null and void. I've wanted his comfort and needed the calm he brings. He pets my hair gently. I feel like I should be crying. I feel like I should feel more than peace. But that's all it is; it's peace and comfort in his arms.

I don't know how long we stand there before he moves me

slowly. Helping me dress. Shirt, pants, and shoes survived the transition. I'm going to need Lena to help scrounge me more clothes. Until . . . until I go home? Is that what I want?

"I'm never going to get used to you swearing." Cade laughs. "I've been reading, and with the transition, it makes sense for you not to be your usual self. I just want you to feel settled. I love you. I only want what's best for you."

Emotions flood me. I look up at Cade. Sunlight drifts through the trees, highlighting his soft brown hair.

He gives me a reassuring smile. "It's all going to be okay. Let's get you cleaned up. We can talk."

INSIDE THE HOUSE, I try to depart from Cade by grabbing the door handle to my suite, but he grabs my other hand and holds tight, stopping me.

"Humor me, please." Cade hits me with his devilish grin.

It sends shivers down my spine.

Circling behind me, he nibbles my ear. Then he gently pulls my fingers from the handle and nudges me down the hall.

My wolf shuffles. She urges me, *Go.*

I step forward. Am I the only one who cares that this isn't permanent? I can't stay here.

We're mad at him. I remind her.

The wolf doesn't seem to care; she radiates enthusiasm, playing along with him as Cade leads us back toward his suite. Wolfish grin takes on a whole new meaning seeing a pleased look in his eye. A hum of understanding and connectedness to him runs through me that wasn't here before.

This suite is massive. Cade pushes me through the bedroom and past an entire seating space before guiding me into a private bathroom. Large and spacious, it's right out of an interior design catalog. He starts running water in a massive tub.

When I turn my attention back to him, Cade's blue eyes slowly ignite to gold.

"Fuck, you're beautiful," Cade whispers as his head tilts slowly to the side.

"You'll have to show me that trick with the eyes," I answer dumbly.

Compliments continue to be my area of weakness.

"What do you mean?" Cade asks, stepping closer.

His hands run up under my shirt. The feeling ignites a fire within me. I want him. I've never stopped wanting him.

"When they turn gold." I gasp as he cups my breast and tugs at my nipple. *Deviously tempting.*

He pulls back for a moment. I catch the quickest smirk and a glint in his eye as he spins me to face the mirror. There are two sets of haunting gold eyes in the mirror.

I barely recognize myself standing in front of Cade.

"Woah."

Cade kisses the top of my head, not taking his eyes from my reflection.

"You're equally beautiful now that you're wolf as you were when you were human."

"You don't prefer me now?" My voice quivers.

Cade's only response is to spin me again, pulling me back from the mirror. His eyes examine my face as he reaches blindly behind himself and turns off the tap. Cade remains silent, slowly lifting my shirt off. His mouth finds my neck, kissing downward as he moves to strip off my jeans. He pulls a nipple into his mouth. As his soft tongue licks against it, I moan. My body pushes forward into his. He steps away from me, standing before pulling off his clothes.

Clearly done with talking, Cade helps me into the tub. The

water's hot, and I draw a sharp breath adjusting to the heat. As I allow the warmth to envelop me, he steps in. We sink into the water.

Still without answer, I sit facing him in the tub. Not for his lack of effort in trying to pull me closer.

I want an answer. I rephrase. "Do you wish they didn't do this to me?"

With a long exhale, Cade runs his hand across the back of his neck. His hand falls away from his neck, and he holds it out flat like he's gifting the information. "Thalia, I'm the one who bit you and turned you wolf. None of them had gifted you an animal. They hadn't done it right. You were dying. If I have to pick between you dead or a wolf? There's no choice for me." Cade's hand falls into the water with a small splash, and he shakes his head. "It should have been something you had a say in. I'm not sorry I saved you. I'm not sorry you're alive."

"Oh." I don't know why, but what he says leaves me speechless.

I catch a softness I've never seen. Cade blinks back moisture as The Leviathan retreats. His eyes fade back to his soulful blue.

He blinks, looking away. "Did I do the right thing?"

"Cade," I call his name, but his gaze doesn't dart back to me. Patiently I wait for him to look at me. I'm holding back the easiest answer I've ever had to a question until I'm sure he's watching. I want him to see me say it. His eyes rise to meet mine. I smile. "Of course you did."

His body relaxes as a weight lifts off his shoulders.

I drop my gaze and say softly, "I didn't think you'd come for me. After . . . everything."

"I'll always come for you." Cade punctuates each word.

I feel it in my entire body.

Regretting sinking so far away from him in the tub, I move

toward him, turning so my back leans against his chest. Cade guides me into his lap. I sink between his legs the best I can.

"Is this tub smaller or what?" I grumble.

"It's smaller. I'll have it replaced tomorrow if you promise to stay." Cade's voice is a vow whispered in my ear.

We'll stay. My wolf whispers, *we'll stay because he loves us, and he would never hurt us.*

"I can't promise to stay here, Cade." I shake my head. My wolf whines, not approving my statement. I draw a deep breath. "I can't stay until you promise me there won't be any more half-truths or lies of omission. No more of this, don't tell the human, because I'm not anymore."

"I'll tell you anything and everything you want to know." Cade's voice is firm and reassuring.

"I want to be your partner, your mate. No more secrets?" I didn't intend for it to be a question.

Cade answers, "No more secrets. But just to be clear, from the day The Leviathan recognized you as ours, you never stopped being my mate."

My wolf murmurs in agreement with Cade's statement.

Shifting to be more comfortable, I keep charge of the conversation. "Why did you do it, the deal with my mom?"

"I had the opportunity to try and help keep us free." He pauses before sighing and shaking his head. "I never thought she'd actually amend the bill. But I had to try."

After a few moments, his body melts against me. Cade doesn't keep talking.

Interrogation it is. I will question him to death if that's what it takes. "What did you bargain to keep me safe for? What was I worth to her?"

"Death penalty for anything under a class C felony for shifters. Removal of language legalizing sterilization of shifters. Increased the requirements for what constitutes dangerous for shifters to be held on suspicious behavior. Removal of all language relating to forced sterilization and limitations on family size." He unfolds one of his long fingers with each phrase, checking them off.

It ends at five. Five really good reasons. Five really big concessions for my mother to make. I wish I could ask what that conversation looked like. *How much negotiating was there?*

Cade doesn't offer any more.

"Why didn't you tell me?"

"I didn't tell you because, at first, it didn't make sense in order to build trust between us. You were already shy and anxious, then the panic attack. What good would have come from telling you? Then, after I fell in love with you, that's all that mattered. I was so focused on you, doing what was right by taking back the throne, and finding a way to make us work." Cade's nose presses into the back of my head.

Some of the tension we've been harboring seems to simmer off. I imagine it like steam dissipating from the tub.

"Are you sorry?" I ask.

His head shakes back and forth. His nose nudges the back of my neck through my hair. "I'm not sorry I made the deal. I'm not sorry that I didn't tell you right away. However, I am sorry I didn't hold you hostage in my living room until you talked to me." He pauses, drawing a deep breath. His next words come out softer. "But I'm not sorry that I bit you. What makes me sorry is that you didn't have a choice in it."

Anger hits me. I growl. It comes naturally. I feel her. My wolf is angry with me. I go to move off him, but Cade wraps his arms around me, holding me in place. I struggle harder, and he growls. My wolf freezes.

Traitor.

"I'm sorry I didn't make you listen to me and that I didn't

tell Peter to let me handle you. I'm sorry that I didn't stay in DC and stalk you until you would listen to me."

Cade keeps holding me. His shoulders shake slightly.

If I could see his face, would he be crying?

The next words come with heavy feelings, hoarse and caught in his throat. "Thalia, I am so sorry I failed to fight to keep you. I should have been a better mate."

"Would a good mate use their gift without the other even knowing what was happening?" I growl, it's an intense rattle in my chest. "In the SUV and with Deacon, I got a . . . feeling, sensation? But when I was human, I couldn't tell if you ever used the command on me. If that makes sense?"

"The only time I've ever used my gift on you was when you were a danger to yourself." Cade pauses. "Including in the SUV on the way here."

"How do I know that's true?"

"Everything I've done has been to protect you. I swear it. Ask your wolf if I'm lying. She'll tell you. She can hear it. She can feel it." Cade instructs.

Our mate is honest. He's been honest. She assures me, and I believe her.

When I move this time, he lets me go. Carefully I step out of the tub.

He scrubs his hands down his face masking more of those deeply felt emotions, effectively tucking them away.

Lena and Deacon said he's not himself. Deacon said Ansel was worried about intervening. What did that mean? My heart hurts, it's crushing seeing him so defeated.

I can't leave him. I don't want to.

I grab a towel off the heated rail and look at him expectantly, but he doesn't move. His eyes are distant, his shoulders hunched. I don't see the fearless and collected man who stared down bears and my mother.

Our mate is hurt. You rejected him, and now he mourns us. We have to keep our mate. My wolf urges me. Sorrow and longing bite at me from the inside out. She urges, *claim him and The Leviathan, and then never leave.*

Her words feel right. They fit in my soul, and all those intense feelings bubble to the surface. I recall the weeks we were together when all I thought about was being with him. And how nothing felt worth having while we were apart because I couldn't celebrate it with him.

I bite my bottom lip. I need him, and from what I'm feeling and understanding, he needs to know that. But it doesn't mean I'm beneath making him work for it. I step forward, and the movement draws his eyes.

When I have his attention, I taunt him with a lip bite. "Convince me to stay."

Fire ignites in Cade's eyes. The sorrow slowly fades as he rises out of the tub.

He pulls me and the towel into his arms. He hugs me before scooping me up into his arms and stalking into the bedroom. Clearly not worried about getting the covers and the bed wet, he lays me on my back so I'm looking at him. There's no pause. He moves, kissing up my leg, trading soft kisses for bites as he gets closer to my wet core.

I moan, squirming myself closer to him.

His eyes meet mine. I take him in slowly. Every piece of him is as I remember. *Almost every piece.* My eyes drift to his left arm draping up me. Where his sleeve now ends neatly in the middle of his forearm.

Cade rotates his arm so I can see the inner side. The scene of trees wraps around with a wolf in the foreground. And, my name, spelled out, in beautiful line work.

My mouth drops open with my gasp. I trace the letters as tears sting my eyes.

It was my name all along.

"There's never going to be anyone else for me but you. If you're here or if you're gone. The Leviathan and I won't ever move on." Cade's words are spoken in his deep velvet timber.

Ours. The voice in my head, my wolf answers. *We are made for The Leviathan. We are his, and he is ours.*

I nod along in understanding.

"I love you. I'm sorry. I should have listened," I whisper, pulling my eyes off the beautiful work of art he's made of my name.

Cade moves closer. The bed shifts with his weight. His tongue brushes inside my thigh, and my head falls back as his nose sinks into my folds. His tongue laps long, languid strokes. Every fiber of my being relaxes under his touch. His arm still draped up my body, meets my breast, and Cade teases the nipple, fingers dancing around it. The other hand slides up the inside of my leg. I lift myself back up to watch him.

He slowly tests me, his finger teasing its way slowly into me. The way Cade works me has desperate, needy noises escaping. I push my hips toward him. I need more. Cade's teeth gently squeezing my clit isn't the more I want. My hips wiggle back and forth, and I try to entice him. Dedicated, Cade sucks on my clit before licking smooth strokes up and down. His second finger slides into me.

"Cade." I'm moaning. "Please. Fuck me."

He laughs. "Oh, no, not yet. I've missed you for three weeks. If you want me to make it up to you, then you'll have to accept my dedication to enough orgasms you'll be too exhausted to leave my bed."

The feeling of his fingers working, fucking deep inside me, matches the ferocity of his promise. I'm panting, the orgasm building deep inside. The heat between my legs grows. He moans as his tongue makes longer strokes getting close to where his fingers are working inside.

He murmurs, "I fucking love how you taste."

I can't focus on his words, the fingers playing with my tits causing me to arch when he pinches my nipples. I'm struggling with where to focus. It all feels so good. I push against him again, grinding. Cade's third finger inside me, curling upward with the others is nearly enough to push me over the edge. The orgasm building inside demands more. I buck my hips against him, encouraging more.

"Mmhmm, I'm not letting you come that easy."

Cade breaks in the licking and tortures me. His face turned into a wicked smile. The Leviathan's eyes meet mine.

I push myself down along him again, needing more.

"Please?" Am I beneath begging? Evidently not. I try again, seeing him squirm. "Please, fuck me."

My request goes unanswered. Cade nibbles against my clit. His teeth tease me with firmer bites.

"Thalia, if I fuck you. I don't know if I'll stop myself from sinking my teeth into your neck and marking you as mine. So, please don't test me unless you're ready to take my bite." Cade's voice is hoarse. His fingers have slowed but haven't stopped moving. "There will be no going back."

My wolf salivates at the idea. *Please let him mark us. We need it. He's given us each other. We need The Leviathan.* My wolf begs. She goes further, *we can claim him back. The Leviathan will belong to us.*

"I'm yours."

CHAPTER 94
CADE

Warmth spreads throughout me with those two sweet words. It rivals the feeling of when she told me she loved me.

The Leviathan fights my slow movements as I withdraw my fingers and stalk up her body. *Claim. Mate. Now.*

He presses the thought of losing her again and the feeling of emptiness and anger threatening me. He'll get his way. *Eventually.*

Each and every movement warrants a kiss or a bite across her warm skin. I nip harder each time, testing her tolerance for pain. Wolf bites hurt, but it's temporary pain. I've heard rumors that past the initial pain of my teeth breaking her skin, she won't feel it anymore.

She bite back. The Leviathan reminds me.

It might not be today.

My heart falls even thinking it, but there's no time to be sad. Even if she doesn't claim me back, I have a lifetime for her to pick me.

I focus on sucking one of the beautiful little buds of her tits into my mouth. She squirms and arches, pressing up. The moan drives me to give her more. My hand finds her throat, and she gasps. Her hand wraps around my forearm, fingers pressing against where I've tattooed her name. Her legs squirm, and her eyes lock on mine. I squeeze a bit tighter and feel her swallow.

Her wolf is right there, focusing on me. The Leviathan presses forward.

My voice comes with a growl as I whisper in her ear, "I'm yours."

Thalia's whole body pushes up to me. Her hips and chest rise as she tries to grind up, taking what she wants. I tease her, my lips just out of reach of hers. She squirms against the hand I have on her neck and tries to kiss me.

I pull away, keeping my hand on her neck as I move to kneel between her legs, pressing them farther apart. She drops her hips to the bed with a whimper. Thalia struggles, her free hand reaching for my cock. I intercept it, shaking my head. I wet my lips.

"What's wrong, draga mea?"

The way she writhes is beautiful. She's so much stronger than before as she fights to get closer to me.

The littlest huff she makes takes me back to the first day I met her. So much has changed. Her hips arch upward again, and I feel her wetness on the head of my cock. The moan that comes from me is almost a pure growl. I can't tease us any longer.

I lower myself into her, pressing my cock into her soft folds. When I tighten my grip around her throat, I hear her gasp for air, but she isn't fighting me off. Her hands pull me closer, digging into me. I sink deeper, letting myself get lost in her smell. The warmth of her pussy wrapped around me.

She pulls her legs up and wraps them around me like she can't keep me close enough. I'm grinding into her deeply, listening to her body's responses. With a desperate sounding whine, I release her throat.

She gasps, and her body shudders, pulling me close.

I nip at the side of her neck, right under her ear, my fangs long since descended. The need to claim her is becoming impossible to fight.

"Fuck yes." Thalia gasps.

The expletive startles me. I pause.

"No," she mewls. "More."

I'm slamming into her, trying to pace against the sounds I'm hearing as her orgasm pushes nearer. Who'd have thought my mate getting a foul mouth would be so hot.

"Cade." She moans, her mouth at the base of my neck. "Don't stop."

There's never been such a sweet command. I do exactly as she asks. My cock is being squeezed tight inside her. I pant heavily against her, trying to wait for her.

Her teeth graze my shoulder along the base of my neck. Then her fangs puncture the flat of my shoulder.

The Leviathan howls, and I come hard. My teeth pierce the skin at the base of her neck.

She screams. The sound is cut short as her teeth sink deeper into me.

My ears are still ringing as her pussy's grip on my cock fades. My vision is blurry. I nuzzle her neck, kissing and licking clean the bite I've given her.

Claimed us back. The Leviathan rumbles with happiness.

No, I correct him, *claimed us first.*

When I slide out of her and roll off, she whines, rolling toward me. She hisses sharply as she moves her shoulder.

"I'm sorry. I know it hurts." I kiss her forehead, pulling her body against mine.

"Why does yours not hurt? Did I do it wrong?" she asks.

Her eyes lock on the bite she placed on my right shoulder.

I smile, kissing her softly before easing her worry. "You didn't do it wrong. It hurts, but you, so far away, hurts more."

I lift her thigh, wrapping it over my legs, entangling us together. She moans, and my cock twitches.

I let the playful growl come out as I threaten, "Keep making those needy little noises and I'll roll you back over and take you from behind so I can watch that glorious ass bounce."

Thalia gives me a devious look, batting her lashes and biting her lips together. I'm mid-contemplation when a knock comes at the door.

"Dude, uh, sorry to interrupt . . . but we've got an issue downstairs." Deacon's hesitancy immediately draws concern.

I squeeze my eyes shut. There are too many things that could be an 'issue.'

I sigh. "What, Deacon?"

"The Clarks are pulling through the front gate." Deacon's footfalls follow his statement as he quickly walks down the hallway.

I don't blame him. I'd escape if I could too.

Thalia is already squirming out from my leg wrapped between hers. Her squirms do nothing. I move quickly, pushing her onto her back again, pinning her in place.

Her eyes are wide, and her breathing is erratic.

She whines, "Cade, what do I do? I don't have anything to wear." She covers her face with her hands.

"Stop, take a breath." I demonstrate.

Hers is more ragged, but she does. I wait to see if her heart will slow down, but it doesn't.

"I had Lauren get you some things to wear. And you don't have to go with them . . ." I don't like this thought. I let her up. "Unless you really want to."

Thalia shakes her head back and forth not looking at me. She sits up, following me off the bed. She's breathing hard.

Between breaths, she gets out, "They can't make me go, right?"

I pull her into my arms. "They can't make you go. You're legally an adult, and you're officially wolf. They've no hold over you."

She's quiet for a minute, letting me hold her.

Holding back the command, I whisper, "Breathe, Thalia. I won't let anyone take you from me."

CHAPTER 95
THALIA

I FOLLOW Cade around his suite as he gets dressed. When he goes to put on a T-shirt, I clear my throat.

Oh, no. No. I shake my head. "It's my parents."

Raising his eyebrows, Cade grabs a polo from the closet. "Better?"

I nod only to catch a glimpse of a major problem. "Oh no."

"What?" Cade moves, and I see his head come into view as he bends to look at me.

I grab his forearm, turning to look at it. "They're going to know."

Cade sighs. "Thalia, would it make you feel better if I wore long sleeves?"

The lack of urgency and understanding of what I mean is aggravating all on its own.

"No, they're going to find out anyway. Might as well let me lay out all the disappointment at once." I scrub my hand over my face.

"Could be worse?" Cade shrugs, then pulls a T-shirt over my head. "You could be with Deacon?"

713

A growl accompanies my scowl, which I wasn't anticipating but is very fitting. "Be nice. We love Deacon. He can't help it that he's eccentric."

Every chance he can, Cade kisses where he claimed me at the base of my neck — when I took off his T-shirt and before I stepped into my dress. And then he pulled my hair aside before placing a necklace around my neck.

After fussing with the bob haircut for a bit, I sigh. *It's hopeless.*

My wolf huffs. *We are fierce and strong. We have the power to bring The Leviathan to his knees.*

Cade's touch is tender as he lifts my hand. "You look beautiful."

I turn to look, and his eyes are soft, happy, and genuine.

He leads me out of the suite, and I wrap my arm around his. My hand rests perfectly on my name.

He smiles and laughs. "Perfect fit. Like you belong here."

Our perfect mate, he will protect us forever. My wolf agrees.

MOM AND DAD are sitting with their backs to the door at the outside dining space, chatting, much to my surprise, with Deacon and Lena. They're both dressed more formally as if they intended to make a good first impression. I hear Dad laugh at something Lena says.

Deacon sees us first and rises from the table. The formality of it feels uncomfortable, but soon Lena does too. My parents follow suit.

"Thalia Ann, what did you do to your hair?" Mom gasps.

My hand flies to my hair. Of course, that's what she sees first.

I lost so much length. I'm sure I look ridiculous, but Cade

tells me it's fine. Lena says it looks hot. But Mom's reaction says otherwise. Over the past several weeks, I've learned that Mom isn't always right. *She might not be right about this too.*

Cade stops walking when we're a few feet from the table. I stay glued to his side. *Do I go to them? Will they still love me when they see me?*

Dad takes a few staggered steps toward me.

He whispers like he's afraid to scare me, "Pumpkin, are you okay?"

I nod and let go of Cade's arm. He encourages me forward with a small nudge to the middle of my back.

When I step toward him, Dad wraps his arms around me. I hug his waist so tight. Before I can stop them, hot tears stream down my face, and I struggle to breathe. But I'm not alone. Dad cries with me. His shoulders heave as he holds me close to him.

He keeps whispering again and again, "Oh, Thalia."

"I'm so sorry, Daddy." There are so many things I want to say, but that's all I can get out.

I don't know how long we stand there, but eventually, my tears stop flowing. Dad lets me go and wipes them off my cheeks before kissing the top of my head.

Cade stood behind me the entire time. When I turn to look at him, his eyes are glassy.

He offers out his right arm, gesturing to the table. "Please, sit. Let's eat."

Lena and Deacon are still standing, waiting for me to be seated before they take their chairs. I don't know or understand the new social norms, but it somehow feels right. How am I supposed to catch up? *Survive lunch. Then learn the sociology.*

Mom, however, sits in her chair, leaning as far away from Lena as possible. She's covering her mouth with her hand. I know from all these years that it's what she does to hide the look of disgust she can't help but express.

Uncharacteristically, Lena charms, "Isn't it lovely to see Thalia so healthy?"

"Please, help yourselves," Cade encourages as he piles food on both of our plates. "Thalia had her first controlled shift today. She needs a hearty lunch. So, don't mind us."

Deacon stifles a laugh and smirks. Lena must pinch him because he sits up straighter. I bite my top lip; they both know. And I'm not sure how I feel about that.

"I don't remember a lot of what happened, but my hair wasn't salvageable. It'll grow back. This was the only solution to make it look presentable." I circle back to Mom's one and only question.

Dad, Lena, and Deacon dish out food, passing plates back and forth. The lunch spread is pasta with steak and chicken, red and white sauces, and vegetables that look fresh off the grill.

Cade has piled more than a little of everything onto my plate. He picks up his fork to eat and lets his left hand rest on my thigh. Him touching me helps.

Obviously, Dad still loves me. But Mom? I guess I shouldn't have expected acceptance.

"I guess if anyone says anything, it was part of your healing process." Mom pulls her hand off her face to gesture at me.

She's fixated on the fact that I'm not perfect looking. I've never been good enough looking for her before, so I'm not sure why she thinks I will be now.

"I don't plan on making any public appearances anytime soon." I shake my head, looking at Cade for guidance. "It won't be that short in a month or two. Lena says my hair will grow faster now."

"It's true. One of the many perks of the wolf. Trips to the

716

salon for pampering are perfectly justifiable," Lena pipes in with a megawatt smile.

Her being nice is almost more terrifying than the angry yelling, *almost.*

"I'm sure your mother is just as happy as I am that you're alive and well." Dad points his fork at us between bites.

He's smiling. I'm not saying I've never seen Dad smile. But never so openly at a table half-full of strangers.

Then, he stands up for me. "And you're absolutely right. If you're not ready to see the public, that is completely alright. Your health comes first."

"Darren, she's going to need to make an appearance. The media is all over the fact that she was abducted. If she hides away too long, it'll be like they've won. We can't hide her away. We must prove that she can be controlled." Mom chides him. She turns her gaze to glare at Cade and reaches down to her purse. She pulls out a stack of papers. With a flick of her wrist, she holds them out across the table toward Cade, shaking her head. When Cade reaches for the stack, she flicks it back momentarily to snap, "You'll find this bill is a lot lighter on restrictions. It's more favorable to the lobbying that your people have been doing."

"Thank you, Senator. I'll review it as soon as I can. I'm glad we've been able to work together." Cade waits for her to lower the stack to his hand. Once it's in his hand, he sets it down on the table between him and Deacon. He defends me, "I have every reason to believe that Thalia will have excellent control of her wolf in the very near future. She's a quick learner. A public appearance may be possible in the coming weeks, but perhaps not directly addressing the media would be easier for her recovery."

Dad nods, taking another bite. "Marie, you should eat. This

is excellent. I'm sure Cade knows her well enough to determine when she's well. He seems very supportive of her."

"I'm not hungry." Mom's voice is flat, and she hasn't taken her eyes off me.

I'm starving, and the food looks amazing, but how can I eat if she's watching me? I push the food around on my plate, having nothing better to do.

My side warms as Cade leans into me. He whispers so quietly it almost feels like it's in my head, "Hungry wolves are dangerous wolves. Eat, please."

I take a small bite, and Cade's hand runs back and forth on my leg.

"Ambassador, I heard you're considering retiring from your post?" Deacon, surprisingly, finds more conversation and knows something I don't.

"Yes. I want to be closer to Thalia more often. This" — he tries to find words. I watch him sit up a bit more — "has made me realize we need to spend more time as a family."

"I don't know that I want to go back to DC." The words come out of my mouth before I know what I'm saying.

Seriously, did I lose the rest of the little filter I had left after becoming a wolf? Before I can make this worse, I put a fork full of food in my mouth. You don't have to answer questions if you're chewing.

"Where else would you possibly go?" Mom scoffs, tossing her hand. She still hasn't even put food on her plate. "You can't finish your schooling or start a career here. We're hours from civilization."

"Commuting to the Twin Cities is very doable. I do so for the university where I'm finishing my master's in biology." Lena highlights her accomplishments and the merits.

And I realize I had no idea she wasn't studying art until just now. *Oof, bad sister-in-law? Mate-in-law?* I make a note to clarify that terminology later. While Lena's tone is a bit rough, it's not completely snippy. *Where did Lena go, and who is this impostor?*

"Are you wanting to stay here, pumpkin?" Dad looks at me and then to Cade.

I nod. "Yeah. I really want to be here. I think I need to learn how to be a wolf, and the people here are wonderful."

For the briefest moment, I think about telling them about the two of us. But outside of Lena and Deacon, and well, Lauren, I don't know who all knows. I don't know what the protocol is. Cade has tattooed my name on his arm, but that doesn't explain how you talk about this sort of thing.

Cade squeezes my leg, another encouragement to eat.

I do while he extends an offer to my parents. "You're more than welcome to stay in the main house, or if Thalia decides to make her stay here more permanent, I would be glad to put together a cabin closer to the main house for you to have your own space when you visit."

"You're not staying here," Mom snaps, losing the tone she'd use in polite company.

All the times she's yelled while we sat at our table at home come flooding back.

"You can't let them win. Taking you from us, making you one of them, and staying here, completely undermine my platform."

The wolf inside me growls. *How dare she? Why should she get to take us from our people?*

My skin tingles like it did just before I shifted.

"I don't care about your platform." I feel my wolf's rage. She's right. I can't stay quiet about this. I feel and hear my growl. "I think your political stance on this is abhorrent, and limiting freedoms of citizens is despicable."

The right side of the table shuffles. Deacon, Lena, and Cade must be conversing.

She doesn't cower in fear of me growling. There's no surprise, no shock. Mom is unfazed. It's not fear running her campaign.

Mom's response is so telling. "You don't have to care about it, but you're very much part of it."

Dad's emitting a sour smell. *Is this what fear smells like?*

"Marie, I don't think now's the time to discuss this. Our daughter nearly died." Dad tries to defuse her. He clears his throat and sits back in his chair a bit. "Let's have lunch and get to know Cade and his family. They've very graciously opened their home to us."

Mom goes to say something but closes her mouth. Is she going to listen to Dad for once?

We eat a bit more.

Lena tries again to start conversation. "Where have you been an ambassador? Thalia mentioned you moved quite a bit as a family when she was younger."

"I started my career as an economist diplomat, so we were able to travel a lot to keep up with markets. We've been everywhere. I remember one year, I think, we had four different posts. Marie hated me those years." Dad laughs.

I remember some of those years. Mom going off and yelling over every little thing. I'm positive the staff everywhere we went talked trash about us. She's always been this way.

As they talk about his work, Cade encourages me to eat. His reminders come in gentle squeezes of my thighs, pushing his food on his plate, then pointing to it before taking bites.

"How long have you been fucking my daughter?" Mom's sneer cuts through the pleasant conversation Dad and Lena are having.

Their heads snap to Mom.

I squirm, and my face flushes red. I feel so hot. I don't want to answer that, so I keep my eyes locked on my plate. Which probably doesn't help in demonstrating a lack of guilt. *Am I guilty?* I mean, yes. I'm doing what she's accusing. But it doesn't feel dirty like she's making it sound. *Why do I even care what she thinks anymore?*

She cannot talk to our mate that way. More and more, it feels like my wolf wants to come out. Those beginning feelings of a shift slither through my body.

"It's been this entire time, hasn't it?" Mom spits those words out as if they taste bad in her mouth. "We left our daughter in your care, and you coerced her into your bed. I won't let you treat her like one of your concubines. Let's not pretend you're anything more than that to them, Thalia. Your eyes aren't even green anymore. I can see the dirty animal they've put in you." Mom's tone drops, and she spits out those last two words.

That's how she sees me. My insides drop.

Deacon snaps. His sharp, uncharacteristic tone comes to my defense. "You do know wolves mate for life, right? We're highly dedicated to our mates. Even after their passing, we tend to remain completely loyal."

"You can't possibly believe he loves you," Mom starts.

I know how this will go. She'll find holes in everything and poke through them until the whole sweater falls apart.

It starts slowly with pointed questions. "That's why you came home, isn't it? He seduced you to keep you happy, and you found out that what? He made a deal with me. If he treated you like an object for his benefit then, what's stopping him from doing the same thing in the future?"

And she does it. Mom nails every single insecurity I've had throughout my entire relationship with Cade. I'm digging my toes into the cement underneath my chair. Cade's hand is firm on my thigh, keeping me seated. She won't take an answer from anyone else. It's got to be me.

I snap. "Yes. That deal was for his people. How could I not love someone who made a deal to fix a bill, that's completely asinine, before it was even truly his job to do so? It's a beautiful, selfless act. He didn't know me when he cut it. We fell in love after. I made a mistake coming home. It luckily didn't cost my life. It gifted me so much more." My words come out with low growls like I've heard Cade do when he's angry.

My wolf feels warm inside me. My chest is rattling with a growl. The warmth tingling against my skin is so intense. It's like she's there, brushing, nearly petting me from the inside out. My body tingles, and I shiver. It feels like approval the way she pushes against me.

I keep my eyes locked on Mom. I'm not looking away. I won't be talked down to anymore. I refuse to be her pawn any longer.

Mom's nose is scrunched, and her forehead wrinkles show as she spews angry words, "Oh, for heaven's sake. Pull your head out of your ass, Thalia. These people are going to use you. That's what they do. They're all abominations. It's unnatural. You can't stay here with him. I refuse to allow it."

"I'm an adult, Mom. You don't control me." The little pep talk from Cade comes back. "Furthermore, I'm one of them. I'm not human."

Dad slams his fork and knife down, rocking the whole table. He folds his hands and looks at her. The Dad I'm familiar with replaces the new fun and happy Dad. He's more cold, professional, and reprimanding. I expect him to chide me as well.

Instead, he turns to Mom. "Marie. Today, let's be happy Thalia is alive. Later, we can discuss whatever your issues are with accepting shifters for who and what they are and how

Cade and Thalia are living together. This isn't something that has to be negotiated now."

"No!" Mom is firm. She shakes her head at me. "We're going home. Thalia, if you stay here with him, you're dead to us."

CHAPTER 96
CADE

SENATOR CLARK DOESN'T KNOW my rule about not casting ultimatums. And it leaves me on the edge of my seat, waiting for Thalia's answer. She sits quietly, shaking her head. I want to believe and trust that Thalia loves me like I do her. But it wasn't even six hours ago that she was still talking about leaving me.

Our mate stays. Her wolf loyal. The Leviathan reassures me. He's more concerned that she's going to shift and overturn the table than leave with her mother. Given Thalia's active growling earlier, I'm believing him more than my own doubts.

Lena catches my eye and pulls her bottom lip up into a speculative look. She isn't concerned about Thalia leaving either.

"Marie, that's cruel. Surely you can't mean that," Thalia's father defends.

Honestly, I'm starting to like Ambassador Clark. As far as a mate's parents go, he wouldn't be so awful.

"It's okay, Dad." Thalia shrugs, and I'm back to focusing on her. "Mom, I'm sorry you feel that way. But I'm staying here. I'd

725

rather be dead to you than give up the happiness I have here. Cade's shown me more compassion and understanding in a few months than I've ever felt from you. You're free from your responsibility for me."

"Fine. If that's how you see it." Senator Clark stands up from the table.

I squeeze my hand on Thalia's thigh. I hope she knows how much I love her and that she's my whole life.

Senator Clark turns to Ambassador Clark. "Darren, are you coming?"

He shakes his head. "No. I'm having lunch with my daughter and her..."

Ambassador Clark looks at me for answers. I glance at Thalia. I'm floored.

Thalia beats me to speaking the words I haven't provided him, "My mate."

"And her mate." Ambassador Clark nods. He does the same little nod Thalia does when she's committing something to memory. "I see no reason to leave. I love our daughter no matter what, and I'm not losing her again."

"Darren, if you don't come with me, we're done. I will not be held back by your progressive views. This is unacceptable," Senator Clark snaps angrily, her finger raised as she holds her purse tightly against her body.

The tension at the table is palpable. Deacon and Lena are both wafting off fear. I feel the static in the air like a nearby shift. Fight and flight mode kicks in. Thalia is holding her breath. Ambassador Clark doesn't get up from the table.

He looks at his wife, and I can no longer see his facial expression, but he speaks, "I'm sure we can find you a car service if you wish to go."

I wish I could see the look on Ambassador Clark's face. It

726

causes Senator Clark to look like she's about to be sick. She storms back across the patio into the house.

The four of us are stunned, looking at Ambassador Clark, mocking his wife's tone and huff as he turns back to his plate. Lena looks at me, raising her eyebrows. Deacon's eyes are locked on Thalia.

"Eat, please. There's no need to let this delicious meal go to waste." Ambassador Clark motions to the table.

"I love you, Daddy," Thalia whispers.

Ambassador Clark reaches over and puts his hand on Thalia's arm. "I love you too, pumpkin. I love you so much."

We've started to adjust post-explosion when Lauren comes out to the table. Her calm and cool formal demeanor has several cracks in it.

She bites back a laugh. "Senator Clark has asked how far the walk is to the nearest airport or the phone number for a town car service."

"Please have one of the sentries take her." I shake my head. Running my free hand down the bridge of my nose. "I'm positive a car service won't drive out this far for her. Can you write down who takes her so I can compensate?"

Lauren walks away, and Lena can't help herself.

She's behaved for too long when she doesn't bother leaning over to whisper loudly to Deacon, "Can you imagine the fees on that if they did?"

Ambassador Clark is the first to laugh at this situation. It's near hysterics like she'd told the most interesting joke he's ever heard. Soon we're all laughing.

The ambassador shakes his head, wiping the tears from his eyes. "You wouldn't have a recommendation for a divorce attorney, would you? Apparently, I'm in need of one."

"I can make the pack's attorneys available to you. If they're

not capable, I'm sure they'll have excellent recommendations."
I nod.

Did all of this really just happen?

Even Thalia's wolf has gone silent. She's retreated into herself.

I move my hand from her thigh for the first time in almost an hour. I drape my arm over the back of her chair, the span of my arm touching her.

I whisper in her ear, "I love you. It'll be okay."

"Also, can I take you up on that offer for a room?" Ambassador Clark nods. "I would like to stay and get to know my daughter's new family."

"*Your* new family." Lena cocks her head with a small acknowledgment.

I need to thank her for being a strong Alpha Female today. I couldn't have done this without her.

"Of course, Ambassador, I'd be glad to get Lauren to make a suite up for you." I assure him.

"Please, just Darren." He smiles at me.

I didn't expect his approval to mean so much to me.

I return the smile. "Darren."

Deacon and Lena are the first to evacuate the table. They cite 'urgent pack business' as their reason for abandoning us. I have no reason not to let them leave, so I take their awful fucking excuse with a thank you for handling matters for me.

"Cade," Darren starts with his eyes trained on me.

Uncomfortable, Thalia shifts in her chair. I run my hand across her shoulder, gently squeezing the place where I marked her as mine. She relaxes just a bit.

"I think it's time we talk about your intentions with my daughter." Darren lowers his chin to look at me through his brow.

"Dad." Thalia tries to stop him. He looks at her in

reprimand, but Thalia continues, "Intention is what they call engagements and dating. It also relates to arranged mating. Cade and I are just mates. There's no intention."

"Thalia." I lean forward and whisper in her ear, "He's doing the thing Dads do where they threaten their child's future mate."

Thalia's mouth forms the cutest little circle, and I want to focus on the memory of how good she looked on her knees before, but now's not the time.

"As I was saying." Darren steeples his fingers before him. "I think it's important that we discuss what exactly you see as your future with my daughter."

"I don't have an answer for that, Darren." I shrug. "I've been trying to take over a small country, coordinate with other small countries, figure out where the wiring issue is in my home, and get over grieving the loss of your daughter."

Darren looks at me, nodding for me to continue.

So I do. "I don't have a plan. My life is too chaotic, and I haven't had the opportunity to discuss with Thalia what she wants her life to look like. I can promise you that she will never want for anything. That she will always be safe. And that if she wants to have a relationship with you, or her mother, I am not here to stand in her way. I'm not here to give anyone an ultimatum."

"Well, that settles it then." Darren smiles and picks up Thalia's hand. "I'm so incredibly happy for you, pumpkin. He seems very nice and with a level head about him."

Darren excuses himself with Lauren when I ask her to prepare a suite for him. She 'just happened' to have one ready on the far end of the house from our suites. And I pull out my phone to write another list.

. . .

FUCKING GET IT DONE, you dumbass:
- Lauren vacation someplace REALLY nice.
- Call legal about divorce for Darren.
- Call builder for cabin for Darren.

THALIA READS OVER MY SHOULDER. She creases her brow. "When did you start writing lists?"

"Oh, about the time I killed my brother, lost my mate, and was spiraling out of control." I kiss her forehead. "Let's go grab a nap."

"Oh, then." Thalia shakes her head, her face contorting into a frown as she averts her gaze. But she snaps her face back to me, and her tone quickly changes. "Wait. Nap nap? Or nap *nap?*" She raises her eyebrows at the end of her question.

"I was talking nap nap but . . ."

"Cade!" Lena shouts out the window of the solarium, "You need to speak to the contractor."

"Mother fucker." I take a sip of water and begrudgingly stand from the table. "Care to join me?"

"Of course." Thalia stands up, following along. "I warn you; I know nothing about house building, other than you promised me a bigger tub."

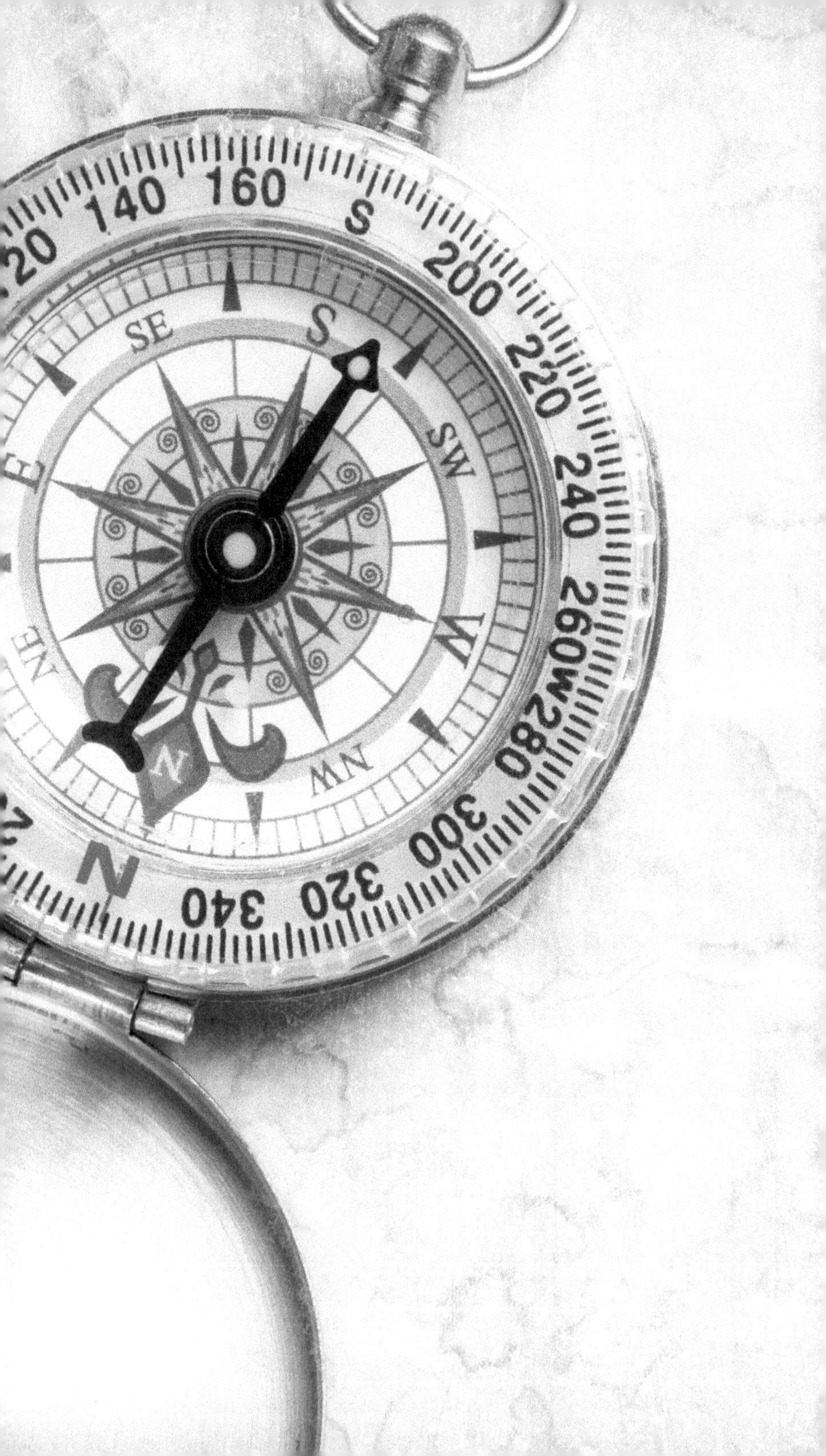

140
160
S
200
220
240
260
W
280
300
320
340
N
SE
SW
NE
NW
E

EPILOGUE
CADE

ALL I WANT to do is sink into bed after we drop Darren off at the airport. He's flying out for two weeks to finalize the divorce papers. But I'm behind the wheel of the SUV again on our way back to the demolition site. When Lena told me about the issue with the house when we were moving in, I didn't want to believe it. I had started a search for why only half the outlets on the main floor of the house worked, and boy, do I regret it now. Opened a fucking wall and found asbestos. There wasn't any building material in the entire place that wasn't in one way or another toxic.

The pack voted unanimously to tear it down, which was the cheapest option. I wholeheartedly agreed with their decision. But the back-and-forth commute from my house in Wisconsin to the Ardelean Territory is wearing more than my tires.

Riding shotgun, Thalia rests her hand on my leg. Her experiences over the last three weeks have been a roller coaster. Being gifted a wolf, becoming my mate, and adjusting to being the pack Luna have been highlights for her. She shifts effortlessly now, and the way she smiles when talking about being wolf and what she's learning warms my insides. But there's a darkness she can't shake, and it worries me.

We had hoped Senator Clark would come around. Thalia wanted to be enough for her mother to put aside politics. Reconciliation isn't happening, and it stings. The only upside is that anytime Thalia comes up in her interviews, she skirts the subject and moves on to the next question. It's better than publicly shaming Thalia, and she's even reduced how much she backhandedly compliments and slings insults at my political agenda. Peace and privacy don't replace the feeling of losing a parent. Time should heal this.

I didn't realize I was driving on autopilot. The sound of my phone ringing over the speakers of the Yukon startles me. The Leviathan bristles.

Reading *Front Gate* on the screen, questions start to swirl. *Who? What? Why?*

Pressing the button, I answer in typical fashion, "This is Cade."

"Sovereign, I've got a woman here, with three other really big wolves. She's claiming to be your sister and some sort of princess? She's demanding I let her in." The gateman sounds very suspicious. "To clarify, she's not Lena."

"The fuck?" I look over at Thalia, and she shrugs.

Why did I expect her to know?

Slowly it dawns on me. "Did she say princess or was it Pricolici?"

"Oh, that one, the second one." The gateman confirms my realization.

"Lovely." The word drips with sarcasm. "I'm ten minutes out. Get them an escort to the build site. Don't leave them unsupervised."

"Roger that." The gateman hangs up.

"Fuck fuck fuckity fuck fuck."

I press the button on the screen harder than I need to. The steering wheel creaks as I white-knuckle it. I press down on the accelerator.

"Cade?" Thalia squeezes my thigh.

"Yeah." I slow down, drawing a slow breath of her fear. "Sorry. Could you text Lena? Under no circumstances should she go to the build site. Tell her I said she's not safe."

I press the button on the screen of the car. Ansel's name is at the top. It only rings twice.

"Hey, cousin, how are you?" Ansel's voice calls out over the speaker of the SUV.

"I'm surviving, you?" I ask quickly.

I owe him more conversation, but time is of the essence.

Ansel blows a raspberry. "I'll be alright. But you don't call to catch up."

"I know. Bad cousin. I'll do better. Maybe." I sigh.

It's honest. I need to work on my communication with the family. It's just been crunch mode dealing with the transitions.

Thalia's hand leaves my lap, pulling on my arm. I drop it from the steering wheel to hold hands with her. She squeezes gently.

"Alright, so, what's the reason for your call? I hope it's not you telling me there's more shit on its way here. Not that I don't appreciate it. But I think my mail carrier hates me." Ansel laughs.

"After . . ." I pause. I don't want to say it out loud. I hope he understands. "Did everything go back to the way it was?"

"Oh." Ansel doesn't answer right away. "I didn't look. I figured you were solid. Let me . . ."

The sound of the tires on the road is all we hear for a moment. Ansel sneezes.

"Yeah. It's all good. Works out how it mostly always has anyway. Why?"

"Because evidently, a Romanian woman just rolled up to the pack property, claiming to be my sister."

I'm shaking my head. I don't want it to be true for so many reasons. It can't possibly be true. *How could I possibly be direct from Romania? I remember nowhere but here.* Maybe if I deny it long enough, she'll just go away?

The Leviathan huffs, fondly remembering his many lives and the many places he's lived.

"Well, that sounds shitty." Ansel snorts.

My stomach sinks. "Hate to abuse your gift and run, but apparently, I'm having a family reunion."

"Have Deacon bring me the cliff notes at Solstice. I've got to get going. Never a bother." Ansel hangs up, apparently in a bigger hurry than I am.

Thalia turns her phone toward me. I look while she talks. "Lena says she understands. She's still at the U."

"I love you very much." The words come out of my mouth, and I'm sure it sounds sappy. I bring her hand to my lips, kissing it gently. "I don't know what's going to happen today. But I know we both make it out of this alive. That's the best I can do for now."

I feel Thalia's wolf pushing forward. She bristles, sitting straighter.

She chooses her words carefully, and her voice wavers. "Cade, who is The Pricolici?"

I let go of the steering wheel as we drive the straight stretch, scratching my head quickly before I come up with an easy explanation. "Alright, so The Pricolici is the equivalent of The Leviathan for Alpha Females. We both have gifts of influence. The difference is that The Pricolici is rumored to be two wolves. In one form."

"What does that mean?" Thalia raises an open palm like she wants to accept the gift of knowledge.

"So, where The Leviathan only comes into the bloodline when he's needed, The Pricolici is constant. As soon as one wolf with her dies, then the next female wolf in the bloodline who has not had her first heat, receives her." I pause. "I don't know what to believe. It's not like I ever anticipated actually meeting her."

"Right, because you're all born with wolves." She pauses. When I look over at her she asks, "If she was wolf, she was born with a wolf, and if she's getting The Pricolici . . . isn't that like getting another wolf? Where did the original wolf go? Does she have two? How would she pick which one to shift into?" Thalia squirms in her seat before pulling at the seatbelt.

"I honestly never thought about that." *Where did her original wolf go?*

The Leviathan doesn't understand and is overall uninterested by my inquiry.

The gateman opens the gate before we even hit the corner to pull off the road.

"Hey," I say sharply, trying to catch her attention. "There's nothing to worry about."

"Then why are you hiding Lena? And why is The Pricolici here?" she sasses back.

We're rounding the last bend of the driveway, and I come up with the most reassurance I can think of. "She can't make me do anything. She has no authority here. Her gift shouldn't work on me."

"Shouldn't?" Thalia's heart beats faster.

We strong. Draga mea should not worry. Draga mea's wolf makes strong, The Leviathan states self-assuredly.

I park the SUV near where the other vehicle is, not convinced this will be a peaceful meeting.

"Stay in the vehicle." I try not to be commanding, but it's not a suggestion either.

She's safer in the metal box if a wolf fight does break out.

I close the door to the SUV behind me. I left it running, hoping that if something goes wrong, Thalia would choose to leave rather than join the fray.

Three large men and a small brunette woman stand on what used to be the front stairs to the house. The wind picks up, and the scent on the breeze tells me all four are wolf.

"Can I help you?"

The bodyguards step back away from her when I approach.

"It's true." She blinks blue eyes at me with clear recognition. The accent I haven't heard since my mother took her life rings out in her voice. "You're The Leviathan."

"I prefer Cade," I inform her. "And you are?"

The Leviathan growls and pushes forward, ready to defend our position between them and where Thalia sits, but I stifle him. There's no need to potentially escalate the situation.

"I'm your sister," the woman answers me.

Like I should know her and everything about her. Her eyes flash golden yellow.

The Pricolici. The Leviathan recognizes her, their centuries together ringing true. *The mother of all wolves.*

"Not to offend, but seat's taken. I already have one." I shrug. *And, despite her flaws, she's a hundred times more personable.*

The Leviathan stays on edge. I can't harness him back. He's intently watching her.

The Pricolici rolls her head to the side, watching me. "The blood tests say otherwise. Given the information and demands Robert was trying to make of our people, I demanded a blood test to prove his claim on the Ardelean bloodline. Imagine my surprise when I didn't receive the sample of Robert Alden, but instead, I received a sample for someone marked 'Cade Alexander,' which must be you."

This can't be happening. There's no way I can have a sister I don't know about. The blood test says I'm a direct match, but that can't possibly mean . . .

The Leviathan and I watch, the gears turning in thought between us. It wasn't the council. *It wasn't all Robert.*

"What were you and Robert up to?" I ask, watchful as she turns her back on me and walks toward the demolition zone of the house.

With careful steps, she picks out a path and wraps her arms behind her.

"Robert claimed that he was the rightful heir to the throne. He had The Leviathan and was ready to return to Romania. He thought the best place for wolves was in our ancestral home. He wanted to start by returning all the wolves there and then take over the entire country." She turns to look at me. "It seemed odd to me that he did not know we are the ruling body of Romania and have been for centuries." She motions to the remains of the house behind her. "Though, I believe dismantling the house was perhaps not the best packing strategy."

"I have The Leviathan, and I'm not going to Romania."

What the fuck Robert? I look up to the sky. Can there be some divine intervention for this craziness? I'd be willing to choose a higher power if I could just catch one small break.

The henchmen stand between me and The Pricolici.

"Of course, you are! The Leviathan cannot live outside of Romania. It's bad enough that you were stolen from us and now pretending to be a king in a foreign land. We need you back home," she snaps at me. Her eyes flood gold. "Leave the less pure bloodlines to rule the colonies."

The henchmen step back toward her. *Protecting her or in fear of us?* I ask The Leviathan.

Cowards. He's pleased with himself.

"I'm sorry you've come all this way to find someone disinterested in meeting you. I don't know anything about being stolen. I have always been here and have the documentation to prove it. I have no business in Romania." I try to be firm but understanding.

I do have the documentation to prove it, right? I shake my head. Of course, I have the documentation. I served in the army for the federal government. It's not like they just let anyone enlist.

"You need to come home. I've come here unofficially without the rest of the family knowing. It will be better if you come home without a fight," she urges. She steps forward in an attempt to intimidate me. "This was a courtesy visit. I needed to see you for myself. I can't believe you're alive."

"I am home," I answer, which was an arguably dumb move.

With a wave of her hand at the remains of the house, she scoffs. "Well, you certainly cannot live in this."

"We're currently moving forward on a rebuild. But that's beside the point. I'm not visiting Romania right now." I try appeasement and give her a shrug. "It is possible to visit for the Winter Solstice."

"I did not say visit. I said to come home, and I meant permanently. The Leviathan belongs to Romania. You will come to Romania and assume your reign. The Sovereign Alpha must rule from Romania as it has always been done."

Her expression delves into a bit of anger but then returns to a cold neutral. It's like she's trying to seem void of all emotions.

"Seems we're at an impasse." I shake my head. "I will not be moving to Romania. Listen, I've had a long day. I would love to offer you a place to stay so we can chat about this further.

But as you have so rightfully stated, I'm short on accommodations."

The Pricolici looks at me with a cold gaze. "You have no memory of me at all? No memory of home?"

"I don't know you. I have a sister. She's shockingly the same level of stubborn as you. But, no, I don't know who you are." I growl, hoping to drive home the point that this scam or strange error of genetic material isn't of interest to me.

"Our parents were murdered, and you were taken. It wasn't until recently that we believed the claims you were alive," she says sharply.

Well, if true, that's an interesting turn of events.

We lost them. The Leviathan pulls at memories and of things I don't understand. *Makes no change. We rule here.* He seems equally settled with maintaining the status quo.

I don't know how to process anything she has said.

I swallow and offer my arms out in a wide expression of understanding. "I'm sorry for your loss. I'm not your brother. Somehow, we may share genetics, but that doesn't give us a life together. I'd be glad to correspond or call or text, but I'm not visiting Romania anytime soon."

"Fine. The next time I arrive, it won't be pleasant, and the rest of our family will know of my visit. You should be sure to have a structure for a home."

The Pricolici looks at me, and her face falls in sadness briefly before she composes herself again.

I nod and carefully choose my words. "You're welcome to visit again. Perhaps next year when the home is finished. But I can't help you with who I am and why I have The Leviathan. I have a family and a pack. Again, I'm sorry for your loss, but I don't have any answers for you."

She doesn't say anything more but instead snaps her fingers, and her guards escort her into her SUV. I wait for them to drive away from the remains of our family home. Once they're out of sight from my place in the driveway, I return to my SUV and my mate.

"You okay?" Thalia asks, having heard our conversation.

I shake my head. "I don't know what's real anymore. I don't know what to believe. The Leviathan recognized her as The Pricolici and then starts giving me information that she might be telling the truth. There are tons of questions about all of this that I don't have answers to."

Thalia reaches her hand out to me. I finally climb in behind the wheel and sit there holding her hand. We're waiting for the architects to pull up to the house.

Thalia says, "You've made it well known that you hold your family together by acts of love for each other. You'll open communication with her, and we'll figure it out together. If it comes down to it that you aren't really blood relatives to Lena and Deacon, then that doesn't make them less family."

"I just don't understand any of this. It always bugged me that Robert was the only one without a gift, but no one else questioned it." I scrub my free hand down my face. With the other, I squeeze her hand tightly. "I don't know what I did to deserve you. But I am forever grateful."

"You can make it up to me." She raises an eyebrow, a devious smirk painted across her face.

I don't know what she has in mind, but I already like the idea.

DESTINATION REACHED

I hope you enjoyed Cade and Thalia. If you'd like to know what happens next sign up for my newsletter. You'll have access to spicy bonus content, other exclusive shorts, and insider information.

The not always so lovely Lena is next and well. Let's just say she's *not* pleased. Pre-Orders are now available on my website and on Amazon.

STAY CONNECTED:
LINKTR.EE/AUTHOR.SARAHJAEGER

Smoke

SARAH JAEGER

Acknowledgments

Alright, if you've signed up for my newsletter you know anything I write free-form can be a wild ride. If you like unhinged declarations of love, buckle up, and let's get this show on the road.

Kelsey — Thank you for every single one of your stop signs, your questions like "How does this advance the plot?" "What are your beats?" and "Okay, but is that necessary?" Because I knew the answers to all of those things and didn't like hearing it, but here we are. I wrote the book.

Dora — I don't know how to ever say thank you that would adequately explain everything you've given me in the last two years; from the push out of the starting block, to finishing the race, and entering the next book. You're the tiger mom I didn't know I needed (wasn't sure I wanted at first... but I love you either way.)

Jeanine — I'm sorry. For everything, for nothing, for commas, spaces, paragraph breaks, the overuse of the word 'gently,' capitalizations, italics, flying commas, and I don't even remember all of the 'great rewrite' drama I've subjected you to. Thank you for sticking it out. Thank you for reminding me they're good characters and that occasionally I know how to tell a story.

Anna Fury — I promised myself I wouldn't cry when I wrote this, but The Stephenses just popped into my head and now here we are. Never, not once, in the history of reading your books did I ever think that I'd make it to this point. But somehow you believed in me. Even if it was terrifying and I'm still a little scared to have you read my book, I hope you did and I hope you liked it–or at the very least break it to me gently.

Nikki – God you walked into a train wreck, didn't you? Great job hanging on for the wild ride – you've had the worst, the best, and the in-between.

Andrea — I cannot tell you the number of times I've said "Oh no" when looking at one of your comments; sometimes it's good, sometimes it's bad. But, every time, I know that you're in my corner and want what's best for the poor tortured little souls of my books.

Caitlen — From mountain men to shifters, you've taken a hell of a leap. Welcome to the dark side! It's okay, we've got cookies. Thank you for every time we inexplicably had to sit in the time-out chair together for thinking something we shouldn't have been.

Josie, Luna, Jes, and Meg — You're fantastic betas. I've had so much love and support from you. The knowledge and information you've provided have been absolutely crucial. I can literally point to passages in the text and go: this was so much better because of each of you.

Marcelle — Thank you for coming in and saving the day. Truly, your help in the 9th hour made a world of difference. I look forward to working together for many books to come.

Mr. Jaeger, Mom, Dad, and Little Brother — Thank you for not reading this (especially Little Brother, you're kinda clumsy with those paws there, bud)

About the Author

Sarah Jaeger is an emerging author of action travel guides. This is Sarah's first book. (Thank you Vellum for this oddly, not entirely wrong, description of me. It is a roadtrip romance novel after all.)

Sarah Jaeger is a human being from the Upper Midwest, even though she is certain she was born to be a shifter. A dreamer since birth, the idea for the Ardelean Bloodlines popped into Sarah's teenage brain and refused to leave. Finally, that idea is taking shape in the form of a fully-fledged paranormal romance series. When she's not writing, Sarah likes to recharge with solid TV show binges, playing cards and games with her family, and caring for her fur babies. Stay in touch with Sarah at www.authorsarahjaeger.com.

ALSO BY SARAH JAEGER

The Ardelean Bloodline, Book Two

Haze

Estimated September 2023

Stay up to date on all things Sarah Jaeger.

Follow me on social media: